THE ROGUE WOLF

MIRRORS IN THE DARK BOOK 2

KT BELT

RUBBER TREE BOOKS

ISBN: 978-1-954913-03-5

Cover design by: Tom Edwards

Visit KT Belt and sign up for the mailing list at:

http://www.ktbeltbooks.com

1

SENTINEL

"Twenty billion. Twenty billion dead!"

"That's the conservative estimate," Admiral Carsono Wright replied after a brief pause.

He then looked into the eyes of his old friend. There was still the shadow of the fierce soldier that was one of his closest comrades in arms. That had not gone to seed; the oceans would turn to dust before that ever happened. Yet the holographic image of Admiral West was hollow in more than one way.

"Are you troubled?" Carsono asked.

West immediately opened his mouth before he bit the comment back. He looked away sheepishly. "How can I not be? Don't get me wrong. I have no love for the sortens—"

"War is war," Carsono interrupted, his tone even but not cold.

He then sighed. Soldiering was all he knew—all that most of the leadership of Space Force knew. They had been forged by the hard fighting during the Terran-Sorten War all those years ago. It would be kind to say the UTE was still recovering from that struggle, despite having decisively won. The memory of that conflict seemed to hang on everything everyone did, whether they realized it or not. And now there was this new war against the sortens, the Eternals, and the arkins. He didn't think it was possible for any society to carry on with the losses that had been suffered on all sides.

"Yes, sir," West said sharply. "But there is a difference between war and razing the enemy's home worlds to the ground."

"There is?" Carsono questioned. He then reached into his desk and pulled out a PDD. "Planet New Athens has fallen. 18 million casualties, 14 million of which were civilian. The enemy systematically hunted down men, women, and children who escaped the bombing of the cities," Carsono read out loud. West shifted uneasily. "Third, eleventh, and fifth fleets have all fallen below ten percent strength with 1.7 million casualties. The recently repulsed attack on the Sol System: Earth SDF is effectively annihilated, Pluto starport was destroyed, the ISS *Stalwart* and countless other ships were lost with all hands. Total casualties are over 6 million and are still being tabulated. Planet Thycol will soon be under siege by the Eternals, and we can't contest their advance. Total population of Thycol: 9 million. Planet—"

"No more. I understand," West interrupted.

"I hope you do," Carsono said. "Medusa will be deployed. We didn't get to this point or come to this decision easily or lightly. Trust me, we have no hope of winning this war without it," he added, raising the PDD for emphasis.

West made no reaction. He simply stared straight ahead for a second before he spoke. "How it's come to this," he said softly under his breath.

Carsono made no response other than to nod, and West looked at him. "Is there something else?"

West didn't say anything at first. His lips pressed together and his jaw tightened, giving a hint at his thoughts. "Why me?" he finally asked. "There are better fleet commanders."

"There are," Carsono admitted. "But if any of them were assigned this mission, the conversation we are having at present would have never happened." He took a deep breath before he continued. "Years from now, if we win or if we only exist in some alien's history book, people will look back at this insane period and try to find the meaning in it all. I don't even know if there is any. But we must go into this with both eyes open."

West's eyes fell for a moment in thought. "I understand," he said. "I will report when it is done."

Carsono nodded again. "Good hunting, Admiral."

West said nothing and shut off his projection. Carsono sighed. His colleagues called him The Bull, and it most certainly was a reputation well earned. Even so, from the moment he masterminded this operation, its objective hung heavy in the pit of his stomach.

He shook his head and then activated his intercom. "What's next?" he asked.

"You have a meeting with Admiral Calbry in main operations, sir," his aide responded smartly. Carsono groaned. *Lance*, he thought. They were on the same side, and Carsono was happy for that, but water and oil weren't meant to mix. "Your escort is standing by outside your door," the aide continued.

Carsono groaned again. "I don't need an escort. I'm just going across the building."

"Sorry, sir. By regulations, all flag officers are subject to mandatory escort, even inside fleet command headquarters."

It was a sensible rule, but having someone follow you to and fro, even to the bathroom, got very tiring. Rules were rules, though. An argument would be futile.

"I'll be out in a minute," he said.

In actuality, he'd be out in less than a minute. The only delay was a brief pause in which he wondered if he should take his pistol. *Don't get paranoid*, he thought, shaking his head. Besides, his pistol was more a pretty ornament than a weapon, loaded or not. It had been a gift from some dignitary that he could no longer remember. He left his office with no further pause.

"Gentlemen," he said.

"Sir," his escorts for the day replied.

This time, it was two Phalanx troopers watching his back. If he had to have an escort, he preferred the troopers to the Sol SDF detachment he was sometimes stuck with. The Self Defense Forces undoubtedly played a vital role, but Space Force preferred to exist on a higher level. Whether his SDF counterparts would agree with that assessment was a different matter. The troopers weren't wearing their trademark armor, but they were armed with M12 rifles, which was more than enough. He'd never met either man before, and he took a moment to study their name tags.

"Sanchez, Taylor, if you'll follow me."

"After you, sir," Taylor replied.

The trio began walking with Carsono in the lead. That was no simple task, as outside his office door was complete chaos. Before the war, the floor his office opened onto was usually a paragon of organization and efficiency. Bureaucratic nonsense was an SDF luxury. But now things were different, and not all fighting was done with bullets and missiles. Nothing all too critical happened here specifically. This was more the building's spinal column than its brain or heart. The computers and cubicles were manned mostly by secretaries, logistics staff, information analysts, and others who considered data, facts, and figures before it was sent somewhere else. His aide was buried in here somewhere.

Admittedly, Carsono had gotten used to the mania by this point. It had only taken a few months. What really threw the grenade and sent the ants scurrying this time was the recently repelled attack by the combined sorten and Eternal fleets. They had also been aided by one single arkin starship, the first time in the war that the arkins had ever gone on the offensive. He hoped and prayed that they kept their usual reticence. That ship was practically a fleet unto itself.

Almost everyone personally knew someone who'd died. Carsono could name several, and it was those aftershocks which caused the disarray before him. They were ill equipped to fill the vacuum left by Sol SDF which, for the most part, no longer existed. Space Force trainers assisted their SDF counterparts in coordinating how and exactly where the replacements for all those lost personnel would come from. The public relations department was working overtime to try to downplay the losses from the battle. In addition, there was the task of scraping together enough resources for the counterattack on the sorten home worlds that Admiral West was leading, while also combating the Eternals in their planet-hopping campaign. His overtaxed colleagues were taking the burden of two, three, and sometimes four people who no longer were.

The trio walked on, and the crowd did their best to make a path. After only two steps, Carsono and his entourage were reduced to walking single file. The reason the troopers didn't wear their trademark armor was obvious now. If they followed protocol, they would have a personal shield—overkill for a place as far from the front line as this. Eventually they were able to escape into a side hall. No one stopped or said anything, though one of the troopers took a breath. Carsono wouldn't fault him for that.

Their pace was relaxed, even though Carsono had never been the slow and steady type. A meeting with Lance always put his preference for haste to the test. He never looked forward to any meeting with that man. Fleet officers and Flight officers were not supposed to mix. Just then, he thought he heard one of his escorts speak, which broke his thoughts of the coming battle—err, meeting.

"Did one of you say something?" he asked.

"No, sir," Taylor said. He looked at Sanchez, which prompted Carsono to do the same, but the trooper only shook his head.

Whatever, he thought. It was probably just one of the other people in the hall. This place couldn't be emptied even if you fumigated it, especially now. As further proof of that point, Carsono had to stop to let a cloud of people walk by. But in due time, the trio reached an elevator farther down the hall, which promised a short respite.

There was that noise again when the elevator doors opened.

"One of you had to have said something this time," Carsono said as they entered the elevator. The sound was too close for it to have been anyone else.

He stared at the two men hard, but the only thing they offered were shrugs. Then the noise could be heard yet again. It was outside the elevator, and Carsono turned to see what it was, but nothing was there. He looked at the two troopers. They glanced at him, shook their heads, and then looked back outside the elevator.

There was a soft voice in the air just as the doors began to close. "Sorry, boys. That was me," it said.

The foggy bewilderment of the moment lifted just enough for Carsono to notice a small, almost imperceptible, distortion shift along the opposite wall. His eyes grew wide, and what happened next was too violently brief to ever really know what transpired. One of the troopers uttered a sharp curse, and then there was a loud noise. The next thing Carsono knew, he was on the ground with someone on top of him. Blood started pooling on the floor.

The doors closed.

"Shit," Carsono said as he bolted to his feet.

His uniform was covered in blood, but he wasn't in any pain. His hands flew over his body anyway. *Everything is where it's supposed to be*, he concluded. He'd seen men get practically blown in half and not realize it.

It was then that he finally noticed the elevator doors had closed. Not only that, but it was moving as well. He saw Taylor's body on the ground. *Poor kid took the bullet for me*, he realized. When Carsono turned, however, he saw that wasn't completely the case. There was one solitary bullet hole in the wall right where he had been standing. The shot would have gone through both of them if Taylor hadn't pushed him out of the way. The trooper had been wearing a personal shield. Few small arms could penetrate one of those in one shot and still have enough energy left to go through someone. Carsono stared at the hole with that in mind. *Personal cloak, high power weapons...* he thought. It was practically a Christmas list of state-of-the-art military equipment. It was quite apparent that this would-be assassin, whoever he was, meant business.

"Yeah, it seems like there's just one of them," Sanchez said into his communicator while the security alarm blared. "He was invisible, probably a Clairvoyant," he added.

Carsono pointed a thumb at the bullet hole. "Clairvoyants

don't use guns," he said. "A Clairvoyant would have just snapped our necks and remained undetected."

Sanchez nodded. "Correction, he's not a Clairvoyant. I say again, not a Clairvoyant. Definitely terran, though. He has a terran voice and is using projectile weaponry with a personal cloaking device."

"Copy, not a Clairvoyant," the voice on the other side of the communicator said. "Is the admiral injured?"

"I'm fine," Carsono said.

Sanchez nodded. "That's a negative," he answered. "However, Taylor is KIA. The son of a bitch got the drop on us right when we got in the elevator."

"Understood. The building is under lockdown, and a particle motion scan is already underway. A squad will meet you to escort the admiral to a safe room."

"Right," Sanchez said. He then looked at Carsono, silently asking if he had anything to add. Carsono simply shook his head. "We'll be getting off on sublevel eight."

"Copy, sublevel eight. Escort is down the side hall, your position in forty seconds."

The doors opened and Sanchez turned to Carsono. "Just stay behind me, Admiral," he said.

Carsono wouldn't waste time arguing with the man whose entire job description was to keep him alive. On the other hand, he also wouldn't stand quietly behind anyone. He picked up Taylor's M12 and spare magazines—the trooper wouldn't be needing them—and then made sure the weapon was set for indoors. When he shot this son of a bitch between the eyes, he preferred that the bullet would not go on to hit some poor bastard cleaning toilets on the other side of the building.

The two of them left the elevator. Their destination was the side hall. The alarm still blared, but Carsono was so

Sentinel | 9

focused that he barely even heard it. He pondered how this person had managed to break into Space Force Headquarters undetected. He saw to it himself that there were PMA scanners at every entry point. Perhaps they had an accomplice on the inside. Carsono would be sure to ask after giving a hearty thanks for getting him out of the meeting with Lance.

They rounded the corner and saw the squad of troopers running toward them. The four men were in full battle dress with Phalanx armor, tactical helmet, and M12 rifle. Even for Carsono, the sight of the troopers was enough to give pause, and they were on his side.

"I am Sergeant Miller," the leader said. "We're here to escort you to safe room S8C," he added. He looked Carsono over before he continued and gave a nod and a small smirk when he noticed the admiral had armed himself. "Foster, Adams, cover our rear. Make sure you're in PMA scan mode. This asshole has a personal cloak. Sanchez."

"Yes, Sergeant," he replied.

"Stay close to the admiral. If he takes a piss, I want you there, holding his dick." Carsono could appreciate the sentiment, but, looking at his rifle, he'd do his own dick holding, thank you very much. "Move out, Phalanx formation."

The troopers responded smartly, two to the front and two to the back with Carsono and Sanchez in the middle. The free-floating, heavily armored and shielded panel that was the Phalanx armor trademark hung like magic in front of each trooper. It only took two men to cover the width of the hall, making the formation almost indestructible from the front, and in this case, the rear as well.

"Corner," a corporal calmly announced. Carsono didn't know his name.

"Shift!" Miller commanded.

The troopers turned into the new hall in perfect unison.

Their precise movements left only the briefest instances of vulnerability. If anything, Carsono found it hard to keep up. The troopers moved like a well-oiled machine, their doctrine and discipline born in the ship-to-ship, corridor-to-corridor fighting of the first Terran-Sorten War.

"Threat, 12 o'clock," the same corporal said. "Verify."

His tone was calm and even, but the callout warranted as much. Particle Motion Analysis, or PMA, scanners worked by tracking air molecules as they bounced off objects. They were notoriously difficult to read and prone to false positives, but they were a surefire way of detecting a cloaked individual.

"Clear. Move out," Miller said, and on they went.

Carsono had never been to safe room S8C. He'd never been to any safe room. He hoped it was close. This section of the hall had offices lining either side. Their glass windows gave a rather pleasing view of almost the entire floor. Well, it would be pleasing any other day. Today, however, it made the team vulnerable. PMA scanners couldn't see past solid structures, glass included. His eyes were peeled for any telltale distortion of a cloak field on the other side of the glass, but he saw none.

The group bunched up at a door at the end of the hall, leaving them vulnerable again. The troopers didn't show any apprehension, though—or, if they did, Carsono couldn't detect it. In seconds, he was rushed through the door with calm professional haste.

"Threat, 12 o'clock."

Miller paused for a moment. "Advance!" he called out. The troopers shuffled forward, and Carsono suspected they would have moved even faster if he wasn't in the middle. "Drop your cloak, place your weapon on the floor, and put your hands in the air."

There was no response. If a pin dropped, it would've sounded like an earthquake. Carsono looked at where the troopers' weapons were pointing. He didn't see anything, though, not even the trademark distortion of a cloaking field. More than likely, the assassin was trying his best to stand still and not be seen.

"Do it now, or we'll open fire," Miller said.

Again, there was nothing.

"All right, light him up!"

Foster and Adams stood firm in their vigil of the rear. Miller and the corporal, however, laid a stream of fire that hit the opposite wall like a sledgehammer. Carsono wasn't a boot trooper; he didn't know every waking detail of the M12 rifle, nor did he care to learn. He knew enough to set his weapon to the indoor setting, but that was it. Sure, he went to target ranges to unwind and read eval reports of the weapon, but he was unprepared for its raw power. Only a buzzsaw could be more gruesome.

Carsono saw something drop to the ground at the other end of the hall, but he couldn't see much behind the two troopers unleashing hell.

"Cease fire. Reload," Miller called out.

"Loaded, set," the corporal said.

"Loaded, set," Miller said as well.

Carsono took a deep breath. The scene was strangely calm in comparison to the last few seconds, but Miller and the corporal looked around the hall nervously. Carsono looked as well, for what he didn't know, but it didn't really matter anyway, since he still couldn't see much from behind them.

"Where's the body? Where's the body?" the corporal asked.

"I don't know," Miller said. "Son of a bitch duped us with a shield generator."

Carsono's eyes narrowed when he heard that. A shield projected into the shape of a man was all it took to set off a PMA scan. It had no way of telling if it was actually a person or not. He looked over one the trooper's shoulders and was able to see the hardware on the ground.

"Has to be here somewhere, bastard," Miller added.

Just then, his communicator cracked to life. "Squad report contact," the voice on the other end said.

"Sergeant Miller reporting. Negative contact. He used a shield to project a silhouette."

"Copy. Do you need any assistance?"

Miller hesitated for a moment. "That's a negative. We'll be at the objective in under a minute." Carsono gripped his M12 tight. He knew what that meant. They'd be running the rest of the way. Miller glanced at all the troopers and Carsono before he spoke. "Move out, double time. Go, go, go!"

The corporal nodded. "Yes—"

A loud noise thundered through the hall. To Carsono, it was like a bomb went off in his skull. He only faintly registered the pieces of the wall he was standing next to pelting him. There was smoke—well, more dust than smoke, now that he was able to consider it more clear-mindedly. His side hurt, and he realized he was lying on the floor. His gaze was listless. It was like being drunk, except the headache didn't wait for the hangover.

He looked at the wall that had showered him with debris. Still groggy, his eyes responded with all the verve of a crippled ocean liner. He could make out a distinct bullet hole with blood splattered all around it.

Carsono groaned and, by reflex and as before, his hands flew over his body to make sure the blood wasn't his. It was a fool's errand, though. The corporal was lying dead right next to him, the front of his helmet ripped open from the impact.

"Fire! Open fire!" one of the troopers yelled. He assumed it was Miller.

Carsono's gun lay next to him as well. He didn't need to be told twice. He grabbed it, head still spinning, and staggered to his feet before Sanchez tackled him to the ground and held him there.

"Stay down, sir."

He would have none of it and growled, "Get the hell off me!" But Sanchez wouldn't budge. Just like that, Carsono was reduced to being a spectator.

Adams and Foster had moved to the front, but the remaining three troopers weren't shooting down the hall. They raked its walls with weapon fire, any notion of reduced power mode for the M12s long forgotten. They weren't as loud as the previous explosion had been, but it was enough. His daughter's stereo could have been on full blast and he wouldn't have heard it. He covered his ears as best he could. He was the only one there without hearing protection.

"Loading!" Adams called out.

Miller said the same a few seconds later, as did Foster, but not one of them stopped shooting. They each put another magazine into the wall before Miller called out a ceasefire. Just like that, there was silence. As before, it hung eerily in the hall as the dust slowly settled back to earth. Carsono breathed too shallowly to cough. His eyes were fixed on the wall now so riddled with bullets that you could practically walk through it. He waited. For what exactly, he didn't know.

"Did we get him? Did we get him?" Foster asked nervously.

"Shit... The PMA is useless in this. I can't tell," Miller said.

A voice reverberated through the air. "Let me give you a clue," it said.

Carsono thought he saw a distortion on the other side of the wall, but he couldn't be sure. There was a bright flash and then that explosion of noise again. Miller reeled back before tumbling to the ground next to the admiral and Sanchez, a hole in the middle of his armored panel. Blood began to pool underneath him.

"Fuck, it went right through the panel. What the hell is he armed wi—"

That noise came again, and then Foster fell to the ground with a scream as he held what was left of his shoulder.

Adams switched to the M12's underslung grenade launcher and lobbed two shells into the wall. "Fall back to the next room! I'll hold him off as long as I can. Go, go, go!" he yelled. He backed up his words by firing a long stream of bullets.

Sanchez struggled to his feet before grabbing Carsono under his arms and pulling the admiral up. "We have to go, sir. Now!" he screamed.

The trooper practically threw him toward the door they had entered the hall from. Both men darted into the next room, another explosion of sound marking the passing. Sanchez closed the door behind him. Carsono noted that he didn't hear any return fire from the other side of it, just the groans and screams of Foster.

Sanchez glanced at him. "Go—run. I'll hold him here."

Carsono's eyes narrowed. "Bullshit," he said firmly.

He'd be damned if he was going to be chased through his own headquarters like a scared rabbit. He dropped to a knee and took aim at the door. Sanchez glanced at him. He must have realized an argument would be a wasted effort, since he made none.

His communicator beeped. "Squad report!"

"This is Sanchez. The squad is dead," he said, his voice rushed and edgy. "I have the admiral with me, but we're pinned down. We need immediate Clairvoyant support."

Sanchez stopped his transmission at the sound of a gunshot on the other side of the door, but it hadn't been aimed at them. They no longer heard Foster screaming. Carsono opened fire with Sanchez a half-step behind him. The glass that lined either side of the hall trembled and shook from the chaos. This wasn't the most glorious place to have a last stand. He had always imagined his final battle would be on the bridge of a starship. By contrast, this was about as prestigious as drowning in a kiddie pool.

Carsono gave himself one chance in three of surviving this. Whoever this guy was, he was good. In any case, a PMA scanner couldn't see through a door. That didn't really matter, though, since neither he nor Sanchez had one. He shifted his fire, hoping they would get lucky. Nothing came back at them, but that didn't mean much, considering the luck of their decimated escort.

The person on the other side of the communicator never stopped talking, even though Sanchez had put it down. "Clairvoyant support on its way! I say again, Clairvoyant support on its way!"

Sanchez slapped a new magazine home. "We should fall back, sir," he said. "I'll cover you."

Carsono glanced at him. "You be right behind me."

"Yes, sir."

The admiral turned to run. Just when he did, that loud noise thundered through the hall, and the glass cracked and shattered. The concussion of the noise alone was enough to knock him to the ground. He turned, head foggy once again, and saw that Sanchez had been nearly ripped in half from the shot. The door had practically been blown off its hinges. It was slight, very slight, but Carsono's aging eyes registered a curve in the doorframe that should have been perfectly straight.

It didn't take long for him to realize it was his cloaked pursuer. He frantically looked for something somewhere that could avail him. The best he could come up with was the slightly open door of the office next to him. He clutched his M12 close and ran into the next room just as automatic rifle fire tore into where he had just been.

Carsono studied his new surroundings. They weren't much better. He used a wooden desk for cover, but that was in no way adequate against the cannon his opposition was packing. It wouldn't even be enough to stop an M12. The glass walls of the offices in this section made it impossible to move without being seen. He checked the remaining rounds for his weapon and then cursed under his breath. He cursed again when he realized he left the communicator both completely open and out of reach next to Sanchez's corpse.

He heard a distinct sigh that was not his own. "I didn't think this job would be easy, but I have to hand it to you, old man. After it's done, I'm going to have to ask my employer for a bonus."

Carsono's eyes narrowed. Many, *many* people wanted him dead—that was never in doubt. But to attack him at Space Force Headquarters? It was a level of insanity beyond description. Someone had paid good money for the job. Whoever his assassin was, he must have talked a good game to be hired over a Clairvoyant. Unfortunately, it seemed like he could back up whatever he promised.

"Oh yeah. You're just wasting your time with hiding." There was the soft twang of someone tapping on metal. "My own creation. Let me introduce you."

Carsono dropped to the ground and flattened himself till he was practically a stain on the carpet. The atom bomb of a bullet tore through the desk he was hiding behind, leaving a watermelon sized hole in its wake. The glass that hadn't been shattered from the shot before now tumbled to the ground. Carsono even felt the pressure wave of the bullet passing over him. His hair ruffled, his clothes billowed, and he was sure blood would be coming out of his ears if his hands weren't clasped to them. The second shot was just as violent as the first, but it missed him by a wider margin.

He took a deep breath. He could sure use that Clairvoyant support, wherever it was. The admiral glanced through one of the holes in the desk but could see nothing, not even the distortion of a cloaking field. He swore under his breath. Shooting blindly hadn't worked for the troopers; he doubted it would be any different for him.

"Still with me, old man?"

Carsono made no reply, though, if he had a grenade, several creative ways for answering the question came to mind. He instead perked his ears to attention. This guy had skill and incredible equipment, but he was a bit of a blabbermouth and getting overconfident.

"Well, let's be sure."

The admiral fell to the ground again, almost on instinct. He wasn't, however, attacked by the cannon. This time, it was small arms fire, probably an M12. Whatever it was, it still ripped through the desk like paper. Wood chips and dust coated the ground like fresh snow fall. But Carsono paid no attention to it. The bullets still passed over him, leaving him relatively safe. Consequently, his attention was bent on trying to ascertain the directions the shots were coming from. He had a general idea at this point, but it was nothing he'd bet his life on.

His opponent stopped firing. "Well, what do you say to that?"

There was a calm silence as Carsono's eyes narrowed. *He's just slightly to my right*, he thought. Experience told him he'd only have one chance. His timing had to be perfect.

"Guess I'll just have to finish you off then," the man said.

Carsono figured that meant he'd use the cannon...or something bigger. It was now or never. He shot to his feet as fast as his aging legs could manage and then he mowed down everything in front of him. An M12 was recoilless in its operation, but he still felt a certain visceral thrill at handling the weapon he had long missed after all his years behind a desk. He swept his fire from side to side, but there was no way of knowing if he was accomplishing anything other than tearing up what remained of the offices. Just then, something cold and hard pressed against his skull.

"Drop the shit," that same voice said calmly.

The admiral stood still for a moment. If this person wanted to just kill him, they would have done so by now. Even with that in mind, he didn't have many options. He dropped the rifle and then slowly turned to face his attacker.

The man had shut off his cloaking field for whatever reason. He was a bit taller than Carsono, which wasn't saying much. A mask covered most of his face, leaving only his eyes as the most prominent feature. They stared out intensely and somewhat coldly. His hair was cut short in the same purposeful fashion as the buzz cut Phalanx troopers, and his skin was dark, on par with Lance's.

The man took a few steps back. His gun, an M12 as Carsono expected, was held firm. He had none of the nervousness or apprehension of an inexperienced killer. Another gun, more than the length of his torso, was slung across his back—obviously the *cannon* that had given everybody so much trouble.

A second passed, maybe two, but it felt like days. No one said anything. Carsono doubted this person was having second thoughts about killing him. He also didn't think this was some brief moment of quiet self-aggrandizement. After a while, he finally realized the purpose of the delay. He gave a small nod in acknowledgement.

The communicator crackled and screamed something about support and holding on. Really, it was a surprise the device had managed to survive the onslaught.

Carsono thought about that for a moment as he closed his eyes. He then took a deep breath. "Those who live by the sword," he said simply as he opened his eyes again.

The man nodded as well. Then he fired once into Carsono's chest. The great leader and warrior tumbled backward to the ground in an undignified tangle. Another bullet was fired into his chest, followed by one to his forehead. The assassin took a moment to ensure the quality of his work before he activated his cloak and escaped down the hall.

2

ONE DAY, EVERY DAY

Subject: Edge Age: 20 Status: Released

The Clairvoyant knifed quietly and efficiently across the room. As always, there was no pause or waver in her actions, like every movement was preordained. She stopped briefly to watch the holonews report on the recent assassination of Admiral Carsono Wright. The extreme loss to the war effort caused everyone to buzz with nervous unease. The Clairvoyant continued about her routine, as unmoved as a boulder in rushing rapids.

Unmoved was an apt description—nothing seemed to touch her. She either didn't hear or didn't acknowledge the whispers about her. She also didn't seem to be aware that the membership of the gym had dropped by almost half in the few short weeks since she'd arrived. It didn't seem to cross her as odd that there was a void around her that none dared enter. The Clairvoyant was blissfully naïve to think that those pretending she wasn't there weren't also plotting and scheming for her downfall. And today, finally, would be the day it happened.

The group watched the Clairvoyant as she carried on with

her exercises. She seemed completely oblivious of the mob as on and on she went about her business. She wasn't bothering anyone directly, but she focused everything in the room on her just because she was in it.

"She's so weird," a member of the mob muttered to herself as they assembled.

"What is she going to do to us?" another asked, his voice trembling.

"We're just going to ask her to leave. There's another gym three blocks down. She can go there," someone else said.

"Yeah," another quipped from the back.

"We should have called the police."

The group fell silent for a moment as they exchanged looks all around.

"They were too scared to come," someone replied.

Carmen heard none of the conversation. She usually didn't. She sighed anyway. Her exercise routine simply wasn't strenuous enough to draw her complete attention.

She hadn't exercised at all for the first few weeks after she graduated. Mind and body were a team, though. The nightmares she experienced from time to time were a constant reminder of those lessons. Allowing half of that team to slowly atrophy made her *uncomfortable*. Her goal wasn't outright physical strength, as no Clairvoyant had any real need for that. She did mess around with free weights sometimes, but her chief concerns were flexibility, joint strengthening, and aerobic efficiency, among other minutiae.

Today it was free weights, her least favorite. The feeling of the weight resisting the movement was especially wretched for a Clairvoyant, and the reactions of those around her were typically bothersome. It was the expectation. They looked at her like they expected her to lift the entire rack of weights with no more than her pinky finger. She could if she wanted to, telekinetically, but what would be the point? Very few seemed to acknowledge that, physically, she was nothing more than a young woman who happened to be in excellent, though not extraordinary, condition.

The gym patrons seemed more agitated than normal. Why now as opposed to any other time was anyone's guess. The lot of them gathered in a corner of the room, but she didn't know why. She could feel their tension; she could *always* feel their tension. Today, though, it could no longer be tucked away in the back of her mind and ignored. It was like a bad case of indigestion.

She retrieved a new weight and began her next routine happy that she'd be going to work soon. All the while, the group in the corner of the room grew larger and larger. Some were people she had never seen before. She could only assume they came on days she did not. The gym owner, staff, and trainers were gathered as well. When she glanced at them, they all shuddered as if hit by a cold wind. Everyone stood frozen. Then, all at once, the mass started walking toward her.

Carmen placed the weight down and stood. At first, this was a curiosity, but now she wasn't sure what to make of it. No words were spoken by either side. The wall of flesh approached, seeming to tower over her. At about average height, she wasn't a short woman, but she felt decidedly small in this instant all the same. She took a step back, and they continued their advance. She took another step and then another, yet the crushing mass came closer still. Eventually, her hand brushed the back wall. Her gaze darted left and right, searching for some way to escape, but she was surrounded. The attack came just as she opened her mouth to speak.

"We don't want you here!" half of them bellowed.

"Get lost!" the other half screamed.

"I...I..." Carmen stammered. She knew she wasn't particularly appreciated here, but she never expected this.

"Yeah, go! We don't want to be around you monsters!"

"I'm not a—"

Someone smacked her then, making her hair, only partially restrained by her ponytail, fall across her face. She didn't see who did it, but it was obvious. The man fell to one knee and held his hand.

"She shocked me! The fucking bitch shocked me!" he said.

Everyone took half a step away from her and fell silent. Carmen ignored them and looked through her hair at the man. She couldn't remember the last time someone had hit her. He looked back at her with a seething terror that, to her, wafted off him like steam. But she made no action. She hadn't intentionally shocked him; it was only a byproduct of the bioelectric field that every Clairvoyant possessed. Her gaze went from him to the rest of the crowd. They reflected his fear but to a lesser degree. Her eyes fell.

"Excuse me," she said softly.

As she walked forward, the group was *nice* enough to clear a path for her. Then they followed a reasonable distance behind. She didn't turn to look but could sense them—hear them, even, as their shuffling steps reverberated off the hard floor like rhythmless drums. Her movements, even now, were graceful and almost otherworldly yet purposeful.

Her first stop was the showers. The mob waited just outside. Carmen tried not to think about them. She would have left immediately if she could. Frankly, she had taken relatively few showers in her life. She usually didn't need to, as it was far more convenient to just cleanse the day's dirt and grime telekinetically. But she couldn't be directly affected by her own energy, and her sweat was as much a part of her as her arm or leg.

The crowd was still waiting for her when she got out. They made a path that led directly to one place and one place only: her locker. She went to it and began emptying it out. The group watched like a flock of vultures over a wounded animal. No one said anything. The scene was too surreal for any words to come to mind. Carmen didn't even wish to ask for a refund of her membership dues. She simply made for the exit with her meager belongings, sans pause or even a look back. She let out a soft sigh when the door was safely shut behind her. Clapping and cheering could be heard from inside the gym. She tried her best to ignore it.

"Is that five or six?" she wondered out loud.

She couldn't really remember, if it even mattered. But this was certainly one of the softer ways she'd been kicked out of a gym. She shook her head as she thought of some of the more ridiculous instances and pulled out her PDD.

There was just enough time for her to make an early bus to work if she flew. She could have flown all the way to work, but, hard as it was to explain to normal people, that was too tiring a mode of transportation to use regularly. She wished she could afford an aerocar, but it seemed that even the luxury of a steady gym was beyond her. Thus, she lowered her shoulder and flew off without a second thought. The bus was only a few blocks away.

Clairvoyants were never known to fly very high if they didn't have to, and she flew only a little above the heads of the people on the street. An outstretched hand would have just been able to touch her. In her time, though, no one had ever tried.

The bus was in sight in seconds. It didn't take much for

her to telekinetically hold the door open long enough to step inside. Payment only took a quick swipe of her credit card. She smiled at the bus driver.

"Hello," she said. The bus driver said nothing back, which was typical. Carmen paid it no mind.

She turned, and the bus fell silent. Actually, she didn't think a sound had been uttered since she stepped onboard. The morning bus, as usual, was packed full. Yet, wherever her eyes fell, the area cleared like a tornado touching down in a wheat field. A solitary step forward was all it took to evacuate the entire forward section. She took the first available seat next to an older man who didn't seem to care about or even know of his new company. She'd seen him before, and she smiled, even though they never actually spoke to one another. She had tried once and got a disturbed mess back—something about the war or some such thing. Either way, it had been enough to caution her from reading him.

His weren't the only thoughts she tried to keep out, either. There were a few regulars on the bus that paid her no serious mind, but their soft song was set against an opera of people who were as wary of her as they would be a smoking volcano. She dropped her eyes to the ground and tried not to look intimidating. That sometimes helped.

Her stop eventually came, and she went. She even heard the bus driver breathe a sigh of relief when she stepped out. Not that Carmen could blame her. After all, she had been sitting near the entrance, and riders were usually reluctant to enter when they noticed her. Anyway, it was only a brisk but brief walk from this point to get to her job. She was a little early, but she had no place else to be.

After walking inside, she sighed yet again. This would be a busy morning; the crowd was wall to wall. The news was on the holo, another report about that admiral assassinated on

Earth. She ignored it completely. She had little interest in the war. It was all so far away, and New Earth was one of the most secure Great Colonies in the UTE. Furthermore, Clairvoyants weren't subject to the draft. Little could be done to *make* them serve, especially on a mass scale. But she also guessed that not being subject to the draft was a small kickback for being locked in a facility and literally tortured until she was eighteen.

She moved into the crowd with a slight smile on her lips despite herself. Times like this were refreshing. Everyone was too busy to notice the Clairvoyant in their midst.

"Excuse me," she said politely as she moved a woman aside. "Pardon me," she muttered to a man as she slipped by him.

And like that it was broken. A different man noticed the precise grace of her movements, her piercing gaze, and the unsettling feeling in his stomach that was not hunger, and he moved out of her way. He bumped into another person who spat a curse in anger, but the offence was forgotten as soon as she noticed Carmen. The rest of the crowd realized their predicament and fell away from the Clairvoyant like dominoes. As a reflex, Carmen's mouth poised to utter an apology before she thought better of it. Instead she calmly walked behind the counter, head held low.

"Hi," she said out loud to none of her coworkers in particular. There were a few equally halfhearted greetings in return, but mostly they were too busy to respond.

She'd been in this situation before and knew what to do. She tossed her bag onto an unused table and telekinetically retrieved her uniform. It was already on by the time she walked back to the counter. Her coworkers moved into position and got ready. She gave them a couple of seconds just in case. They always said it was hard for them to keep up.

The first customer to step up was a young teenager of maybe thirteen years old. The girl approached boldly. It was hard to tell if she didn't notice the Clairvoyant of if she just didn't care. Carmen raised an eyebrow at the atypical girl. She was rare in more than one way too, since she was of Asian descent. There weren't many of that heritage on New Earth. Kali was the only one Carmen personally knew.

"May I take your order?" she asked.

The question was a pointless formality, but she had somehow gotten into the habit of asking it for the first customer of the day. The girl opened her mouth to answer. Carmen took over from there.

"A number one and a number three, extra-large," Carmen said. It was momentary, but the girl's eyes narrowed in obvious confusion. Carmen responded before she could open her mouth. "Hold the sides," she added.

The girl blinked a few times. "Right..." she muttered. "Cool," she said, her lips forming a pleased smile.

Carmen smiled too. "That's 8.75."

"Yeah, okay."

The girl paid, and Carmen attended to the next person in line. It was a Space Force enlisted man. His uniform indicated that he was in the Fleet Command branch. As with the girl, he approached boldly. Carmen expected as much, as most Space Force personnel she met were well used to Clairvoyants and weren't unduly afraid of them. Space Force was always eager for Clairvoyant recruits, especially with the war. She received at least one piece of mail from them each day.

He looked at the now awestruck girl and then turned to Carmen and smiled. "Guess I don't have to tell you what I want," he said, chuckling lightly.

She couldn't help a self-satisfied smirk. "A number four

with everything. On the house." Active-duty soldiers weren't charged.

"Thank you," he said.

"You're welcome," she said back.

The next pair was a married couple. Carmen took a deep breath and let her finger tap the counter.

"What should I have, Bob?"

"I don't know, Mortina. Pick one," Bob replied.

Carmen stood by and waited…and waited…and waited some more. It was always rather hard to know when to interject, even for her.

"But I always have the same thing. I want to try something different," Mortina said.

"Umm," Carmen tried to say, but they ignored her.

"Why don't you try this one?" Bob said, pointing.

"But I don't think I'd like that."

"Umm, excuse me," Carmen tried again.

"Hold on, we're almost ready," Bob said without even looking at her. Mortina didn't pay her any mind either.

"Excuse me," Carmen said with a bit more force.

"What?" they both asked simultaneously, so annoyed that even a comatose dog would be able to tell.

She was unfazed. "Salad," she said simply.

There was a long pause. "I guess I'll have that," Mortina said. Her voice was a pathetic whine.

Carmen rolled her eyes as they paid. *Sorry. I guess I should have just read your mind and known what you wanted,* she thought sarcastically. They looked at her hesitantly over their shoulders as they walked away. Carmen ignored them. She instead fixed her attention on the next person in line, a woman with a small child. Her arm was wrapped around her son while she tried her best to shield him behind her leg. She didn't even step up to the counter. Carmen took a second to consider the ridiculousness.

"Can someone else help me?" the woman asked.

"A number two and a number one off the kids' menu," Carmen said with a sigh. There was no point in even dignifying the question.

The woman hesitated, and Carmen realized what the problem was. She had no way of paying without getting closer. The Clairvoyant sighed again before she telekinetically lifted the woman's credit card from out of her purse. The woman gave what could best be called a mouse squeak at that. Even Carmen would admit she was stepping over the bounds of acceptable behavior, but her line was getting too long for anything else. She replaced the card and looked the woman in the eye.

I could snap your neck with a thought, but... "I don't bite," Carmen said simply. She doubted the woman believed her.

The next person in line was no better. He stared at the Clairvoyant and swallowed hard. Carmen looked at him then glanced at the rest of the line and noted the same. Her little display, while expedient, wasn't very wise. By this point, though, the cat was out of the bag, running across the room, and climbing up a tree. No way was it coming back.

"Why play around anymore?" she said to herself.

She turned to her computer and rung up the next five people in sequence. Shortly after, five credit cards zoomed through the air and into her hand. A few people screamed, but Carmen paid no mind to the hysterics. She wasn't stealing anything. Their cards were flying back to them in only a few seconds. Nevertheless, two people left the line and then the building at a fast walk. The next group in line stood still, too confused and nervous to know what to do. Their state made them a little harder than usual to read, but only a little bit. In due time, another convoy of cards were flying toward her.

"She's never done this before," she thought she heard one of her coworkers mutter to another.

That was true, but it worked. It took less than ten minutes to clear the entire line. Carmen eventually folded her arms and smiled. *All done*, she thought. There'd be some ruffled feathers, but whatever. She turned around and saw everyone scrambling to fill the backlog of orders. She turned again at no conscious prompting. Someone was coming to place an order. Carmen smiled.

* * *

Hours later, she took a deep breath. It had been the epitome of a busy day. She went to retrieve her bag with a weary sigh. Someone reached out an arm to place a hand on her shoulder only to stop short. Carmen turned anyway.

"Carmen…" It was the manager.

"Yes?" she asked.

He hesitated before he spoke. She didn't even have to read him for her spirits to fall. "What was that? Why'd you pull people's cards without even asking them?" There was no heat behind his words—he was too nervous for that—but it seemed like he wanted to yell if he could.

"Everyone was afraid of me. It would have taken too much time to just ask," she said. *I already know what they want anyway*, she thought with a bit of frustration.

"I would've preferred if you had taken your time. Half of them said they're never coming back after what you did. Almost all of them complained. Some are even saying they're going to write letters to corporate." He paused. "You do a good job. Damn good. Please, *please* don't be angry. I have kids. But...I'm going to have to let you go."

Carmen took a deep breath. *I have kids?* she wondered while clenching her jaw. She was a Clairvoyant, not an ogre.

"I'm not angry," she said simply. She thought about saying something on her behalf but decided against it. "Anything else?" she asked, already knowing the answer.

He said something, but she had already moved off. There was no reason to stay and listen. She found herself outside and in the flower shop next to her former employer almost as if she were on autopilot.

"Eight...I think," she muttered.

But who was she kidding? She'd long since lost count of how many jobs she'd lost. Maybe if she considered only the times that were strictly her fault, like today, she could keep the number to one hand. She groaned, regretting her stupid decision with the credit cards, and tried not to think about it. The flower shopkeeper walked toward her.

He smiled. "Hey, Carmen. The usual?"

As usual, it had taken a few minutes for him to get to her. The store had been doing record business since the start of the war. Most of the supply went to cemeteries and funerals.

"Yeah, sure," she replied. She then considered the contents of her bank account and the fact that it wasn't going to be filled by much of anything in the near future. "Just give me half," she added.

Flowers in hand, she set off for her next destination. It was always her favorite and her most dreaded. Another bus ride was involved. It was longer than before, but since she'd be looking for new work and a new gym, the regulars on this line would be spared the company of the Clairvoyant after today. She once again sat alone. The void around her was more apparent this time, since the bus was only half filled to begin with. At least she was able to give the flowers their own seat.

What am I going to do? she thought over and over again. She needed money, and it had been hard enough to get that job, meager though it may have been. She, like all Clairvoyants, had one best skill—a very lucrative one at that—but she promised herself that she'd never go into *that* market. Her stop came, though no answers came with it. The only thing she could think to do in the meantime was to try her best to sound hopeful, for what it was worth.

She got off and then paused in front of the building for a moment. She hated places like this. They brought back too many memories. Its counterpart was like her second dorm at the facility.

She walked inside and, as expected, the air was both stale and dry. No one stopped her or questioned her. She was here so often that she didn't even have to check in. She could probably draw a map for the entire hospital without really thinking about it. Certainly, she could find the intensive care ward with her eyes closed. From there, she could probably find Michael's room in her sleep.

She entered. Michael lay in bed unmoving, not saying a word, comatose. Part of her always hoped his bright smiling face would greet her when she opened the door or that she'd finally open her eyes and learn that the past year had been nothing but a bad dream or a cruel practical joke. But she looked at him and knew he was just a step up from dead. The doctor told her, when he was first admitted, that talking to him might improve his condition; that he could be aware of her presence even in his state. She didn't know if that was the case for other coma victims, but for Michael, they were hollow words. The impression he gave her was just as much a shell as all those Constructs she fought when she was younger. She had no doubt he was alive. The medical monitoring systems and her own senses could easily tell that. There was hardly anything else, though.

"Hello," she greeted as pleasantly as she could.

There was no response in any manner. All things considered, she wondered why she went through the motions. She was painfully aware that they meant nothing to him.

She walked over and kissed him on the forehead. A few loose strands of hair fell on his face. She apologized and changed the flowers out of the vase. After that, she took a chair and sat down next to him.

Carmen took a deep breath. She was happy his parents weren't here. She wanted some time alone with him. She'd be the first to say that they had warmed to her over time. Sure, they were wary as most people were, but at least they didn't cling to the ceiling every time she coughed. She remembered the look on their faces when she and Michael revealed that they were going to live together. It seemed like such a long time ago.

Stackett Syndrome, as was the case with Michael, could be swift in its onset. The post-natal genetic messaging update to generation three, which she had received not too long after she was born, didn't take as well for everybody. It was exceedingly rare and at times seemingly random, but a select few suffered a complete breakdown of major organs, as well as immune system failure and a host of other ailments that basically amounted to the body rejecting the outside genetic tempering. She guessed progress of all kinds wasn't without a bit of sacrifice.

The bigger issue, though, was that treatment was expensive and the cure exorbitantly so. If he wasn't sick, it would have been cheaper to shoot him, let him go cold for an hour, and then revive him. She was living barely above subsistence, and his parents were only doing a little better, just to keep him going.

She took another deep breath. Then she leaned forward to rest her arms on the bed rail. "I had quite a day," she said. "I got thrown out of another gym. It was a little ratty there, so I guess I don't mind."

She paused for a few seconds before she continued. The gym, in reality, wasn't all that bad. Not perfect, but not bad either. Carmen rested her head on her arms and closed her eyes. She thought about her trips on the bus and figured she'd stay here a little longer than normal. It was comforting. At least everything was still here. No one stared at her. No one fought to get away from her.

"I was pretty stupid at work, though. We had a long line, and everybody was moving real slow. So, I just took their orders and telekinetically lifted their cards. I don't think I've ever seen the manager madder. But he was too scared of me to really say anything." She paused again. "Everything will be okay," she said, trying her best to sound hopeful. "Everything will be fine." She was only able to mutter the last part a bit above a whisper.

She opened her eyes and looked at him. There was no response, no murmur, nothing. There was just the beeps and hums of the medical equipment that was keeping him alive. She once again wondered why she went through the motions. She sensed nothing from him, just a numbness that filled the room, chilling everything about her.

"I, I—" she started, but there was someone at the door.

She turned to face it just as it started to open. Carmen knew who the person was and her name, Elaine. She wasn't happy to see her, though. She was a nice person, for as much as Carmen ever cared to read, but she wasn't the giver of good news.

"Ms. Grey, can I speak to you for a moment?"

"Yes," Carmen said. She turned to Michael. "I'll be right back," she said softly.

Elaine led her into the hallway and closed the door to the room. "About the bill… The account is now a month overdue and will soon be two months. We'd like to know when we can expect payment."

"I don't know. I lost one of my jobs. I don't really have anything to give."

"That's unfortunate," Elaine said. Carmen licked her lips nervously. The woman took a subconscious step back. "We've been as flexible as we possibly can, but with the war, we need all the space we can get. We've reviewed all delinquent accounts for—"

"So, you're basically saying that, if I don't pay you, you'll kick him out?"

Elaine retreated a step farther. Carmen noticed and felt her entire body wilt. She had attempted to ask the question with as polite a tone as she could muster. If she offered it with a bowl of sugar, people would probably still cower.

"Unfortunately, yes, that's what I'm saying."

"That would kill him."

"I know," Elaine said. "I'm sorry. I don't enjoy this, but you and his family can barely afford to keep him here, let alone what it would cost to fully treat him. The reality of the situation is that it's time to let go. You all suffer in living this disjointedly."

There was visible worry on Elaine's face. Carmen noticed the entire hall was clear of people. She couldn't remember that ever being the case. The poor soul in front of her was sent to face down the Clairvoyant, and not even the janitors had the courage to be on the same floor. *What power I wield*, she thought dejectedly.

"You aren't angry, are you?" Elaine eventually asked after swallowing hard.

Carmen didn't answer right away. Her Dark, her emotions, and her thoughts were all essential ingredients, but none was more important than the other. She'd received endless lessons on that. Anger, though? Janus and even Kali had never much mentioned it, or what to do with it specifically.

"I'm feeling a lot of things," she said. "I guess anger too. But that doesn't help me. I can fly, read your mind, snap your neck where you stand, or burn this building to the ground with a thought—"

"Ms. Grey, please!" Elaine said with a start, holding her hands up in a vain attempt to defend herself.

Carmen saw her reaction to the simple truth both of them had pretended, until now, didn't exist. She took a deep breath and her eyes fell before she spoke again.

"I'm sorry. I didn't mean to alarm you with what I said," she spoke softly. "My point is, it doesn't matter if I'm angry. For all those things I can do, right here and right now, you're more powerful than me." She was quiet for a few seconds. Elaine just stared at her. "I'll try harder." She then walked back into the room and closed the door.

3

HOW TO PLAY

Carmen's eyes narrowed. She knew what was coming.

"I'm so angry."

She considered her charge's words and could only shake her head. "So, why are you angry, Phaethon?" she asked. "This time, anyway," she added.

Phaethon noted his handler's tone and winced. It didn't occur all too often, but he made that reaction from time to time. She was always at a loss as to why. She never thought she came across as a cold, overbearing tyrant like Janus had with her, nor did she think she possessed Kali's quiet intimidation or even her calm persuasiveness. But somehow she affected Phaethon just as strongly as they had affected her.

How she came to be his handler was a special case, mainly because he was a difficult one. He'd only been her charge for a few months—her first and only. She wasn't all too keen on being a handler. The idea of it left a bad taste in her mouth. She had never liked the facility nor had any real interest in coming back, let alone helping it. However, the money was good, and that was always in short supply. Her conversation with Elaine from a couple days ago still echoed in her head. She'd need every credit she could scrounge up now more than ever. She only had to the end of the month to pay the hospital bill.

She tried not to think about it too much. For the here and now, her focus was on her charge, but she and Phaethon were just so unalike. It was like they'd been deliberately selected to be together because they were opposites. It also didn't help that they were relatively close in age. Kali and even Janus, to a lesser extent, had seemed so wise, so knowing. But what more did she know than someone four years her junior? She hadn't named him. She hadn't collected him from his birth family. In fact, he killed the handler who'd done those things, which was a bit disconcerting, since he and Carmen didn't get along like she had with Kali. At best, they were still feeling each other out.

Phaethon's moment of weakness was brief. After, he stared her in the eye, his gaze fiery and fierce. It seemed like he would spontaneously combust at any second. Yet it was not like Artemis all those years ago. She was raw, extremely raw, but it was focused aggression. Phaethon's blaze was not as coherent. Carmen was unfazed, though. She simply leaned back and calmly rested her head on an open palm.

"Well?" she asked.

He said nothing, as she expected. If nothing else, being a handler was definitely a test in patience. This time, she was able to keep herself to just a sigh before turning back to the game. It was chess. Kali had suggested it. Carmen never really played it before. Calling her a novice would be charitable. Phaethon was worse, and most of the time he didn't even want to play. More games than not ended with the board and pieces thrown on the ground.

It was her turn. She picked up a piece, considered it for a moment, and then carefully placed it back on the board. Phaethon looked at her. His brown hair was a mess. He never really cared about tending it. His soft, almost babylike features, offered an odd contrast to his muscled, athletic body. He shifted slightly in his chair. That was nothing new or unusual. She considered it a foregone conclusion that he was incapable of being truly at rest. A thought or two definitely raged madly in his head. She didn't know what they were, as he was too strong to read, but it was obvious his neurons were lighting off in rapid fire. It even looked like he was going to say something, but in the end they were words she'd never hear, since he turned his attention to the game and ignored her for a moment. His hand hovered over the board, tentative and uncertain.

Carmen's eyes wandered while he took his time. As usual, they sat outside. Most of the assets, and she herself, preferred it after spending years trapped underground. The grounds and facility had been updated and expanded since her attendance. The courtyard was larger to allow the assets more space in their attempts to socialize. There was also now a library, among other new buildings. The protective concrete wall topped by barbed wire still ringed the facility. She swore its height had been raised.

The barrier was still no such thing to her and all the Clairvoyants here. There were no attempts to breach it, that she personally witnessed, from the outside. Even so, that loathsome wall did limit one thing: any view beyond it. Inside the grounds, assets mingled self-consciously and handlers managed them, but that was it. There was just this place. That was almost all there was to see and interact with. She had no care for it. It wasn't much help either that it was almost an outright war to get Phaethon to go to the bluff or the field trips she and Kali used to go on. The only true vista that could be seen was the nearby Haven City. Its cold skyscrapers were just as intimating now as when Carmen saw them all those years ago. Their perpetual shadow menaced the court-yard even on the best days.

Carmen looked at the city in the distance and then turned back to Phaethon. His hand still hovered over the board. He was biting his lip. She'd been told that he was one of the fiercest Clairvoyants to have ever been brought here. She'd never questioned that. But looking at him now?

"So?" she asked, trying to get him to finally make his move. They could be sitting here for the next half hour if she didn't give some sort of prompting. She'd put a timer on their games more than once just for that purpose.

"I just am. I don't know why," he said.

"What are you talking about?"

Phaethon looked at her strangely. "Being angry."

"Oh," she muttered. She'd forgotten about that conversation.

She looked at him and considered what she'd say in response, but his attention was fixed on the chessboard and what move he'd make. It could wait. He moved a rook one hesitant square forward. His hand remained on the piece while he made sure it was free from danger. He removed his hand a few seconds later and sat back. Carmen gave a thoughtful nod. Phaethon was always so eager to rush into things that it was nice to see him at least try to think his play out. But after the nod, she used a pawn to capture the piece. Phaethon frowned.

"Damn it!" he yelled.

Stupid, Carmen thought as she braced herself for the

explosion. She didn't need to take the piece. In fact, she wished she hadn't taken the piece. It was no real secret that a major reason she'd been selected to be his handler was because she had some hope of defending herself. She wasn't afraid of him. His rage never truly turned against her, but it was prudent to be prepared.

This time, his ire was directed at the chessboard. He stood up, and a quick swipe sent it to the ground. Then he glared at her and took a step forward, fist balled. She stared back, her expression casually thoughtful. Phaethon sat back down after a few tense seconds. He then slouched in a huff with his head resting on his hands. Carmen had been in this situation enough times by now to know it was safe to proceed. She telekinetically gathered the pieces and reset the board and then waved for him to take his turn.

"Why do we have to play this stupid game anyway?" he asked as he half-heartedly moved a pawn forward.

Carmen studied the strategic situation before she spoke. "In all honesty, I don't really know," she said, moving her own pawn forward. It could have been brilliant or clumsy— she couldn't really tell either way. It was simply the best move she could make that she was aware of. "My old handler suggested it," she continued.

Phaethon groaned, and Carmen tried her best to hide a wince. *Stupid*, she thought again. Kali and her advice were a constant source of discussion and contention. Phaethon was tired of hearing it. Carmen, unfortunately, had no other real source to draw upon. Her charge had referred to her as "the messenger" more than once in a fit of frustration. Carmen didn't think any of that was fair, though. She never reiterated Kali's advice verbatim. No, she changed a word or two when she said exactly the same thing.

He leaned back and ignored the game for a moment as he stared off into the sky. "And why did she suggest this stupid waste of time?" he asked dismissively.

"She said it helps you to think," Carmen replied.

"We're Clairvoyants. We don't have to think."

She stared at him hard. Try as she might, she couldn't piece together his reasoning. "Umm…"

"You know what I meant," he said, glancing at her. "*My* old handler said that, because of our Darks, we don't need to consciously think. We just do."

"I don't think it's that simple," she replied.

Phaethon looked at her but said nothing. Slowly, his demeanor changed from dismissive indifference to, well… something else. If she didn't know better, he even seemed curious.

"Really?" he eventually asked. "What do *you* think? Not Kali."

"Well…" Carmen muttered, not knowing where to start.

It wasn't the first time he'd wanted her unfiltered opinion. She, however, was always hesitant to give it. Her advice didn't help her any. Her life, such as it was, could only be called a rousing success in a tragic comedy.

"I like to think that our Dark is what gets us going—what gets us actually motivated. But we still need reason to decide what to do and how to do it." Phaethon began to nod, yet the nodding was soon replaced by a growing frown. Carmen decided to change tact. "It's kind of like this game," she said. "You want to win…right?"

Phaethon said nothing. Carmen stared at him hard and then rolled her eyes, which prompted the proper response. "Yeah, I guess so," he said.

"Right," she said with a quick nod. "But just because you

want to win and you take action to win doesn't mean you know how to win. That has nothing to do with your Dark. You have to actually think and make choices. Your Dark can't do that. Like, you may have a favorite flavor of ice cream, but you have to decide whether you eat it and even how to eat it." She considered what she was going to say next, thought against it, and then figured why not? "Or like when you realized you were losing and decided to throw the board to the ground. It was stupid, but you were thinking," she said, her tone light and teasing.

Phaethon was quiet and serious while she spoke. Then, in an ever so rare event, he laughed lightly. "No, it wasn't. You always beat me," he said. Carmen shrugged. He turned back to the board, his hand hovering over it. "You sure Kali doesn't think the same thing?" he asked, adopting a teasing air as well.

Carmen didn't notice it. "I don't know," she said.

Phaethon nodded. "Hmm." He placed his hand on a piece and hesitantly moved it forward. He leaned back after a sigh. "I wish I knew what to do."

You and me both, kid, Carmen thought. She considered saying as much but thought better of it. "I think it's something we have to practice, just like anything else," she said instead as she moved her own piece. "At least, I hope it works that way," she muttered under her breath. Phaethon heard her and nodded.

His next move lacked the hesitant caution of his previous few. He could never keep to that for long. Despite that, it completely changed the landscape. Carmen paused for a moment as she worked out what her response would be. Nothing immediately came to mind, but what did come were the first elements of anxiety.

Phaethon stared at her, and though there was no clock, she felt pressed to act. She moved her piece and then winced as soon as she was finished. Phaethon, in turn, smiled, and capitalized on her mistake. Mercy never even entered the equation. After his move, he stared at her again, ready and waiting. Carmen, however, looked at the board.

The shadows of Haven City and all contained therein muted her features. There was anxiety and maybe even fear; either way, her Dark let itself be known. She leaned back for a moment. Her next manipulation of the chessboard was simple, direct. It wasn't a very good play, though. Phaethon captured the piece, and the strategic situation changed again, for the worse.

Carmen considered the new layout for a few seconds and then made her move. It was just as bad as the previous one. Phaethon didn't capture another piece, but he did greatly enhance his position. She frowned. She thought about how he always overturned the board when things weren't going well. It was tempting, but just then she saw an opportunity, though a small one.

At first, Phaethon didn't realize what had just happened. He smiled as he took another piece. But he and elation parted ways soon after. With each move, he became more unsure and more frantic. His actions took a sporadic quality in contrast to his handler's calm focus. Till, at last, boxed in a corner, he heard the word he couldn't stand to hear.

"Check," Carmen said simply.

Her charge stared at the board. His face fell and his body slackened. At first, she worried he'd overturn the board again or worse. But no, he'd given up trying. There were other moves he could have taken, other options, but he took none of them. Instead, Phaethon knocked his own king over and sat back in his chair.

"You always win," he muttered softly.

Carmen glanced at him. "I wish that were the case," she said under her breath.

He didn't hear her as she began rearranging the board. "I'm tired of this game," he said.

She glanced at him again. That wasn't an unusual complaint. They wouldn't play for days and he'd still say it as soon as she broke out the board. But maybe he had really had enough for the day. Her eyes turned to Haven City and then back to him.

"We could take a field trip?"

Phaethon turned his head slowly to look at that great metropolis. It had been one of the main tourist centers of New Earth before the war. While Carmen had never done it, one could get lost for weeks sampling its vistas, cuisine, and unique entertainment. Phaethon swallowed hard.

"I'd rather not," he said meekly. Carmen couldn't help raising an eyebrow. "What of it?" he spat, noticing his handler's wayward eyebrow.

That's the Phaethon I know, she thought. "Don't worry about it," she said simply. "We'll go another time."

He nodded, then leaned toward her and rested his foot on top of the board. He knocked the pieces to the ground again, which made Carmen frown, but she otherwise kept her composure.

"We should spar." His voice carried steel-like confidence.

She shook her head. "I don't want to fight you."

Phaethon laughed and rested his arm on his knee. "Come on, we don't have to fight to the death. My handler said Clairvoyants fight to the death, but we don't *always* have to."

So did mine, Carmen thought. "I don't want to do that either."

Her charge gave an annoyed groan and sat back in his

chair again. "You're no fun. Me and the other assets spar all the time—" Carmen looked at him hard. They weren't supposed to do that. "No one gets hurt," he said quickly. "Too badly," he added under his breath. "But why not?"

She took a few seconds to think about it. She doubted simply saying she didn't want to would satisfy him, despite all his lessons on Darks.

"I'm you're handler—"

"So?" he interrupted.

Carmen raised a hand to hold him off. It had become a reflex by the second day of knowing him. "That means I'm responsible for your wellbeing. I don't think beating you up falls in line with that."

"Beating me up?" Phaethon mused. "What makes you think you'd win? People say you're pretty strong, but I always win. That's what I'm good at, not this stupid game," he added, glancing at the board. "I'll prove it to you."

"No," Carmen said firmly. She was about to respond to what he said till she realized they had both missed the point. She took a second to gather herself before she spoke again. "I said I'm responsible for your wellbeing. And really, your wellbeing *is* about this game," she said, motioning her head toward the city. "And that fight. Not about...not about showing off."

"Is that another message from Kali?"

"No," Carmen replied. "She only tells me every other thing to say," she added, chancing a joke. It didn't work, although she wasn't surprised. She didn't have much practice in making jokes.

"Well, that's bullshit," he said. Carmen looked at him hard again. Almost everyone knew not to curse around her. "That's stupid," he corrected himself.

"Why?"

"'Cause I don't need any of that," he said. Carmen looked at him hard for about the tenth time today before she shook her head. He continued anyway. "We don't need to play that stupid game. And it's not showing off. We're practicing. You know as well as I do that we're all going to become mercenaries, soldiers, or something like that. Why'd they spend so much time training us to fight if we were supposed to play chess?"

"I don't know," Carmen said. "But why am I here if all you're supposed to do is fight?"

"…Stop confusing everything."

She shook her head again and sat back in her chair. She said nothing, however. Perhaps she was being confusing? Either way, this conversation wasn't going anywhere. Carmen glanced at the other assets and then looked at Phaethon.

"Maybe we should take a little break?"

He glanced at them as well and knew exactly what she meant. "That would be good," he said as he stood.

He added nothing else and began to walk off. "I'll find you later," Carmen said before he was out of ear shot. She saw him nod in response, and then she was alone.

Her first thought was to go to the bluff. It had been a while since she last visited. But she didn't really have the time for it, so instead, with a sigh, she pulled out her PDD. She hated trying to find a job, despite her extensive practice at it. Things were worse now that she needed something that paid a lot very quickly.

She'd long since assigned a hot key to the local job listings. The first pulled were, of course, offers to join various mercenary bands. The occupation was on the extralegal side, but the authorities tended to look the other way, especially with the war, since they were the prime clients. For years, some of the larger mercenary groups had even been trying to set up recruitment centers at the facility. Clairvoyants were always in high demand.

Although the job search engine was smart enough to sort by her personal skills and aptitude, it wasn't as good in responding to her tastes. The listings were projected out in front of her in a large hologram. She studied the image, hoping to find something that didn't fit her best skill. She found nothing on the current page, so she went to the next. It was filled with recruitment ads for Space Force and various planetary self-defense forces. Carmen had seen them so many times that they may as well have been tattooed on the back of her eyelids. The signing bonuses were tempting, though. She went to the next page before her willpower could completely fail. Then she grabbed a clump of her hair and pulled in frustration.

"This is impossible," she muttered to herself.

After leaning back in her chair, Carmen took a deep breath and then let it go in an annoyed huff. If she gave both her arms and legs, she still wouldn't have enough money. Just then, she smiled. She turned and saw her old handler walking toward her. She waved so fast that it was a wonder her arm didn't fly off; she just couldn't help herself. Kali smiled modestly and waved back in the same fashion. Carmen ensnared her in a hug when she was close enough.

"And how is my favorite former charge?" Kali asked after taking a step back.

Carmen paused for a moment. She could practically feel the small spurt of elation drain from her body. "Battered," she muttered.

Kali nodded slowly and then took a seat, which prompted Carmen to do the same. "No luck on the job hunt then?"

Carmen's PDD started randomly scrolling through the listings. She didn't really care enough by this point to stop it or even check them. "Luck…" she said, rolling her eyes. "I think it's a bit beyond luck. I need a miracle."

"Well, I'd be happy to—"

"No," Carmen said sharply. "I said I don't want to do that. How many times do I have to tell you?"

Kali raised an eyebrow at her former charge and let the look simmer. Carmen wilted much as Phaethon had with her. Although Kali held no formal power over her now, the effort to even look at her old handler could break infinium.

"Edge, why do you always make things so difficult for yourself?" Kali asked, though it sounded rhetorical.

"I'm not," Carmen said anyway. "Everything was fine before the hospital needed more money."

"Everything was fine? Lie to yourself, but don't lie to me, please. Actually, don't even lie to yourself. You should know better."

"I guess you're right," she muttered. "But I don't want to fight anymore."

Kali studied her former charge for a moment. "I'm only trying to help you," she said softly.

"I know," Carmen replied.

"Edge…my Edge," she went on, slowly shaking her head. "If he did anything, Janus named you well. So, what do you plan to do?"

Carmen couldn't help a small shudder. She thought about her answer and simply shrugged when nothing good came to mind. Kali opened her mouth but closed it just as quickly. She glanced at the chessboard.

"How's your play?" she asked.

"Terrible," Carmen admitted.

Kali gave an amused smirk at that then waved at the board. Carmen's PDD rested on the board and was still on. It continued to flip through the job listings, but Kali said nothing about it. Carmen didn't think it would get in the way, so she didn't move it. The board was set in moments, and Kali made the first move. Carmen took a deep breath before she made hers. They'd played each other only a few times, and even then it had just been to teach Carmen how to play. Carmen knew she had no hope whatsoever in winning, but it would help take her mind off things.

"How are you handling your charge?" Kali asked.

"I don't even know," Carmen said. "I wish it was just like…you and me," she added, glancing at her.

"And how are you and I?"

Carmen looked at her through the job listings. "Well, for one thing, he doesn't get up and hug me when he sees me."

"I see your point," Kali said after a quick nod. "But that really shouldn't matter."

Carmen frowned as one of her bishops was captured. She was already doing badly enough before she lost it. "What do you mean?" she asked.

"A handler is not a parent or even a teacher," Kali explained. "Our chief concern is the wellbeing of our charge. It doesn't make much difference if they actually like us or not."

"It certainly makes things easier, though," Carmen said with a groan.

Kali made no reply other than a smile. Their game continued, though Carmen would say it was more of a rout. When it was finished, inevitably with her defeat, they started again. Their play was different from hers with Phaethon. Kali was almost toying with her, teasing her into action before closing an unseen trap. The second match ended much like the first.

"Have you heard the latest news?" her old handler asked casually, changing the subject.

"About the admiral, yeah. What of it?"

Kali glanced at her and slowly shook her head. "No, I don't mean him."

"Then what are you talking about?"

"Earth was attacked."

Carmen paused as she considered her first move. Her hand hovered over almost every piece in turn. "Everybody heard about that. News talks about it all the time. They said a lot of people were killed."

"A lot of people killed?" Kali mused with a shrug. Then she looked at the city in the distance, at the courtyard, and lastly at Carmen. "You'd never know," she said simply. "Everything is so calm here. It's hard to tell that everything has its price."

Carmen's hand hovered over the board for a few brief seconds. "Price? Since when are people currency?" she asked casually.

"Everyone has a value, especially in war," Kali said, her tone vastly more serious than Carmen's.

"So what is being bought?" Carmen asked, only half paying attention to the conversation. The game required most of her focus.

"Hmm… I don't know," Kali said. "I don't think anyone really knows."

"So, then what's the point?" Carmen asked, glancing at her.

She glanced back. "Edge, do you remember what you told me after your first flight? That the people in the town seemed disjointed?"

"I remember." It was obvious that she was going to lose this game as well.

Kali nodded slowly. "Individual people aren't rational, let alone billions of them committed to an effort. They're scared now, more like frightened beasts than anything civilized. The reason is easy to figure out. They don't want to be killed. But why? Life is more than just fear of death. It has a point—everything has a point—but I don't think anyone can know what it is," she said. "You've been out there for a couple of years now," she began again, motioning toward the city. "Do you really understand any of it?"

"No," Carmen admitted.

"No one does. It can probably never be understood. There are benefits to that, though."

"How does anyone benefit from that?"

"Hmm." Kali smiled broadly. "Terrans are as much a wildfire as anything—uncontrollable and utterly destructive. And if the sortens are dumb enough to throw away their worthless lives fighting it, we're all better off."

It wasn't the first time Kali had said something like that since the war started. Her words, as always, flowed so smoothly that they may as well have been dipped in honey. The words, just as the style in which they were said, were not unusual. Most of the Clairvoyants of her generation detested sortens. Carmen had never met any.

"I don't pay much attention to the war. I have enough to worry about as it is. I just wish I knew what to do," she said after a sigh.

"You don't need to make things so hard on yourself. You do have options," Kali said.

"Doesn't mean I have to choose them," Carmen said back.

She then slumped in her chair and stared at the chessboard. In retrospect, she couldn't really blame Phaethon for never wanting to play. It wasn't very fun when you always lost.

"So, what will you do?"

Carmen looked at her old handler through the image

projected by the PDD. Kali's face was mixture of concern with a touch of impatience. She had seen the expression more than once. But just when she was about to respond, Carmen stopped short. Her focus changed from Kali to the image itself. She smiled.

"Well, there's an option I can live with."

4

LONG SHOT

A dab here, a dab there. The effort drew Carmen's full focus, as the precision required in this sphere of life was beyond her normally deft hand. She was progressing slowly, but progress was still progress. That was, until she looked at her reflection, frowned, and decided to start over. This had to be the third or fourth attempt; she'd lost count. Makeup wasn't a weapon she had all too much experience with, nor was it one of those skills she just knew. Kali had tried to give her some practical lessons with it when she was younger, but her handler had been just as hopeless. The guides Carmen found with her PDD were helpful, though. Now she looked like a circus clown only when you squinted.

She shook her head and then continued with the construction of her new face. Everything would have to be perfect for a change. She'd been on countless job interviews and thought nothing of them, but this time she swore she'd see a guillotine hanging over her head if she looked up. If not over her head, it was certainly over Michael's.

She found it a bit hard to optimistically gauge her chances. Her clothes, unfortunately, were rather modest, though that was due more to lack of funds than bad taste or meager skill in dressing herself. She styled her hair to the best of her ability, which meant it was in a ponytail. Considering her hair, clothes, and haphazard makeup, it would come down to her charming personality to make a good impression.

"This is impossible," Carmen said after a groan.

She checked her watch and noted the time. She needed to catch her bus. It would be improper to be late to a fruitless job interview. She could be there in a matter of minutes if she flew, and in fact she had recently abstained from public transportation to save a little money. Every credit helped. Today, though, she would take the bus. It was too tiring to fly, and she wanted to be at her sharpest. Furthermore, flying fast had an annoying tendency to turn her hair into a frizzed mess, which wouldn't do at all.

She looked at her reflection again, wanting and hoping everything was in order. She remembered when she had melted the thing once when her reflection gave a bad review. The memory made her smirk as she left the bathroom.

The floor boards were so loose in the apartment that even the Clairvoyant caused squeaks and groans as she made her way to the door. It was the best she was able to afford. Having a roommate was out. She had tried a couple times, but no one wanted to live with a Clairvoyant. The cockroaches she couldn't see but knew were there didn't count. She entered the elevator, pressed the button to the ground floor, and sighed.

"Not impossible," she said to herself, hoping.

When the elevator opened, the building's super, Anthony, was standing in front of her. She had never said anything to him, nor he her. But they did have some semblance of a relationship. He sneered at her and she tried her best to ignore him. She glanced at him, and he her. She walked by him, not gracing him with another glance. Once, she had overheard him saying to another tenant that occupancy had dropped fifteen percent since Carmen rented there. That, of course, was her fault, but for what it was worth, she figured it had more to do with the war draft than run-of-the-mill Clairvoyant fear. Whatever the case, someone she was actually pleased to see was in the lobby.

"Theodore," she called.

The boy glanced up at her and smiled, but he was too preoccupied with whatever he was doing to hug her leg as he usually did.

"Hello," he squealed.

Theodore was four. None of the other children ever played with him, and none of the other adults, as far as she knew, ever talked to him. His parents were terrified of him. He never seemed to notice, though. He just did his own thing. At present, he had a collection of some of his toy people and cars in the center of the lobby telekinetically swirling the lobby dirt in a funnel.

Carmen fell to her knees next to him as she watched the scene. "What are you doing?" she asked.

"Playing tornado," he said proudly.

"Tornado?"

"Yeah, look."

Right after that, the spinning dirt engulfed one of the toy people. Round and round the toy went until it was kicked out of the tornado. Theodore laughed impishly, and Carmen smiled. *Why did I never think of that?* Certainly, it seemed more fun than making the dolls dance.

She didn't know if Theodore was destined for the facility when he turned six. She'd learned since she was released that the rules governing which children were taken were quite complicated. She couldn't ask his parents, as they tried to avoid talking to her, even though she regularly babysat for them. She was the only person, for as far as she knew, who would agree to babysit him. She guessed he would be taken. Either way, she wished she'd had someone to talk to when she was his age. Every Clairvoyant she knew wished they had

"So, how do I look?" she asked after his demonstration was done. "I'm going to a job interview."

"Another one?" he asked in complete disbelief.

"Yes, another one," Carmen replied, rolling her eyes. "So, how do I look?" she asked again, turning her head from side to side in exaggerated fashion and puckering her lips. "Pretty, right?"

Theodore looked her up and down, examining every inch of her carefully. He started giggling before he spoke. "Ew," he said.

"Ew!" Carmen said back. "Ew!" she said again. Theodore giggled louder. "I'll show you ew!"

Then she grabbed him and gave him a big wet kiss on the cheek. It hurt a bit to do so. He wasn't very good at lowering his bioelectric field to touch anyone or when they touched him. In any case, Theodore squealed like he'd been stabbed.

"Yuck!" he screamed as he pulled away, furiously rubbing his cheek with his shirt sleeve. Then he pushed her telekinetically.

"Ah, ah, ah, no. I told you not to do that to anyone. That's not nice." Theodore looked at her but gave no response. Carmen stood up and then leaned forward so they were face to face. "Listen to your mom and dad, and I'll see you when I get back."

He smiled. "Okay!"

"Good," she replied, standing straight again. "Don't blow down the building," she added as she began to walk off.

He laughed and, a moment later, sicced the tornado on

her. She made a show of running away until she was safely outside. This time, Carmen sighed contentedly as she leaned against the glass door. She turned to wave goodbye and was greeted by her reflection. *Ew indeed,* she thought dismally.

"This *is* impossible," she muttered to herself as she started walking toward the bus.

The journey would be quick. She thought she heard someone mutter, "Monster," or some such thing when she entered, but she wasn't sure. Either way, the ride was more or less sedate. No one was unnerved like they usually were—cause for celebration, if she wasn't so anxious. It was hard to remember the last time her Dark had made her suffer that rather annoying malady. Anxiety to a Clairvoyant was like water to a cat. She took a deep breath when the bus lurched to a stop. At least executions had some sort of ceremony involved. Her only luxury was the long walk before the end.

The stage that would be removing Carmen's head was a nondescript office building in an old section of the city. She didn't know why she expected a construction company to be housed in a compound that looked like an industrial palace, or that it would be some perpetually half-built hulk. She took one last moment to look herself over and then walked inside.

"May I help you?" a receptionist behind a desk asked.

The room was large and squarish. The floor was tile, and the walls were adorned with pictures of various completed construction projects and people she didn't know. There wasn't much decoration other than that.

"I'm Carmen Grey. I have an interview scheduled for today."

"The Clairvoyant candidate, right?" the receptionist asked.

"…Yes," Carmen responded. She listed on the application that she was Clairvoyant. She usually didn't, for what good it did, but in this instance, it was the only way, in her mind, that she could get the job. All the same, it always made her uneasy that it was a fact worth mentioning.

"Please fill this out. You can sit over there with the other candidates," she said, pointing. "Please wait until you are called."

Carmen glanced at her opponents. She was one of the youngest. Most were in their fifties or sixties, which wasn't very surprising, given the war effort. A higher-than-normal percentage of women was just as expected. She took a seat amongst them. They looked at her and then uncomfortably shifted away.

"Off to such a great start," she said to herself after demurely resting her head on an open hand. Maybe it was her makeup?

No one really talked to each other, and Carmen didn't mind it. Most, as she did, just filled out their forms without saying a word. When the time came, she stood a few seconds before she was actually called.

"Ms. Grey—" the recruiter started, but she cut him off.

"I know," she said simply. "Neil, isn't it?" she asked as she walked closer.

Everyone looked at her, but Carmen paid them no mind. Frankly, she found the reaction strange. What was so odd about a Clairvoyant acting like a Clairvoyant?

Neil took her hand and gave it a firm shake. "Clairvoyant, huh? We were talking about you."

Carmen smiled. "I know," she said. She started walking toward the interview room in the back with no prompting.

Neil scratched his head. "I guess I'll follow you," he muttered.

She gave a self-satisfied smirk that he couldn't see and figured that would be enough showing off. They had talked about her, but those discussions were more out of curiosity than fear or disdain. She could glean at least that from a cursory read. All in all, she thought she made a good first impression. She opened the door telekinetically when they got to the interview room, and then she sat in her designated seat before he told her which it was. Well, maybe she could show off that one last time. Neil sat opposite her.

The office was stuffy and small. It probably had a previous life as a supply closet. Carmen well knew the like. She could probably write a book about all the places she'd been interviewed. Neil looked her over for a few brief seconds, which was fair, since she had given him a read just as long. She made sure, however, not to read him now. Reading the mind of someone considering her could some-times be messy. She'd be the first to say there were some opinions of herself she'd rather not know.

Neil leaned back in his chair and pulled out his PDD. "You have an interesting work record," he said as he consulted her resume. "But it seems like you never stay in one job for more than a few months. Would you mind explaining that please?" he asked.

Carmen opened her mouth but closed it just as quickly. An easier explanation was possible. She telekinetically lifted a pen off his desk, twirled it a few times in front of him, and then replaced it. She punctuated the display with a small smirk and rolled her eyes.

"Do you want me to tell you what you had for breakfast this morning? Or which of your kids you love more?" she added for effect.

Neil looked at her, nonplused, till he chuckled lightly. "Yeah, I can kind of see your point," he muttered. "Clairvoy-ants can make grown men crap their pants. You don't read people's minds all the time, do you?" he asked nervously.

"No. It's not very pleasant," she replied.

"Hmm. Why?" he asked, curious.

"Do you want to know everything someone's thinking or has thought?" she answered after a brief pause.

Neil nodded slowly. "Have you ever had any work incidents?"

"Not with coworkers," Carmen answered. "They kind of get used to me after a while," she added, which was a small stretch of the truth but nothing her references would disagree with.

Neil nodded again while he wrote something on his PDD. "Well, you definitely seem more normal than I expected."

"What's normal?" Carmen asked. It was a semi-serious question that she just blurted out. She smiled to turn it into a joke before he could notice.

He laughed. "Yeah, you'd fit in well here," he muttered. "All the other candidates are so rigid. Must be the war," he added. Carmen smiled again. "Anyway, you indicated that you're interested in being a crane operator, but you have no experience in construction whatsoever."

"No, but I can telekinetically lift more than 180,000 kilograms to an altitude of…" She would have continued, but her voice trailed off when he began staring at her like she was a dog that had just said hello.

He sat still for a long moment while Carmen shifted uncomfortably in her chair. "Really?" he asked.

She swallowed hard. He had to have a chopping block around here somewhere. Surely a man with a black hood was sharpening his axe in the next room. Being a Clairvoyant, however, did have its perks. She gave him a quick read to know where she stood, and then she breathed easy.

"Yes," Carmen said with confidence.

Neil blinked a few times while he shook his head. "That's

ridiculous," he muttered, rubbing his eyes. "One thing, though. Our equipment is capable of lifting a lot more than that—"

"But with anti-grav systems, that won't really matter. I don't need maintenance, I'm more precise, and I don't break down." She didn't add the fact that machines didn't get tired and she did, but there was no reason to remind him of that.

Neil sat back in his chair and nodded. As before, she abstained from reading him. He eventually smiled, so she figured it wasn't the end of the world just yet.

"Clairvoyant, huh? Shit, I should tell HR to hire ten more of you," he said with a chuckle. Carmen couldn't help a grin. "I must say you definitely did your homework. Still, even if you can do it, you don't know anything about construction. There will be things we have to teach you... But we have a good crew, and I'm sure they'll be able to get you up to speed in no time."

"They won't even need to *tell* me what to do," she cut in.

Neil stared at her for a moment or two until he understood what she meant. "But I thought you said you don't like reading people?"

Carmen shrugged. "I'm a big girl. I can handle it." She added a knowing smile.

Neil laughed lightly, nodding. "When can you start?"

"Immediately."

"Excellent. With this war, demand has been stretched so far beyond our limits that I doubt we'll ever catch up. We build factories which build arms which our troopers use to fight. None of it is going well," he added after a sigh. "We can definitely use you."

Carmen nodded. *Good*, she thought. Then her spirits fell a touch as she focused on the second most worrying part of this ordeal.

"I hate to have to ask, especially so soon, but I'm going to need an advance," she said.

Neil paused for a moment. "That's not something we normally do, especially for a new hire, but how much are we talking about?"

She told him a conservative estimate after swallowing hard. The request was met by the same look of perplexed disbelief.

"I'm sorry, but we'd never be able to authorize any sort of advance in amounts that high."

"I wouldn't ask if it wasn't important," Carmen said. "My boyfriend is very sick. If I don't get the money somehow, he could die."

Neil didn't say anything, not at first. He took a deep breath before he spoke. "I would if I could. You should know that as a Clairvoyant. But we can't give an advance that high. I'll see if we can get you something, but I doubt it. In the meantime, let's get you to HR so we can start your paperwork right away. That would help, at least."

He wasn't lying, as Carmen well knew. He would if he could. She guessed she should take what she could get.

"Thank you," she said. "Can I make a call before we start the paperwork?"

"Sure, take your time," Neil responded.

Carmen nodded and then stepped out of the room into an unoccupied section of the hall. She stared at the phone in her hand. It shook slightly. The device seemed to have somehow turned into granite. If she dropped it, it would surely fall through the floor and take residence in the center of the planet. She had been wrong. The interview in and of itself hadn't been worrisome. Asking for an advance had been barely a bother. This, however, rained dread like her own personal typhoon.

Somehow, she was able to place the phone next to her ear without its gravity scrambling her brain.

"Hello?" she heard from the other end of the line.

"It's…it's Edge," she said.

"Oh, how did it go?" Kali asked.

"Well, I have a new job."

"And?" Kali asked expectantly.

Carmen had never had much luck reading someone through a phone. Really, she never heard of any Clairvoyant that did. Kali, however, would probably know what her old charge was thinking half a universe away.

"And I think I'm going to need your help after all," she said.

They were simple words which flowed out of her mouth like a public service announcement. A few of her soon-to-be coworkers even heard them when they walked by, and they paid them no notice. But there was a long silence on the other end of the line. Possibly Kali was as surprised by the request as Carmen was loath to make it?

When Kali finally spoke, her tone was slow and soothing. "All right. There's someone I'd like you to meet."

5

THE ROGUE WOLVES

As Carmen's hand hovered over the board, she didn't notice that it was shaking. The pieces and the game itself only registered faintly, despite her best attempts to focus. It wasn't like she didn't know what to do. She could have checked Phaethon five moves ago. But her effort in the game was about as deliberate as breathing.

Her hand started to descend upon a piece till she stopped short. Her attention then turned to another, where she did the same thing. There would not be a third attempt. She sighed and then sat back and tried to assess the board. Her first impulse had been the best she could make, but it wasn't the only choice, or at least it didn't seem to be. She studied the board. Traces of desperation clouded her thoughts. *What else can I do?* she wondered. Her hand was on her next impulse before she even realized it. The piece greeted her touch with hard coldness. There was no getting out of it now. She moved the piece forward and then leaned back in her chair in a heap.

Phaethon didn't take his turn. He instead looked his handler up and down, utterly confused. He cocked his head to the side. "What's the matter with you?"

"Nothing," Carmen said, glancing at him.

"I thought Clairvoyants didn't lie," he said pointedly.

She rolled her eyes more at herself than anything but kept her peace other than that. Phaethon waited for a response and continued to wait until it became obvious that she wouldn't say anything. He turned his attention back to the game, guessing the probing questions were the sole province of handlers. Carmen watched him make his move, but her heart just wasn't in it. She looked at the board and could only shake her head.

"I think we should stop for today," she said.

Phaethon frowned. "You would say that when I'm finally starting to win."

She shook her head again and forced a smirk. "So, you're telling me you actually want to play chess for a change?"

"No, no, no," he said quickly after he realized how his handler maneuvered around his words. He opened his mouth to complain further, but Carmen raised her hand.

"I actually have to see someone," she said.

"Now?"

"Basically." Really, she had an open appointment, but there was no point in delaying the inevitable.

Phaethon eyed her and then looked at the board. "All right, but don't put the board away. I want to win for once."

"Fine. You can flip it over when I get back," she teased.

There was only a hint of it, if any, but Carmen saw him blush for the briefest of moments before he stood. "We'll see," he said. He looked at her again. "Take care of yourself." Then he walked off.

Carmen could only gawk at him. *Take care of yourself?* she reflected. New Earth was off its axis—had to be. She seemed to be the only person who noticed, though. *Phaethon,* she thought with a groan as she considered him. She wondered if she had ever vexed her handlers as much as he did her. He'd probably try to punch her the next time they met to make up for it.

But she ignored that entirely likely possibility and looked at the board one last time. *What can I do?* she thought. On and on, she considered every step and outcome, questioning each and every moment. *What can I do?*

She stood after a sigh and left the board in place as Phaethon asked. Everyone knew they played chess there, so she didn't think anyone would mess with it. She saw Kali as she made her way across the field. They passed close enough to hear a word between them if one was spoken. They certainly could have spoken telepathically. But they barely waved to each other. Carmen wasn't in the mood to talk. Perhaps Kali wasn't either, or maybe she could sense as much from her former charge or tell from the plodding determination of her steps. Whatever it was, Carmen walked right past her, though she could practically feel Kali's stare as she walked away.

She was in the facility proper a short moment later. It always took her aback at just how numbing a place it was. Most of the assets preferred to be outside when they could, and she couldn't blame them. The hall, just like when Kali had taken her out for the first time all those years ago, was dull and windowless. A little girl and her handler were walking toward her at the other end of it. The girl was maybe eleven or twelve. Carmen was never very good at guessing ages. She looked about nervously while she followed her handler. Maybe she was going to have her first flight? Carmen wasn't sure, but it made her think of the first time she'd been brought to this level with Kali. The memory stood out as much as the skyscrapers of Haven City.

The girl stared at Carmen as they approached each other.

The girl's body quaked with anxious indecision with each step forward. Carmen could sympathize, and she smiled down at the girl when she was close enough. The gesture wasn't returned with the same courtesy. After a flash of surprise, the girl raised her fists and then took a few hesitant steps away. Carmen would be hard pressed to say the reaction was unexpected; kids just greeted smiles as an invitation for a fight here. The girl's handler, for his part, nodded Carmen's way, to which she replied with a nod of her own. They passed each other after that. The girl watched Carmen over her shoulder. Carmen gave her a backwards glance. She looked away just when the girl paused in shocked amazement at her handler opening the door to the outside world.

Carmen then transitioned to the heart of the facility's administration. There were no assets here, just the technicians, scientists, handlers, and others who allowed the facility to function from day to day. Carmen spent very little time here. She spent as little time inside the facility as possible, but her duties rarely carried her to this place in particular. At least there were windows, one of the perks of it being an above-ground level. Her destination eventually came into sight. She didn't sense anyone inside the room and there wasn't a note on the door, but he had said that, if he wasn't there, she should just wait for him. She walked inside to do just that.

It was a Clairvoyant's office through and through. The decor was purposeful, clean. No attempts had been made to *soften* the space or make it feel more like home, as she found in most workplaces. It wasn't cold or robotic in nature, but there was a quiet intensity and focus that was hard to place.

Carmen took a seat as she waited for Gungnir. He had to be along shortly. He knew she was coming. It helped that the office had a window with a rather spectacular view of Haven

City. You could see almost all of it. In the foreground, the courtyard of the facility was close enough that you could just barely make out individual assets' faces in their bumbling attempts to socially fit in. As always, the ever-present mass of skyscrapers towered over them, existing almost like a growth of the landscape.

She was just starting to get a full taste of the scene when the door opened. The Clairvoyant's head shot toward it in surprise. She hadn't sensed anyone approaching. Gungnir, however, made no reaction to her. He was noticeably taller than herself, if she'd been standing. Like her, he was blond, though his hair was almost white in color, and like her it was tied into a ponytail, though his was quite a bit shorter. She couldn't read him no matter how hard she tried. But there was a measured focus to his power that was quite obvious, like a high-powered laser compared to an atom bomb. It was different from most of the Clairvoyants she had met. It seemed...mature. Carmen considered herself in that instant and wondered if Phaethon looked at her in the same way. She doubted it.

He walked into the room and took a seat behind his desk. "Edge, it's a pleasure to meet you," he said with a slow nod.

Carmen looked at him hard, as curious as she was confused. It was a simple statement, but it was so...to the point. He had to be the most Clairvoyant Clairvoyant she had ever met. His words, both spoken and unspoken, said every-thing that needed to be conveyed yet carried little of their intrinsic meaning.

"Can you help me?" she asked simply and directly.

"And what's your problem?"

"I need money," she said, confused. "Didn't Kali tell you?"

"Yes and no," Gungnir answered after a pause.

"So—"

"So, Edge," Gungnir said, interrupting her. "Kali informed me of your situation. However, I asked you what's your problem?"

"And I answered. I need money," Carmen said again with more emphasis.

Gungnir sat back in his chair, nodding slowly once more. She wished she could read him. "And how is that a problem?" he asked.

The briefest of frowns graced her face. "I don't need it for me. My boyfriend could...*will* die without it."

"Do you care for him?" Gungnir asked.

Carmen hesitated for the briefest of instants. "Yes, of course," she said confidently. "I wouldn't be here otherwise."

"Why?"

"Why?" she asked back. She'd never reasoned it out before. "I love him. Why else?"

"Why?" Gungnir asked again.

Carmen didn't say anything for a short while. "I guess he was the first to see me as..." Her voice trailed off in a quiver as she thought about what she was about to say.

Her mind went to that day on the bluff when she had first met him. Every second of that all too brief moment stayed with her always, ever present and all encompassing. Every day since, however, had been no more than a fragmented blur. She recomposed her thoughts.

"I want him to live. I need him to live. I *need* him to."

She stopped talking, yet Gungnir seemed completely unmoved by her conviction. In truth, she was as well.

"I need to know...I need to know that I can do this," she continued.

"This?"

"Everything I've been trying to do for the past two years. Since I left," she said, "it hasn't been easy." She looked away from Gungnir for a moment. "Sometimes I have dreams that he just wakes up and the rest of my life is…"

"Is what?"

"Happy." She nodded slowly. "I have to keep trying. No matter what it takes," she said more to herself than to him.

Gungnir nodded. "Your predicament is not a problem," he said without missing a beat. "Your boyfriend will just be another body for the foundations. No one will notice."

Carmen's lips pressed together into an outright frown. He spoke before she could say anything.

"I can't read you, but I'd say you look angry."

What made you guess that? she thought. But she said, "No."

"We Clairvoyants are always so bad at lying," he remarked. "I don't know why we try. Anger, however, is good…at least for some."

"Well, I don't need anger. I need money. Can you help me?"

"No. Unfortunately, I cannot," he said.

Carmen was about to leave right then and there, but Gungnir must have sensed as much because he gave her a look that pinned her in place. It reminded her of the halting glares Janus used to give her. The two men weren't physically alike, nor did they *feel* in any way similar, but that look… She was happy Kali had never used it. He said nothing, though. Carmen waited while he got out of his chair and walked to the window. He looked at the cityscape, crossing his arms behind his back. Carmen watched it as well.

"I can't help you, Edge, because there is nothing wrong with you. You don't have a problem," he said slowly.

"I don't have a problem!" Carmen said with a start.

Gungnir glanced at her over his shoulder, and she held herself to just that outburst. He turned to look back out the window while she took a deep breath. "What Kali told you—why I'm here—is a problem for me," she said simply.

Gungnir didn't speak. Instead, the two of them watched a group of assets attempt to organize some sort of ball catching game, obviously prompted by their handlers. After a few frustrated tries, the group scattered when the rules couldn't be agreed upon. Carmen's gaze then went to a handler and asset returning from a field trip in Haven City. She didn't know what Gungnir was looking at. The asset fell to the ground in tears after reaching the grounds of the facility. Carmen couldn't tell if the asset was happy to be back or upset at whatever happened during the trip. Either way, she made no response to her handler's best attempts at consoling her. She looked at Gungnir, who simply watched all that transpired calmly and dispassionately yet somehow calculatingly.

"That, I'm sorry to say, is the point," he muttered, half turning to face her.

"The point of what?" she asked.

Gungnir motioned to the walls all around them. "This place."

Carmen dropped her head into an open palm and then looked at him. "So, the people who run this facility want my Michael to die?" she asked, unable to help a bit of sarcasm. "And why would they want that?"

"Edge, you forget why you're here?" he asked as he turned to look back outside. His tone was even. Carmen didn't know what to make of it. He already turned her down but had yet to tell her to leave, for what that was worth.

"Why am I here?"

Yet again, Gungnir said nothing. He surveyed the city and

the grounds, his head turning slightly from side to side as his gaze leapt from feature to feature.

"Impressive, isn't it?" he finally asked. Carmen couldn't help but agree with a small nod. "I must admit most of the reason I chose this office was because of the view. It's fitting."

"How?" she asked simply.

He glanced at her over his shoulder. "Did you know that, eons ago, on Earth, people were afraid to go into the forests?"

"No."

"It's ridiculous, but they believed monsters and horrible beasts lived in the forests and other dark places." He paused before he continued. "A war is raging, but if you haven't noticed, none of that war is taking place here or on any world with a large Clairvoyant population. When the sortens or Eternals attack other worlds, they have to kill every last man, woman, and child to be certain they can hold the territory. That is why we are here. We are wolves," he said, turning around. Behind him, Carmen could see the clouds break, once again covering the facility in the shadows of Haven City. "And we aren't able to give pause to those who want to enter the forest if we aren't vicious. More than that, we can never *leave* the forest, otherwise those taking refuge within it would be rendered defenseless."

Carmen couldn't help but think about her time with Janus and Kali, her thus far failed attempts at reaching Phaethon, and how much trouble she had with finding a job.

"And this has what to do with me and my problem?" she asked.

"As I said, you have no problem, since you are acting exactly as you were trained. It is not something I can really fix. I was trained similarly," he said. "You said you need money. I can help you get that. But I can't do anything to help with why you need money and can't get it other than through people like me. Before you and I go any further, I want you to understand that."

"It's just a job. I don't have any choice."

"It's not *just a job*, and there is always a choice," Gungnir said.

Carmen looked at him hard and then said slowly, "I don't have any choice."

"You can let him die," he said. His tone wasn't cold nor was it comforting, just even and factual.

She said nothing to that and simply waited. Gungnir sat back at his desk and nodded slowly.

"Fine," he said. "What did your old handler tell you about me?"

"Not very much. Just that you know about jobs that pay very well…and that they skirt the outer edge of the law."

"Hmm. Odd," he muttered with a shrug. "Kali and I were close. We were interned together during the sorten occupation. We even named each other…though I must admit that we and the rest of our generation were a little grandiose with our selections. I figured she would have mentioned at least how we knew each other."

"No."

"Hmm," he muttered again, nodding. "She told me a fair amount about you."

"Like what?" Carmen asked.

"I'll just say that she says you live true to your name, for as much as that helps and hurts you. Nevertheless, she knows I'm always on the lookout for talent and recommended you to me based on that."

"So, you'll help me then?" she asked. He frowned, which extinguished her small glimmer of hope like a candle placed under a waterfall.

"If that's how you want to consider it," he eventually remarked. "But I want you to be clear that this is what you want before you agree to anything."

Carmen didn't hesitate. "It is," she said.

Gungnir nodded. "All right. You will be hearing from me within the next few days. You should pack your bags."

6

MOUSE AND CAT

Evonea was always a noisy muddle. Its natives, a group that included himself, were brash enough to call the chaos *cosmopolitan*. Everyone else simply called the sensory over-load what it was: pandemonium. He couldn't see what the problem was. How could you not have cities whose lights were visible a galaxy away? Peace and quiet—what was that, a terrible myth? Any other type of life was an insipid, point-less bother.

Carson—at least his name would be Carson till he stole another ID—nimbly moved his big frame through the crowded sidewalk as he took in all the sights and sounds. He tried to draw as little attention to himself as possible. There was no need to be careless, even if this was his home planet. Business was too good thanks to the war to waste being on the run for a month or so. His dress and manner were nonde-script. He knew what was required; this wasn't the first time.

The meeting wouldn't be in person. None of them had been. He'd write a book about all the idiosyncrasies of his various employers if he could do it without landing in jail. His latest client, Charon, as a Clairvoyant, could certainly fill a chapter or two. There were perks for being in a Clairvoy-ant's employ, though. The pay always arrived on time, and he was never lied to, even if he didn't know the whole story. He was told the job, and all that mattered was that he completed it, no bullshit.

But Charon never showed his face. He never met in person. And, as somewhat of a curiosity, he never said who *he* was working for. Carson guessed it was the sortens, considering the targets, which was unusual, since most Clair-voyants detested sortens. There was no way to be sure, though, nor was it even worthwhile to know. In this business, some modicum of ignorance at times meant surviving to see another day. So, he'd never really cared to ask.

He rounded a corner and disappeared into a new crowd. The meeting site was about a block away, but he preferred to take his time, just in case he had a tail. Unfortunately, the gaggle of people that made him hard to follow also made it hard to know whether he was being followed. He had his pistol for any shadow. You always had to be careful, even if you hadn't been nor planned to be planetside for very long.

The meeting was in an old hotel—at least old for Evonea. There was older bellybutton lint on Earth than buildings on Evonea. Carson paused for a moment before he went inside. He just had one of those feelings. It was difficult to know how Clairvoyants could stand them all the time. He casually glanced around himself for a time, but there was nothing to see, so he walked inside a few seconds later.

The places changed, but the method always remained the same. He never knew exactly what room to go to. A key would be waiting for him at the check-in desk. The clerk this time was a young man who could pass for being in his late teens. It was amazing he hadn't been drafted yet.

"May I help you, sir?" he asked.

"Yes," Carson said. "I have a reservation. Name is Decker."

"Okay, please say your name into this microphone."

Carson leaned forward. "Decker," he said.

"Thank you. It will be room 110. Just say your name at the door to open it. I hope you enjoy your stay."

He nodded. The room was down the hall. He always insisted on having meetings on ground floors. His hand found his pistol, though he didn't pull it out. He'd take meetings outside in the open if he had his ultimate preference; enclosed spaces were bad for the health of someone in his profession.

"Decker," he said when he reached the room, but only after giving the hall one last glance.

The room was the most basic of a typical hotel. He'd been in so many by now that he could close his eyes and still find everything of consequence. The only thing that didn't belong was a pad in the center of the floor. That, however, was expected, so he paid it no mind. He instead went about surveying the room. He always arrived early specifically for that purpose. Surprises never involved clowns or good cheer, in his experience. But the room appeared clear, so he waited.

A wispy, ghostlike image of a person appeared on the pad minutes later. After a few seconds, it was hard to discern the image from a *real* man. Charon was quite a bit shorter than Carson. His face was covered by a metal mask obviously designed to intimidate. Carson wouldn't think much of it, except it tended to reflect his image in several grotesque distortions. It was such a simple thing, but for some reason the faux mirror was disconcerting. Charon's clothes were just as wispy as his image had been. They were dark and tattered and hung off his body in a way that exaggerated every move-ment, making him look like he was always in motion. It was obviously just another part of the costume that was meant to intimidate.

"We've sent your payment to the accounts you've specified. Have you verified the amounts yet?" Charon asked.

"Yes, I have. It looks good."

Charon nodded. "We have a new target for you. Are you ready?" he asked, producing a PDD as he spoke.

Carson took out his own and then waited. Charon sent the information. Carson could only blink in disbelief at what he read. "Admiral Lance Calbry?" he asked.

"Yes."

"Why didn't you just tell me to take care of him at the same time as Admiral Wright?"

"Could you have done it?" Charon asked simply.

Carson thought about it for a minute. "No, probably not. I barely escaped as it was."

"We figured not. Frankly, I would take care of this myself, but I have other business to deal with. Will this be a problem for you?"

"No, I don't believe so."

"Standard rate?" Charon asked.

"No," Carson said. "I underbid the previous job. Double or I walk."

The image of the man was silent for a few seconds. "Done. Inform me when it's finished through the normal channels. Our timetable necessitates no more than a standard month."

Carson nodded as the transmission cut out. Straight and to the point. If only every one of his employers were Clairvoyants.

He left the room. Someone he didn't know would be by to collect the pad. The bill for the room had already been taken care of. He exited the building from a different door than he entered, yet there was that odd feeling again. He looked around and, as before, there was nothing. Whether something was actually there or not, the feeling was enough to give haste. He was no Clairvoyant, but it did feel like he was being watched. No, it felt like something was stalking him.

He gripped his pistol as he moved quickly and deftly through the city streets. It was always wise to heed odd feelings. He had planned to get off planet as soon as possible, even before the hairs on the back of his neck started standing on end. It was never good to stay in one place for long. He just needed to get to one of his stash houses and then book passage back to Earth.

He was parked only a few blocks away, out in the open. He could already see his aerocar. Procuring the Corvette was probably the least nondescript thing he'd ever done. Its sleek, aerodynamic body and bright red paint screamed "HERE I AM!" better than any bullhorn. He always lied to himself that it was his way of hiding in the open, for what that was worth. At least it was fast enough to get him to various locations on the planet in only a matter of hours. The sportscar practically put any aircraft short of a starfighter to shame.

It rose to ground-cruising altitude as he approached. Its onboard mood-sensing and personality-detecting devices automatically set the air conditioning to his subconscious preference. The turbine engine whined to life when he sat in the cockpit. The trip would be short enough to not need to leave ground level. He accessed the car's communications gear to make a few arrangements on the way.

"Thank you for connecting with Milky Way Starlines, the one-stop destination for all your travel needs." Carson couldn't help a small groan. He'd heard various starlines' menu systems so often that he had almost memorized them. "Please be advised that, due to the ongoing war effort, travel restrictions may apply. If your travel plans are affected, please speak to a representative for assistance. Please say the destination planet or system."

Carson guided his car through traffic as he wondered what equipment he'd need. It would be too risky to attempt to break into Space Force Headquarters again. Any competent military would have found and fixed the weaknesses he'd exploited by now. He'd have to find another way. Maybe he could simply shoot Calbry on the way to his car or something? It was hard to be sure. He figured he'd take his usual kit with a little extra, just to be safe.

"I'm sorry. Can you please state your destination?" the automated representative said.

"Earth," he barked.

He was already outside the majority of the city. All he needed to do now was cross the bridge before he could get his equipment. The view was scenic and a tourist attraction, but he was in no mood to notice. He was still trying to figure out what kit he'd need.

"Please say your desired departure time."

"Immediately," he answered.

The system asked another question. He didn't pay it much attention. Instead, he wondered why traffic was slowing in front of him. People were abruptly swerving out of the way of something maybe a hundred yards ahead. He couldn't see what it was. Such was his focus that he didn't realize the hair on his arm was standing straight out. More cars swerved out of the way. He too began turning, since there was no point in staying put.

Then he saw it—her. There was about thirty feet between

them now. She wore a dark red hood and cloak. Clairvoyants and their theatrics… There was no doubt whatsoever that a Clairvoyant was what she was. He often wondered if the theater happened consciously or if it was just a natural part of their personalities. Either way, this performance was certainly having an effect.

Her eyes were locked on his like a snake about to strike. For a moment, he could only stare back and tremble. Her stance was rigid, hard. He was well aware, in the back of his mind, that Clairvoyants limited themselves. She could crush his head like a grape with just a thought if she wanted to. That wasn't likely to happen, though. There was some weird unspoken rule that Clairvoyants had to fight on their opponent's level. He didn't complain about that, especially now, since the only thing he had to defend himself with was a handgun. It may as well have been a water pistol.

"Shit," he muttered under his breath.

There was no question in his mind that he was her prey. He had only one chance. A flick of a dial on the control yoke vaulted the Corvette into the air. He pointed the sportscar toward open sky and then let all the power he paid for do its work. The aerocar was supersonic in seconds, the acceleration sinking him into his seat at least half an inch, despite the inertial inhibitor. Moments later, the city was a distant memory in the rearview mirror. He didn't think even all that would be enough.

A Clairvoyant really didn't have a speed limit when they pushed themselves—at least, that was what people said. No one really knew. Almost everything about Clairvoyants was rumor and innuendo. He wished he'd asked Charon or some other Clairvoyant about it. For now, at least, she was still with him. The flickering gauges in his car were a clear enough tell. Another thing he'd heard was that Clairvoyants had difficulty breathing at high speed. Perhaps he could tire her out.

His first instinct made him thunder the Corvette through a hard turn. The car had already transitioned to RACE mode and adjusted the inertial inhibitor accordingly. The turn grayed his vision even with the system, but it was comforting to know that Clairvoyants had no inertial systems and were just as physically limited as he was. If the turn didn't black her out or even kill her, it certainly sapped some of her stamina.

He turned again, waited a few seconds to open the distance, and then made another turn. The maneuver was so violent that he had to stop for a moment to catch his breath. Just then, a bright shaft of light streaked by his canopy. He cursed. She was still with him. He dove the Vette toward the ground and then shot it back up to a few thousand feet. Their twists and turns brought the city in front of them again, barely visible on the horizon. He could just see its air traffic streaming at different levels above it like a multilayered blanket.

Outright speed did nothing to avail him, nor did violent turns. The only other option he could think of was to climb. He pulled the control yoke into his lap, and the altimeter scrolled upward so fast that it was unreadable. The clouds thinned to nothingness. Even the curvature of the planet became more easily discernable as the Corvette shot upward.

All of a sudden, the car shuddered and shook and warning chimes blared. He hadn't hit anything. He'd probably be dead if he did at this speed. Nevertheless, the car twisted and bent, and now he saw why. It was being literally ripped apart around him. This Clairvoyant was no longer playing by artificial limits. He felt cold. He had no chance now.

The sportscar eventually sensed a catastrophic failure and

started the auto-ejection system. The sequence lasted a mere second or two and the inertial inhibitor spooled to full power. Such was its effect that he didn't even feel the seatbelts pull tight. Next, the canopy turned solid black. Some safety engineer somewhere had thought it would be a good idea for the occupants to not be able to see that they were falling through the sky. Carson hated it. That, combined with the inertial inhibitor, made him unaware that he'd already been blasted clear of his crippled Corvette.

The escape pod's automatic systems steadied the fall to resemble the flight of a well-controlled anvil. Carson could only sit and wait, though he didn't do so comfortably. *What is she waiting for?* he wondered over and over again. He should have been blasted from the sky or crushed by now. It was with some surprise that the canopy opened and he found himself safely on the ground.

"Emergency vehicles are on their way. Please stay with the escape pod. If you are injured, please state the nature of your injury now."

Carson paid no attention to the emergency systems and found some meager comfort when his hand rested on his pistol. The pod had landed only a few miles outside the city limits. Several apartment buildings were a short distance away. He could even see people running out to help him. He didn't have much time.

He scrambled out of the pod so fast that he tripped twice.

"Hey, mister, are you all right?" a man asked.

"There's a Clairvoyant after me! She's crazy! Call the police!" Carson screamed in panic. He wasn't much of an actor, but he could win awards in a pinch.

"Oh wait, I see her! Let's get out of here," the man said.

No shit, Carson thought. He sprinted toward the closest alley, leaving the bystander in the dust. The police would never try to match against a Clairvoyant, but it was worth a try. He didn't have anything else left. Hiding would be no use against her. He slid to a stop and took a deep breath.

What to do? What to do? he thought. He pulled his pistol and looked back the way he had come. The Clairvoyant had just landed. She looked ridiculous. Her hair reminded him of a cat that had been electrocuted. She telekinetically slicked it back and then tied it into a ponytail after a sigh. Just then, the police and an ambulance arrived.

"Please, we don't want any harm. Please surrender," Carson could just barely hear one of the officers say.

The Clairvoyant cautiously raised her hand, which made his mouth drop open. "I don't want to hurt anyone. Just leave me be," she said.

Carson looked at her crossed-eyed. She was actually trying to reason with them. What Clairvoyant anywhere would waste their time on that? Every one he'd ever met would just kill them or simply walk away—anything more efficient than talking.

"We will open fire if you don't stand down," the police said.

"No, wait—" the Clairvoyant yelled, for all the good it did.

The police emptied their weapons on her. The gunshots echoed through the alley and the entire block. Carson thought he even heard a woman scream in the building he was standing next to. Throughout, though, the Clairvoyant stood still. He didn't think the police would be able to drop her, as telekinesis could do amazing things. He received another shock, however, when she gave no retaliation. She even seemed bothered when they ran away in fear. *Maybe I can use this.*

"I didn't think I could pull the last job without some sort

of reprisal!" he yelled. She looked in his direction and walked quickly toward him. He pulled back before he could be spotted. "At least they sent a cute one," he added, now that he got a better look at her.

She made no reply.

"How'd you find me anyway?" he asked as he ran down the block.

She still didn't answer, though that wasn't much of a surprise. All the same, he was curious. He thought he was good at covering his tracks.

"What did they think it would take to bring me down, anyway? Twenty percenter?" he mused as he ran down yet another alley. "Fifteen percenter?"

Carson looked back the way he had come and didn't see anyone. It was too much to hope that he'd lost her. She had to be here somewhere.

"Dare I ask…a ten?" he called.

When he turned around, she was standing in front of him. He backed away by reflex and half raised his pistol. She looked at him and the weapon and then cocked her head to the side and rolled her eyes.

He looked at the gun and couldn't help a small chuckle. "Yeah, this would be pretty worthless against you," he said. After throwing the gun away, he took another step back and then slowly raised his hands. "Would it be vain for me to think you're a five percenter?" She pointedly rolled her eyes again, which made Carson let go a small smirk. "Stronger? Wow, I'm honored."

"Do you ever shut up?" Carmen barked as she started toward him.

Carson raised his hands even higher. "Why? Does it bother you?" She said nothing, but he noted the briefest of hesitation. "Nah, no way. Not you. Hope they're paying you well for this job. I'm no easy mark."

"Shut up!" Carmen said again.

"Shit, I wouldn't take a job against me. You must be a real monster," he said.

"Shut up! Shut up!" Carmen yelled. "Turn around and get down on your knees, now!"

Carson looked at her and smirked. "No," he said simply.

She glared at him. "Turn around and get down on your knees," she said firmly.

"How many people have you killed?" he asked. "A hundred? Two hundred? Certainly more than I have. It must be easy for you by now. Just between you and me," he began, making a show of looking around the alley to see if they were really alone, "sometimes my hands still shake just before."

"Just shut your mouth," Carmen said as she grabbed him by the shoulder and forced him to the ground.

He could only look up at her. "Weren't expecting this, were you?" he asked. "Killing me in some violent struggle is one thing, but murdering a man who surrenders? Well, that's something else, isn't it? Did they even tell you anything about me?" he continued. "Whether I have a wife, kids, whatever? Ahh, both you and me know none of that shit matters. A job's a job, right? Doesn't matter how you come by the money."

Carmen said nothing. She took a step back and telekinetically turned him to face the other way. Then she pointed two fingers at the back of his head.

He took a deep breath. "Those who live by the sword," Carson muttered.

Then he waited...and waited. He wished he could look at the Clairvoyant, if only to have some clue as to what was going through her head. A few more seconds passed. Then she spoke.

"Disappear," she said with a shaky voice.

Carson slowly turned around to find that she was gone. He looked up and down the alley and searched the sky, but the Clairvoyant was nowhere to be seen. He took a deep breath.

"Shit, that was close."

7

GREAT NEWS

A sharp pain hung in the pit of Carmen's stomach, and there was nothing she could think to do to be rid of it. It reminded her of when she killed Mikayla. It was a bit ironic that her lack of a conscience had cost her dog her life but that the interference of her conscience had spared the Sentinel's.

It wasn't like he was some kind of saint. She'd insisted on learning everything she possibly could about him. As it turned out, she didn't think the Sentinel, as he was code-named, was anything special. He was a former Space Force Special Forces elite turned mercenary after the first Terran-Sorten War. There were many like him. From what she'd read in his dossier, she guessed his many exploits were impressive. She didn't really have a point of reference, as it was a world she previously barely knew existed, but she would be surprised if they weren't impressive. No one would hire a Clairvoyant at their premium price to take care of someone who had simply robbed an ice cream booth. It was all so much death, though. She hadn't even been able to finish reading the dossier. But now all of that was neither here nor there. Now, all that mattered was that she had choked and Michael was as good as dead.

The thought made the sharp pain in her stomach feel like someone was twisting the knife. Carmen looked around the bar, hoping for some distraction, if however brief. She sat in a quiet, dimly lit section with a forest of empty chairs arrayed around her. It was tempting to leave for somewhere else or even find a street corner to just be by herself, but she didn't have the heart for it. It was still a few hours till her transport back to New Earth, and she didn't want to spend that time alone, even though she effectively was. She remembered when she had laid almost comatose in her room after Mikayla's death, utterly and completely alone. It wasn't a time she wanted to relive, even distantly.

She knew very little about Evonea and even less about this bar. There weren't many patrons. It was still early, though. The size of the establishment suggested that it regularly saw large crowds, but she had no way of knowing for sure without asking someone. She had just come upon it while she was walking.

The atmosphere was tensely joyful. It wasn't like the patrons weren't having fun, but they seemed keenly aware of just how fragile the moment was. The desperation in their revelry was becoming more and more commonplace for everybody, thanks to the war. Even the holo, at ear-splitting volume, could barely be heard over the anxious din. Carmen simply sat and soaked in the ambiance as she was mostly ignored.

Her phone rang.

"Hello," she answered, telekinetically damping the background noise by reflex.

"You missed your check-in."

It was Gungnir. She took a quick glance around to make

sure no one was in earshot and let go an annoyed sigh. *Who in the world would sit near me?* she mused.

"Sorry," she said.

"Are you all right?"

"Yes. I'm actually waiting for a transport back."

"It's done then?" Gungnir asked as casually as he would ask if she had finished trimming the hedges.

She paused. It wasn't that Clairvoyants never lied, as was the stereotype. She lied from time to time when required, and now would be a good opportunity. If the Sentinel disappeared, as she told him to do, no one would ever know.

"No. I couldn't do it," she answered. There was no point in having a clean conscious by refraining from killing someone to dirty it by lying that she did. "I'm sorry," she added.

The other end was silent for a few seconds. "Was this a momentary lapse? Could you track him down again?"

"No," Carmen said. "Not without your help, like before. But I wouldn't do it even if I could. I'm sorry I wasted your time. It's not for me."

There was more silence. "What's done is done," Gungnir eventually said. "He'll be taken care of in due course. As for you—"

"Yes?" Carmen interrupted, feeling suddenly nervous.

She had never stopped to think about what would happen if she failed. It wasn't an option, for Michael's sake. She had thought the only way she could fail was if the Sentinel killed her.

Gungnir said nothing at first. It was possible that he'd also never considered that she could fail. "This is a bit complicated," he began. "I have to be honest. I am…sympathetic to your situation. This is what we'll do. You will be paid the same as what was initially promised. We'll discuss how you'll compensate me when you get planetside. It won't be anything like your previous assignment—maybe bodyguard duty or something like that for a time. Is this arrangement acceptable for you?"

Carmen was so shocked that it was a miracle she didn't drop the phone. The cheers and jeers of the bar patrons echoed in her head, but she was still too disbelieving to do the same.

"You can't be serious?"

"I never thought another Clairvoyant would ask me that," Gungnir said. Carmen laughed in response. In fact, her laughter made her laugh harder. "But yes, I am being serious."

"Good. That's good," Carmen said, still exorcising her last remaining giggles. "Thank you."

"You're welcome," Gungnir replied. "Make sure you see me when you get back."

Carmen nodded. "Right." Then he hung up, and it was done.

She looked at the phone in her hands and smiled. This was just so hard to believe, and for once in her life, it was hard to believe in a good way. Forget just seeing him—she'd probably give Gungnir a hug and a big, sloppy kiss when she got back. As she looked around the room at all the tensely happy people, Carmen felt less distant from them than before. Sure, their elation had nothing to do with hers, but it made her smile to pretend otherwise.

Just then, the holo stopped the program it was running with a special report.

"This is channel five news with the latest on the ongoing war effort," the newscaster said.

Everyone stopped what they were doing and watched. Carmen did as well but only nonchalantly. She didn't have much interest in the war. She couldn't read anything from the newscaster, since holograms were simply a transmission, but his voice was rushed and excited.

"According to information just released, elements of various Space Force fleets have just struck the sorten home worlds with a new weapon called Medusa, destroying them completely."

A thunderous cheer reverberated through the bar, and people screamed obscenities Carmen didn't care to hear. All the tension she sensed earlier exploded into a rawer, more benign form that reminded her of squeezing a balloon until it burst.

"Our sources also speak of sorten diplomats wanting to open peace talks. Even with continued Eternal and arkin pressure, this just may be the turning point of the war," the newscaster continued. "Here to discuss that and the future of the Sorten Empire with me is Captain Zahn of Space Force Fleet Command."

Carmen stopped paying attention about there, though she did hear a couple people say they wished Captain Brown was the consultant. She remembered the name, but nothing other than that came to mind.

She looked at the bartender before he spoke. "Drinks are on the house!" Another cheer broke out, almost as loud as the first.

Carmen smiled, if weakly. She guessed free drinks were a good thing, but alcohol and other drugs had reduced effect on Clairvoyants. It had something to do with separating oneself from reality, which Clairvoyants were resistant to. She had no real idea. What she did know was that it always made anesthesia an experience. Her doses when she was in the medical wing back at the facility were best described as multiples of horse.

A group of men walked in just then. They were about her age or maybe a little older.

"Everybody hear the news?" one of them asked the crowd.

"Yeah, blew those bastards straight to hell!" someone answered back.

The men then glanced in Carmen's direction. After casually pointing her way, they whispered something to each other. They had her full attention seconds before they began walking toward her. They smiled at her, she politely smiled back, and they took seats near but not with her.

"Buy you a drink?" one of them asked.

Carmen gave a bewildered smirk. "They're on the house," she pointed out. "But you don't know what I am?" she asked, somewhat surprised. Sure, she got attention from time to time, but it was rare for someone to just start talking to her.

"I know you're hot," he said.

She smirked again and then held up two fingers in the peace sign. A spark of electricity arced between her fingertips, and the mood changed.

"Sorry. Didn't know," the man said as he held up his hands. "Hey guys, let's get out of here." With that, the group left.

Carmen smiled and slowly shook her head. Then she picked up her phone and made another call.

"Hope Memorial Hospital. How may I help you?"

"This is Carmen Grey. I'm calling about Michael—"

"Yes, we've been trying to reach you. I'll transfer you now," the receptionist said.

"Ms. Grey, this is Elaine. I've been trying to reach you for days."

"Sorry about that. I'm off planet," Carmen said.

"You didn't leave a forwarding number?"

"I...couldn't," Carmen replied. "Anyway, I have the money. I can send it right now."

There was a long pause on the other end of the line. "That's why we were trying to reach you," Elaine finally said. "Michael died four days ago due to complications—"

"What?"

"I'm sorry, Ms. Grey, but you know as well as I do that the situation had been deteriorating for months. We wouldn't have wanted to transfer him out if the case had been different. There was nothing we could do. His family already had the funeral. Understandably, they tried their best to reach you too."

Carmen's lips quivered. It took effort to even hold the phone.

"If you'd like to speak to our grief counselors," Elaine continued, "we'd be happy to provide—"

Carmen turned off the phone and let it fall to the table. Her senses were numb, her body deadened. She couldn't think. She sat in her chair with dim eyes, looking at the ground in front of her, surrounded by the forest of chairs. People passed back and forth, yet she didn't really perceive them and they didn't notice her, at least not consciously. If anything, they just seemed happy that she stayed where she was.

She rested her head in an open palm. It was too much at this point to sit up straight. It was too much to keep her composure in public. She moved her hand to her forehead, covering her eyes, and tried at least to be quiet. It wasn't much of a concern for anybody there, though. Everyone cheered too loudly to notice the Clairvoyant crying in the back of the bar.

8

NO MORE WALLS

"How does she keep beating me?" Phaethon muttered to himself.

He stared at the chessboard, his perpetual source of defeat, with a sneer. It was such a stupid game. That Edge thought it had something to teach him was laughably remote. He just wanted to fight, or fly, or do something—anything but this fucking waste of time.

"How?" he muttered again. It couldn't be complicated, yet by some trick, he just couldn't win.

He didn't need to play now. He didn't want to play now. Edge would be gone for the next few days. He had to fight back a smile when she told him that. But he had no doubt whatsoever that playing chess would be the first thing they did when she got back. Consequently, he took time every day to practice. Perhaps if he beat her and she finally tasted what it was like to lose, she wouldn't be so eager to play again? It was worth a try. Reasoning against her or outright complaining about it definitely didn't work. He would have just killed her and been done with it if she wasn't so nice to him otherwise. But maybe if she forced him to play checkers as well as chess, he'd finally snap her neck?

Phaethon smiled weakly and then went back to it. His practice would be more effective if he could get his friends to play against him. They, however, took one look at the board and wisely shied away. Edge had to be the only handler who insisted on this pointlessness. So, his opponent was the computer. Unfortunately, it put his handler to shame in both skill and, most obvious of all, ruthlessness. At least Edge would lay off a little when he was being especially creamed.

This time, it was a quick if brutal beating. He reset the board and then started again, hoping for better. It was almost impossible to know how the game would turn out, despite all his senses and abilities. He was well aware that Clairvoyants couldn't tell the future, nor did they have much insight into the random pains and triumphs of chance. That more than anything made him anxious. He'd always hated the feeling.

The computer played White, just like Edge usually played White against him. She said that even Clairvoyants only rarely had the initiative and that they could only react, same as everyone else. Whether that was Kali talking or if the idea came purely from his handler was hard to tell.

The computer's first move thrust right toward him from the center of the board. He could only stare at the piece, which didn't help since this was a timed match. His play with Edge was either timed or untimed depending on her mood. He looked at the board and then the empty chair opposite him. Whether with Edge or against the computer, he had no idea what he was doing. That was painfully obvious at this point in his life. The best response didn't just come to him the same way everything else had.

He tried to think about what Edge and his handler before

her had told him. Nothing came to mind, other than platitudes that were as easy to remember as they were worthless in practice. That wasn't really the case with Edge, but it seemed like everyone here wasn't even trying to teach him anything—at least not anything useful. All his life, there had always seemed to be limitless options available. He was one of the most powerful beings to have ever existed and was maybe even *special*, so he was constantly told. There was almost nothing he couldn't do. Yet everything seemed so hollow now.

He leaned back in his chair, still having yet to make a move. He didn't really notice the time remaining in the match despite the clocks ringing in his ears. *I only have two years left*, he reflected. The thought made him lightheaded. His hands even shook slightly like they did over the chessboard when he was flummoxed. He turned to Haven City looming just outside the compound. Perhaps it would be a good idea to not turn down every field trip Edge suggested?

Eventually the buzzer for the game went off. He lost… again. If he just sat here and didn't bother with any of it, maybe he could at least get a stalemate? Admitting that fighting the inevitable was futile had to count as some sort of victory at this point. The only other way he could see was endless fighting, endless loss. He shut off the buzzer and sighed. What was the use?

Just then, Phaethon looked to his left with a start. In fact, every asset and handler turned almost at once. He couldn't remember that ever happening before. What caught his attention was far too unusual for him to spend much time pondering that, though. Clairvoyants—many of them—were approaching the facility and rapidly. A mass of them not from this place was strange enough, but there was something else as well. Almost all energies of the approaching Clairvoyants felt similar if not exactly the same. The feeling that revelation produced was oddly disgusting. It was so...*unnatural*. Even twins didn't feel exactly alike. Everyone's energy was unique in some way, no matter how minor. This horde felt like they had come off an assembly line.

"What's going on?" one of his peers nearby asked no one in particular.

Phaethon stood and could only shrug. "I don't know."

A second later, there was an explosion. He felt the shockwave coming before it actually hit, though the effect was quite light. Any normal person would have just noticed a brief, slight tremor on the chessboard. He guessed it was an aerocar crash; it was hard to know for sure. A pillar of smoke rose outside the facility, but that was all that could be seen.

A hint of a possible threat came when half a dozen handlers wearing body armor exited the facility with a host of security personnel right behind them. *What is going on?* Phaethon thought. Each handler's primary aim was the wellbeing of their charge, but that only rarely extended to their physical wellbeing. Most assets, especially those who were allowed outside, could take care of themselves. He considered the impossible even further. *This can't be an attack. Who in their right mind would attack here?*

Whoever these approaching Clairvoyants were, it felt like they were just outside the compound now. It wasn't like he was afraid or anything. He'd beaten everyone he had ever fought quite easily, in fact. Some of the assets looked about nervously and even shied away. That was probably the oddest thing of all. Clairvoyants were the strongest beings in the known galaxy. Sure, they felt fear, but it just wasn't the same as everyone else. He only wished Edge was here so he could show her what he could do. Yeah, that had to be what his Dark was telling him. His hands were only slightly shaking.

"I think I'm going to go back to my dorm," a kid next to him said.

"Yeah," another agreed.

Phaethon and the other assets around his age looked at them and sneered. He even saw a few of his friends coming outside while the first group retreated.

"Do you have any idea what's going on?" they asked.

"No," one of the assets near him answered. Phaethon nodded.

"Wait…what's that?" someone asked.

He turned to see that a section of the wall was glowing bright red. He could only assume that this force was trying to burn down the wall, which he found strange, since Clairvoyants could just fly over the barrier.

The wall crumbled in moments and out poured a small army. Phaethon's mouth fell open. They were Clairvoyants, there was no doubt about that, but they also weren't. They all looked the same—not broadly similar, but exactly alike. They were all men quite a bit taller than he was. In fact, it would be better to compare their bulk to mountains. Their hair was jet-black, and there was a steely coldness about their gaze. Its intensity reminded him of a spotlight. Their movement was just as alien. Clairvoyants were direct, but not mechanical. These *people* moved like robots. There was none of the grace or fluidity that defined Phaethon and his kin. He'd never seen anything like it.

He was snapped back to the here and now when one of the security members fell to the ground dead, her neck telekinetically broken without pause or restraint. Phaethon looked at the other assets near him, and they all leapt into action.

As always, there was no real conscious thought. Action, reaction, force, will, the Dark—all words from his education that came together as easily as breathing for him, at least in *this* game. These clones, for lack of a better name, were fast like Clairvoyants. They seemed to have telekinetically-amplified strength as well. It even seemed like they could anticipate some of his movements, but they weren't efficient nor even very powerful. Phaethon could feel the energy of the environment flowing through everyone, and these clones were as porous as a filter of rocks.

He fought two with barely any effort at all. Each second the contest went on, the more behind they fell due to fatigue. His fist landed before he consciously realized it was time to strike. His opponent reeled back, and a second harder attack killed him. The other clone lasted only a scant bit longer.

"*Impressive. I think you'll do,*" a voice said in Phaethon's head. "*You're a credit to our kind, even though you miss the point,*" it added with a bit of sarcasm.

Phaethon defended himself while also trying to look for whoever was speaking. Telepathy wasn't like talking with the strumming of vocal cords; it was difficult if not impossible to tell direction.

"*Who are you? What do you want?*" he asked.

"*Who I am doesn't really matter. But—Phaethon, is it? Yes, you will do nicely.*"

"*What? How do you know my name?*"

"*How I know you is unimportant,*" the voice said. "*But you are needed for something grander than this middling education. This is a dark time. Our enemies stand on the brink of annihilation. All it will take is a little push.*"

Phaethon felled another clone, though it seemed that the battle was slowly being lost. There were just too many. He could only pay them so much attention, though.

"*Our enemies? I don't have any enemies,*" he spoke.

There was a long pause before the voice spoke again. "*You are a foolish, foolish boy. What's happened to our self-*

respect? If this is what I must do, it is without regret. This will be the end of everything."

"*You're crazy!*"

Phaethon turned around and was immediately pinned in place. The Clairvoyant standing before him was no clone. He was different from any he'd ever seen. He wasn't very tall and was rather slimly built. His clothes were dark, tattered, and hung wispily off him like dead skin. But his metal mask was as unnerving as it was captivating. It completely shrouded his features while also reflecting the scene around Phaethon as a distorted mess. The mirrorlike finish warped the young Clairvoyant's image into a feeble tangle.

"Crazy?" Charon asked. "I'm simply burdened with a sharper view."

"Well, whatever. I'm tired of you," Phaethon said as he assumed a guard.

Charon was armed with a Taper, which was attached to his waist. The weapon was collapsed for now, and if he was any sort of Clairvoyant, he would fight on his opponent's level. Phaethon hoped for as much, since he was bare fisted.

"You want to fight me, boy?" Charon asked with an amused tone.

Phaethon made no reply other than a kick that missed badly, but he never expected it to connect. Charon's movements were effortlessly direct in execution. A small step on his part took Phaethon's best counter away before it could even be made. He decided to try a punch, and the next thing he knew, he was flipping through the air. A quick reaction with telekinesis let him land on his feet.

"There is fire in you," Charon remarked. "Foolish."

Phaethon gritted his teeth and went on the attack again. He never fought so hard in his life, but it was like Charon was three moves ahead. He'd fought other Clairvoyants before.

He'd never lost a sparring match. All those battles, however, were child's play compared to this. Charon was just so smooth, almost perfectly efficient. His movements were precise and focused. The disparity only grew over time. Phaethon wobbled and his form grew messy as a mixture of conscious thought and rage marred his action. He wanted to kill his opponent. But the further that bitter reality seemed from fruition, the angrier and more desperate he became. The feelings fed on each other.

"It seems you were miseducated. I make you angry. Anger, however, is not a Clairvoyant's salve," Charon said as he blocked the boy's blows. "We are meant to impose our will—direct it—not scream at the unyielding. That conflict is what makes us what we are."

Just like that, Charon went on the attack. Phaethon wasn't ready for it. The hits weren't very hard, but the blows were starting to add up.

"We revel in it," Charon continued as the young Clairvoyant spat blood. "It's every sting shapes our vision as we bend it to ours."

Phaethon looked at his distorted image on the metal face mask. He didn't think he could defend himself much longer.

"Then...then, we get the one thing we've wanted, when the previously unyielding breaks. It's a look—a hopeless, defeated self-reflection—that signals the triumph of our Dark and gives the true rush of its power."

Phaethon threw a punch that Charon's open hand caught. He watched in horror as a beam of heat seared away his arm to the elbow. He staggered, falling to one knee. Then he looked up at Charon, which made the man pause.

"That's the look exactly!" Charon declared.

9

GAME OVER

Carmen had felt uncomfortable from the moment she stepped off the transport shuttle. The feeling was new to her Clairvoyant senses. It was like someone was watching her. That didn't mean much, since people had been watching her all day, both on the shuttle itself and while on her way to Michael's grave. The feeling persisted, though. She tried to ignore it. It wouldn't be the first time she had sensed something irrelevant.

There was only one thing on her mind anyway: That she had just bought her last bouquet of flowers. She'd been buying them for Michael for so long. The realization that they would no longer be needed was halting in a strangely distant way. It was like the rug had been pulled out from under her, but after she came back to her feet, it didn't really matter that the floor was bare. Part of her was still crying in that bar on Evonea. She accepted it, though, just like she accepted that the sky was blue. He'd been dying for so long that she supposed she had long before prepared herself for his final day without even realizing it. She hadn't even tried to stop the flowers she had placed on his grave from blowing away in the wind. After everything she'd done—after all the trying and hoping—that was how it ended.

She left the cemetery with her head held low. *What now?* she wondered. She had no real want for money with Michael dead. Her first step would be to resign as Phaethon's handler. She'd never had any idea what she was doing, and it was obvious she was no good for him. He'd be better off with someone else. He certainly wouldn't miss the chess games. She guessed she could still stay with her new construction job —until they fired her, at least, which she figured would be in maybe a month and a half. She considered that possibility and found the worry a little odd now that she had just herself to look out for. It had been a constant source of dread. Money, money, money—she never had enough. It hadn't been out of the ordinary for her to skip a few meals to save a credit or two.

Just then, the sum total of her life to this point, especially the past two years, made her ball her hands into angry fists. Yet it also made her feel weak at the same time. All she could do—all her abilities and all her training—counted for as much as spit on a burning blaze. No one could say she hadn't tried. Myths and legends could be written about her determination. But now, with the unreachable summit still far in the distance, lost wasn't just a word; it seemed to be an inescapable state of being.

She got on her bus, and everyone stared at her, as usual, while she moved to an open seat. She decided to do them all a favor by sitting as far away from them as possible. As Carmen glanced at everyone tensely trying to pretend she wasn't there, she came to one conclusion. She had a month and a half probably, maybe two or even three if she was lucky with her new job. Then she would start over, possibly on another planet. There were too many memories here.

It was a while till she got back to the city, as it was another bus after the first to get within walking distance of the facility. As always, it was too tiring to fly everywhere. She had to have slept for a straight day after the chase on Evonea.

As she began the last leg of her journey on foot, she reflected that this was going to be quite the day of goodbyes. She had said goodbye to Michael, and she'd be saying goodbye to Phaethon. She paused for a moment when she realized she also wouldn't be coming back to the facility ever again after today. She'd thought that before, but this time there was absolutely nothing at all tying her to anything on this planet. Her mood took her mind to when Kali had first brought her to the bluff. Just as she had then, she stood at a precipice now. Unfortunately, there were no friendly shores in sight this time.

A soft sigh put her frenzied thoughts to rest for the moment. The walls of the facility were in view, and several police cars were parked outside, along with other emergency vehicles. *Strange*, Carmen thought. She couldn't see a lot of activity from this distance, but something had certainly happened. One of the few personnel dorms that lay outside the main compound was destroyed. Workers tended to the rubble as she walked by. They didn't seem to be looking for survivors; she couldn't sense anyone alive in the rubble at all.

She turned her attention back to the facility proper, more curious than concerned. Everyone she cared about now was a Clairvoyant, and they could take care of themselves if anything serious happened. The only things she could think of that could affect them were a major fight among the assets, some sort of accident, or the place being shut down. Her curiosity prompted her to fly over the walls rather than take the time with the usual check-in procedures. It wasn't like anyone would try to stop her.

Her eyebrows furrowed when she saw what was on the other side. The place looked like a warzone. One whole section of the wall was missing, and blood stains covered the field for as far as she could see, as did hologram projections of dead bodies. She gave up counting after two dozen. Most of the bodies looked exactly the same. If she didn't know better, Carmen would say they were clones, but that made no sense.

She walked aimlessly through it all, weaving through the agents and detectives trying to make sense of the carnage. It was only after a few minutes that she realized the quiet dread rising within her could be sated more easily than using her eyes.

"Excuse me," she said to the closest agent.

"Yes?" He paused when he realized he was talking to a Clairvoyant. "Yes, ma'am. How may I help you?" he asked.

"Are—" she began, but then she stopped short. It would be easier to just read him. She wanted to be sure.

Her eyebrows furrowed again when she finally understood what had happened. *I should have been here*, she thought. The answer to her next question wasn't as easy to determine. All that really mattered to her was whether Kali and Phaethon were okay. Regrettably, people couldn't be read like a book. Thoughts weren't arranged so conveniently and were often fragmented, chaotic. She peered through the layers of the agent's mind before stopping at memories of the first Terran-Sorten War. Even now, her time with Eli occasionally kept her up at night, and she preferred not to go through it again with someone else. If Kali and Phaethon were alive or dead, this man didn't know.

"Thank you," she said, walking away.

"Yeah, right. Sure," he muttered, confused.

Carmen shook her head at the next thing he thought. She always wondered why people thought it would be fun to read minds. There were many thoughts she'd rather not know. A moment later, something caught her eye across the field. She was surprised no one had moved it, with everything going on. Maybe they wanted to keep everything as it was for evidence collection?

She came upon the chessboard as she had dozens of times before. This time, though, the board and table it always rested on were overturned. She felt the need to reset the board. Perhaps with all the times Phaethon had turned it over, it had become a reflex. Her first instinct was to do so telekinetically. She knelt down, however, and fixed the mess with her own two hands. Carmen appreciated the added focus of using muscles and sinew in this instance. A small smirk graced her lips when she noticed the board's computer was set to training mode. *He was practicing for me*, she thought. Well, she liked to think as much. Phaethon probably hadn't even been using it at all.

She sat on one of the previously overturned chairs, needing a moment before she made her next move. *Everything has been such a nightmare lately*, she noted. She had traveled across the galaxy to kill someone she didn't even know, Michael had died, and now this. She looked at the overturned chair on the other side of the board. *Administration has to know what happened to them*, she thought, as the uncomfortable feeling that'd been her company almost all day returned.

She turned her head. It was Kali. Carmen rushed toward her.

"I was worried," she said as she hugged her former handler tightly. Carmen didn't see her smile weakly in response. "Are you okay?" she asked as she pulled away.

"I'm fine."

"Phaethon?"

Kali paused with a quick sigh. Carmen swallowed hard. "I don't know," she said simply.

Carmen opened her mouth to speak, but Kali waved to one of the chairs. Carmen nodded, and they sat down.

"We were attacked by a veritable army of Clairvoyants," Kali explained. "They seemed to be clones. We'll know for sure once the bodies are finished being analyzed. But one was a normal Clairvoyant. Phaethon was last seen fighting him."

Carmen looked at her old handler hard. "No one knows what happened to him?" she asked. She already knew about the attack from reading the investigator, but it was difficult for her to believe that Phaethon, as fiery as he was, would just up and disappear during a fight.

"No, we don't," Kali said. "These clones may not have been very strong, but they had to have outnumbered us by at least five to one. No one was really able to keep track of anybody."

"Who is this Clairvoyant?"

"I don't know. I never saw him."

Carmen nodded slowly while taking a deep breath. She looked at the agent and detectives surveying the aftermath and then turned back to Kali. "Is anyone else missing?"

"Only the dead," Kali answered.

"And you're sure he isn't dead? Has somebody—" Carmen paused for a moment. She was unprepared for the emotions her next words created. "Has somebody checked all the bodies?" she finally asked as matter-of-factly as she could. She didn't think the question would bother her. Things she cared about died around her all the time. Just a few minutes ago, she'd been quite comfortable with never seeing Phaethon again.

Kali noted the momentary influence of Carmen's Dark but decided to say nothing about it. "We checked. We're sure," she said. "He's not here. Whether he'll be declared dead is still up in the air," she added.

"He's alive," Carmen said after a few seconds of musing. "If there's any mercy at all in the galaxy, he is alive."

Kali gave her former charge a sidewise glance. "Edge?"

"Michael's dead," she muttered. "He died while I was away. In fact, I just came from the cemetery."

"…I'm sorry."

Carmen nodded meekly. "It was a long time coming," she said, resting her head on an open palm. She didn't care that she knocked down some of the chess pieces she had just picked up.

"Yeah, but that doesn't change anything," Kali remarked.

"I know."

"How did you trip go anyway?"

"I'd rather not talk about it," Carmen said timidly.

Kali sat still for a moment before she leaned back in her chair with a raised eyebrow. "I don't think you've ever told me that before," she said. "It wasn't that bad, was it?"

Carmen glanced at her and then shied away when the look was returned. No, she never had told Kali that before. Everything between them till now had been freely shared. It made her feel guilty, but she still didn't want to talk about it.

"Why would they take Phaethon?" she asked instead, trying to change the subject.

Kali watched the asset she was once responsible for shift

uncomfortably under her gaze. "I don't know," she finally said. "This attack was too random to know much of anything."

"It's not like Clairvoyants don't make guesses," Carmen remarked.

Kali smiled weakly. "I don't think they were trying to kill us. At least, not all of us," she added after glancing around the compound and surveying the damage.

"What makes you say that?" Carmen asked, but by this point she wasn't paying much attention to the conversation. She stared at the chessboard in front of her, wondering if Phaethon would still be alive if she hadn't been such a waste of a handler. *I can't believe I made him play this*, she thought.

"There was no point to," Kali said. "Anyone can be a Clairvoyant. You can't stop Clairvoyants by destroying this place."

"Tell that to the protestors," Carmen remarked.

Kali shook her head. "They don't know what they do. They're scared. This was different. It was planned and had purpose. If the point was to kill us all, they would have just used a bomb, not these *Clairvoyant* clones," she added. Derision bled into her voice.

"I don't understand how that's possible," Carmen said.

Her old handler sat back in her chair and rolled her eyes. "I can't read you, Edge. You don't understand how what is possible? It's almost like talking to a *normal* person sometimes."

Carmen gave a pained smirk at that. "Clairvoyant clones. I don't understand how that is possible. Janus said no one knows how or why Clairvoyants are clairvoyant. He said that, if you cloned me, for instance, it wouldn't *be* me. It wouldn't have the same Dark as me, the same experiences, or any of my other intangibles. We would be genetically identical, but we wouldn't be the same."

"Well, it seems like someone figured it out," Kali said, her voice growing harsher after each word. "If there is any consolation to all this, it's that most of these abominations died in the attack." Her tone became much the same as when she spoke of the sortens, with bitter hate turning her soft, melodic voice into thorns. Carmen hated when she talked like that; she sounded like a completely different person. Yet the wrath fit her former handler just as surely as her sweetest smile.

"I guess so," she muttered disbelievingly under her breath. Kali heard her anyway, and Carmen saw her eyes narrow, but she kept whatever comment was brewing to herself. "What about the mystery Clairvoyant? What happened to him?" Carmen asked. "Was he killed?"

"No, no one saw him after he started fighting Phaethon." Carmen nodded slowly, and Kali continued. "It's a pity that he didn't die as well. I despise Clairvoyants like that."

Carmen glanced at her old handler, looked away, and shifted uncomfortably again. She didn't say anything, though.

"Don't start with me, Edge," Kali said, ignoring her prudence. "If you think this was bad…" She waved her finger all around her. "You don't know. You really, really don't know what it was like with the sortens. You don't know what kind of vile creatures they are. We deserve blood for blood for their crimes—for what they turned us into. And if this Clairvoyant, whoever he is, is helping them in any way, he must suffer as well. If you lived a life that approached anything like mine, you would feel the same."

"…I'm sorry," Carmen said.

"Everyone is sorry. You I actually believe."

Carmen said nothing to that. She gave Kali a hesitant glance and noticed her features beginning to soften.

"Edge, these are old wounds," Kali continued with her usual comforting tone. "Forgive my forcefulness, but I wouldn't burden you if I didn't think it was important for you to know. The galaxy doesn't look kindly on Clairvoyants. It probably never will. You're only just starting to understand that."

"I know," Carmen said simply.

"Good. We need to always stick together. There isn't much we have left after that," Kali said. "So, enough about me. I told the administration to wait till you got back before clearing Phaethon's room. If there are any personal effects you want, now would be the time to take them."

Carmen sat back in her chair and took a moment to think. "Shouldn't that go to his family?" she asked.

"You are his family," Kali shot back. "At least, the closest to it any of us can have."

Then she stood and gave Carmen, who was still sitting, a hug. Carmen was quick to realize that usually she was the one to hug Kali and not the other way around. Her former handler let her go and smiled down at her.

"Remember that," she said softly. She then turned and left.

Carmen watched her leave till she caught sight of the chessboard out of the corner of her eye. She bent down and picked up one of the pieces she'd knocked over. It was the king and the color Phaethon usually played.

"Checkmate," she said softly to herself, noting the irony.

She placed the piece back on the board on its side, the position it had always assumed after a match. Then she studied it for a moment. If there was anything she'd like to keep from Phaethon, it would be the chess set. It was the most fitting symbol of her total failure as a handler. Perhaps she'd also chip off a piece of Michael's headstone, somehow find a tuft of Mikayla's fur, and start a collection. But it wasn't Phaethon's or even her chess set. It belonged to the facility, and she couldn't just take it without asking someone first.

Maybe there's something in his room, Carmen thought as she began walking. She had no doubt whatsoever that she'd never forget Phaethon, no matter how many of his trinkets she did or didn't have. This trek was prompted more by Kali's suggestion than anything.

Carmen had been to his room numerous times to collect him. She had never really been *inside* his room before, though. It was an unspoken taboo for a handler to do so. The assets were allowed to maintain that modicum of personal space. Someone somewhere had probably realized they'd all go insane if they didn't have at least that. Now that she thought about it, Janus and even Kali had never really entered her room. If they had, they'd certainly never gone looking around in it.

She stopped outside the door to Phaethon's dorm, keenly aware that she only knew her charge on the barest, almost completely impersonal level. Either he resisted her attempts to bridge the gap, or she was just too incompetent to be able to. It was hard to know whether this would be her final jump across that chasm or a violation of what little progress she had made. Carmen had half a mind to let the janitor see to the clearing of her charge's room, but she thought, *I may as well be a complete failure*, and took a deep breath before she entered.

The lights came on automatically. The dorms, like almost everything at the facility as she had long since learned, were standardized. She didn't know what, exactly, she could take that had anything to do with his person.

She walked toward his work desk. *I had that same notebook*, she thought as she thumbed it open. *Algebra...* She'd hated algebra. By reflex, her hand went to her cheek. She remembered, dimly, when she had been hit after worrying to the point of distraction over an algebra test. She couldn't even remember how well she'd done on it.

Carmen looked through some of his things, but nothing really stood out for her. What would she do with his comb? She thought of her own room, both when she was here and at her apartment. The only thing she ever really had was the essentials. She stopped in front of his mirror at that moment.

"Why in the world *do* I always have a ponytail?" she muttered to her reflection.

She pulled the tie and let her hair fall, if just for now. Then she explored the room a little more, choosing to ignore the bathroom. There was, however, nothing of consequence to be found. It didn't help that her thoughts wandered as she looked, but there was no point in trying to stop them. Eventually, she sat on his bed and let her mind roam.

Carmen had only been out of the facility for a couple of years. Her rousing success during that time was definitely worthy of awe. With a sigh, she lay down and stared at the ceiling. She couldn't compose her thoughts, though. *What is that?* she suddenly wondered. Something hard was under the pillow. She pulled it out to find it was another notebook. After opening it curiously, she read the first page.

I don't know where I am. What did I do wrong? The man shot me!

Her eyes grew wide as she slowly understood the words. *Phaethon journaled?* she thought in disbelief. She rapidly flipped through more pages, and sure enough they had writing on them too. The realization was so strange that Carmen wondered if the next duck she saw would meow at her. There were no dates on any of the entries, though, on further consideration, she had never really known what day it was when she lived here either. Time had just seemed to pass.

The man's name is Adamantine, Carmen read. It took her a while to figure out what he was trying to spell. Phaethon had to have been six or seven when he wrote it. *He wants me to hurt people and do bad things. He said I'm special.*

I woke up in the hospital today. I don't know how I got there. Adamantine wanted me to fight some other man. It hurt.

Carmen skipped ahead a few pages. The entries brought back too many memories that she thought she'd buried long ago. The next entry brought a smile, though.

Grammar. I hate grammar. I'd rather just learn algebra.

"I guess everyone really is different," Carmen muttered to herself as she read the next entry.

I'm good at this, the violence. It's all starting to make sense now. I'm just an animal. This room is my cage. That's why everyone was always afraid of me. That's why Adamantine is called a handler. A part of me, I think, even enjoys this. But why do I still cry every night?

"Why indeed," Carmen said.

I'm going to kill Adamantine or bash my skull open against the wall. Nothing I ever do is good enough for him. He wants me to kill, so I kill. Then he says "Clairvoyants are monsters, not savages. We kill because there are those foolish enough to get in our way. We don't seek destruction." That's complete bullshit. I didn't kidnap myself.

Carmen turned the page.

I killed Adamantine. He took me to some bluff or whatever and told me to jump off. I flew to some town a little ways away. I was so scared that I had to fly back here. Why didn't Adamantine tell me all this was out there? I don't want to go back to the world. I thought it was a dream. I was happy down in my hole.

I don't like the new handler they assigned me. I may kill her too. She talks a lot but says nothing. I'm a monster, a Clairvoyant. Just leave me in my hole. I don't want to come out. I don't deserve to. I don't want to graduate, either. I should have crashed against the rocks for my first flight. All I can do well is kill. At least here I'm just killing other monsters like me.

I killed her. They haven't given me a new handler yet. They just keep me locked in my room all day. I don't think they know what to do with me. I've been alone for a long time. It's hard to know what day it is. I may bash my head against the wall again. Everything makes me so angry. I don't know if something is wrong with me or if this is how I'm supposed to be. I don't sleep well and keep waking up. My graduation date is only a couple years away. I'm so scared.

Carmen's lips pressed together in a bemused sneer when she read the next entry.

I have a new handler. Her name is Edge. I'm definitely going to kill this one.

I wish she'd leave me alone like everyone else does. I can't scare her away. She just looks at me and waits. She's really strong. I don't know if she can read me, but it's like she's looking right through me when she does that. I want to strangle her, but I can't.

Fuck, she has no idea what she's doing. Why did they assign me to her? She doesn't shut up about her old handler. She's making me play chess. For shit's sake, CHESS!

"Yeah, I know it was bad," Carmen said under her breath. But she fell silent at what she read next.

She still has no idea what she's doing, but she's different somehow. I don't know. It seems like she's actually trying... like she actually cares about me. She at least listens to me. Must be my imagination. I'm a piece of shit.

Edge had to go off planet for some reason. She wouldn't tell me why. I think I miss her. I hope she isn't trying to run away from me. She said she'd be back, but everyone here lies. I'm such a piece of shit. She tries so hard, but I just don't know what to do. I don't know any other way to be. Why hasn't she given up on me? Maybe if I get good at chess while she's gone, she'll know that I'm trying too. But it's such a stupid game.

That was the last entry. Carmen stared at it without reading for a long while. Her thoughts were too muddled to think clearly. She placed the notebook on her lap and stared at the ceiling, letting the fragments of ideas play through her mind. None of them coalesced into any sort of conclusion, but eventually she felt prompted to leave the room, notebook in hand. The lights shut off behind her, but she didn't notice.

Her journey through the facility was swift and direct. She only paused briefly when she saw Gungnir talking to a detective. He glanced at her. She opened her mouth to speak but closed it just as quickly, sure that she was absolutely crazy. The ideas circling through the maze that was her mind in its present state were too ludicrous to give voice to. He paid her no attention.

She noted that the bizarre uncomfortable feeling returned when she was outside again. It was stronger than before and felt strangely anxious. It was close company on her bus trip home. No one sat near her, as usual, but someone complained about running into something. She wasn't paying any attention, though.

I can't do it, Carmen thought as she stepped off the bus,

though it was more of a plea to herself. The uncomfortable feeling plaguing her almost all day promptly vanished for no discernible reason. That, however, did nothing to change her mood. *I can't*, she thought over and over. Maybe she'd just sleep on it and everything wouldn't feel so…immediate? She didn't know why, but for some reason she doubted that would be the case.

When she approached her apartment building, she sighed. She'd had enough of people for the day—enough of people staring at her, enough of people terrified of her, and enough of trying to block out their thoughts. Just the idea of bumping into Anthony or anyone else in the lobby made her groan. She gave Phaethon's notebook a squeeze, happy that the same abilities that were the source of most of her troubles allowed her, on occasion, to also circumvent those troubles. She eyed the window to her apartment and flew to it. A thought opened the window, which she kept unlocked for such instances, and she stepped inside.

The empty nothingness that was her apartment greeted her. It had been her normal since Michael got sick, but for the first time it gave her pause. More than that, it actually made her shudder. She sat on the windowsill, scarcely able to even look at it, as a sickening feeling took hold. She looked away sharply, held the notebook tight to her chest, closed her eyes, and took a deep breath. A million thoughts bounced around her skull, and she ignored them as she usually did.

Carmen opened her eyes to watch the city. The sun was beginning to set and the sky was clear. She took a deep breath again and tried to get comfortable, as difficult as that was when straddling a windowsill with a leg dangling outside and simultaneously trying to ignore her lifeless life inside. But then she experienced another feeling. It wasn't roused from deep in her core, as most of her nightmares were. This was more immediate, though just as terrible. It screamed at her as she looked back into the apartment.

No! she thought as the mounting dread took her.

There was a brief flash, and the apartment rumbled and shook as the glass in all the windows shattered. It was only the beginning. Bright lights weren't much of a bother for Clairvoyants, but her eyes sealed shut out of pure instinct at the flash of the second, more violent explosion. Carmen screamed as she was overcome, yet the advancing heat was absorbed by the Clairvoyant like an old friend. The concussion wave flowed around her body by trained telekinetic reflex, muffling the sound and the force till they felt like a stiff breeze. If but for that subconscious thought, its kinetic energy could have injured or killed her the same as anyone else.

The next thing she knew, she was tumbling through the air. She only dimly registered that she had been blown out of the window. The apartment building crumbled next to her as she fell. The strain and snap as its structural members failed seemed to play in slow motion for her heightened perception as the ground rushed to meet her. She landed gracefully enough, twisting in the air like a cat to land on her feet, but there was no respite. She turned, and the cloud of the apartment's debris crashed on her like a wave. All she could think to do was cover her face with her arms and grit her teeth.

Brick, glass, and metal were redirected away from the Clairvoyant by some unseen force. Parked aerocars were flattened and then exploded. The entire side of an adjacent building was ripped to the bare frame. And Carmen stood against it all like a rock in rushing rapids. When it was over, there was utter silence.

She opened her eyes slowly. Her sleeves were in tatters. Her hair was frayed. It took a second for her to notice that the bottom of her pants was on fire, and she snuffed it out teleki-netically. It was hard to see. Dust slowly fell to the earth. She looked at where her apartment had once been, using all of her senses, but there was nothing left. Her mouth was dry. She tried to swallow and found it near impossible. Thoughts flooded back on her as her lips contorted in vain attempts to give them voice, till at last she could think of only one thing to say.

"Ew…" she muttered softly.

Her fingernails dug into Phaethon's notebook, which miraculously stayed with her during the fall. *Why did this happen?* she wondered over and over. She could hear distant sirens and could sense others approaching the scene, but there was also something else.

With no thinking on her part, she turned her head in its direction even before it came. The bullet sped toward her at hypersonic speed. She stopped it in midair, and it hung in front of her face. The extraordinarily loud report from the weapon registered an instant later. She stared past the bullet to the rooftop it had come from. She couldn't see who'd fired it, but she knew she was looking right at him. His anxiety filled the air, thicker than the smoke from the explosion.

She flew to the rooftop in seconds. A large gun was aimed down at the street, but there was nothing else, other than that odd feeling from before. This time, though, it attached an alarm to Carmen's nervous system and begged for her atten-tion so completely that her hands shook.

"Shrewd," she said softly when she realized what was happening.

He let out a piercing scream as she telekinetically crushed his arms and legs. It was tempting to do more, but she held herself to that. Another thought ripped the cloaking system clean off him. With his protective shroud gone, the Sentinel appeared at her feet, completely crippled. His pistol lay next to him. She wondered how long he had been stalking her. She guessed she'd been too preoccupied to fully sense him.

He stared up at her, and she could practically taste his fear. It was well warranted. Carmen glanced down at Phaethon's notebook and then looked at the Sentinel. His face reflected the quiet truth of the situation. There would be no mercy this time.

10

A PAWN STEPS FORWARD

"Is this phone secure?"

"Yes," Gungnir said simply.

His job contacts always changed, but he was quite aware that his chief employers were certain members or even certain branches of the United Terran Empire. They were too prompt and rigid for anything but government work.

"Good," the contact said. There was a pause before he continued. Gungnir didn't waste his time by asking what his name was. Any answer would probably be an alias anyway. "We have the preliminary autopsy analysis."

"And?"

"They are genetically identical. Every single one of them. Until now, we've had vague reports of Clairvoyant clones, but nothing like this. This was almost completely without warning. The fact that whoever organized this was able to strike in force at a colony as secure as New Earth with mass Clairvoyants is...disturbing."

Gungnir nodded to himself as he turned to look out the window. "Is this related to the war?" he asked as he surveyed the damage to the facility. Admittedly, it wasn't much, and not many people had been injured or killed.

"We believe so, but we don't know how. Attacking civilians like this, even Clairvoyant civilians, serves no military purpose. There are softer targets in the system that would have yielded greater effect."

"There really wasn't any effect," Gungnir remarked.

"Quite true," his contact agreed. "We have no idea, no answers. That is where you and your team come in. We need you to find out, by any means, what is going on out there, and either report it back to us or destroy it, if required and possible. You'll have a blank check."

"Fine," Gungnir said simply. "Are there any leads, no matter how small?"

"Nothing. They could strike Earth or Leevi and we wouldn't know anything about it till it was all over."

"That doesn't give us much to go on," Gungnir said.

"No, it doesn't."

Just then, Gungnir's door burst open. It was Carmen, her clothes burnt and frayed. What had Gungnir's complete attention, however, was the man telekinetically suspended next to her. She dropped him to the ground, doing nothing to blunt the fall. He groaned when he made impact.

"We need to talk," she said.

Gungnir sat in stunned silence for several seconds. The Clairvoyant couldn't remember any instance in his life in which this had ever happened. He let out an annoyed sigh.

"I'll get back to you," he said to his contact on the phone before he hung up. Then he looked at Carmen. "Who is that bleeding on my floor?"

"The Sentinel," she said matter-of-factly. The man groaned when she telekinetically wrenched his head to allow Gungnir a better look at his face. One of Gungnir's eyebrows rose at the news. "Somehow he figured out who I was, followed me back here, and tried to take me out."

Gungnir looked her up and down, noting her tattered clothes. "Are you—"

"I'm fine," Carmen said sharply. She glanced down at the Sentinel lying at her feet and sneered. "The scum planted some sort of bomb at my apartment. Completely leveled the building. Killed everyone. There was no warning," she said, anger tainting her voice. Then she took a deep breath, which did nothing to calm her, before she continued. "If I had just killed him, all those people would still be alive." It looked like she wanted to say something else, but she allowed her statement to hang on the air like a bad smell. Gungnir watched her. She eventually looked away, wearing a pained expression she wasn't able to hide.

He nodded slowly and then picked up his phone again. Carmen didn't know who he called, and she didn't pay any attention to what he said. The accumulation of the past few hours made her body shake with rage while also making her feel weak.

She was broken of her trance when a security team entered the room. They took the Sentinel away with little fanfare. Carmen didn't watch and instead considered the one thought that consumed her. It was one impossible thought— the insane idea that had brought her here. Her eyes came to rest on Phaethon's journal, now slightly burned, still in her hand.

"I need your help," she said to Gungnir.

"Edge."

"Yes?" she said quickly.

"I don't know what you need," he began. "For the moment, I don't even care. You should clean yourself up and calm down. Then we can talk."

Carmen rolled her eyes and shook her head. "I said I was fine."

"Fine? Just look at yourself. There's still debris in your hair. You—"

She rolled her eyes again and pointedly took a seat across from him. "They took Phaethon," she said in a rush.

"They? Wait, I don't want you to answer that," he added, just as she was opening her mouth. He walked over to her and pulled her to her feet. They both winced from the interaction of their bioelectric fields. "At least take a shower and get a change of clothes."

"I don't think you heard me. My apartment was blown up. I don't have anything!" she remarked, anger once again bathing her words.

"Then I will find you something."

Carmen stared at him, her jaw clenched tight. Gungnir stared right back. When it was obvious that he wouldn't yield, her gaze fell and her body slackened.

"All right," she said softly.

He nodded. "Come on."

She said nothing but followed without protest, and the two Clairvoyants made their way through the facility. Their haste was notable, even for those of their ilk. Gungnir stopped outside the staff bathroom. Carmen turned to him.

Something about her was different than when they had first met. There was anger, shame, and maybe even a hint of fear, but now there was more to her than that. Now there was poise and decisiveness to her manner—more so than the average Clairvoyant and certainly more than he'd ever seen in her. She seemed…serious.

They continued to stare at each other. Carmen swallowed hard, and it looked like she wished to say something. Gungnir readied himself for the stream of words she was obviously considering. But, when they finally came forth, they were such a simple thing.

"Thank you," she said, looking both expectant and worried at the same time.

She spoke with such genuine gratitude that Gungnir nearly missed that what she said was also an apology. He nodded slowly and gave the most reassuring smile he could. Carmen responded in kind.

"I'll have someone bring you something to wear. See me in my office when you are done. I'll wait for you there."

She nodded and then walked into the dark bathroom alone. She tried the lights several times, but they just wouldn't turn on. She could only guess that power in this part of the facility had been damaged by the attack. Although Carmen was tempted to ask Gungnir if she could use a different bathroom, she thought better of it. It wasn't actually a bother, as the Clairvoyant moved deftly through the black nothingness.

She shed her clothes after a few steps. She did not know if the air was hot or cold; she was too apart from everything to ever truly know. Indeed, she had to consciously allow the water to touch her. Yet, as the calming warmth washed over her, taking with it the grime of the day, she was not comforted.

In the dark, there was nothing to aim her focus, allowing her mind to think of nothing and everything. Time entered the same dimension. In that state, fully exposed and vulnerable with no one to care, Carmen considered her charge. She wasn't sure what she could do. Perhaps no one could do anything. Her thoughts turned to Michael in his coma. Her middling efforts had kept her former lover alive as much as the machines he'd been attached to. Except now he wasn't alive—no more than the dolls she had used to play with in a make-believe life she could never have. His parents had given up long before his last moments. The hospital well knew he couldn't be saved. Kali knew it. And here, now, Carmen had to admit that she knew it as well. She had always known. In the end, the whole escapade had never really been about him.

"I never loved him," she concluded softly to herself. The words landed like an anvil, but here, in the dark, that truth was accepted just like the knowledge that she had to eat to live.

She paused for a long second, shut off the water, and then rested against the wall. Doubt crept into her being. As she stood in the black nothingness, the faces of Theodore, Anthony the super, and everyone else who had lived in her apartment building could be seen all around her, sure as she was breathing. Mikayla was among them, as was Michael. Countless constructs reached for her to draw her down to their level. Death seemed able to follow her, despite whatever twists and turns she took to elude it. And now Phaethon was out there somewhere.

Her eyes narrowed as she telekinetically dried herself. She still had no idea what she could do or where she could go. She had no idea if there was anything else but this. All the same, she was completely certain she could no longer stay here.

Gungnir was true to his word, and a set of clothes waited for her. She brought the items into the bathroom telekinetically and dressed in the dark. When she finally stepped out into the hallway, she was miffed to learn she was dressed in the same uniform assets wore. She figured they were the only clothes Gungnir could find on such short notice.

She received several confused looks as she made her way back to his office. There was no explicit rule that assets weren't allowed in the administrative sections of the facility, but it was a place they never ventured. She moved with such verve, however, that no one felt pressed to challenge her. Even other Clairvoyants made way on her approach. She took a deep breath. When she opened Gungnir's door, she saw him standing with his back to her, surveying the grounds of the facility as he usually did. He turned and sat at his desk when she entered.

"Much better," he said. Carmen nodded as she took a seat. "Now, what is this about someone taking Phaethon?"

"I don't know who took him, but he has been missing since the attack," she said. "I need to find him."

"He could be dead," Gungnir replied.

Carmen slowly shook her head. "He's not dead. Don't ask me how I know... I don't. But...but he's not dead. He can't be."

"So why come to me? Why do you think I can find him?"

"I have no idea whether you can, but I want him back. He's my responsibility. If you can't deliver, I'll try something else."

"Like what?"

She paused for a few seconds and then slowly shook her head. "I haven't gotten that far yet," she admitted. "I'll try something else if you can't help me. I don't know what, but if I have to sell my soul, I will."

"Why?" he asked.

"No one else will," she answered. "No one ever will."

Gungnir sat still as he considered her words. She stared at him expectantly and waited. Her expression suggested he'd be able to just wave his hands and produce Phaethon before her. He slowly turned to look out his window. By now, the sun was well past the horizon, and it was getting harder and harder to see the damage to the grounds.

"I may not be able to help you," he said.

"You told me that before."

"And I meant it then, just like I do now."

He continued looking out his office window while Carmen's eyes drilled into the back of his chair. His tone, even and accurate as always, did nothing to dissuade her.

"I don't believe you," she said.

"Clairvoyants aren't prone to lies."

Carmen remained undaunted. "You're not like the other Clairvoyants here. You're different."

"As are you," Gungnir said simply.

"I know," she responded without missing a beat. "But everything you said to me before about forests and wolves, the view being fitting, and that you couldn't help me wasn't just talk. You really are on the outside looking in...by choice."

Gungnir turned slowly in his chair to look her in the eye. If she didn't know better, it seemed that, for the first time, he was truly interested in what she was saying.

"Continue," he encouraged, almost as a dare.

Carmen swallowed hard and did just that. "For all the talk of power and force of will, Clairvoyants still only have a rote self-awareness. We still follow all the same ruts and predetermined paths everyone else follows. We all flew to the same town on our first flight. We all become mercenaries of some sort—even me. We never leave the forest, even if we're aware of it."

"And you think I have?" Gungnir asked.

"I...don't know," Carmen said. "But you talk like you have. I think you took this position at the facility to see if there is anyone else like you. Even if all you are is talk, you at least know there's something other than this," she said, gesturing around herself for effect. "I think you can help me, even if you say you can't."

"But that has nothing to do with Phaethon," Gungnir pointed out.

"It has everything to do with Phaethon."

"What do you mean?" he asked.

Carmen shuddered and then looked away. After a few seconds of searching, she muttered, "I can't really say."

"Can't or won't?"

"Both," she replied. "It's important…to me. He's my charge." Gungnir looked at her hard but said nothing. "I have to know. Why did you elect to pay me, even though I failed my mission?"

"I've already told you why. I was sympathetic to your situation."

"Why?"

Gungnir opened his mouth to answer and then paused. He said nothing but started nodding slowly. "I can't really say," he eventually answered. Carmen nodded as well. "Speaking of which, you don't want to stay here while your boyfriend recovers?"

Her eyes dropped just then. "Michael died while I was gone," she said, her voice hollow.

"And then this with Phaethon," Gungnir said more to himself than to her. Carmen nodded. "I understand."

"Can you help me?" she asked.

He sat silently, and Carmen could only watch and wait. "Maybe," he finally said. "In this instance, you catch me in an awkward position. I have no leads." She gave a dejected sigh at that. "Except for one thing," he added quickly. "It is ironic, but the fact that you didn't kill the Sentinel before makes us strangely fortunate now. He was taken by Space Force. My contacts there will forward anything useful from his interrogation. I doubt he'd know much of anything, but it's the only thing we have to go off of." Carmen nodded.

"This won't be like before. For now, I'll just say you should stay close to your phone and I'll contact you."

"My apartment blew up," she reminded him. "I don't even own these clothes."

Gungnir dropped his forehead into his hand and sighed. "Yes, I forgot about that. Take a room here, and I'll contact you when the time comes."

Carmen took a deep breath and then nodded slowly. "Okay."

11

UNSEEN WORLDS

She stared at the ceiling of her temporary quarters at the facility. It wasn't her old dorm room; it wasn't even a dorm. Yet, just like then, her eyes drilled into the ceiling while she awaited her next trial. Just like then, she had no idea what it would be. As she waited, the time between then and now seemed separated by no more than a breath.

A knock came at her door.

"Yes?" she answered.

The door opened slowly to reveal Gungnir. "Edge, it's time."

Carmen already knew he was coming and was dressed with her hair tied in a ponytail. All the same, his words caused a subconscious shudder. He didn't notice.

"I'm sorry you had to wait so long," he continued as they started walking down the hall.

Life in the facility was slowly returning to normal. It no longer crawled with detectives and investigators, just repair techs and others of that sort. Some of the outside contractors visibly shied away as the two Clairvoyants passed them. How they weren't used to the principal inhabitants of the facility by now was beyond her.

"It was only a couple days," Carmen said with a shrug, turning her attention back to Gungnir. "So, what do we know?" she asked.

"Still not much. The Sentinel was more resilient than expected." Carmen frowned, which he caught out of the corner of his eye. "We know enough, Edge," he reassured her. "He's a professional working for professionals. His ability to resist Clairvoyant interrogation is no surprise, nor is it that he doesn't know major operational details. He's just a tool, even if an extremely skilled one."

Carmen nodded. "So, what do we know?" she asked again. It was a rarity for a Clairvoyant to repeat themselves. The inefficiency was grating to the nerves.

"We know who hired him."

She waited for him to say more. When it was obvious nothing else would be forthcoming, she asked, "That's it?"

"For now, yes," Gungnir said.

When they stepped out of an elevator, it was quite apparent that they were heading outside. For what, she had no idea. That question could wait till later.

"I thought you said he worked for the sortens. Does he?"

"We don't know. We suspected that he worked for the sortens or Eternals, considering his target on Earth. However, it was and still is just a guess." Carmen took a deep breath and then let it go in a loud sigh. Gungnir glanced at her as they walked. "This should interest you, though. The person who hired him and his only contact was a Clairvoyant. A Clairvoyant matching the description of the one who attacked here."

Carmen stopped in place. Gungnir stopped as well and then turned.

"Are you certain?" she asked.

He gave a smirking smile. "What, no sighs?" he joked. She nodded several times, trying her best to hide an embarrassed frown. "Quite," he finally answered.

"What do we know about the Clairvoyant?" she asked hurriedly.

"Just the name: Charon," Gungnir said calmly.

Carmen thought back to her history classes and swallowed hard. Not every Clairvoyant's name perfectly described the person. Most Clairvoyants' names were just a general reflection of who or what the person was. Of course, some names were grandiose or overly dramatic, but no one was extreme enough to be named Destroyer or something equally ridiculous. Janus had told her, and Kali had reiterated, that the truly crazy Clairvoyants—the type ones—didn't last very long. She hoped this Charon wasn't a type one. *Why can't the Clairvoyant who attacks other Clairvoyants be named something like Puffy Cloud?* she thought.

"What can we do with just a name?" she asked.

"I don't want to say anything that will get your hopes up, but it just might be enough to get started," Gungnir said after a brief pause. "I've never heard of this Clairvoyant before though, which is odd. We might not typically do much to advertise ourselves, but we aren't exactly secretive. There's no reason to be." Carmen nodded. She couldn't hide, despite her many attempts to. People just knew what she was. "In the circles I travel, most everyone knows each other or at least knows of each other. But his attack strikes as some kind of statement." He continued walking again, and Carmen followed.

"What makes you say that?"

"The theatrics, the attire, the mask," Gungnir answered. "It's not unique. Most of us have our props. It's just odd that they come from a Clairvoyant no one has ever heard of in an attack that, as far as we know, had no real purpose. I keep thinking this attack was designed to fail, despite all the effort. Nothing of substance was achieved."

Carmen shrugged. She hadn't the faintest clue. "What does any of that have to do with taking Phaethon?" she asked.

"Difficult to say. We're getting unsubstantiated reports that the sortens are looking to hire strong Clairvoyants in large numbers."

"For mercenaries?" she asked as they stepped into the parking lot.

"I doubt it. There's no need. They surrendered to us just a few days ago. The war is over for them. Besides, Clairvoyants have a casual…*dislike* for sortens. They'd never willingly join them."

"…Yeah," Carmen said.

Gungnir nodded solemnly and then stopped at his aerocar. He looked at Carmen. "If anything is certain, it's that something big is going on. No one knows what, but all my contacts are buzzing…and they're nervous." Carmen thought back a few days to when she had barged into his office. He'd been talking to someone. It was pretty easy to guess the subject of conversation now. "Charon is not the center of it. He is, however, its most visible element. It stands to reason that, if we can find him, we'll at least have another piece of the puzzle."

She nodded. "So, where are we going now?"

"I greatly appreciate your help, but this is more than you can handle by yourself, Edge. I told you before that this will not be like your first contract. No one swims alone in the deep end."

Carmen made no response. She wasn't naïve enough to believe Gungnir was the only individual involved in his operation. Still, for whatever reason, she had assumed this would be like before, where she was given a destination and a set of instructions. She nodded slowly as the full scope of what she was undertaking came into view.

They got inside the aerocar, and Gungnir handed her a blindfold.

"What's this for?" she asked.

"Your protection," he answered. "Knowledge is a double-edged sword," he added.

Carmen nodded again as she understood his intent. However, she waved the mask away and swallowed hard. "I'm in this all the way, no matter what happens," she said, looking ahead.

"Very well," Gungnir muttered as he started the car.

She didn't often get to ride in cars. The vehicle leapt into the sky and shot off to the west, and Carmen knew immediately that this wouldn't be a short trip. They were quickly above the clouds as they joined the intercontinental traffic. A quick glance outside was all she needed to see that the ground was moving by quickly. It reminded her of all those years ago when she had been brought to the facility by Janus, which started her thinking.

"Gungnir," she began, "when I had my problem before, Kali knew I should go to you. You had precise information on how to find a, as you said, professional who didn't want to be found. When I walked into your office a few days ago, you were talking with someone about this even before I came to you. You talked about the circles you travel in... What are they?"

He looked at her. The car was under autopilot anyway. "You said you're in this all the way, so I won't be coy." She nodded. "Have you heard of the Rogue Wolves?" he asked.

"A little," Carmen said. "It's a group of powerful Clairvoyants who work solely for the highest bidder."

"Essentially that's true. There are several of us. I won't go into those details. But not everyone is a Clairvoyant, nor do we all work full time, like when you initially went after the Sentinel."

Carmen nodded slowly. "I imagine the facility is a good place to scout talent," she mused out loud.

"It is, but that's not the primary reason I'm there. Most of my business at the facility pertains to the operations of the facility itself. I try my best, given what it is. It's difficult. Objectively, I must admit that the facility, at its foundational level, seems touched by madness."

"Why don't you do anything about it?"

Gungnir slowly shook his head with a tight jaw. "Edge, you don't understand." She raised an eyebrow. "When all who are around you are crazy, what is the sane individual?" he asked rhetorically. "Trust me, I do what I can. There are a few handlers like Kali who steer people like you my way when they need the type of help I can provide—"

"Do they all get the same speech I got?" Carmen interrupted, noting that her hunch about him was at least partially correct.

"Yes, but you're one of the few to pay attention to it. Most, to use your words, are on the inside looking out but think they are on the outside looking in. They don't realize how trapped in their perspective they are," he said. Carmen considered that and nodded. "Trust me, it is no easy task to convince such people that, no matter how they move, they are going in circles," he continued. "Once again, madness."

"I think I understand," Carmen said. "So, who do you— who do *we* work for?"

"I work for myself, you work for me, and you serve yourself, as all do," Gungnir said simply. "Most of my contracts are government work, principally for the UTE. I suspect the...*requests* come from the upper if not top levels, but I have no way of being sure."

Carmen nodded as she felt the car wobble slightly from turbulence. Its inertial inhibitor was designed so she would never notice such disturbances, but although she didn't feel them physically, she was keenly aware of every time the system stepped in. Maybe luxury cars had a setting for a Clairvoyant's particular sensitivities? Her mind, however, was shifting through less immediate discomforts.

"Have you ever done anything you regret?" she asked.

Gungnir glanced at her before he started their descent. "Regret is practically a curse word for a Clairvoyant," he said simply.

Carmen agreed with every fiber of her being, but she also noted that he didn't answer her question. She looked at him and wondered. She couldn't read him, and she knew hardly anything about him. What twists and turns had his life taken? She did know that Kali trusted him, though, and that was probably good enough.

As the car entered the clouds, she considered her own twists and turns over the past two years. She had never thought she'd ever be in a position like this. She had never thought she'd ever, in her wildest imagination, be a handler, let alone for a charge like Phaethon. It had all seemed impossible, but it made complete sense now that she was living it. It was like something was guiding her as she stumbled through life. She didn't know if that was actually true, and she didn't know if it was a good thing if so, but she did remember her conversations with Phaethon on the Dark over all those games of chess. She sighed as she wished *she* could overturn the board.

They broke through the clouds over a vast forest cradled in a valley. It looked like a great hand had hollowed out the earth. The remoteness of the location was quite apparent, as not a single trace of civilization could be seen. Carmen had no idea where they were, which made her wonder why the blindfold was even considered necessary. Large outcroppings of rocks dotted the valley like pimples. They sped toward a rather large one.

After stopping to hover over it, Gungnir flipped some switch on the dash, and they then started downward. The walls appeared to have eroded away to make a large cave. She looked up just as the roof closed shut. Artificial running lights illuminated to guide their trip till they set down on a landing platform. It was the smaller of two. The other was at least three times bigger and presently occupied by an arrow-head-shaped starship. She knew nothing about starships, though, and could only guess what it was.

"I welcome you to the Lair," Gungnir said as he opened his door.

Carmen was only a half-step behind in opening hers. She followed him obediently while she glanced at the starship and everything else in the room. There was no point in being shy. As she said, she was in this all the way.

"How long have you been doing this?" she asked as they reached a door.

"A long time," he responded after a brief pause. He motioned to the ship. "*The Lady* is almost as old as you are," he continued as he opened the door.

Carmen nodded, and they walked into the next room. It wasn't all too big, maybe a healthy fraction of the fight rooms she had so loathed. The chaos contained here, however, rivaled the battles she once waged in those rooms. Computers and PDDs were strewn about on tables like the bodies of the slain. Papers also littered the room with notes she could read quite easily but couldn't make sense of. They were fragmented in their logic almost to the point of being gibberish. She figured they weren't worth paying too much mind.

Her attention then turned to a woman sitting at a desk in the center of the pile. She faced them but gave no greeting, even to Gungnir. She wasn't very old, maybe Kali's age. It was always so hard to guess. Her dark brown hair was about the only thing neat and tidy about her. She wasn't at all dirty or disheveled, but her clothes clashed...badly. Carmen, as was typical for Clairvoyants, had little care for fashion. Her dress—in fact, everything about her—was purposeful and didn't attract attention unless it needed to. This woman was surely visible half a system away. She didn't look ridiculous per se, but it was like someone screaming just to scream.

Carmen was quick to note that she couldn't be read. Well, not exactly. The woman wasn't a Clairvoyant, but from what Carmen could tell, her psyche seemed muddled, like the notes she saw earlier. There was no making sense of it. And unless Carmen missed her guess, it seemed deliberate.

"Edge, this is Widget. She's in charge of logistics, among other things," Gungnir said.

Carmen nodded slowly. Widget, however, made no response as she continued typing out whatever she was working on. The silence persisted for almost a minute before Carmen had enough.

"*Is she always like this?*" she asked Gungnir telepathically.

Just then, Widget looked at her. "Absolutely," she answered casually. Then she looked away and went on with whatever she was doing.

"Excuse me?" Carmen muttered.

"Speaking," Widget said a little louder than required. "I

don't speak—not at all—unless I'm speaking, and then I'm speaking all the time, because I'm speaking. Past, present, future. Got it?" she asked.

"Um…no," Carmen said.

"Oh well," Widget said with a shrug. "You looked smart."

Bewilderment practically leaked from Carmen's pores. Gungnir stepped in. "To answer your question, Edge," he said, "yes, she is always like this. Don't let it bother you. It's just a little Clairvoyant paranoia. It's not to be taken pers—"

"Truth. It's wonderful," Widget interrupted.

"I…don't get it," Carmen said.

"Despite my many attempts to convince her otherwise, Widget believes that we are always trying to read her mind," Gungnir said, giving the woman an affectionate glare. "It's an old technique but still quite effective. Constantly shifting your thoughts, thinking in incomplete thoughts, and using nonlinear logic makes it very difficult for a Clairvoyant to read you. The Sentinel tried the same techniques during his interrogation. Usually pain forces enough focus to break it."

Carmen noticed a rifle lying next to Widget on the table. "And that's for?" she asked.

"Flies, of course," the woman responded with an amused smirk.

"Unfortunately, I think Widget has been doing it for so long that she's been permanently afflicted… Or she's just toying with me. I can't really tell," Gungnir continued.

"The only thing I do seriously is play cards…and lie. Oh yeah, not flies, caterpillars. Or was it scorpions?" she said, tapping a finger against her chin.

Carmen had to force herself to not roll her eyes. "Why would a Clairvoyant want to read your mind? Believe me, we try hard to not read anyone's mind."

"Can't take that chance. Too important," Widget shot back.

"What's too important?"

Widget's head snapped right toward her, and Carmen had never seen anyone with a face so serious. "I don't want every Clairvoyant I meet to know my underwear is pink. It's not, by the way."

"Figured as much," Carmen muttered under her breath.

The woman pointed a thumb at her and looked at Gungnir. "She's definitely smarter than the last dumb one you brought by."

Gungnir rolled his eyes so Carmen didn't have to. "Enough, Widget. Have you found anything more on Charon?"

"If you want a trained monkey to do this job, I have an umbrella and a ticket to the zoo. Thankfully, you're stuck with me," Widget said. "They're closed, for now. Find nothing, yes did I. Perhaps better luck when pigs eat ducks."

Carmen gave Gungnir a hesitant glance.

"She's very good at her job," he said firmly. "You can trust me on that. She wouldn't be here otherwise. You can trust me on that as well."

"My pet goldfish cries a single tear," Widget remarked.

"Uhh...yeah, right," Carmen muttered under her breath. "So, what now?"

"Now we take another avenue. I doubted this could be dealt with directly. Please come with me."

Carmen nodded and followed him out of the room. They passed through a short corridor and into another slightly larger room. It was the complete antithesis of the first: orderly and focused, despite its more casual fittings. It had several couches that looked rather comfortable and even a holoprojector, which currently showed the news.

There was also a lone man sitting on one of the couches. He turned to look at them. He was Clairvoyant through and through, muscled in the same purposeful fashion as most of the Clairvoyants she met. He was direct if graceful in all his movements and had steely eyes that, for the moment, were fixed directly on her. He seemed to be not much older than she was. His African descent marked him as relatively unique on New Earth, much like Kali with her Asian descent. There was a relaxed tenseness about him. She couldn't describe it as similar to Gungnir's focused precision; it was more like a lack of concern.

He walked toward them and only turned his attention away from her long enough to nod to Gungnir. "She's a little different from what I expected," he said. Carmen noted that he didn't have a New Earth accent. She couldn't place it, though that didn't mean much, since she wasn't well travelled. "Will she be reliable?" he asked Gungnir, though he looked at her when he spoke.

She frowned. She was used to perceiving the thoughts of people who thought about her. She was well experienced with people talking about her behind her back. But this was annoyingly direct. Her reaction seemed to cause a response in this man that could be best described as curiosity.

"I believe she will be, but we shall see," Gungnir said.

They both looked at her now. She glanced at the two of them, wondering if she had somehow turned transparent. *Who are these people?* she wondered. First Widget, and now this.

"I'm right here," she said with a hint of irritation when she couldn't take it anymore.

"I know," the man said simply.

Gungnir took that moment to cut in. "Edge, this is my second-in-command, Inertia," he said, looking back and forth between the two of them. They stared at each other with not the friendliest of spirits. "It's nothing personal, Edge," he added after a sigh. "You just have to give everyone some time. They're not bad to work with."

Carmen wasn't sure if that was true, but just then Inertia extended his hand. She paused. Clairvoyants didn't usually touch people in casual circumstances. It required conscious thought to lower their static charge enough to not shock the other person. She hugged Kali, of course, but it was a bit odd for two Clairvoyants who didn't even know each other to bother with a social ritual as pointless as shaking hands, especially after the rather off-putting first impression.

She thought about it and then took his hand. His grip was a firm but agreeable. He smiled politely, even if it was slight, and she couldn't help a small if puzzled smile in return. Inertia wasn't anything she was expecting, but this was better than Widget at least.

"So, round two?" Carmen asked hesitantly.

Inertia smirked slightly. "If that's what you want to think," he remarked.

Carmen didn't really know how to take the comment, but Gungnir looked at them again and nodded slowly. Widget walked into the room a few seconds later. She didn't say anything, choosing instead to sit on the back of a couch nearby but not with the group. Carmen ignored her as Gungnir started speaking again.

"Anyway, this is a complex puzzle and we only have a few of the pieces," he began. "It seems that there are two main parts that we don't see the full extent of. The most visible element is, of course, Charon. We don't know what his goals actually are, but they are either desperate enough or he is confident enough to operate out in the open. Personally, I think he's just an agent for something else, much like the

Sentinel was. Either way, we can't be concerned about him for the moment."

Carmen's eyebrows furrowed. "Can't be concerned?" she asked. Inertia looked at her but said nothing. If anything, it seemed like he was assessing her. She had no clue why. "Well?" she asked Gungnir when he didn't answer right away.

"We're not forgetting about him. We just have to wait until we can make our move," he said.

"Why am I here, then, if all we're going to do is wait?" Carmen asked, trying to hide her frustration.

"I talked about other avenues," Gungnir replied.

"Yes…" she responded slowly.

"And that is why you are here. You're to accompany Inertia in tackling the second part of the puzzle."

That's why he was pressing me, Carmen realized, reflecting on how Inertia had first behaved. She had assumed she'd be with Gungnir every step of the way. Then she thought of the first impression—the *real* first impression— she'd made without even knowing it. Both Widget and Inertia had to know that she let the Sentinel go in their first encounter. *I'm the biggest liability of this mission.* With that in mind, she took a deep breath and looked at everyone in the room, also watching her just as intently. *Round two indeed*, she thought, realizing how stupid she must have sounded.

"What is the second part of the puzzle?" she asked.

"The sortens' bid to recruit Clairvoyant mercenaries. The two of you will seek employment."

"How does that help to get Phaethon back?" she asked. "Or help to get Charon?"

Inertia cut in. "Who hired Charon?" he asked simply.

"I don't know. You said you don't either," she added, addressing Gungnir.

"But if you were to guess?" Inertia asked.

"I'd say the sortens," Carmen answered without much thought.

Gungnir nodded slowly. "There's an old Earth saying that is appropriate here. 'Follow the money.' Charon, by all rights, may as well not even exist. None of our contacts can track him down," he remarked with a bit of frustration . "As I said, Charon is the most visible element of the puzzle, but I doubt he's a critical piece. If he is connected with the sortens, the need to capture him for more information could be circumvented by dealing directly with them."

"So, what will you be doing while we're dealing with the sortens?" Carmen asked.

"Widget and I will be here, waiting for Charon to show himself. Charon could make a mistake or another attack that we can capitalize on if we are in position to act," Gungnir answered.

Carmen paused and then turned to look at Widget. The woman waved back with one hand, gave her the finger with the other, and smiled broadly.

She turned away sharply. "Wouldn't it be better if I stayed here?" she asked. "All things considered," she added with a wayward glance Widget's way.

"No," Gungnir said forcefully, which caught Carmen off guard. "Inertia is as strong as you are, but whoever goes will be going into the lion's den alone with no assistance. I need the two of you."

She thought of Gungnir and, more distressingly, Widget standing up to Charon as he wielded the same army of Clairvoyant clones he attacked the facility with. *This is a stupid plan.* Unfortunately, she wasn't in any position to object.

"Just follow Inertia's lead, and the two of you should be fine," Gungnir continued.

Carmen glanced at Inertia, who gave her a nod. If he had any doubt, it didn't show. Unfortunately, his confidence did nothing to hearten her. She took a deep breath, closed her eyes, and then let it go slowly, reminding herself that this was the best and only course available.

"So, what now?" she asked.

"Now I'll discuss details with Inertia before you both depart. You, however…" Gungnir said, turning his attention to something behind her.

Carmen gritted her teeth. *You're looking at Widget, aren't you?* she guessed. She took a step forward before turning around.

Widget didn't adjust her position to be practically on top of Carmen as was her plan. She simply recognized Carmen's preemptive measure for what it was and frowned. "I've seen more flying unicorns than surprised Clairvoyants," she muttered to herself.

"What color were they?" Carmen muttered back sarcastically.

"Were what?"

Why do I do this to myself? Carmen wondered. "Never mind."

Widget smiled and then slowly shook her head, and Carmen now knew exactly what Gungnir meant by not knowing if the woman was toying with her or not. The idea of mentally teasing a Clairvoyant was strange, but it didn't seem intentionally harmful, if that was worth anything.

"Me come with girl of less years than petrified rats," Widget said.

Carmen followed close behind, rolling her eyes the entire way, though their destination was just across the room. Widget stopped at a table against the wall. Carmen hadn't noticed it before. Widget turned around after picking up a suit off the table.

"This is for you," she said.

She took it and gave it a quick look-over. The body armor was a bit on the heavy side, but it wasn't unexpected, nor was its amazing flexibility. She thought back to the incident with Artemis at Crystal Palace Mall, when she had worn similar. Then she thought of Artemis. No one knew what happened to her after her escape. It was like the galaxy had swallowed her entire existence. All that remained was memory.

This armor was dark grey in color with lighter grey parts that gave it a texture similar to fur. *Rogue Wolves*, Carmen thought. She expected the suit would fit her perfectly after laying it against herself for a quick check. She didn't remember Gungnir explicitly asking her for her measurements, but she paid it no mind. She handed the suit back to Widget, who replaced it on the table.

Carmen's eyes noticeably widened, however, when the woman picked up the next item on the table. This prompted a smile from Widget. It was a long sword, and Carmen couldn't remember the last time she'd even been near one. It had to have been several years at least. She removed the weapon from its sheath and noted that, once again, it seemed tailored for her. Its length, weight, and hilt—everything about it about it—just felt perfect. She looked at Widget for a second or two before the woman spoke.

"If you haven't noticed yet, it's also conductive to your particular energy signature and resistive to everything else."

Carmen hadn't noticed, but she was quite curious now that she was aware. She wasn't exactly sure what *energy conductivity* meant or what she could do with that ability—all questions for later—but she wondered if the sword could do something easy like transmit heat. She tried to do so pyrokinetically, and the sword responded in due course, warming with little of the resistance expected for a piece of metal its size. *Neat.* But it was too tiring to be practical. It had always been easier to project heat than to simply set something on fire. She had no real idea why. With that in mind, she had the idea to place her finger on the blade and try the exercise all over again. The metal responded again, but this time with less effort. *Neater.*

"How?" she asked.

A Clairvoyant's energy was as unique as a fingerprint. She hadn't seen Janus in years, but if he was in the next room, she'd know he was there. There were machines that were able to track and catalogue the telltale signatures; the detectives at the facility had such devices. She knew it was possible to make materials *sympathetic* to a certain Clairvoyant. She'd just never seen a working example. Much like with the suit, she also couldn't figure out when or how Widget had been able to get enough data on her energy signature to make the sword.

"How do I do my job so badly, or how do birds fly loops?" Widget asked.

Carmen gave a soft groan. "Guess," she said.

"Birds can't fly loops, silly. They'd just flop in circles."

Carmen rolled her eyes and then smirked. "You're not unpredictable when you pick the obviously stupid choice," she pointed out.

"When did I do that?" Widget asked with a bit of distress. Carmen let go a small laugh, which made the woman smile. "What shock. You can frown," Widget pointed out. Carmen felt her mouth, and indeed she was smiling. It had to have been on Evonea that the expression last graced her lips. "You have to be one of the most studied Clairvoyants to ever live," Widget continued more seriously—for her at least.

"Remember when you played Patty-cake with Artemis? I had to have thrown up on that video twelve times."

She nodded, and Widget kept talking, even though Carmen was no longer paying attention. Everything she said was complete nonsense anyway. She instead marveled at one of Widget's hairs, which floated freely in the air, as if by magic. Then it was pulled out suddenly with a quick jerk.

"Ahhh!" Widget screamed more out of surprise than anything. "Which one of you did that?" she yelled across the room at Gungnir and Inertia, who were still casually talking. They completely ignored her.

Carmen's mouth fell open. In that one brief moment, the muddled ridiculousness of Widget's mind coalesced into sharp, unwavering clarity. It was enough that Carmen couldn't help a quick read. It ended a few seconds later as the dams were rebuilt.

"I hate it when you guys do that," Widget said as she turned back to Carmen.

"It's blue," Carmen said simply.

"What?" Widget asked.

"Your underwear. It's blue."

The woman paused as her face turned white, her eyes widening with actual fear. Then her cheeks flushed a shade of pink. "See? See! I'm right to be paranoid! That's all you people care about."

Carmen grinned. "At least I know it goes both ways," she said as she telekinetically played with a clump of Widget's hair. The woman screamed, and Carmen laughed lightly. She had never thought of messing with someone like that before. *All the opportunities I missed...* she mused. "What else do you have to show me?" she asked, forcing herself to be a bit more serious.

Widget sneered at her, though the look seemed more

playful than angry. She also glanced at the rifle still sitting on the table in the next room. Carmen very much doubted she'd use it and figured it was just another in the long line of actions Widget took for *effect*.

"You people won't be happy till I shave myself bald," she grumbled as she picked up another item from the table.

12

THRESHOLDS

Carmen felt a tingle along her spine that caused her tongue to go numb for a moment. It was hard for her not to grin. She knew absolutely nothing about starships, but she did rather enjoy being around them. Their power existed in her perception like an ultra-dense but utterly raw explosion. It couldn't really be sampled like most other energies, but it could be sensed. The intensity felt like walking on the surface of the sun. She sat in the bridge of *The Lady*, marveling at how it was even possible to harness so much in seemingly so little. Math had never been her strong suit. Her understanding of engineering fared even worse. Still, it was obvious that it wasn't just Clairvoyants who harnessed the energy around them to their own ends. She had always found the technology that adorned her daily life more amazing than any talent a Clairvoyant could possess.

For now, she just waited. Inertia was in some other part of the ship, doing what she did not know. She would have helped if she could. When he started giving her instructions on how everything worked, though, she was so confused that an egg could have been fried on her forehead. Things were moving, at least. Actually, things were moving faster than she expected. It was only a matter of minutes after the meeting that Gungnir told her to get ready to go.

The body armor Widget gave her fit perfectly, as expected. Carmen's other new toy rested comfortably next to her on the floor. She glanced at the sword from time to time, wondering when she'd need it and, more importantly, if she could bring herself to use it. A distant look came to her eye as she considered her new path. Inertia entered the bridge a minute or two later and, fortunately or unfortunately, ended her thoughts on her many probable futures.

"We ready?" she asked as he took the seat next to her.

"Yes," he said simply, looking at her. His gaze lingered, though he said nothing else. It didn't take long for Carmen to realize she was being evaluated yet again.

She pursed her lips in a small frown. "Why do you keep looking at me like that?" she asked, her tone more curious than annoyed.

Inertia didn't even blink. "You aren't going to fuck me over, are you?" he responded.

Carmen paused, unable to answer right away. There was no anger or even worry in his question. She didn't know what he thought of her. Still, and she had no idea why, she didn't think his opinion of her was anything negative. His question caught her off guard anyway.

"I hope not," she finally said, which was the most truthful answer.

Inertia nodded slowly. "You're in this all the way?" he asked.

Carmen looked away from him for a second and then nodded sharply when she looked back at him again.

He nodded slowly one more time and then turned his attention to the ship, fiddling with something on his console.

She had no idea how any of the systems in the starship worked. A few seconds later, the ship started humming to life. Her pulse quickened and she swallowed hard. Inertia noticed.

"Gungnir told me you're doing this for your charge?" he asked, glancing at her briefly as he spoke.

Carmen nodded, even though he was no longer looking at her. His attention was divided between her and the ship. She could only assume *The Lady* was relatively easy for one person to operate. It didn't seem like it was designed to accommodate a crew of any real size.

"Do you think that's stupid?" she asked coyly.

"No," he said. "I wouldn't do it. But it's not stupid." He paused. "It might be the only thing in this whole operation that makes any sense."

"What do you mean?" Carmen asked.

Inertia gave her a quick glance. "Nothing. Don't worry about it."

She made no reply but looked at him intently. He cracked a wry grimace in return. "It's just a few musings here and there. Grumbles, really. As I said, nothing to worry about, at least for now."

Carmen looked away and her eyebrows furrowed as she considered everything he said. "You don't think the plan will work?"

"I didn't say that," he said simply. "However, I have experience in these sorts of things. And this mission seems like a rathole if there ever was one," he continued. Then he looked at her just as intently as she had earlier. "The problem with ratholes is that, once you stick your arm down one, you never know what you're going to pull out. What you want, though, and why you're here is simple, direct, binary."

"I see," Carmen muttered softly. "How many ratholes have you stuck your arm down?"

"Many."

She sat quietly for a few seconds. "And how bad were they?"

"I think I know what you're asking. It's probably better that you don't know," he said without looking at her.

Carmen nodded glumly. Inertia looked at her then, and she caught his concern out of the corner of her eye. "I'm in this all the way," she remarked, raising a hand to hold off the question again. "It's just...why do you do this?" she asked. "This job. I don't get it."

"Somebody has to," he replied.

"That's not an answer."

"No, it's not," he admitted. Then he turned his entire body to face her, which prompted her to do the same. "But why are *you* here?"

She looked at him, confused. "You know why. To rescue my charge."

"But why you?" he asked again.

Carmen paused as she realized where he was leading her. "Somebody has to. No one else would."

Inertia nodded. "Let me ask you this, Edge. You want to save a life, and that's very noble, but how many will you take to save it? I hope you don't expect me to do it for you."

"No, I don't expect you to do it for me," Carmen said quickly. "As for the rest, I hope I don't have to take any. Don't think I'll be that lucky, though," she added under her breath.

He nodded again. "I have taken many lives. I don't count," he began. "I guess it can be thought that I have saved many lives as well. I'll never know. I don't really think about it," he added with a shrug. "But, if you need a reason, I guess that why I'm here isn't too dissimilar from why you are here. I just can't give a name to who I'm saving."

Carmen got a faraway look in her eye. She signaled her understanding with a nod when she realized he was still watching her. "I think I understand," she said softly.

Inertia went back to tending to the ship. "Unfortunately, I have a feeling that the rats down this hole are going to be particularly vicious," he said calmly.

Carmen said nothing to that as she slouched in her chair with a look that while not defeated, betrayed growing apprehension. She regained herself after a moment. Then her gaze moved around the bridge, taking in all the details of *The Lady* and where, exactly, she was. She took a deep breath and let it out slowly.

"I'm in this all the way," she mouthed silently to herself. She steeled herself with another deep breath after a pause. "So, where are we going now? Gungnir really didn't say in the briefing."

"We're going to get recruited," he replied.

"How?"

"We ask, of course."

Carmen looked at him for a few seconds till her tensely pressed lips broke into a slight smile. *So, everyone has a sense of humor*, she thought as she rolled her eyes. Either way, it lightened her mood, which was a welcome change.

"You're not like Widget, are you?" she asked. Inertia, confused for a moment, looked at her hard. "Didn't think so," she muttered. "So, how are we going to do this?" she asked again.

"Just a second. Almost done," Inertia said as he turned his attention to the ship once more. A minute or two passed before he spoke again. "As I said, we just ask. Most really aren't shy about seeking out Clairvoyant talent."

Carmen frowned. "So...we just look in the classifieds? That sounds too simple."

"It isn't. We aren't looking here," Inertia said. "We need to be recruited by sortens. The problem with that is we need to find them. And if we find them, we need them to trust us. The last part will be difficult. It is very rare for a Clairvoyant to openly work for or with sortens."

Carmen nodded slowly. "Where do we find them?"

Inertia didn't answer her right away and instead pressed something on his console. *The Lady* began trembling. She gasped as the starship's power started to flow. Her skin tingled. In this case, she couldn't use any of the energy she felt. It wasn't direct enough. She still enjoyed being around starships, though, and this was exquisite.

"Not many people know this, but there are freighters that travel throughout the galaxy that are beacons and a source for…what I guess we'll call the less savory," he said. "These ships are cheap and nondescript, and it doesn't take much to convert their decks into a veritable city. They can also move to another territory if a local government gets too curious or pushy. The UTE doesn't really make much effort to stop them when they enter our own space."

"Why is that?" Carmen asked.

She could feel the inertial inhibitor power up. They were moving. She glanced at the console in front of her. She couldn't understand half of what it said, but she did see a button marked EXTERNAL VIEW. Inertia had never said she couldn't touch anything. A quick tap on the touch screen changed her display to a rather close-up view of the wall of the dormant volcano that housed the base. The wall scrolled downward slowly. *We're flying out*, she realized.

"They can't really be policed, and they are too useful to be worth doing so," Inertia answered her question.

"Kind of like how they don't stop the Rogue Wolves. They employ them from time to time," she cut in.

He gave a sharp nod. "Exactly."

"Umm, different question… It might be a stupid one, but it's been bothering me since I came here. Don't people see you fly out of the volcano all the time? Don't they get curious?"

"If anyone lived out here, they might, if the ship wasn't cloaked," he said. "*The Lady* doesn't have much in the way of armament, but she does have some of the best stealth systems money can buy."

"Okay," Carmen said.

"Anyway," Inertia continued, "our destination is a ship that goes by the roughly translated name *Last Resort*. She is currently deep in vellian space. Thankfully, Widget was able to get us an invitation."

"We need an invitation?"

"No, but it does affect the greeting we'll receive. We'll probably be ignored, mostly."

"What if we weren't invited?"

Inertia glanced at her, smiled dryly, and tipped his head in her direction as he looked back at his console. "You'd probably need that sword sooner rather than later," he said simply.

After a few seconds of quiet reflection, Carmen said, "I don't like your world."

Inertia nodded several times. His reaction seemed like she'd just told him water was wet. "All you need to do is follow my lead. We'll have to figure it out as we go," he said. There was a slight change in the tone of his voice. It sounded almost…comforting. She nodded slowly. "Ghosting now," he said after pressing something on his console.

She looked at her own console. Her display was still set to external view and captured the breach of the lightspeed barrier in perfect detail. The first sensation, however, was being pressed hard enough into her seat that Carmen wondered if there would be a permanent indentation. She knew little about starships and had no idea that the ship's main engine was belching fire for hundreds of miles in their wake. The inertial inhibitor eventually trimmed the force till she just felt a weight on her chest.

On her display screen, an ethereal light built on the edges. Then, all at once, it was gone—the light, the G forces, everything. Her display showed nothing but solid black. She did know enough about starships to know that was all normal, even if she didn't know how any of it worked. They were still accelerating.

"Going fast," Inertia announced after a couple minutes.

A second passed. He took a deep breath. Carmen noticed her display now showed a star field. She glanced at him.

"We're here," he said.

Carmen took a deep breath herself. "Now what?"

"I don't know," he muttered. "*Last Resort*, this is incoming Corvette squawking 77535," he said.

Carmen didn't know how to control the view cameras. She wished she could have seen what the freighter looked like.

"To incoming Corvette, squawk code recognized. Invitation confirmed. Standby for tractor beam," came the reply.

"Ready," Inertia said in turn.

"Tractor beam engaged. Welcome. You have an unlimited pass. Give no trouble, expect none."

"Thank you," Inertia said.

Carmen looked at him. "Well, that was easy."

He looked back and smirked. "Day isn't over yet," he pointed out. "Come on, it will only take a couple minutes till we're docked."

She nodded and stood with him. They were halfway to the door when she stopped.

"Should I take my sword?" she asked. It still sat on the floor next to her chair. "Give no trouble, expect none," she added with a questioning tone.

"Yes, you should."

"Are we here to give trouble?" she asked.

"No," he said. "Despite the pleasantry, there is no reason to expect we'll receive none. In places like this, even the janitors wouldn't have qualms about challenging a pair of Clairvoyants."

Carmen nodded. "Okay."

On that cue, her sword telekinetically flew to her hand, and she tied it on her back as they made their way out of *The Lady*.

13

LAST RESORT

Carmen stood just before the exit hatch of *The Lady* and frowned. "The deck is vibrating," she said.

"It's the music," Inertia casually replied.

She looked at him and smiled hesitantly. "You're joking."

He stared at her for a moment, his face serious and determined. It was quite obvious that the vibrating deck wasn't on the forefront of his mind. Yet, after a second or so, he gave a knowing smirk and then turned to open the hatch. *He has to be joking*, she thought. She couldn't hear any music. There was no way they could be playing music that loud. All the same, she was at a loss for any other explanation.

Inertia walked out of the ship, and she followed a half step behind. She'd never been in a starship hangar before, let alone one this large. The sheer inconceivable scale of it all made her lightheaded.

What is this place? she thought.

The Lady didn't rest alone. Starships were lined as far as she could see in both directions. The seemingly endless rows simply faded into blurry nothingness. *The Lady* was one of the smaller vessels and also the least colorful. Carmen had heard of people decorating starships, though she never really understood the reason for doing so. In any case, they had parked next to a shuttle painted in bright red and orange flames. Another ship, maybe twice the size of *The Lady,* was more tastefully covered in logos for some security company she'd never heard of.

Overhead, a pair of starfighters cruised past to their landing spots. A freighter that was maybe a quarter mile long was being loaded with a line of goods and what she guessed were slaves or prisoners. She had no interest in reading any of them to find out, but their hands were bound, and they were prodded forward in an...*ungentle* manner.

She turned away and looked at the people all around her who were just as elaborate and varied as the starships they crewed. Most were not terran. She didn't know many alien species. It had never been something she had any interest in studying. Now, with the bizarre and exotic right in front of her, it was hard not to stare. She even stopped in place to look at one group.

The tallest stood no higher than her knee. Their lanky gait made their heads sway from side to side with each step they took. A sack on the top of their heads bulged outward when they breathed, like the throat of a frog. She looked away sharply when they eventually noticed her interest. It was then, before she could catch up to Inertia, that a group of sortens passed in front of her. She figured that was a good sign.

"Look at that," she whispered to him when she was close enough, motioning at the sortens with her head.

Inertia nodded slowly. "Sortens in places like this aren't out of the ordinary, but I guess it's better to see some than none," he said.

Carmen nodded as she watched them walk away. "Now what?"

"Nothing," he said simply. "This place is too busy to do any business here."

Carmen guessed she could agree with that. The sort of extralegal work they were seeking undoubtedly took place in the more shadowy realms of the ship. Here, there were people —all types of people—all over the place. It was tempting to take to the air just to not have to deal with them.

"Come on," Inertia said, joining a crowd that was leaving the hangar. "*From now on, if you have anything to say about our mission, say it telepathically*," he added.

"*Of course*," she replied after a quick nod.

Half the universe wanted to exit the hangar along with them it seemed. The number of individuals present reminded her of blades of grass in a meadow. Eventually, the lot of them entered the next corridor, and Carmen's eyes grew wide. The only thing they found was the other half of the universe. The corridor was as wide as a highway. Despite that, there was so much and so many people that the traffic flowed like frozen molasses. She'd never seen anything like it.

Someone bumped into her in that moment. She couldn't prevent it. He cried out in pain and then glared at her. He wasn't terran. His widely spaced eyes, which were mounted on stalks that protruded from his thin head, fixed on her. She was surprised when the color of his skin changed from a dull brown to a milky pale white.

"Damn Clairvoyant," he muttered before continuing.

She moved quickly to Inertia, grabbed his hand, and held tight. She was shocked just as the alien, whatever he was, had been, but she gritted her teeth and tolerated it till Inertia lowered his static charge.

He glanced at her, and she said, "You're crazy if you think I'm losing you in this." It would be her luck. He gave an amused smile, and they continued on.

They reached a large grand foyer. Several corridors like the one they were just in came together here. The traffic turned into an almost solid mass of people. Carmen looked around when she could. No real business or much of anything was happening here. The room seemed to be designed to steer and direct people to wherever they wanted to go. They peeled off into another corridor, and the number of people thinned to no more than would be on an average city street. She was vastly more comfortable now than before, but she held onto Inertia regardless. It was only now, relatively comfortable and not having to think about where she was going, that she noticed the subtle details in the long tunnel they were walking down.

The walls, such as they were, were...such as they were. Their construction seemed hasty and weak yet deliberate. If she breathed on them hard, they'd probably come tumbling down. She remembered what Inertia had said about how a freighter's decks could be converted. It only took a glance to realize this would simply be an open space if but for the conversion. And it didn't take long after for her that to realize that individual spaces and corridors could be easily and quickly changed if required.

Her curiosity had her looking down each corridor whenever they branched off to who-knew-where. Occasionally, she even heard some of the fabled music, though distantly. The vibrations through the deck were certainly getting stronger. Her feet were vibrating at this point.

They left the main corridor, and Carmen knew they had to be getting close. She could feel the music in her gut now. Her fingers were practically tuning forks. Even considering that, it was getting a bit odd. She had expected the people that were traveling in their general direction to be, well...less *savory* by this point. She thought they'd be armed at least. But few were. There weren't many terrans, but that was no longer a surprise. Neither was the exotic and, at times, bizarre alien life that she still sometimes stared at, though she was getting better at not being so obvious whenever she gawked.

Everything seemed so…casual. The conversations she heard were light and fun, even by the people who were actually armed. If anything, her body armor and sword seemed horribly inappropriate. It was like she'd been invited to a costume party but she was the only one who actually dressed up. Yet, for all that, she and Inertia didn't draw any more than the usual Clairvoyant attention, and even that was muted. She didn't know what that meant. The odd and profane was a matter of course here. She'd always wondered what it must be like to be *normal*, to not have people cower, scream, or run away just because she was there. She just didn't want to be considered normal in a place like this.

Just then, the movement in the corridor slowed but didn't stop. It seemed to Carmen that they had joined the end of a long line. Others joined behind them as Inertia squeezed her hand just a touch tighter.

"Is this it?" she asked. He glanced at her and nodded, which prompted her to take a deep breath.

Just before they entered the room, they passed two terrasaur guards. They were maybe twice as tall as she was, and it was all too obvious that they were meant to intimidate. They did a good job of that. Terrasaurs weren't known for being violent, but their imposing size was backed up by teeth almost as long as one of her fingers and claws that could slice through her bones like butter. Only in the back of her mind did she know she could crush them into small balls with just a thought. The idea of terrasaurs had always made her nervous when she was a kid. It was easy to remember why, now that she was face to face with one.

For all that, the terrasaurs didn't even give her and Inertia a passing glance. Carmen watched them over her shoulder. She'd never formally met a terrasaur before. She'd only seen them rarely. Earth was their favorite terran tourist spot. New Earth didn't have much history with non-terran visitors.

She looked forward again, wherein her brain exploded. The lights were bright enough to sear their image into her retinas. The thundering music hit her like waves on a beach. Every sense screamed like it was on fire. The ludicrous overwhelming stupefaction of it all made her wonder if they cooked with nuclear weapons. It wasn't just the raw sights and sounds of the club, either. The atmosphere was easily their equal.

Women of all manner of species danced on multilevel poles in various stages of undress. Carmen stepped aside to allow a terrasaur to throw out an alien that had been beaten to a pulp. Tables throughout the room were piled high with food she'd never even heard of. Large groups ravaged their meals with all the delicacy of fishing with dynamite while servers tried their best to refill the table without getting their arms ripped off.

This had to be the most unbelievable place she'd ever heard of. She looked at Inertia. He couldn't be serious about wanting to come here. They'd have better luck finding sorten recruiters at an elementary school.

"*So...*" she said telepathically. She didn't think he'd hear her speak out loud even if she screamed in his ear.

Inertia let her hand go. "*You know what we're looking for,*" he said.

Carmen thought about it for a moment. "*Umm...no, I don't. I thought this would be more...formal.*"

"*This is,*" he remarked after taking a second to look around the room.

She noted that they had very different ideas of what the word formal meant. "*What are we looking for exactly?*" she asked. "*How do we even know it's here?*" she added.

"*I don't really know. At this point, we have to figure it out as we go along,*" he responded. Carmen frowned, which prompted him to smile. "*You're a Clairvoyant, aren't you?*" She didn't say anything but unknowingly furrowed her eyebrows as she nodded slowly. "*That has to be worth something,*" he spoke, walking away.

"I'm still not sure about that," she said to herself as he disappeared into the crowd.

She entered the raging storm herself with no real direction. It was a bit annoying that people didn't get out of her way as she was used to. Sure, they moved, but only just enough to avoid being shocked by touching her. If there were sortens here, it was impossible for her to tell in the crowd. She glanced around the room quickly and then spotted an easy solution. The VIP section on the third floor overlooked the entire establishment. The curving, serpentine stairway to get to that level, however, prompted a quiet groan from her. It would be too much of a bother to walk through it all. *Besides, it might help*, she thought. A little advertisement couldn't hurt.

A thought telekinetically whisked her straight to the third floor. She made a show of flipping over the guardrail onto her feet. Once again, the advertisement couldn't hurt. It was certainly effective. Attention flew at her in such volleys that she may as well have been a dartboard. Outwardly, at least, she paid it no mind. She instead turned to survey the floor. She hadn't sensed anything of any interest anyway.

All she could use for the moment were her eyes. There was too much *noise* to really understand anything else she was sensing. It was like trying to read Widget. Too much was going on in the foreground to know if there was anything relevant in the background. She had never been one for places like this. She didn't think any Clairvoyant was fond of the overstimulation. What would be the point? In any case, she allowed her eyes to drift with no active thought on her part.

Unfortunately, she couldn't see much of anything, even from this perch. The darkness colored the plainly visible below. Smoke billowed in from machines she couldn't see, making the foggy soup altogether worse. Her new perspective was simply a broader view of what she'd been in the midst of mere moments before. There was no real making sense of it. Even the random flashes from the lights overhead, while giving a few seconds of insight, were too unpredictable to be useful.

She couldn't help a small sigh. "No one can figure it out," she said, her words instantly lost in the din of her surroundings.

She turned around before she was called. As always, what prompted her Clairvoyant intuition was beyond her. In this instance, it was a terrasaur guard running toward her. He was out of breath, and she guessed he'd run up the stairs.

"I don't care what you are. Everyone pays for VIP!" he yelled.

She didn't have any money, nor did she know how much the privilege cost. "I won't be long," she said, testing how much reason was worth.

Not much, apparently, because his claws swiped at her. A casual step back and slight turn of her head was all it took to make him miss. She didn't even consciously think about it. His jaws then snapped open to bite her in half, and all she could do was wonder how it was that she was looking down a terrasaur's throat on a freighter in the middle of nowhere when all she had wanted to do was look off a balcony. The thought came and went. She grabbed his mouth by reflex to hold him off, turned her body, and with her greater leverage threw him over the guardrail. It was as easy as taking a breath.

She watched him fall in the dark while a quiet thought whispered in her ear. The seconds stretched out almost comically as she weighed whether to let him die or not. Clairvoyants weren't exactly known for showing mercy, outside of a quick and clean death, to those who challenged them. She doubted, however, that the sortens were interested in gentle Clairvoyant mercenaries. But... She slowed his fall enough that, on impact, he broke his arm and a few ribs but nothing more. Several graceful steps later, she disappeared into the dark and out of sight. There was no reason to go through a needless fight again. That kind of advertising *did* hurt—if not her directly then certainly someone else.

She considered what she'd do next and then stopped. It was obvious by now that her search couldn't be logically reasoned. Not in this place. Pure reason wasn't supposed to exist here. It couldn't. The numbing, ethereal haze of it all made sure of that.

She started walking with no aim or direction. The pulsing music guided her as much as anything. Ghosts in the dark, illuminated by the flashing lights, caught and then lost her attention. Everything seemed like an interesting lead when it could only be seen for a split second, which was frustrating. She even thought she saw Inertia for a moment, but she guessed that didn't matter. Despite all the effort of getting into the VIP section, Carmen casually walked back down the stairs. It just felt better to be in the midst of everyone. And then it didn't, and she flitted into a mostly empty corridor. There, shrouded in the darkest of the dark, she stopped and thought again.

What do I do now? she wondered. She'd done this more times than she cared to remember. Probably every Clairvoyant had. Her thoughts shifted rapidly through…nothing. It was like she'd stepped out of herself. She perceived everything, yet the immediate was no more than a dim haze. Oddly, the only thing that stood out in particular was her games of chess with Phaethon, mixed with some of Janus's sermons. Despite what she had said to her charge and despite what Janus had said, or Kali, or Gungnir, she had to admit that, at times, even Clairvoyants had to rely on nothing more than pure serendipity. She closed her eyes and took a deep breath. Such things could never be forced.

As she leaned against the wall, the feeling of her sword resting in its scabbard and pressing against her back took almost the whole of her attention. There was no real reason; it just did, as did a few strands of hair covering her face. A passerby glanced at the motionless Clairvoyant with her eyes closed, paused a moment, and then continued on. There was no rhyme or reason to how Carmen knew of the event; she just did. And then a new feeling came slowly. It was difficult to give words to. The best way she could describe it was anxiety, yet it was different from the conscious anxiety she felt about getting a job or finding Phaethon. That feeling was well worn company. This she'd experienced only once or twice before, and for some reason it made her think of ice cream.

Her eyes snapped open when the moment to act came. She didn't know why it had to be that instant, but she felt prompted just as surely as if someone rang a bell. Purpose, focus, and economy, the Clairvoyant hallmarks, returned almost naturally. A few quick steps brought her back into the open. She was in no way surprised when Inertia appeared next to her. She glanced at him, and his face mirrored hers.

"Come on," he said.

Carmen neither needed to nod nor give verbal affirmation. She simply became his shadow. The two followed far enough away behind a sorten that they wouldn't be noticed. To their Clairvoyant senses, however, the sorten stood out like a giraffe at a dog show. There was just something *different* about him.

She'd only seen a sorten a few times before today. The people weren't the epitome of grace or poise. She'd describe them as gangly if she were being charitable. She guessed their form could be considered sleek if she were being even more polite. Their shaggy white fur hid much of their bodies, giving mass that actually wasn't there. But their lean, thin proportions always seemed to suggest they'd be far taller than the foot and a half advantage they held on her when they stood upright. They rarely stood upright, though, preferring to walk on all four of their legs. In such instances, they typically wrapped their two arms around their neck. There was something frail or sickly about them, like a stiff breeze could blow them apart.

But this sorten was all that and, well…not. He looked around the room with the same nervous anticipation of a deer. Carmen wouldn't say he was scared, per se. She certainly wasn't going to read him to find out for certain. By her guess, though, he seemed anxiously expectant, which was odd for a denizen of this place. There was a tense readiness about his movements. He wasn't wearing a uniform of any kind, for what that was worth. In fact, there was nothing official about him. She'd always assumed that the sortens they were seeking would be representatives from some central sorten authority. Perhaps she was just being naïve? The Rogue Wolves weren't officially part of anything themselves. But, all the same, it was obvious that this sorten's purpose for

being here, like hers and Inertia's, wasn't rest and entertainment.

They followed the sorten to the other end of the room,
where he sat next to another sorten at a table. The second
gave her much the same feel as the first. She figured that was
a good sign. She glanced at Inertia, who neither slowed nor
stopped till they were standing right in front of the sortens.

What now? she thought again.

There were no rules on how to go about this, as far as she
knew. She couldn't even be exactly sure that these sortens
would be of help. For now, the two sides simply stared at
each other. The sortens stiffened noticeably before one of
them spoke.

"Would you like direction, terrans?" he asked.

"Yes," Carmen blurted out by reflex.

She caught Inertia smile and then shake his head out of the
corner of her eye. She couldn't help but blush as they sat down. It
was only a minor humiliation, though. He telekinetically grabbed
two chairs from another table. The sortens noticeably stiffened
again as the confirmed Clairvoyants joined them, yet they also
wilted, even under her gaze. She did her best to soften it, but it
was a futile effort. She turned her attention to Inertia. There was
no reason to make their prospective employers nervous.

"I've never worked with sortens before. Do they always
ask stupid questions?" Inertia asked. There was no anger in
his voice, but there was arrogance and noticeable contempt.

She didn't know enough about Inertia to tell if that was an
act; she did, however, roll her eyes and groan at her previous
desire to be polite. It was a wonder sometimes if she did
anything right.

"And what is your work? Gardening, perhaps?" the sorten
asked.

Inertia's eyes narrowed for a moment on the sorten who had spoken, who wilted again. "Don't waste my time," Inertia said. The authority barked out of his mouth as strong as a punch.

Carmen flashed him a look. She didn't think the aggression was necessary, but she held her peace. What did she know?

"I apologize, terran. You catch us at a disadvantage," the other sorten began. "It appears you take us for something we are not."

"So, what are you?" Carmen asked, following Inertia's rather direct style. He even gave an approving nod.

The sortens glanced at each other before one of them answered. "Merchants."

Inertia stood almost immediately and walked away. Carmen was caught off guard, but she was just a step behind.

"*What are you doing?*" she asked telepathically.

"*Playing along. I hoped you didn't think this would be straight forward,*" he spoke.

"*No, I didn't,*" she replied.

"*Good. Actually, we are doing rather well,*" he continued. "*If they are merchants, they'll let us go and count their blessings that they emerged from encountering two Clairvoyants unscathed. If they are what we are seeking, they'll realize they overplayed their hand and call us back.*"

He turned to her and smirked. She smirked as well a half second before it came.

"Terrans!" one of the sortens called. "Please excuse us, and don't be hasty." Carmen and Inertia turned around. She was about to walk back, but he stayed put, so she did as well. "We would like it if you could join us."

Carmen and Inertia glanced at each other again and then returned to the table and sat down. Inertia said nothing.

Neither did she. The music pulsed and pounded. The lights flashed all around them. The scantily clad and profane vied for everyone's attention. Quite frankly, she was used to the chaotic, grimy mess by this point.

"If you could forgive us, it turns out that we might have use for your services," one of the sortens said.

"Not finding many gardeners who are willing to work for you?" Carmen asked.

"*Don't play too hard,*" Inertia warned.

She gave a quick nod, and the sortens offered no reply, which was enough of an answer for her. Kali was right that Clairvoyants didn't work with or even really consort with sortens. It made her wonder what motivated Charon to do so.

"What do you need us to garden?" Inertia asked.

"We don't know," one of the sortens answered. Carmen looked at Inertia, ready to get up and leave again, but he remained unfazed. The sorten continued. "We're only looking for…good gardeners."

"Where?" Inertia asked.

"Do you have your own ship?" the sorten questioned. Inertia answered with a nod. "Where? I don't know that either. But I happen to have some coordinates—deep space. Perhaps someone there can tell you more?"

Carmen gave a satisfied nod and leaned back in her chair.

Inertia was more focused. "That will do," he said.

14

SUBMERGED

The dark was all encompassing and ever present, as always. Nothing could be seen in any direction. In this forsaken hell, breaths reverberated out in echoing pants. Their only company was the slowly quickening beat of the heart. All thought that wasn't transfixed on the immediately worthwhile faded away to barely remembered dreams. By contrast, fears, worries, hopes, pleasures, and the like, morphed into a sublime, ethereally distant yet all-pervading veil. This state was blind and deaf but not dumb. No, there was too much awareness to call the stupefaction dumb. The active will, always seeking and forever unsatisfied, meant that they weren't lost, at least not completely.

The Lady dispelled her ghost field after going fast. Carmen removed a few strands of hair from her face and took a deep breath. The exhale joined the various hums and whirrs ever present on the bridge of *The Lady*. She'd never get used to ghost drives; it was such a disorienting means of travel. She couldn't wrap her mind around the fact that they had just travelled hundreds, if not thousands, of light-years in a mere moment. It didn't feel like they'd even gone anywhere. At least now she'd finally be able to see what they had been searching for. She turned on the external view camera, which had fast become her favorite button, and then sighed. The screen reported nothing, other than a completely black image.

"We did go fast, right?" she asked Inertia. It seemed like they were still in the ghost field.

"Yes," he replied without pause. "We're exactly where we're supposed to be."

Carmen frowned and looked back at the screen. "I don't see anything."

Though, upon a more detailed look, she could see stars dotted amongst the dark. The pathetically small pinpoints of light only served as a reminder of just how alone they truly were.

"You're not supposed to see anything," Inertia said casually as he glanced at her. Then he slowly shook his head. "Sons of bitches..." he muttered. "No one would ever find this."

"What are you talking about?" she asked. Inertia answered by hitting a few buttons on the console in front of him. He then motioned for Carmen to look at her external view screen. "I still don't see anything," she replied after a few seconds.

"Press the button marked infrared," he said, pointing.

Carmen dutifully complied, and it became quite obvious now that something was out there. The object was roughly spherical in shape and several hundred miles in diameter. The infrared camera also showed several areas that were noticeably, though not especially, hotter than the others. The color display made the thing look like a horribly painted Easter egg.

"It's a rogue planetoid," he said.

"I'm sorry, but...so what?"

Inertia shook his head again. "We're nowhere near any systems or anything else, really. This anonymous rock is just floating free in deep space, dim as a speck of dirt in a dark well. It's a wonder the sortens even found it. Unless they towed it out here…" he added after a second thought.

"So, no one else will be able to find it either?" Carmen more stated than asked.

"Yes, exactly," Inertia replied anyway.

"Why do this?"

"I don't know. Could be anything. That's what we're here to find out."

"So, what now?" she asked without missing a beat.

Inertia opened his mouth but closed it a moment later. Then he turned to her, after slowly rolling his eyes. She looked at him expectantly, wondering what the problem was. His face was serious and meditative.

"You really do like asking that question, don't you?" he asked casually. Carmen gave a guilty smile. She had never thought about it before. Inertia also smiled for a moment before becoming more serious again. "Well, it's a good one. We were given a destination but no real instructions after that."

"Could they have just been leading us on?" Carmen wondered out loud.

Inertia shook his head again. "No," he said simply. "Not like this. Random coordinates wouldn't drop us right in front of a planetoid in the middle of nowhere."

"So—"

"So," Inertia interrupted, aping her tone. "I'm at a loss." He sat back in his chair and thought for a moment. "Let's try hailing them, at least."

He made his hail and there was no response. Carmen looked at him, and he looked at her. She opened her mouth as a certain question came to the fore. Then she thought better of it. *I really do ask that question a lot*, she reflected. She turned her attention to her external view screen and figured she'd try to be more productive. She didn't know much about anything in this realm, but perhaps some common sense would suffice? This was just a rock lost in the dark, no doubt about that. She looked at the screen over and over again and could come up with no other conclusion. Maybe the obvious was too much so. The little spots of extra heat on the screen caught her attention.

"Inertia, why would a planetoid have hot spots like that?" she asked, pointing at her screen.

"Any number of reasons," he said. "But if I were to guess, I'd say a heat source like that is coming from some sort of artificial device on or just beneath the surface."

Carmen nodded slowly. She had assumed as much. "So —" Inertia glanced at her, and she sheepishly closed her mouth. "Excuse me," she muttered, choosing different wording. "But is there anything on the surface?"

Inertia turned to his console and pressed a few buttons. "No."

"What about under the surface?"

"There's no way to tell definitively with the sensors we have," he answered.

She still couldn't accept the situation as presented. Inertia had to be right. There was no way the sortens had given them random coordinates that just happened to lead to a random planetoid in the middle of nowhere.

After a minute or so of quiet thought, she asked, "How did you hail them?"

"There is a standard agreed upon interstellar greeting when encountering unknown vessels. I transmitted it on all channels."

Carmen nodded again. "There was a little boy who used to come to my apartment," she began, thinking of Theodore. "He'd tease me by knocking on the door and then running away. It got to the point that I never answered the door when he knocked. He'd make such a racket. Used to drive my neighbors crazy," she added with a smile. "I'd catch him by sensing him before he knocked or by looking down the hall through the peephole to see him coming."

"What are you suggesting?" Inertia asked.

"That we should walk up to the door," Carmen replied after a shrug. "If they're not listening, maybe someone's watching."

He looked around the room as he mulled it over and then threw up his hands after a sigh. "As good a plan as any," he uttered as he started maneuvering *The Lady* closer.

Nothing happened, at least not at first. Carmen watched her screen, since there was nothing else for her to do. Then there was a change—a distinct hot spot on her screen. It grew steadily till it peaked and then died off to its previous level.

Inertia sat still for a moment. "They opened the door," he said simply.

Carmen wasn't sure what he was referring to, so she switched the cameras on her external view screen back to the visible light spectrum. The dark mass of the planetoid now had a lighted hole cut into its depths. Her victories in life being what they were, she couldn't help a small smile of triumph.

"Well, there it is," Inertia said. "It helps that some part-ners are better than others," he added, glancing at her. She smiled again, this time more fully.

The mood decidedly changed after that. There was no more smiling, and all casual banter ceased. Carmen even glanced down at her sword resting next to her.

"I'm taking her in," Inertia said. After a moment, he asked nonchalantly, "What happened to that boy?"

Carmen swallowed hard. "He's dead," she said evenly.

"I'm sorry about that."

"So am I."

A brief blast from the thrusters glided *The Lady* steadily, if cautiously, into the planetoid. From Carmen's view screen, the approaching black mass appeared to swallow them whole. The small tunnel of light that was their unambiguous welcome was the only hedge against crashing into the dark bare rock. The stars were slowly ripped away as the lights guided them deeper. It reminded Carmen of the long elevator ride down into the facility. She was quite happy when the ship eventually settled on a landing platform at the bottom. At least now they wouldn't hit anything—just one worry among her thousands.

Inertia studied his console. "There's breathable atmosphere here," he said.

She nodded and turned to her display, too curious to stop herself from looking around. "I see a door," she said.

Inertia glanced at her screen and nodded as well. "Let's disembark."

"All right," she muttered as she gripped her sword. This time, there was no question in her mind that she should bring it. Whether it would be needed she couldn't say.

She followed Inertia out of the relative safety of the ship. It wasn't a very big vessel, but here and now, it felt like it took hours for them to reach the exit ramp. This place —this rock in the middle of nowhere—seemed so cold, so alien. There was nothing to sense or perceive. Forgotten grains of sand had greater stories to tell than this...construct.

Inertia stopped at the exit ramp but made no move to

actually open it. Carmen looked at him expectantly. He returned the look.

"Edge," he started. He didn't usually address her by name. He always had her complete attention, now her atoms snapped to the ready. "Follow my lead no matter what happens or what it is," he said. Carmen nodded thoughtfully. "No hesitation. We're all alone out here, and I'm sure you know what that means if anything happens," he added with real worry in his voice.

She looked at him as she considered everything. "What do you think we'll find?"

"I don't know," he said. Then he pressed the button to open the ramp.

The dry, almost dead, air of the landing platform flooded into *The Lady*. Even the Clairvoyants subconsciously raised their hands to shield themselves from it. All was still afterward. They walked down the platform, accompanied by no sound, no nothing. Carmen couldn't recall ever experiencing such a scene. It was like she was watching everything through a telescope. The lights never wavered, and the air was dry and unmoving yet thick like a fog. Even her Clairvoyant senses were dulled. She perceived distantly, if at all.

She looked up just in time to see the entrance to the tunnel close. The stars, though steady like the lights all around her, were not of the static artificial edifice she was currently encased within. The stars were much too far away to feel, unlike the power surging in *The Lady's* main reactor. Yet Carmen felt a painful lamentation when the tunnel sealed shut and the view was taken away.

Rather than dwelling on their situation, she turned her attention to the door they were walking toward. Inertia stopped just in front of it.

"Do you sense anything on the other side?" he asked.

"I don't sense anything," Carmen replied glumly.

He nodded slowly, and that was all she needed to know that he experienced the same. Neither of them moved to open the door. There was no visible means to open it, which prompted Inertia to rip it open telekinetically. This new corridor looked much like the tunnel *The Lady* had descended through. It was dimly lit, and the air was just as dead as on the landing platform. Carmen wondered how this place could exist without some sort of ventilation system. Nothing moved, nothing happened. Everything just sat…still.

She glanced at Inertia. He gave her a look and then walked inside. She followed slightly behind. The tunnel was a nondescript gray and seemed machine-cast as a solid piece. She looked back at *The Lady* and was reminded of the stars from earlier. Just then, they rounded a corner, and the starship was gone as well.

They walked on. The path was straight, yet Carmen felt utterly lost. Time and distance were hard to determine. She tried to count the lights they passed to keep track of how far they travelled, but when the count got to the triple digits, she gave up. *I hate this place*, she thought over and over again. If anything was readily apparent, it was that. This was so numbing yet so eternal that it was worse than the horrors of the facility. It seemed like this place could consume the whole of her life on a triviality. It was then that they came upon some choices, as the corridor branched into three others.

There was no sign, marking, or anything to indicate a direction or place. There was, however, one difference between the paths. Only one was lighted. It would be quite a stretch to call the nondescript, bare corridor inviting, but it seemed the better option than walking in the dark. Carmen glanced at Inertia. She said nothing, though several comments and questions came to mind. He turned to look at her then. It was brief, only a second or so, but she knew she was being evaluated again. Their eyes met without challenge or waver. As his eyebrows rose and his jaw relaxed, she realized it wasn't an evaluation of her state but of her opinion. She gave a small nod, and he began walking down the lighted corridor.

She followed, and was tempted to ask if he'd ever experienced something like this before. But her surroundings were so dimly perceived, so unreal in their stark reality, that giving voice to it made her worry that the universe, such as it was presently, would shatter all around her. *Nonsense*, she thought. But Carmen's lips stayed still nonetheless.

She only subconsciously felt herself lean back as the slope of the corridor changed to lead them deeper. It turned slightly, possibly doubling back on itself. The Clairvoyants dutifully followed. Even they were past the point of questioning this. There were no other options to make such a query worthwhile. The corridor eventually straightened, and the sheer extent of it, for as far as could be seen, made Carmen's eyes grow wide. She stopped in place.

Carmen looked in both directions. If she closed her eyes, spun in place, and then opened them again, she wouldn't have any idea the direction in which they had come.

"Inertia, I—" she began, but she stopped when the lights cut out all of a sudden.

The dark was unmerciful in its completeness. There was nothing other than the black. Her Clairvoyant senses flared to life by reflex, and it was then that she finally became aware of one thing. Someone else was here.

A distinct, pained groan in front of her filled the corridor. She was able to recognize the voice as Inertia's and could even discern him falling to the ground. But there was no time to be concerned. She had barely raised her hands to defend herself before she was reeling back into the wall.

The surprise stung more than the pain. She was hit again, and fear began to take her. They were under siege by a Clairvoyant; she had no doubt about that. The precision and speed of their assailant was akin to nothing she had seen before. And the presence—the unmistakable verve, focus, and purposeful violence—could only be from a monster of the Dark.

Her mind raced. She had expected to fight. She had even mentally prepared herself to fight. But now fighting was not her first reflex. Carmen's arms flailed in front of her in a useless attempt to protect herself. She shuffled back, away from the threat, and into a wall, for the good that did. She was hit once more and, for one brief moment, she thought there were tears in her eyes.

Where was Inertia? Why wasn't he helping her? She'd heard him get hurt. She'd heard him fall. Was he dead? Her entire body ached, but she hadn't been hit hard enough to be broken. A painful hit to her midsection, however, put that to the test. Carmen fell to one knee and wrapped her arms around her body, cradling it. A punch to her face dropped her to the ground. A kick sent her sailing across it. She couldn't think anymore. She couldn't even feel anymore. Her emotions were a jumbled, irrational mess of fear and worry, but most prominent of all, doubt. Instinct was all that remained and all that was needed.

A long-sleeping beast stirred, called to action by the plight of its master. It had been forgotten, hated even, and made to think it no longer existed. Now it was deemed quite necessary. Carmen didn't even notice the brief illumination of the corridor from a spark along her arm. She'd come upon this moment before in her life, the pause before she was unleashed. When she was a child, she'd considered the power, the surge, and the focus, completely natural. After

Mikayla's death, that moment became mixed with quiet dread for the consequences. Now, she let go a contented sigh.

Carmen got to her feet. Her power flowed from her core to her extremities in brilliant electrical sparks which attenuated to nothingness at her fingertips. Their light, however, let her plainly if dimly see her enemy.

It was a Clairvoyant. He was functionally muscled, as was typical, and noticeably taller than her. He looked similar to the Clairvoyant Constructs that had attacked the facility. At least, of all that was happening, that final clue that they were on the right track was comforting.

He stood before her in a guard. There was nothing wrong with it, but there was something wrong with him. He felt different from every other Clairvoyant she had ever sensed. He had the same vibrancy and focus that every Clairvoyant possessed, but it seemed muted somehow. The dynamism just did not compare. It didn't ebb and flow. It didn't change, grow, adapt, get weaker, or surge forth. He didn't seem alive, just a well-made approximation. For some reason, just looking at the abomination disgusted her. Carmen pursed her lips as she remembered her fundamental hatred for all the Constructs she had slayed. A moment later, her bioelectric field rebalanced, ending the sparks, and the two were recloaked in the dark.

A singular punch rushed toward her. She knew by means she could not say that another would follow soon thereafter. A casual block deflected the first blow. A step to the side, a tilt of her head, and a masterfully timed counterpunch made her opponent's follow-up attack a fool's errand. Clairvoyants recovered differently from physical trauma than the normals. They most assuredly felt pain, but it could be ignored and even used as fuel for more power. She felt his face deform under the pressure of her fist, but all he did was stagger back and then come at her again with renewed fury.

She stepped around his next attack. Each of her movements was graceful and full of poise but direct in its economy. A kick at the optimum moment doubled him over. A hard, precise punch broke his cheek and jaw, knocked four teeth loose, and sent blood invisibly spraying across the darkened walls. He came at her again, but it was obvious that his reserves were gone. The attack lacked any semblance of speed and contained a hint of desperation. It was time to end it. Her final attack's swiftness belied its simplicity. He lunged at her. She took a step back and punched him as hard as was necessary in the chest. He fell forward and didn't get up again.

And then it happened. His body failed, and the last breath of his consciousness assaulted hers. She groaned uncomfortably. It had been too long since her last time. She had forgotten that she'd feel everything. Worse, long buried memories and sensations came flooding back in that instant. She closed her eyes and gritted her teeth through a scream.

When Carmen opened her eyes, the lights were on, and they were no longer alone. Metal panels exploded out from the bare, nondescript walls of the corridor and in poured dozens of armed sortens from both the front and behind. Their formation and demeanor, for what it was worth, was chillingly professional. Their thoughts didn't waver, from what Carmen could read. All weapons were trained, and the intent was clear: kill the Clairvoyant by any means necessary.

Carmen regained her composure and then looked at the group arrayed in front her. She turned and looked at the group set against her back. Then she rolled her eyes and placed her hands on her hips while she tapped an impatient foot. Body language didn't always translate as well as words to alien mentalities, but a few of her opposition gave the sorten equivalent of a sneer. She guessed her message was well received.

She ignored them and turned her attention to Inertia. His face was bloody. In fact, his face was a gruesome mess, but only superficially so. There was a cut on his forehead and that was it. She looked at him hard when he stood up. She just couldn't figure out how his injury had been so debilitating. Gungnir said the two of them were roughly equal in power. Till now, there had been nothing to suggest otherwise. She didn't think she'd be incapacitated by the attack he suffered. He seemed fine now, though. Whatever the truth was, a Clairvoyant couldn't be affected by their own energy, so she telekinetically lifted the blood and temporarily sealed his cut with heat.

He walked to stand side by side with her. They glanced at each other, wondering how long they needed to wait. The answer came soon enough.

"Clairvoyants… Formidable creatures," a voice in front of them and out of sight said. "Don't be fooled by their discipline."

The voice moved toward them from the front. The soldiers parted in trained unison, and their obvious leader came into view. He didn't wear the battle armor of his counterparts, just enough to protect the vitals. He was just as well armed though. A projectile rifle mounted on his shoulder tracked them, Carmen in particular.

He stopped in front of the dead Clairvoyant Construct and didn't speak while he examined the body. He looked up at her and then almost respectfully backed away.

"See how easily they defeated one of our best copies?" he continued. "If they wanted to fight us, I'd give our chances at five percent. Everyone, study the tapes of their battle at half speed at most until every movement can be described in your sleep. We begin new battle readiness drills in the morning."

No one else spoke. That was, until a soft voice shattered the silence. "Battle readiness drills. That would be prudent, Director Mugal."

This one emerged from behind the soldiers just as the director had, but this sorten was different. He walked toward them on his hind legs, which wasn't too unusual. Sortens did walk upright from time to time, even if it wasn't a matter of course. However, his right arm and leg were robotized prosthetics. Carmen couldn't help but stare. Lost limbs could be regrown. It had to be an active choice to be hobbled by such clunky alternatives.

He stopped next to Mugal and looked at the Clairvoyants for a moment. His stare didn't carry the hearty respect of the director's, nor was it afraid or even worried. He seemed...amused.

"Yes, I do rather enjoy your drills," he said. "To watch is to see ants running in circles to turn back the sun."

Mugal glanced at him but made no response. It was then that Carmen noticed this sorten's face had patches without fur. The skin there was badly burned, leathery blisters. He walked toward them and stopped halfway. Not a single step hesitated. He even turned his back to them to look directly at the director.

"Do the Clairvoyant beasts look wary entering here, Mugal?" he asked. Then he turned and looked at Carmen, at Inertia, and finally at the dead Clairvoyant Construct. "We stand at the edge of their realm, scared to even look at it. While they play, understanding, knowing, and laughing." He paused before he spoke again. "The Dark cannot be controlled, only survived," he said under his breath as he patted his prosthetic arm. Then he sauntered off. The sorten ranks broke to allow him to pass, but he didn't seem to notice or care.

Well, that was strange, Carmen thought as she glanced at Inertia. He returned her look, and it was obvious that he didn't know what to make of it either. The assembled soldiers broke ranks on some unheard command and retreated back into the walls. Another sorten bounded toward them, stopping next to Mugal who had remained. The new sorten wasn't armed or especially unusual.

"Please forgive our project leader, Caelus. He is one of the most gifted among us, but it appears genius has its cost," he said. "Since I'm sure no one made any formal introductions, the fearsome individual next to me is Security Director Mugal," he continued. "My name is Rauon; I'm the head technician. We were told that you were interested in being employed by us?"

Carmen looked at Inertia. It was tempting to answer the rather simple question herself, but he had said she should follow his lead.

"Yes, that is correct," he answered.

"Excellent," Rauon replied enthusiastically. "Speak to me for anything you need. And since not all of us wish to refer to you as Clairvoyant beasts," he said with a hint of annoyance, "what are your names?"

Carmen was ready for this. "I was named Psyche," she said.

Inertia glanced at her and slowly shook his head. "Inertia," he said simply.

Carmen flashed him a look. "*Why are you using your real name? Won't they be able to track you down with it?*" she asked telepathically.

"*Trust me, it won't matter,*" he replied.

"We're pleased to have you. Now, if you'll follow me, I'll show each of you—"

"Excuse me," Inertia interrupted. "We're married. We *will* be roomed together," he added with emphasis.

Rauon looked at Mugal, who nodded after a time. "Yes, of course," Rauon replied.

Carmen spun in place to look at Inertia as her mouth fell open. "*Wait, what?*"

15

PINPOINTS OF LIGHT

Carmen studied every move Inertia made as they walked. His movements, while direct and flowing like all Clairvoyants, also held a certain weight and power that was subtle but obvious to those who were looking. Inertia moved just like the way he spoke: slow, methodical, and seemingly care-free...yet also not. He had her complete attention now. She didn't care where they were going. She didn't care what was happening. They could have just walked past the fiery gates of hell, for all she'd notice.

"*Married,*" she said telepathically for about the millionth time. "*What do you mean we're married?*"

He still gave no words in response. She glared at him, though she wasn't actually angry. Well, she was, but the emotion couldn't be described so simply. She could think of no one in her life who had ever treated her as he did. Most everyone existed as a prisoner of her mood, placating her and trying their best to please her, even to the point of her exas-peration. They feared that one day, someway, somehow, she'd snap and go on a killing spree. Carmen did her best to give no proof that such a day would ever come, but she guessed she had just gotten used to the terrified deference of everyone around her. Even Michael, before he'd gotten sick, was quietly wary of her. Inertia was no such thing. He prodded her. He challenged her. And she didn't like any of it. Though she also had to admit she'd do anything he said without a second thought. She couldn't make much sense of the dynamic.

"*Well?*" she asked again.

He said nothing. He didn't even seem to hear her, except for one sign. It was ever so slight, but he gave a small smirk. Carmen grinded her teeth.

"This is not funny!" she spat.

Rauon and Mugal, who walked in front of them, turned to look at her. Mugal's face rivaled a stone statue's for hardness. Rauon simply looked confused.

"Pardon me, Psyche, but what isn't funny?" he asked.

Inertia smirked again, and Carmen could only sigh. "So many, many things," she said dejectedly. Rauon looked even more confused, but he questioned no further. After a few seconds of awkward silence, the group continued on.

Carmen, unfortunately, had to divide her attention between Inertia and the sortens. The layout of this place would never allow anyone to walk aimlessly and get to wherever they intended. She had learned that the main corridor really did continue on forever, subtly doubling back and curving in on itself in one continuous loop. Rooms and secondary corridors were hidden behind doors built into the walls of the main corridor to be as nondescript as possible. If she and Inertia didn't follow closely, they'd be lost in a matter of moments.

"*Why did you say we were married?*" Carmen asked again.

Inertia glanced at her. "*So, what now?*" he teased.

Her eyes narrowed and she pressed her lips together. She didn't ask that question *that* much. "*Now you'll talk to me,*" she responded.

"*Yes, we can talk now,*" Inertia said after a thoughtful nod.

"*So, why did you tell them that?*"

"*Edge, if you thought* Last Resort *was bad, you need to look around,*" he spoke. "*No matter how strong we may be, if we get lost here, we'll never get out. I want to make sure they don't separate us.*"

"*All right, I get it,*" she said back. "*But why didn't you tell me earlier?*"

Inertia paused for a moment. "*If you could have seen your face when I said it, you wouldn't ask that question,*" he responded simply.

Ha ha ha, Carmen thought, but even she had to admit it probably would be funny if it were happening to someone else.

As they went through another door hidden in the walls, she thought about their current situation. The seriousness of it all made her eyebrows scrunch together as her mind was invaded by one and only one thought.

"*Married? I don't even know your real name,*" she said as she fought a dry smile.

Inertia gave her a quick glance. "*That's what my ex-wife said too.*"

Carmen laughed lightly. It was nice to be able to laugh in a time like this, in a place like this. And it was now that a place like this finally stood at the forefront of her attention. This new corridor was no different from the last one, the one before, or the one before that. She looked at the two sortens in front her, walking as if this were a pleasant stroll through the park.

"Excuse me, Rauon," she began. He seemed the more reasonable of the two. "Where are you taking us?"

She waited for the inevitable remark of, "You don't already know?" She wondered why everyone thought Clairvoyants were omnipotent, all-knowing gods, but this time the comment never came. Neither Rauon nor Mugal seemed surprised by her question.

"*Excuse me?*" Inertia asked her telepathically before Rauon could respond.

"*What? I shouldn't be polite?*"

"*And if they took Phaethon?*"

Carmen shrugged but said nothing else. There was no real reason not to be polite, at least for now.

"We are taking you to our medical center for an examination," Rauon answered simply.

"Why?" she asked without really thinking.

Mugal abruptly looked at her over his shoulder and Rauon paused. Carmen wondered why they reacted as they did. It was a perfectly legitimate question, as far as she could tell.

"We want to make sure that neither of you were injured from your fight with our copy," the head technician eventually said.

"Oh…yeah," Carmen muttered, rubbing her bruised chin. She'd forgotten all about that. She looked at Inertia and examined his large cut. He gave her a thoughtful nod, apparently knowing what she was thinking, so she assumed he wasn't badly hurt either.

"They're even more formidable than I first assumed," Mugal growled under his breath.

Carmen ignored him, there were other things on her mind. She looked up and down the corridor, unable to contain her curiosity now that they were talking.

"Rauon, why is this place designed like this?" she asked.

"It's so…vexing," she eventually added when she found the right word.

The security director responded, even though the question wasn't directed at him. "Of what you speak, of everything around us, it is all a personal touch of our project leader," Mugal said. "Caelus is utterly obsessed with what your kind calls the Dark. He's been studying Clairvoyants since before the first war. He says this, all of this, gives him focus. We've taken to calling this facility Solitary."

"Is that its actual name?" Carmen asked.

"No," Mugal said simply.

"What is it called?"

"No one can remember," he said. "It has had many names in different eras."

She frowned but didn't challenge the statement. He wasn't lying.

Rauon chose that moment to cut in. "That's completely true. No one knows anymore. But the last Clairvoyant here said the architecture was…*fitting*," he added.

The conversation ceased being a casual means to satiate Carmen's curiosity in that moment. "Last Clairvoyant? What last Clairvoyant? What was his name? Why was he here?" she asked breathlessly.

"Interesting," Mugal said to himself, still loudly enough to be heard clearly. "The Clairvoyant doesn't even know why she is here, yet she is at attention about the purpose of another."

Carmen looked at Mugal, who calmly stared back at her as he walked. "Are my questions a problem?" she asked Rauon, though the words weren't aimed at him.

"Questions? No, never. As always, the only potential problem is why the knowledge is sought and what you plan to do with the answers," Mugal said. "What is your plan, Psyche?"

Carmen looked the sorten in the eye. He made no attempt to hide his lack of trust. Every fiber of his every muscle stood at the ready, waiting for the call to action. She didn't doubt that he had spent countless hours studying how to fight and defeat someone exactly like her. But she didn't need to lie for this test.

"I wish I knew," she said simply, and then she looked at Inertia. Mugal's eyes swiveled to him like turrets on a battleship, but Rauon spoke first.

"With respect to the security director, if our new guests were set against us, I doubt we would be standing here right now. Am I correct?"

"Yeah," Carmen said almost immediately.

Mugal stopped and looked at her. He then looked at Inertia. Inertia stared back. Despite her Clairvoyant senses, Carmen could only guess what understanding was exchanged in those few wordless moments. Mugal broke contact first and turned to the head technician.

"It's always cold in the deep dark places," he said quietly. He pressed an unseen button on the wall. A door opened and he stepped inside. "Remember that, Rauon," he added before he disappeared from view.

Rauon watched him leave. Carmen still didn't have a full read on sorten facial expressions, but she distinctly registered disappointment before he turned to face them.

"I apologize for the security director. I hope you understand that he's spent most of his career as a soldier, training to fight Clairvoyants," Rauon said. Carmen gave a nod, but Inertia made no response. "This is the medical center. If you'll please step inside, the examination won't take too long."

She nodded again and entered the room. She was instantly reminded of the medical wing at the facility. The layout was quite similar, with rows and rows of beds in a large central room. Doctors casually roamed the room, poking and prodding where needed. And that was where the similarities ended.

The place just didn't feel right. It looked like a war was happening and that whatever side was being cared for here was losing. Healing didn't appear to be the main priority, though. Almost every bed was taken by dead or badly maimed Clairvoyant Constructs. The smell of it all made Carmen subconsciously raise her hand to her face while she consciously kept the most offensive odors at bay by telekinesis. But the plight of the Clairvoyant Constructs didn't seem to be anyone's real concern. One of them died right in front of her, and his doctor simply took notes. Piles of corpses were carted out as unceremoniously as one would take out the trash. She could only assume the bodies were on the way to some sort of disposal.

She looked around the room with a thought and a wonder in her mind, but the grim truth was quite easy to see. No sorten reacted whatsoever to the horror around them. She could neither see nor sense any emotion when one of their test subjects expired. Deafening cries of pain from the suffering were heard by the sortens as loudly as a boulder dropped into a bottomless pit. She looked at Inertia and, when he returned her gaze, she could see seriousness mount in his features.

"Psyche, please sit here," Rauon said.

Carmen nodded and sat on the bed. Inertia sat next to her. A doctor came for each of them soon enough, while the head technician waited a little way off. The Clairvoyants waited for the doctors to begin their work. And they waited...and waited. Carmen's doctor didn't say anything, which struck her as odd. He simply scanned her over and over again with his PDD. It was like she wasn't even there. She leaned forward and cocked her head to the side to give her *healer* a hard stare.

"Don't move," the doctor said tersely.

Carmen sat up straight by reflex before she wondered why she was doing it. "Umm, what are you doing?" she asked.

"Don't move," the doctor said again.

All right then, I won't move, Carmen thought. She sat as still as humanly possible, staring at the doctor while hesitating to blink. It was then that she heard someone approach. It was hard to sense who exactly it was. They weren't a Clairvoyant, but they were quite hard to read nonetheless.

"The Clairvoyant beast doesn't like our methods. I remember when we used to be more...invasive."

It was a pretty easy guess as to who it was now. She turned her head to look without even thinking about it.

"Don't move!" the doctor said again.

Carmen sighed and turned her head forward again. Caelus chuckled lightly. He walked in front of her, and she looked up at him while he looked down.

"Is this better, monster?" the sorten asked. She said nothing. She was tired of the doctor snapping at her. "It's fascinating how the beasts often prefer to use their primitive eyes instead of their extrasensory gifts. Our tests with the copies prove the same."

Carmen's primitive eyes narrowed, yet her lips stayed still. Her thoughts turned to Inertia. "*How should I react?*" she asked him telepathically.

"*I'm not sure*," he responded as a doctor tended to the cut on his head. "*Run with it.*"

"*Run with it?*"

"*Keep him talking,*" Inertia explained.

She didn't think she'd be able to get him to stop talking, even if she snapped his neck. It certainly didn't take long before he continued.

"Are you angered, terran?" Caelus asked with a mocking tone.

She was not. He made her more annoyed than angry, but she ran with it by pressing her lips together into an obvious but not exaggerated sneer. Caelus looked her in the eye, and she looked back. But then his condescension and arrogance broke to allow the keen intellect of the scientist to show through. He looked quickly at the PDD.

"Psyche, is it? I will have to research that name," he said. Carmen was surprised by the rapid change in his demeanor, and her eyebrows scrunched together. "Oh no, terran, don't think you're special, just unexpected. You have my attention."

She could only agree that she wasn't special, but that still didn't answer why he was suddenly so interested in her. She was about to ask more directly when Caelus continued.

"There is an incongruity about you that's hard to place," he said. "I cannot tell if that is a natural occurrence in you or evidence of some conscious subterfuge that you've failed to conceal. No Clairvoyant beast that I've ever known has bothered with the effort of a self-cloaking ruse, though. It is superfluous, isn't it?" he asked. "You cannot hide your true nature with itself."

Carmen made no response other than a nervous subconscious twitch of her eyes in Inertia's direction.

The sorten didn't seem to notice the tell. In fact, he appeared lost in his own thoughts. "Yes, yes," he muttered to himself. "Your time here will be fruitful indeed."

"Analysis complete, Project Leader," the doctor said.

"Very well. I'll look at the findings later. You may go." The doctor left, and Caelus turned his attention back to Carmen. "Speak," he said simply.

"Analysis?" she asked.

"Yes. We were studying your bioelectric field. It's unfortunate that we don't have many...*natural* baselines to work from. I hope that, with enough data, we'll be able to completely map the Dark, as your kind calls it," Caelus said. "The Dark," he repeated. "We came up with many designations for that unknowable void but produced nothing so accurate. Terrans, at least, can be credited with a degree of creativity among their many vices."

He didn't speak again, at least not right away. Instead, he reached out and casually gripped Carmen's chin with his artificial hand. Clairvoyants didn't feel heat and cold like normals did, as their bioelectric field shielded them from changes in temperature in the air. That was not the case, however, with direct contact. She shuddered as the cold metal pressed against her soft flesh.

"Terran genetic messaging is most interesting to me," he said. "Generation three," he added as she allowed him to turn her head. "I wish I could have seen a terran before you began fiddling with your construction. The baseline would probably be useful."

"If I remember correctly, sortens did some fiddling of their own," Carmen pointed out as he turned her head the other way.

She was quite tired by this point of him holding her face. It was probably the longest time that anyone other than Michael had ever touched her. But his artificial limb prevented him from getting shocked.

"Yes, quite right, beast," Caelus said. "I even made some

contributions myself while we were in possession of your kind. However, I campaigned quite strongly against it until I was overruled." He then ran a finger through her hair, which particularly made her shudder. She almost vomited when he leaned in close to get a good look at the individual strands. "Hmm… So there are some differences," he remarked as he let her go.

"What do you mean?" she asked, putting her hair back into a ponytail.

Inertia watched the back and forth between her and Caelus more intently than she ever could and even answered for him.

"On average, we have clearer skin and healthier hair than generation two. It's very, very slight but quite visible if you know what to look for. Almost nothing else is as readily apparent," he said.

"Oh, so he can speak," Caelus said. "And this one appears to have a mind as well. What else can you say?"

"Lots, when it suits me," Inertia remarked.

"Indeed," the sorten muttered to himself. He looked at Carmen, who stared back at him. He was completely undeterred. "And what secrets does your more powerful companion hold?" he asked rhetorically.

"You're so condescending that I imagine you know them already," she blurted out.

She just couldn't help herself. Being called a beast all the time, him touching her hair, he was still *only* annoying her, but that didn't mean it was painless. After that brief moment of emotional self-defense, the gravity of what she did made her eyes grow wide. The ruse was over now. They were no longer the naïve or desperate Clairvoyants seeking the employment of their enemy. The low level of their commitment was obvious to all. Mugal would be attacking them any second. She had just enough time to give Inertia a hesitant glance.

Yet Caelus laughed. Or at least he gave the sorten equivalent of laughter. In fact, he laughed quite hard.

"Clairvoyant," he began, "your appraisal falls short. There is more collected knowledge on the Clairvoyant scourge here, in this place, than in the rest of the galaxy combined. I've dedicated almost my entire life to studying creatures like you. Nonetheless, I would never dream, even in my wildest, most awe-inspiring fantasies of having a single clue about the nature or magnitude of your secrets," he said, laughing again before he continued. "I condescend to you? You, who engage me in such petty talk when you could rip your answers from my mind and crush me to pulp with but a thought? Is that the joke you wish to mock me with?"

"Umm…" Carmen muttered, at a loss.

"The Clairvoyant beast is suddenly unable to speak. She never even thought of any perspective but her own, always a curious happenstance," he added with a sneer. Carmen sneered back despite her best efforts not to. Caelus observed that tell quite easily, and his sneer morphed into a wry smile. "I like the truth in your eyes, Psyche. All else about you may be a lie, but your eyes can't hide their purity. There is a simple efficiency to what they express that would be a waste of so many words. But let me tell you of another truth. Terrans, all of them, are at their most dangerous when they feel they are powerless. For my safety and that of my team, I will continue reminding you of your reality for the entirety of your stay here." With that, he turned and left.

Carmen watched him leave. She had never really met a sorten until today. She didn't know what to think of Caelus, other than to be wary. Her attention turned to Rauon, who began walking toward them.

"Once again, please forgive—" he started saying, but she stopped him by raising her hand. Clairvoyant or not, she well knew what he was going to say.

"Is he like that with everyone?" Carmen asked.

"As I said, only one other Clairvoyant has volunteered to work with us," the head technician said. "And it was worse with him. That one always threatened to kill us all for even the slightest annoyance, which only seemed to make Caelus more eager."

"I meant is he like that with all of you?" she asked again.

"Forgive me," Rauon said. "I misunderstood. But, of the project leader, I'll say—"

"Why didn't this Clairvoyant kill you all as he said he would?" Inertia interrupted.

Rauon wasn't prepared for his entry into the conversation and visibly jumped when Inertia spoke. "I don't know. You'd have to ask him," he answered after he regained his composure. "Caelus found it quite interesting, in his amused sort of way. I'm sure he has detailed notes of every encounter, much like what he'll be writing about what happened here. But I will say that whenever Charon got completely frustrated, he'd get really quiet and then he'd look at us all and say one word. *Wait,*" Rauon added after pausing to look at them both. "I'm quite happy he won't be back here for some time."

Carmen couldn't help a soft groan when she heard that. "So, what now?" she asked no one in particular.

"If you'll allow it, I'd like to show you to your room," the sorten answered promptly, to which she stood immediately.

Rauon's quick response to *that question* only served to make Inertia smile. He finally came to his feet when Carmen turned, obviously curious about his lack of haste. The trio left the room with no further delay. Mugal left as well, walking slightly in front of them. He eventually departed down a different corridor and was gone. Carmen watched him leave, but he didn't even give them a backward glance. She guessed that meant they had passed some bare minimum level of trust to be left alone with only the head technician.

"I must say that this is a very different experience from what I expected," Rauon said as they entered an elevator.

"What do you mean?" Carmen asked. Inertia listened intently.

"If you don't mind me saying, you're some of the most docile Clairvoyants I've ever met. Nothing like Charon. He was very cold, very calculating. The only time I took him at his word was when he said he was going to kill me. Obviously, he never did," he said. Carmen nodded, and he continued. "It's hard to know what to expect with your kind. Caelus councils us that the more powerful Clairvoyants are *finicky*— his exact words. All of our copies behave similarly to each other, so the transition can be difficult."

The elevator opened, and they started down the corridor. It was as similar and nondescript as every corridor in Solitary.

"How many copies do you have?" Inertia asked.

Rauon didn't answer right away. The delay continued, and Carmen wondered if he was contemplating whether to answer. "I'm not exactly sure," he finally said. "There's another facility capable of manufacturing Clairvoyant Constructs in addition to this one."

Carmen shot an alarmed look in Inertia's direction. His features hardened from the news. "Another facility? Is it like this one?" he asked. The tenseness and edge in his question was only partially reined in, but Rauon didn't seem to notice the sudden interest.

"I don't know anything about it, other than that it exists," the sorten said casually. "I didn't even know it existed till

Charon mentioned it offhandedly," he added with some degree of bitterness.

The two Clairvoyants glanced at each other. No words or thoughts were explicitly shared, but the doubling of their task was keenly seen in the worry on Carmen's face and the seriousness on Inertia's. The reality that she might never find Phaethon made her shudder.

"Here is your room. Once again, I'm available for anything you need. I'll come for you in the morning," Rauon said.

Carmen simply nodded. Her thoughts were too disjointed to pay attention to much of anything. She entered the room with Inertia a half step behind. It was relatively empty only the bare necessities. In comparison, her room in the facility back on New Earth was a luxury apartment. None of that, however, actually mattered for the moment. She placed her sword down and sat on a table opposite Inertia.

After taking a deep breath, she rested her head on her hand. "What do you think?" she asked.

"A lot," he replied. "But I know what you're asking. For now, we play the hand we've been dealt."

"Yes, but for how long?" Carmen asked.

"That I don't know, and that is the tricky part. If and when the moment comes, I imagine it will happen rapidly. You need to act accordingly," he said.

She took another deep breath and thought about their situation before she turned to him again. "What makes you say that?" she asked simply.

Inertia shrugged. "A hunch. Nothing more."

Carmen nodded. "What should I do till then?"

"Just be yourself."

"I don't think Caelus believes my act, though," she pointed out. "You heard what he said, how he talked to me."

"I know, and I'm counting on it."

Carmen looked at him for a moment, noted that he was being serious, and sighed. "Okay," she said simply.

"Get some sleep. We might need it for whatever they have planned for us."

She nodded again and said to herself, "I hope Phaethon's okay."

16

DECEPTIVE FOUNDATIONS

Waking up was never a quiet event for a Clairvoyant. Their bioelectric fields, energized by irrational dreams and nightmares, raged madly though invisibly while they slept. Then, by the slightest stir of the conscious mind from its stupor, the fields exploded into spectacular disarray. Visible sparks coursed along both of their bodies, getting wilder and wilder till they eventually filled the corner of the room where they slept. The two Clairvoyants' respective fields played with each other, challenged each other, retreated, and gave way like a superhuman duel between two angry specters. And then it stopped. The only evidence that remained of the monster within was a slight whitish-blue tint to their eyes when they were opened, but it went away after a second or two.

Carmen sat up in bed and then glanced at Inertia waking up next to her. "Good morning," she said nonchalantly.

"Yeah," he muttered back.

They were forced by the circumstance of their ruse to sleep in the same bed. Neither she nor Inertia knew if sorten couples slept together, and they certainly didn't know if the sortens knew it was odd for a terran couple to not sleep in the same bed. Thankfully, it was easily large enough for both of them to forget that the other was there, so their modesty didn't have to suffer much.

She got out of bed and wondered how she'd get ready for a day that could bring anything. The first step, of course, was to get fully dressed. She heard Inertia casually stir as she went for her change of clothes the sortens had been kind enough to bring from *The Lady*.

"What do you think they're going to do with us?" she asked.

"I don't know. It's difficult to say," he answered. "We still don't have their full trust."

Carmen agreed with a nod. "Well, I'm hungry. There's nothing in here to eat," she said. Inertia shrugged in response, and she was quick to recognize that when they were fed was quite out of his control. "What do you think about what Rauon said about there being another facility?"

He didn't say anything. It was obvious he was thinking hard.

"Well?" she asked again after a minute or so.

"Oh…yeah," he muttered as if distracted. "I guess we shouldn't be surprised. It's not like the sortens are ever sloppy with anything they do," he said. He remained in bed after he spoke, obviously still thinking.

Carmen looked at him for a moment. He sat unmoving and barely breathing, lost in thought. "All right…" she muttered, her voice trailing off. Then she continued getting ready.

There was no question as to whether she'd wear the body armor. The sortens *might* not trust her, but she certainly didn't trust them. She wasn't all too keen on eating their food either, but she needed to keep her strength up. If they had mind to poison her, it was a risk she had to take. Carmen sighed at that thought and then turned her attention back to her partner, who still sat in bed.

"Are you going to get ready?" she asked.

"Yeah," Inertia responded and slowly started getting up. Small as it was, she was pleased with that small progress in their mission.

"Should I bring my sword?" she asked.

"I don't think you'll need it," he said simply. But his attention was so obviously elsewhere that she was surprised he even heard her.

She looked at him sidelong. "Is—"

"No, nothing's wrong," he said, cutting her off.

Carmen nodded and reminded herself that even an unfocused Clairvoyant was still aware. She tied her hair into a ponytail and was pretty much ready. Inertia moved slowly, so she took a seat and waited.

"What's on your mind?" she asked, her tone calm but curious.

"Charon," he said.

Carmen nodded. "I was thinking about him too." That was a bit of an understatement. She thought about him all the time. "Where did he come from? What do you think he wants?" she asked, voicing only a few of her many questions.

"I don't know. It's damn strange," he responded.

"Even the sortens were surprised that a Clairvoyant wanted to work with them," Carmen continued.

"Yes, it doesn't make sense," Inertia agreed.

She nodded again and then thought about another thing that troubled her. "In the medical center, did you notice something?" She waited, but Inertia made no response. He didn't even look at her. She continued anyway. "Every Clairvoyant in there was a copy. They've had other Clairvoyants here—they must have. Brought against their will, of course. But I wonder what happened to them? I wouldn't be surprised if they dissected them or something, considering how they treated us," she added, stopping short of mentioning that fate for Phaethon.

Inertia glanced at her as he walked across the room to retrieve his body armor. His mind was clearly still racing with what she didn't know, but she could discern some worry. She didn't think he had much care for Phaethon, if she were honest, but it was undeniable that being dissected was a terrible fate.

She thought about her charge, imagining him being brought to this forsaken place beaten, broken, and lonely. She wondered if the sortens would even be humane enough to kill him before they started cutting him up. She didn't have any real firsthand experience with sortens. The stories she'd heard when she was younger spoke of their unending ruthlessness. Kali had several personal examples. Everyone Carmen knew who wasn't a Clairvoyant treated Clairvoyants like they were violent animals too, though. How true were stories? It was difficult to say.

What she did know for sure was that one sorten in particular was obsessed with Clairvoyants. *Caelus*, she thought. She wouldn't put any horror past him, as long as it could further his research. Who knew? Maybe Phaethon needed to be screaming in agony for Caelus to get the data he needed. She shook her head as her thoughts strayed to even darker depths.

"If Phaethon isn't here, do you think we could get them to transfer us to the other facility without arousing suspicion?" she asked, unable to keep the question from coming out. "Maybe Charon is there too."

Finally ready, Inertia took a seat across from her, still thinking. "I doubt it," he said simply.

"But what if what we're looking for isn't here?" she asked quickly, though she wasn't exactly sure what they were looking for. She didn't think Inertia knew either. "What if Charon attacks again while we're waiting for something to happen here? We have to think of some way to get to the other facility if we need to. The sortens wouldn't take us to their main site if they don't fully trust us," she added, not believing he could be so unmoved by the possibility.

"That is not our central issue," he said.

"Then what is?"

"I never heard of it happening before, but there must be some reason for it—"

"What? Reason for what?" Carmen asked, cutting him off. It was like he was talking to himself.

Inertia glanced at her. "Charon."

"What about him?"

"Rauon said that Charon threatened to kill them several times but never did. Why?" he asked as he rubbed his chin.

Carmen looked at him, her eyes glazed over in disbelief. "Come again?" she muttered.

"What kind of Clairvoyant does that—promise an action but not follow through? It doesn't make any sense," he said, looking away from her.

She gazed around the room and took in her surroundings. She contemplated the fact that she was literally in the middle of some forgotten planetoid lost in a forgotten sector of the galaxy. She remembered why she was here: to rescue her charge and to stop a maniac from harming anyone else. Carmen also reflected on the grim reality that she was surrounded by aliens who had more than half a mind to kill her, and who had trained for most of their adult lives to do just that. In the midst of all this, her only ally in the maelstrom, her only guide and the only person she could trust—and even then just barely—was searching for clues with tweezers in a darkened room.

"Does it really make any difference?" she asked him. "Maybe Charon just changed his mind? It's not like I never have."

Inertia looked at her hard, and Carmen felt every molecule in her body freeze in that brief instant. "Clairvoyants don't do that," he said simply but with a slight edge to his voice. "We change our minds, sure, but there is always a reason for it. We don't make a threat, change our minds and not carry it out, make the same threat again, and not carry it out yet again."

She considered his words and could see what he saying. Now that she thought about it, she'd never acted that way ever in her life. "Clairvoyants aren't all the same, though," she said. "Yes, we have similarities, but weren't not completely alike in everything. Clairvoyants don't work for or with sortens, for instance, yet Charon has."

"And I'm sure there's a reason for that as well. Just because we don't understand it doesn't mean it doesn't exist," he said. "It might even be connected."

Carmen looked away for a moment before she turned back to Inertia. Rauon was coming. The discussion would have to wait for another time.

"I still don't think it's important," she said.

"Perhaps it's not."

Just then, Rauon opened the door and stood in the doorway, silhouetted by the light in the corridor. Carmen gave a subconscious shudder.

"Greetings. I hope you slept well," the sorten said. Neither Clairvoyant answered. "Are you ready?"

"When are we going to be fed?" Carmen asked.

"I apologize, Psyche, but not for some time. Hunger gives more accurate test results," Rauon replied.

"What type of tests?" Inertia asked.

"I'm not at liberty to say," he answered simply. "It would distort the test results. I must also ask that you don't read me for the same purpose."

Carmen glanced at Inertia, who gave the silent go-ahead. She stood and went to retrieve her sword.

"Your weapon is not necessary, Psyche," Rauon said.

She frowned but said nothing, and the two Clairvoyants obediently followed the sorten out of the room. Four guards waited for them in the corridor. They were heavily armed. They weren't, however, at the nervous hair-trigger as most guards were when near Clairvoyants. She didn't see the point; the sortens had to know the soldiers were no match against them. Despite that, the group started walking with the guards trailing slightly behind.

"What's with the company?" she asked, unable to stay quiet.

"Oh, that's Mugal's doing. They are here to observe you," Rauon said.

"For what?" She turned to look at them, and a pair of guards simply watched her, completely stone-faced. The other pair watched Inertia with equally as much poise.

"Treachery," the head technician answered.

Carmen glanced at Inertia, who shared her look. She then looked at Rauon, who walked in front of them and couldn't see her interest.

"Do you suspect anything?" she asked casually.

"Do I personally?" Rauon questioned, turning to look at her.

She shook her head. "No, I mean all of you in general."

He looked forward again and called for the elevator. Then

he turned to face the Clairvoyants as they waited. "I don't want to speak for anyone," he said, "but…in general, there is no real reason we should trust you. Clairvoyants speak quite openly of their animosity toward us. It would be prudent to be cautious."

Carmen nodded. "That does make some sense. What about you, though? What do you think?"

Rauon paused for a moment. It didn't seem like he was ready for the question just yet, but then his face slowly turned more serious, almost meditative. "Your kind terrifies me," he said frankly. "They have always terrified me." Carmen looked at him curiously, which prompted him to elaborate. "I remember when I was first shown the training vids," he continued. "They were made back when we first discovered you. In one of them, we had a Clairvoyant child of about five or six of your years old in a room with a tau beast—"

"What's a tau beast?" Carmen asked.

"Fearsome creatures. We genetically engineered them to control an invasive introduced species on one of our colonies. They're about the most cunning animal you could ever face. Their claws can gore even steel," the sorten answered. She nodded, and he continued once they stepped inside the elevator.

"The test was simple. Could the Clairvoyant survive? I watched the video with a group, and no one expected much. I assumed the child would survive only a short moment at most. Indeed, one swipe of the tau beast's claws ripped off half of the Clairvoyant's face." He paused for a second. "I distinctly remember one of his eyeballs swaying back and forth by the optic nerve."

Rauon spoke in a calm and direct manner, and Carmen got the impression that he was trying not to think about what he was talking about. For her part, she couldn't help a disgusted frown.

"That attack would have killed any normal being," he said. "But the test readings indicated no stress response. It was like the Clairvoyant was hit by no more than a stiff breeze. I've seen test animals with deactivated pain receptors give a stronger reaction to physical damage. The tau beast never really had a chance. The Clairvoyant set it on fire pyro-kinetically," he said.

"But that wasn't all. After the tau beast was dead, the boy gave a stare," Rauon continued, talking more to himself at this point. "He was drenched in blood, his eyeball hung loose, and he just stood there and silently watched the creature madly flail about. Then he looked at the camera. He shouldn't have known it was there, but his working eye seemed to just bore into you. I remember it almost made me leave the room the first time I watched it. Now I shut off the video before it gets to that part."

"Why?" Carmen asked.

Rauon turned to look at her. "I'm not sure you can fully understand," he said. "It requires some understanding of our history, which I doubt you are a student of." Carmen shrugged and shook her head, which prompted him to give the sorten equivalent of a nod. "Our past—our distant past—was a violent one. It approached nothing of your terran history, but a certain degree of brutality is still brutality." He stopped talking for a moment as the elevator doors opened and the group started walking down the corridor. "Our ancient ancestors believed in a spirit both good and evil, as you would understand it. It lived in every being, and its domain was both knowledge and destruction."

"What do you mean?" Carmen asked.

"I think knowledge is the wrong word. Terranese is an

imprecise language," Rauon said. "Perhaps it is more accurate to say self-knowledge."

She couldn't help a bemused frown. "Now I really don't understand."

"One is not granted without the other," the head technician said matter-of-factly. "Our forebearers were wise enough to see that the more we learned about ourselves—the more we learned of our fears, what could hurt us, and what we were vulnerable to—the more destructive we could be to others and them to us. First, we learned that if we were crushed, we would die, and there were clubs. Then we learned that if we were cut, we would bleed, and edged weapons were spawned. After that were poisonous gasses, explosives, and other best forgotten monsters," he said, looking at her as they walked.

"I have always wanted to work with Clairvoyants," Rauon continued. "Terrans didn't even know their own potential before our two species met." Carmen raised an eyebrow, noting the very *polite* way he phrased the first contact between terrans and sortens.

Rauon didn't speak for a long time after that. It was like he was lost in thought. The sorten looked into the distance, and his breathing even slowed. The few seconds seemed like a lifetime. A gentle cough on her part snapped him back to the present.

"I just worried what we were teaching you about yourselves," he added. "What we may be unleashing by furthering our research."

Carmen considered everything he had said. "That spirit sounds a little like the Dark."

"I've never really thought of it that way," Rauon said. "Yet, I can see your meaning."

"What happened to the boy?" she asked softly.

"He died not long after he killed the tau beast," he answered. "The video didn't say, but I imagine his body was studied. In fact, full research of your kind was taken shortly after that video was made."

She nodded and then thought of Phaethon again...and herself. But her thoughts were cut short when Inertia spoke.

"Do you think we are here to destroy you?" he asked Rauon.

"Excuse me?" the sorten muttered.

"Do you think we are here to destroy you?" Inertia asked again.

Rauon grew visibly uncomfortable again. Every sorten here was experienced enough with Clairvoyants to know they hated repeating themselves. Inertia looked at Rauon intently but merely out of curiosity. The head technician relaxed upon reading his features.

"I don't know why you are here," he said simply.

"We're not working for free," Carmen pointed out.

"True," Rauon admitted. "It is certainly less...*alarming* to be around you since you are voluntarily in our service." He paused for a few seconds. "Though I must say that wasn't the case with Charon. Anyway, I'm sure the precise reason you chose to help us instead of taking another contract will reveal itself in due time. I don't think it matters, though," he said as he stopped to look at both of them. "Every encounter with a Clairvoyant is akin to staring into the unknown. We should not fear, even if we are terrified. I'll say especially if we're terrified. It is an exciting test." Rauon took a deep breath. "Caelus used to always say that...long ago," he added after a short pause.

Carmen nodded, and with that, the conversation appeared to be effectively over. The group continued on. She reflected on what Gungnir had said about wolves in the forest and giving pause. Her biggest day to day worry for the past few years had been nothing more than making enough money to get by while paying Michael's medical bills. She looked all around her, thinking of the planetoid they were presently encased inside. She knew sortens and others studied Clairvoyants. She was even distantly aware of the lengths they went to. But the reality of her life and the sheer dread of what she was capable of causing were laughably nowhere near each other. Would the sortens be so worried if they knew how difficult it was for her to hold down a gym membership?

Rauon stopped in place and opened one of the hidden doors on the wall of the corridor. "This is it. Can you please step inside?"

Carmen glanced into the room before she made any other move. She wasn't completely surprised by what she saw. In fact, she was such a finely tuned weapon by this point in her life that she didn't even notice her heart rate quicken, her breath shorten, or her hands ball into fists. The walls of the room were padded with heat resistant material. It was perfectly square and a little larger than what she was used to at the facility.

Rauon prompted them into the fight room and then followed them inside. Carmen glanced at one of the several blood stains on the ground and wondered why the sortens didn't bother cleaning it up like her previous captors had. Then she turned to look at the wall behind her. High on it, near the ceiling, was a large observation booth with a commanding view of the entire room. Caelus stood in its center, intently staring down at them as he stood on his hind legs. She had been well aware that she was observed, recorded, and catalogued back at the facility, and she had no doubt that she was being studied now. How obvious the sortens were about it, however, took her aback.

"I will come to collect you when the test is complete," Rauon said.

Carmen watched him leave. She then looked at Inertia before her gaze finally rested on a door at the other end of the room. In just a brief moment, four Clairvoyant Constructs emerged. They all looked the same with jet-black hair and a mechanical directness about their movement. She took a few steps away from Inertia to have room to move if she needed to. The purpose of this test was quite clear.

"Defend yourself only," Caelus said through the room's speaker system. "Do not attack back. This is a nonlethal test. But they will kill you if they are able."

Carmen sighed. She already wasn't looking forward to it. "Why do we have to fight?" she muttered under her breath.

"Did you say something, Psyche? If so, I want to hear it," Caelus said.

She hadn't thought he'd be able to hear her, but the microphones in here were apparently stronger than she expected. Even so, she wasn't in the mood to be shy.

"I said why do we have to fight? Why is it always fighting?" she replied, staring at her opponents who stood by at the other end of the room.

"Do you not want to fight?" the sorten asked.

The observation booth was behind her, so Carmen couldn't see him, but his words were soaked with the inquisitive mind of a scientist pulling wings off a fly. Her response would be noted somewhere for further study. She wasn't exactly sure how to respond, causing her eyes to glance Inertia's direction.

Caelus spoke again. "Well, let me answer your question then—"

"Fighting involves the whole self," Inertia said, cutting him off mid-speech. "There is no other task or endeavor that stresses the consciousness and the Dark so completely, maybe other than being in love. The Dark can't be hidden in battle; it is always called upon. I'm sure they have preliminary readings on our bioelectric fields cross-referenced with our genetic makeups. By now, I'm sure they've made projections based on those readings with whatever computer model they've developed. This test is meant to verify the accuracy of the computer model so they can make more powerful Clairvoyant Constructs. They don't want us to kill these Constructs because I'm sure they are expensive to produce."

Carmen turned her head slowly to stare at him for a moment. "Oh…" she muttered.

It was a few seconds before Caelus finally spoke. "So, the weak one does have a brain after all. Most unexpected among the Clairvoyant beasts. As I asked yesterday, what else is there?"

Inertia half turned to face him. "More than you want to admit," he said. "You will never succeed. You don't know the correct questions to ask. The final secret can't be uncovered through science. You know this and you're still lost. Everyone else, though, hasn't realized the obvious yet. That surprises you."

There was a long silence. Carmen looked back at Inertia and Caelus as they stared at each other. She only somewhat understood what they were talking about, and she certainly couldn't see how it was relevant, especially now. With that in mind, she glanced at the Clairvoyant Constructs, just in case they made a move.

"Bring him here," the sorten said.

The door burst open, and the guards that had accompanied them immediately entered. Carmen watched the scene, completely frozen in place. She had no idea what to do. Were they attacking Inertia? Was this a good thing? The indecision bounced around in her skull till he gave her a reassuring nod.

"*What do I do?*" she asked him telepathically.

"*Exactly what you are doing*," he said back. "*Be yourself and follow my lead.*"

Carmen considered the advice and all the travails it had so far caused. "*That's not exactly easy.*"

He had already begun to leave with the guards, though. She had never really realized till this moment how comforting it was to not be completely alone. Now her face fell further and further with each step he took.

"*I know*," he replied as he glanced at her over his shoulder. With that, he left the room.

Carmen turned to face her remaining company and rolled her eyes.

* * *

The sortens moved quickly, but Inertia noted everything—every inch of this place, every light, every twist and turn they made, the added haste from the command of their leader, everything. In short order, he was shepherded into an elevator and then they were walking down a new corridor. A few steps later, he was inside a midsized room. Caelus stared at him from the other end of it, but Inertia paid him no notice. Dozens of sorten technicians were busy behind computers, analyzing every possible detail of his partner and her opposition. He was well aware that Caelus was almost madly eager to talk to him, as always by means that couldn't be obviously discerned, but that was not why he was here.

He walked intentionally slowly toward Caelus. Mugal was also near, like a steadfastly loyal dog ready to defend his master. For now, though, the security director was quiet and observing. Inertia didn't even waste his time glancing at him. His attention was on the computers. He was less interested in what they were reading and instead keenly curious as to how they worked. As discretely as he could, Inertia took in every detail of their operation. Unfortunately, it was a system he'd never personally used before, and when he looked at Caelus, it was with a frown. This would take longer than he'd thought.

He walked right past Caelus, stopping to look down into the room he had just vacated. Edge was thankfully okay. If anything, it looked like she hadn't even moved. She had to know he was here, watching her. She never turned to look, though, so it wasn't a guess he could confirm. He allowed a second or two of silent consideration. Thus far, his plan was strategy at its most raw and basic. They weren't at the point, yet, where they could do anything other than react to what was happening to them. As if on cue, Edge's head turned slightly toward him, and even he wondered, *So, what now?*

Inertia turned around from the imperceptible prompt Clairvoyants lived by. Caelus towered over him. The terran looked up at the sorten, who stared back with fiery intelligence in his eyes.

"There was a building I used to walk past every day," Caelus began. "It was part of a complex built more than a hundred of your years ago. All of its kin were impressive in their physical height, but the one I passed every day was the most well known. I can't really describe it for you now. It had elegance in proportion and other subtleties that can only be appreciated when seen in person," Caelus said. Then he closed his eyes, and Inertia just watched and waited. "Even people familiar with it would stop and appreciate the masterwork in its construction before they went on their way. I would often spend entire days just studying every detail.

"And I couldn't understand it," he continued after a brief pause. "That building was functionally the same as the rest around it. They had the same general shape and ultimate purpose. Yet this one was elevated above them all. It deserved to be elevated, but I could never explain how it was what it was, nor did its creator ever say why he built it the way he did. For years I walked past that building, marveling at every inch of its genius. I even took it upon myself to master as much of the science of architecture as anyone could possibly teach themselves.

"Most of this facility was designed by me personally. I fully understand the discipline's principles and am painfully aware of its limitations. I can describe the minutest detail of any edifice with perfect mathematical precision. Nevertheless..." His voice trailed off and his face grew blank as his thoughts retreated in on themselves. "Nevertheless, that building guarded its secrets well." Caelus looked down at Inertia after a deep breath. "You say I will never succeed," he said simply.

Inertia didn't answer right away. He looked behind the sorten to the dozens upon dozens of computer technicians working diligently in the background.

"Never," he finally said.

"What makes you so certain?"

"You're asking for too much—"

"Explain," Caelus interrupted.

"Every terran can become a Clairvoyant," Inertia said. "Everyone. The only reason Clairvoyants are special is because of how many people choose not to become one."

"It may not be special to some to be able to melt a solid block of metal with just a thought," Mugal snorted.

Inertia glanced at him before he turned his attention back to Caelus. "I must ask. How many buildings did you see every day on your way to work that you took no note of what-soever? How many buildings in your life inspired you in the same way as that one?" He paused for a moment, and the scientist waited. "Of all those buildings, there was only one you could say was truly exceptional, and you cannot explain why, it just is. My partner is exceptional. She cannot be recreated out of science."

"What are you saying?" Mugal asked hurriedly.

"Put simply," Inertia began, glancing at him and then back at Caelus, "your copies are almost a match to an average Clairvoyant. They will not, however, progress much further. Natural talent and the forces that nurture it can only be observed. It can't be mapped, distilled, and packaged. What makes Edg—Psyche—what she is is unique to her and her alone. Even if she had a twin, they would not be capable of the same and certainly not in the same way. No two dishes of food taste exactly the same, even with the same ingredients and prepared the same way."

The sorten stood completely still for a long while. He stared at Inertia, but it wasn't with disbelief or a critical eye. "I have mapped every possible attribute of your kind down to your last molecule," Caelus said. "My models have accurately predicted every vagary of your primitive psyches—"

"Yet you will not succeed," Inertia said.

"I will admit there have been a great many pains, but even you admit our copies approach the strength of the average Clairvoyant. To say never?" Caelus questioned.

Inertia smiled.

"Why do you smile?" the security director asked with obvious anger bleeding into his voice.

"If only you could see and understand the depths of your ignorance," the Clairvoyant answered simply. "Unleash the beast then, if you don't believe me," he said, turning around to look down at Edge. "Expect her to injure one of your copies in only a few moves."

"How do you know what she will do?" Caelus asked.

"Knowing a thing is not the same as cataloging a thing," he remarked.

The two sortens fell silent, unable to do anything but watch him. Mugal eventually looked to his master, who nodded.

"Begin," the security director barked to the army of computer technicians behind them.

"*Edge, I need your help,*" Inertia spoke to her telepathically.

He could almost feel her mind actively studying every move the Clairvoyant Constructs made as they slowly surrounded her.

"*How exactly does that work?*" she asked him.

"*I need you to injure one of them when they attack you.*"

She paused for a moment. "*I thought they said not to fight back?*"

"*I'm aware,*" he replied. "*But it will help my credibility.*"

Carmen gave a slight nod. A nanosecond later, it began.

The speed and savagery of the contest was evident from the first twitch of a muscle. The four Clairvoyant Constructs attacked in well-timed unison. Carmen feigned a counterattack, but none of her opposition took the bait. She was quite certain they knew she wasn't supposed to attack them.

In any case, a step back moved her out of the way of a kick. A block saved her face from a punch from her side. She telekinetically threw herself out of the way of another punch; there was no other way to avoid it. The room chilled a degree or two. It wasn't a sensation she consciously registered, nor was the thought to twist her body out of the way of a heat beam. Her eyes narrowed, but other than that split second, she gave no sign of her annoyance.

The first Construct came at her again. She matched his rhythm as he aggressively struck forward. A slight move of her head sent his lead hand sailing over her shoulder. Then she changed the beat, taking an extra half step and moving out of the line of attack. His power hand rushed out to where she was supposed to be. At the same time, she intercepted his outstretched arm at the elbow with a counterpunch in one fluid movement.

The sound of the Clairvoyant Construct's arm breaking was only a loud crack, but it froze every soul in the observation booth and the fight room, save one. Inertia couldn't help a slight nod of approval. Caelus's stare bored into him, but he ignored it for now.

The next movement of the battle had an entirely different tempo. This time, a feint by Carmen stopped all the Constructs in their tracks, allowing her to reposition herself along the wall. She gave up controlling the fight with distance, but at least she only had to defend herself from one direction. In fact, she could only really be attacked by one of them at a time. The first's fist cratered the wall as she moved her head out of the way.

It was like fighting in a phone booth. Her arms, shoulders, and body responded in split-second saves that were only belied in their intensity by their awesome gracefulness and accuracy, such to the point that everything she did seemed almost preordained. Subtle sidesteps forced her opponents to stop and reset for a new attack. Yet a moment later, she felt a sharp pain, and the room spun from a blow she didn't see coming.

Her entire body quaked and everything became...uncoordinated. Her thoughts were still as sharp as ever and she knew exactly what she wanted to do, but her body simply didn't respond with its usual haste. *Bound to happen sometime*, she thought. She gave her head a brisk shake and everything became clear enough that she was dangerous again. A quick survey of her situation was the only other thing Carmen needed.

Three of the Constructs took turns attacking her to conserve their stamina and wear her out. The fourth, the Construct with the broken arm, stood by, ready to blast her with a heat beam the moment she was vulnerable.

A punch that just grazed her cheek, however, soon reminded her that she needed to stay focused on the immediate. She smothered the follow-up attack by stepping forward. She then ducked out of the way of another, moving ever so deftly to position the third Construct exactly where she wanted him. He came at her as expected in a lunging attack that closed the distance. She was ready for him and what came next; she had already conducted the orchestra in her head.

A step to the side and back made him miss and placed them exactly where she wanted to be. He, of course, responded with the only offensive option available to him, which was what she was waiting for. Carmen stepped into him, grabbing him in exactly the right moment, and pulled him around her body to shield herself from an onrushing beam of heat. The Construct screamed and, a few seconds later, she dropped his charred body to the ground. Then she placed her hands on her hips.

"She's...she's not supposed to do that!" Mugal exclaimed.

Caelus glanced at him but didn't add to the protest. Inertia half turned to look at Caelus, who studied him for a moment before finally turning his attention to one of his technicians.

"Report," he said simply.

"Data is still streaming, Project Leader. But…" he trailed off and then paused. "But—"

"Yes?" Caelus pressed.

"There's only a thirty percent correlation with our model," the technician answered.

"That is incorrect. Recalibrate," the sorten said after powerfully stomping his foot. The technician went to work immediately, and Caelus snarled when the new data began streaming in. He ran at Inertia, stopping just short to tower over him. "Why?" he screamed. Inertia made no reply, other than a smirk. "Answer me, beast!"

"I told you why."

"Then tell me again."

Inertia nodded and turned to look down into the fight room. "Fighting involves the whole self. The Dark can't be hidden in battle; it is always called upon."

"I know that already," Caelus said. "There have been countless battles in this facility proving exactly that."

"But you don't really understand the principle," Inertia countered. "You don't even understand the battle itself. You think the fight is between the Clairvoyant and their opponent, but that is never the case. The battle is within the Clairvoyant themself."

"Project Leader, do not be seduced by this nonsense," Mugal cut in. "There must be some problem with the sensing equipment. Let's run a check and then start the test again."

"Mugal, silence." The security director shuffled and groaned but said nothing else, and Caelus turned his attention back to Inertia. "Continue," he said, regaining his normal calm state.

"A Clairvoyant's will and desire is what gives their Dark its potency and generative force," he explained as if it was obvious. "That's why it's ever-changing, never static, and difficult to quantify. Every moment of every day, it's responding to the slightest challenge or difficulty, reshaping itself, evolving, conquering."

"But our copies match our model to ninety-eight percent accuracy," Caelus said.

"They are robots," Inertia replied. "Well made robots, but they are only what you programmed them to be."

"That didn't stop them from besting you," Mugal muttered under his breath.

He glanced at the sorten but didn't challenge the statement. "Look in there," Inertia said to Caelus while motioning to the fight room. The scientist took a step forward and did just that. "You see a battle. You see a beast. But what do you think she sees? What do you think is going through her head?" he continued. "Do you think she's determining every move and countermove she'll make? No, it's simpler than that. She doesn't particularly want to be in there. She doesn't particularly want them to attack her. Everything about her is focused on that. Everything she does or doesn't do, every memory she's ever had, and even when she takes a breath… Everything is concentrated on that one desire."

The sorten said nothing and just watched the battle. He noted how Carmen was able to move about the room almost with complete impunity. A potential attack was stifled with a feint, a subtle change in her positioning, or even just a turn of her head. For a short while, the Clairvoyant Copies didn't even dare to throw so much as a punch.

It was then that Caelus saw the details in his latest subject's masterwork. Not one thing she did repeated itself, at least not in exactly the same way. Every movement and indeed every breath was ever so slightly different from the last. In comparison, his creations could only be described as the clunky abominations they were. She almost danced around and through them, like a whimsical muse conducting an opera. It would be difficult to say that a single thing happened in that room that she didn't intend. His eyes grew wide upon the revelation.

"Stop the test," he said as he walked away from the window. "It's all wrong. We're going to have to start again," he muttered to himself as he moved toward the exit.

"Project Leader!" Mugal called.

If Caelus heard him, he paid no mind. "All wrong…" he continued to mutter as he left.

The Clairvoyant Constructs stopped their attack instantly. Carmen kept her guard till a subconscious cue told her it was over. She took a deep breath. The ordeal was by no means the worst she'd ever suffered, but all the same she didn't care for it. Her eyes lingered on the dead Construct for a second as she turned to look at Inertia in the observation booth.

"*Are you okay?*" he asked telepathically.

"*Yeah, I'm fine.*"

She saw him nod. "*Good,*" he spoke. "*This is just the first day.*"

17

THE DARK DEPTHS

The aches and pains of the past worked through Carmen as she stretched. It was somewhat maddening that, for most of her life, she was constantly prepared to fight yet never knew when her next battle would be. She no longer noticed the unremitting state of readiness, at least not consciously. Though her fight yesterday with the four Clairvoyant Constructs had been relatively light work, mind and body were a team, and her body was quick to remind her this morning that it needed to be focused and primed before it was so stressed. She couldn't control much here—they had yet to be fed again—but she could do something about being sore in the morning.

Inertia watched her warm up but made no move to join her.

"You know, they probably won't have you fight today," he remarked.

"And what if they do?" she said without looking at him.

"Then what you're doing is prudent," Inertia replied. "But if you don't fight, it'll just be a waste of time."

Carmen couldn't help a momentary quake. Wasting time

was practically sacrilegious to Clairvoyants. She didn't stop her warm up, though; she just looked at him and frowned at the suggestion.

After a few seconds of silence, she said, "We'll see."

She then went about her business, missing his thoughtful nod in reply. Though the conversation was over, his words stayed with her. *I have to fight*, she reflected. *What else do Clairvoyants do? What else does anyone want them for?* Occasional oddly timed frowns gave voice to the thoughts roaming her mind, but she said nothing else, and Inertia didn't seem to notice. She finished her warm-up a few minutes later. She could sense the sortens coming.

"You like going the direction you're pointed," Inertia said when she turned to face him.

Carmen frowned again. She had an inkling of what he meant, but she didn't get a chance to say anything as Rauon walked into the room.

"Clairvoyants, if you may," he said simply.

Carmen glanced at Inertia, who got up, and the two of them walked out of the room. Mugal was waiting for them with a security contingent.

She looked at the formidable force arrayed against them and then looked at Inertia sidelong. "*No fighting*," she said telepathically with a sarcastic tone.

He said nothing back. He simply raised a hand, and Carmen held herself from making any further barbs. She'd met countless Clairvoyants from her time as a handler and, on the whole, the lot of them were as calm as a forgotten lake on a tranquil night. Inertia was an order of magnitude more. Her heart rate had to drop three beats a minute just being around him.

"Inertia, please go with the security director. Psyche, you are with me," Rauon said.

"Why the division?" Carmen asked.

"The project leader has taken an interest in you," Mugal answered, looking at Inertia as he spoke. "His machinations may vex me from time to time, but this is his order, so it will be done. But mind yourself, Clairvoyant. You may bedazzle him. However, that grants you nothing. At the slightest provocation, I'd obliterate this rock and everyone in it to terminate you, if need be."

Inertia made no response to that. Carmen had seen people have bigger reactions to an unreturned smile. With no hesitation, her partner went with Mugal and the security detail. She noticed his head turn slightly toward her as they walked away, which was as much of a goodbye as she'd get.

She turned to Rauon. "So, what now?"

"We have a full day," the sorten said.

"Am I going to fight again?" she asked with a degree of hesitation.

"No, that's not needed for today. It'll just be some simple tests," he answered.

Carmen let go a soft sigh. She wasn't completely sure, however, if she was relieved because of the answer or annoyed because, as Inertia had said, she'd wasted her time. It didn't really matter.

"If you may," Rauon said, and the two began walking.

Carmen was quick to note a difference between now and yesterday and even just a minute ago. "No escort?" she asked.

"I don't think I need it," he replied. "Your mate terrifies me, quite frankly. But you...there's something different about you. I can't really say why. Honestly, that's part of what these tests are designed to figure out."

"I'm not special," she cut in quickly.

"No, that's not what I meant to imply. You are very much

a Clairvoyant and act in their typical manner. On the other hand, it seems that you try not to. It's…curious."

"You sound almost like Caelus when you say that," Carmen pointed out.

Rauon said nothing else for a long moment. He seemed troubled. "I know you don't particularly care for the project leader. His drive can be…off-putting," he said, pausing to find the right words. "However, we are both scientists. We both want the same thing—"

"You do?" Carmen interrupted.

"Of course we do."

"And what's that?"

"Answers. Always answers," Rauon said without missing a beat. "There are always new questions."

"But why ask them?"

The sorten turned to her, clearly amused. She'd never seen him look that way before. But his manner wasn't the demeaning, superior attitude of Caelus; it was almost child-ishly innocent by comparison.

"Typical Clairvoyant. Few of us *just know* like you do," he said.

"There's very little I *just know*. Trust me."

Rauon gave her the same amused look again. "Perhaps, and that's what makes you interesting. I think I'm going to like working with you."

She had no idea what to say in response, so she simply nodded and shrugged at the same time. They said nothing after that as they entered an elevator. It was difficult to know what exactly she should be doing now. Inertia's only advice had been to be herself. Just then, Rauon muttered a curse under his breath that didn't have a direct translation.

Carmen glanced at him.

"It's nothing," he said. She raised an eyebrow. "I left

some of my research materials in my quarters. I can reference some of it by memory, but it would be difficult."

"We can go get it," she said.

"You don't mind?" Rauon asked with hesitant surprise.

Carmen couldn't help a small chuckle. "Why would I mind? Is there some place I need to be?"

"Yes, that was a foolish question," he muttered softly. "This will only take a few minutes."

She nodded, and he redirected the elevator at the press of a button. She still had no real idea of where anything was located in the planetoid. Its bewildering design made it difficult to find any reference points. Still, it felt like they were sinking deep into the pit of the thing, deeper than her quarters, and when the elevator doors opened, it was obvious that she'd never been on this level before.

"Follow me," Rauon said.

Carmen dutifully complied. This part of the facility didn't have meandering, endless halls. No, the elevator opened to a large circular room with several identical doors equidistant from each other. She turned to note that the elevator doors were just as identical.

Several sortens were present. Each of them paused in turn when they noticed the Clairvoyant in their midst. As Carmen looked at the chaos of it all, it was crystal clear just what a total hell this planetoid was. Each sorten needed a short while to get their bearings before they determined where they needed to go. It seemed that knowing which door was the elevator, now that someone stepped out of it, was a big help.

Carmen had always assumed the madness of Solitary was limited to the levels she'd previously seen. Surely deeper, in the dark heart of the mass, the sortens would revert to more logical ordering. Shockingly, that didn't appear to be the case.

Indeed, Carmen, whose task was simply to follow Rauon, was the only person who didn't appear to be lost.

"It's this way...I think," the head technician said.

They joined a small group exiting through one of the doors. After a few steps down that corridor, however, Rauon groaned and then peeled off with the other aimless sortens who had guessed incorrectly. As they walked back to try another door, he looked at her with a hint of embarrassment on his face. She didn't really think it was warranted. Two tries later, they were on their way.

This section was more straightforward, like the winding, meandering corridors in the rest of the planetoid. The most intriguing aspect here was how the sortens reacted to her. The affront of her existence first produced alarmed disbelief that then transitioned to curiosity aimed Rauon's way. His only response was to politely tell anyone questioning him not to mind. Despite that, Carmen had to stifle more than a couple of laughs when some of the sortens jumped in fearful surprise.

"Here it is. Once again, I apologize for the delay," Rauon said when they finally reached his quarters. She shook her head and waved the apology away.

He went inside, and Carmen hesitated to follow. She thought back to how Janus and Kali had rarely if ever entered her room back at the facility. Despite everything that had been taken from her, she'd still been allowed one space free from intrusion. Thus, out of respect, she waited at the entrance to his quarters while he found his forgotten items. It only took her a minute or so to realize why the sorten had been coy about coming here as he rummaged through his belongings, obviously unsure of where what he was looking for was located.

"Sorry, sorry," he muttered a few times when a fresh search turned up nothing. "I'll be brief."

"It's okay," Carmen replied.

Still, her wait was long enough for her to give up repeatedly studying the empty, endless corridor to instead look into his room more directly. It was a cold, rather barren place. She didn't know if all the living spaces for the sortens here were like this one. Actually, she didn't know what any living space for any sorten anywhere was like. Still, there was a surprising lack of personal definition about the room. It was hard to believe Rauon retired from a day's work to…this.

The room was filled with work related material and almost nothing else. The walls were covered by long, drawn-out theories and mathematical equations that, to her, looked like gibberish. Handwritten notes annotated his labor: "Work Harder," "Failure," "Not Good Enough," "Keep Working." She couldn't help but wonder if they had somehow stumbled into Caelus's quarters. The single-minded obsession certainly fit that android more than one of the politest people she'd ever met, sorten or otherwise. But Rauon was slowly finding his things, making that possibility less and less likely. And then her eyes fell on one of his work desks and the picture laid front and center on it. She recognized Rauon in the picture but none of the other sortens. It was annotated with the words "Never Forget."

"All right, I've found what I needed. Sorry for the delay," he said as he walked toward her. Carmen held short of commenting on his quarters. Unable to think of anything else to say, she nodded. "Now we just need to figure out how to get back," he added with a groan.

"I don't know how you work here without being driven mad," she remarked as they started walking back.

Rauon laughed lightly. "Perhaps that's why the project

leader designed this place like this. It's as good a reason as any."

"He really designed all of this?" Carmen asked.

"Essentially," the sorten answered. "The project leader is greatly respected for his research. If he requires his labs and facilities to be constructed in a certain way, no one will question why."

"Perhaps they should have," she remarked.

"Perhaps. However, Solitary has been the birthplace of countless breakthroughs. Results are results. Caelus has never really given any detailed rationale for why this facility is built this way, but he often says we need to push to the edge of reason and beyond to unravel the great mystery."

"He's definitely a bit beyond reason," Carmen said under her breath.

The head technician eyed her as she spoke and then seemed visibly disappointed. "To be fair to him, there is nothing rational about Clairvoyants and their abilities."

She shrugged. "I guess that's true."

Rauon looked Carmen up and down several times then, which prompted a quizzical look from her in return.

"Yes?" she asked.

"No, that would be stupid," he said to himself.

She raised an eyebrow. "What are you talking about?"

"Psyche, would you be interested in an experiment?"

She was curious—in fact, quite so. Prudence, however, was not hard to muster. "What kind of experiment?"

"This conversation got me thinking. If you don't mind, I'd like to see just how clairvoyant the Clairvoyant is."

"Come again?"

"I'd like to see if you can get us to where we need to go with no input from me," he elaborated.

Carmen looked at him, her face completely blank. "You can't be serious."

"Quite," Rauon replied as he took out his PDD to take notes. "And don't read me or anyone else. That would obviously invalidate the results."

"Have you ever done this before?"

"Never. I'm not really sure what to expect," he said.

"Okay," Carmen muttered softly to herself.

She started walking down the hall in the direction they were already going. That was easy enough. Rauon followed her, purposely out of sight and taking notes the entire time. She wasn't sure what to expect either. She got directions the same as everyone else whenever she needed to get somewhere.

They entered the large circular room from before, and her first test was upon her. The sortens visibly jumped when she entered.

"Never mind us. Just an experiment," Rauon reassured them.

Carmen ignored the sortens. Her mind raced and her Clairvoyant senses were at full alert, yet she still had no clue what their destination was or how to get there. The only thing she did know was that they needed to get in the elevator. Several sortens aimlessly made their best guess as to which door it was, same as she did. She heard several talking amongst themselves about their personal methods for figuring out this abhorrent room. To her, the conversations seemed like nothing more than admissions that they too had no idea how to get anywhere. But, unlike the sortens, Carmen didn't waste her time trying to explicate the nonsensical. She simply walked toward a door that seemed as good a prospect as any.

She approached the door, hand outstretched. Doubt, for whatever reason, was her overwhelming feeling. The confirmation for her intuition came when the elevator door opened…at the other end of the room. A fresh group of sortens were offloaded into the maelstrom, and Carmen walked toward the elevator. The sortens, however, stood in place while the Clairvoyant knifed through the crowd. None dared to join her and Rauon in the elevator, despite his reassurances. It was quite obvious that being stuck in the room for another few minutes was a better alternative than being stuck in an elevator with a Clairvoyant. Despite that, she noted their longing though wary looks as the elevator door closed.

Rauon furiously took notes next to her. She ignored him while she tried to figure out what floor they were supposed to go to. Just then, the elevator door opened again, since they had yet to move. The sortens waiting in the room looked at her in shock, surprised she was still in the elevator.

"Sorry," she muttered, frustrated that she couldn't remember which button Rauon had initially pressed.

The door eventually closed again, and she was left with the sound of the sorten's note-taking. She noticed that the volume of his notes was different depending on which button her finger hovered over. The elevator opened again.

"Sorry, sorry," she said, annoyed.

Then Carmen pressed a button and hoped for the best. When the door opened again, it was at the requested level. She looked at Rauon before she stepped out. His look in return was encouraging, like a parent urging their child to take their first steps.

She walked out of the elevator with him in tow and entered the meandering corridors of Solitary. This one was just as empty and nondescript as its kin. It was hard to know if she'd ever been on this level before. It was harder to know if where they needed to go was even some place she'd been before. The doubt that was with her in the elevator remained her company, but now she felt oddly pressed to continue.

Her pace was not swift. To anyone watching, it seemed like the Clairvoyant was feeling out every step she took. She ran her hand along the wall for no particular reason. Then that felt wrong, and she walked over to the opposite side of the corridor and did the same thing with her other hand.

She could have been walking in circles over and over again without knowing it in this hell. It was hard to be completely sure; everything looked just slightly different in its sheer sameness. That subtle aspect of Solitary's design was just as vexing as everything else about it. She sighed softly and, perhaps as silent protest, suddenly felt the need to walk on the ceiling. Rauon's PDD nearly melted from his note-taking when she continued the trek upside down. She had her fill in only a few seconds and returned to the floor to walk like everyone else.

Carmen glanced at Rauon before she continued. His eager, bright eyes met hers, but he said nothing. She decided it was a pretty fair guess that the little experiment wasn't over. Her hand soon found a seam for one of the panels hidden in the walls, and she walked into the next corridor after another soft sigh.

The new corridor looked exactly the same, which made her eyes grow wide.

She went through another hidden exit built into the walls and entered another corridor that looked exactly the same as the previous two. This time, she sneered, though her feelings of doubt didn't grow in intensity, which was as good a sign as any. It was the only thing she had to go on at this point.

On they went till the corridor split into two. Of course, they looked exactly the same. She started down one of them before abruptly stopping for reasons she'd never consciously know. Then she chose the other. It wasn't a pinprick on her consciousness, which was at times a Clairvoyant's closest company that made her change her mind. There was no prompting at all, as far as she could tell. It just seemed right.

Her head turned slowly back and forth as she went. She had no idea what she was looking for. Nevertheless, a determined focus came to Carmen's face. Her pace slowed for no particular reason, and her eyes fixed on a section of the wall. She was certain there was a panel behind it. Her hands felt along the wall yet discovered nothing. She rolled her eyes when she realized the panel was a half-step to her left.

"No, Psyche, don't," Rauon said when she moved to open it, but his words came too late.

Carmen froze in place. This wasn't a new corridor that looked exactly the same as every other, nor even an elevator. The space was darkened, and she could hear people talking even though she couldn't make out what they were saying. She walked inside, entranced. Rauon made another protest she didn't acknowledge. The room opened up after a short hallway. A couple more steps let her see banks upon banks of computers. A few sorten technicians were talking with someone on some sort of comlink system.

"We've completed the latest batch of tests. Arch Angel Alpha is now eighty percent the overall capability of Phoenix," the person they were communicating with said. "Arch Angel Beta is at eighty-seven percent," he continued.

"Did you receive subjects 143 to 149?" one of the technicians asked.

"Yes," the person on the comlink said. "They will be ready for tests with Arch Angel Prime in no more than two days."

Carmen had no idea what they were talking about. Rauon

was doing everything short of grabbing her to get her to leave. She ignored him, but it was a short-lived effort.

"What are you doing here!" a sorten guard yelled at them. He trained his weapon on her, and she raised her hands to show she wasn't looking for a fight. "Director Mu—" he began, activating his intercom.

"No, no, the security director is not needed," Rauon said hurriedly, cutting him off.

"Explain yourself!" the guard spat.

Rauon stood between him and Carmen. "We're just conducting an experiment. She walked inside before I could stop her," he answered quickly. "She didn't know this was a restricted area."

The guard looked at him and then eyed Carmen suspiciously. "Terrans can't be trusted. You know what they are capable of."

"You can trust her," Rauon said. "If she wanted to kill us, she would have done so already. Do you honestly think you'd be able to stop her alone otherwise?" The guard paused for a moment and looked between the two of them again. "We'll be on our way. Report this to the project leader if you must, but do not saying anything to Mugal." Then Rauon turned to Carmen. "Let's go."

"Why don't you want him telling Mugal?" Carmen asked as he tried to rush her out of the room.

"Because this would be all the excuse he needs to terminate the two of you," Rauon responded. "Come on, get going," he said.

She took her time nonetheless, her eyes and ears at complete attention.

"Transiting to new position. Next communication in a standard week," the person on the other end of the comlink said.

Carmen heard no response. In only a few seconds, Rauon ushered her out of the room, and the panel was closed behind them. She stood still for a moment and stared at the wall while she came to grips with what had just happened.

"What is that room?" she asked.

Rauon hesitated. "Comm room." Carmen nodded. "Let me lead," he continued as he began walking, making it quite apparent that it wasn't a request. "We don't need any other surprises."

She nodded again and dutifully followed, and the two of them walked in silence. It amazed her that anyone was able to have any sense of direction in this place. Rauon kept glancing in her direction. After about the fourth or fifth time, she gave him a curious look.

Tentative, he asked, "You didn't go there on purpose, did you?"

"You can't be serious," she said. "I really don't know how anyone is able to find anything here."

Rauon nodded slowly. "I didn't think so."

His pace quickened after that exchange, and he seemed to regain his cautiously optimistic confidence again. They were back at the elevator sooner than Carmen thought possible. She had only been off by a floor from where they were supposed to be. Rauon kept his fast pace. She guessed their diversion had put them a little behind. Wandering the feature-less corridors for only a few more minutes brought them to the medical bay. She wondered why they were back here but didn't think it was worth asking. Rauon walked inside without pause. She was unable to do so as casually.

The dying or dead Clairvoyant Constructs were arrayed in gruesome efficiency. Pieces of some sat on the beds and in isolation chambers all around her. The medical bay seemed more a lab than a place of healing.

"Please wait a moment. I must set up some equipment," Rauon said, not appearing to notice her reticence.

Carmen nodded glumly, though he wasn't looking at her. She hadn't ventured much past the entrance. Her Clairvoyant senses were fully aware and there was nothing she could think to do to mute them. Her arms came to her on their own accord, wrapping around her chest in a hug. Yet, she could not avert her eyes from the horror. From her first step, she was submerged in it.

The top part of a Construct's skull was removed and his chest cavity was split open. One of the doctors walked by her then. His clothes were covered in blood. The only clue that the sorten even noticed was when he dropped the clothes into a biowaste bin and retrieved another set. Then a Construct who was very much alive weakly reached out to her. The doctor tending him spoke into some sort of voice recording device.

"Subject 137 was exposed to a Clairvoyant heat radiation beam that had a recorded temperature of 500,000 Jkals, sufficient to vaporize all known materials," the doctor said.

Carmen didn't pay much attention. The Construct lay in the bed, making pained moans from time to time. He didn't say anything, if he was even able to speak. His face…she couldn't really describe. She'd never seen such an expression of fear and anguish in a living being before. She brought her hand to her face to hide her disgust as best she could. Then she looked at the doctor.

"Aren't you going to do anything?"

The doctor ignored her. "Subject 137 has severe category burns over sixty-seven percent of his body. While subject will expire without direct intervention, bioelectric burn mitigation showed a thirteen percent improvement over prior batch of subjects."

The Construct moaned particularly loud but stopped reaching for her when it was obvious that she wouldn't do anything to help him.

"At least give him something for the pain," Carmen said more insistently.

The doctor glared at her over his shoulder. "Don't be preposterous. He is an asset. He has served his purpose. We will make another."

She gave no reply. She just looked at the asset on the table, and he looked back. She could feel him straining to hold on, but his hold was only getting weaker. She looked away and swallowed hard when he finally died in front of her.

"Psyche," Rauon called. "I need you here."

Carmen left the now dead Construct and walked toward the head technician, but her thoughts still lingered.

"Please sit here," he said, gesturing to one of the few open beds.

Carmen didn't do so immediately. Instead, she stared at Rauon for a second or two while he got comfortable across from her. If anything here bothered him, it didn't show. She guessed it was best not to mention it. He pulled out a device to scan her bioelectric field and got to work.

"I thought you did that already?" she asked. He frowned a little. "Yes, I know, don't move. But I have to ask," she said.

"You can talk; it just makes the scan take longer," Rauon said. Carmen nodded, which caused him to frown again.

"Sorry," she said sheepishly.

Rauon batted her apology away. "Just try to stay as still as you can. But, to answer your question, Caelus wants a follow-up scan after the readings from your fight yesterday—"

"To make sure the first scan was done correctly?" Carmen cut in.

"Exactly. Good science is as much about eliminating assumptions as it is about making good theories."

"So, what's your theory?" she asked.

The scan required Rauon to move around her slowly. "It's a bit early to postulate," he replied as he moved beside her. Carmen looked at him pointedly and rolled her eyes at his answer. "If I must guess," he continued after her prompting, "I simply believe the same thing I always have. That your kind is more complex than you first appear. There may be a hundred variables that we don't even know we don't even know."

"We don't even know how we work," Carmen said. "In a practical sense, I mean."

He appeared to be amused by her reply, which was a little surprising. "That is to be expected. If you don't mind me saying, sorten science is more advanced than terran. And we've had longer to study the…issue," he said, trying to find the right word. "It's a pity we don't get more natural Clairvoyants to study. It's difficult to form a baseline from the data we have so far."

Carmen turned her head to look at the dead Clairvoyant Constructs all around her. Rauon groaned.

"Psyche, please keep your head still."

"Natural baselines?" she asked coldly.

He didn't detect her change in tone. "Yes. Clairvoyants that are not clones or Constructs," he said as he moved to her back. "It's always exciting when we get a new Clairvoyant to examine. Your bioelectric fields are all unique, if only slightly in some cases. It makes for very interesting study, but it also makes it very difficult to make predictions or models. Honestly, our models were looking very promising till you came along. Now, well…you know." He paused to allow her to respond, but she said nothing. "I've always found it absolutely fascinating that an individual Clairvoyant's bioelectric field never changes, even as they get older. Did you know that?"

"Yes," Carmen answered, though her mind was too preoccupied to really pay attention to what he was saying. "We can sense it. It's like knowing someone's face but deeper. You always remember a Clairvoyant you've met before," she added.

"Interesting. I'd like to discuss that further, if we may."

Carmen nodded out of reflex, but she wasn't thinking about a word he said. She instead thought about the dead Clairvoyant Constructs. She thought about Phaethon, and what Caelus and maybe even Rauon may have done to him. On and on, the idea turned in the corridors of her mind till she had to give voice to it.

"Where do you get the natural Clairvoyants?" she asked, interrupting whatever he was saying.

"Oh, them? No one place in particular," he said. "Some are prisoners of war, but we get very few of those for obvious reasons. Most are children, bought from slavers or mercenary groups."

"Children?" Carmen asked, surprised. "How young?"

"We don't discriminate by age. It's hard enough to get Clairvoyants to study as it is," he answered. "I believe the youngest ever brought here was around three or four standard months old." Rauon was still behind her and couldn't see her grimace. "I don't know where they get them from. I always assumed they were kidnapped in civilian raids, probably on less well-defended colonies."

"So, these groups invade some outlying colony and steal their children?" Carmen asked, turning to face him. He stopped what he was doing and groaned again. "Sorry," she muttered after a sigh. Then she faced forward and redoubled her efforts to stay still.

"I can't say for certain. It's just a guess," he said. "Clairvoyants are in high demand. You should know that. Even, if not especially, children."

"Why does anyone want children?"

"As I said, we take what we can get," Rauon said. "I'd like to have statistically relevant numbers of multiple age groups if I could. Now, for any specific preferences, I can only make educated guesses."

"Guess, please," she said as she pondered the possibilities herself.

"Well, there are many ways a young Clairvoyant can be an asset," he began. "Despite a Clairvoyant's inherent intuition, young and especially very young Clairvoyants can still be influenced and even controlled into a certain way of thinking or acting, which can be beneficial. The mind is fragile and can be irrational. I believe terrans call it the 'carrot and the stick,' for whatever reason. The right abuses in the right ways—pressure applied in just the right points and in just the right amount—can make an individual do or become anything you want them to be. Some methods are more brutal than others." He paused for a moment as he fiddled with something on his PDD. "It is interesting science that I've thankfully never had to undertake. But I do have some studies I can give you, if you'd like to read them."

Carmen felt a chill along her spine. Rauon walked in front of her, and she watched him with her eyes. "I'd rather not," she said with a hollow voice.

He made no reply as he sat down. He was still dealing with his PDD. Carmen waited patiently.

"Scan is complete," he eventually said. "I do apologize. I know it's difficult to stay still for so long." Carmen raised her hand and shook her head. "But, if you don't mind, I'd like to ask you some questions. Please answer as truthfully and completely as you can."

She leaned back slightly, caught off guard by the change in focus. "What type of questions?" she asked, curious.

"Tell me about your parents?"

"My parents?" Carmen asked.

"Yes. There is a component of what makes a Clairvoyant clairvoyant that is genetic, though it is difficult to say how much. We will sequence your genes, but for now, anything you can tell me will be helpful. Honestly, I prefer interviewing. Raw data never gives the complete picture."

"Oh," she muttered.

"And you can skip any physical description. That doesn't really matter. Tell me about their personality, history... anything you can," he added before she could get started.

Carmen sat quietly for a long moment. It wasn't really a question anyone had ever asked her before. Clairvoyants, and most normals who weren't terrified of her, knew better than to ask. Even Michael had never asked her about her parents. She looked at Rauon. His face was eager and curious, as it always was. Her gaze dropped as her thoughts turned inward.

"I don't really know my parents," she said. "Potential Clairvoyants are taken at a very young age to a special facility for training and...adjustment," she continued, trying to find the most accurate description of the process. "I was taken when I was six, which is about standard."

"Yes, yes, I know of this practice," Rauon said. "However, I hoped you'd be able to tell me something about them. Is there really nothing you can say?"

Carmen looked down again as she thought. "I know they were sad."

"What do you mean?"

"I don't really know," she said. "I don't remember much from…before, but when I think of them, I know they were sad. They never said anything to me about it. I just knew. Just…sadness, all the time."

Rauon paused to write something down. "Did you ever try to reconnect with them as an adult?"

"No," Carmen said simply.

"Why not?"

Her eyes looked away from his and searched. She'd never really thought about it before. She knew of no Clairvoyant who had done such a thing. It was difficult to find the right words so that he'd understand.

"They are my parents," she said, looking at him again. "But everything I am, everything I have become, has nothing to do with them." Rauon opened his mouth to speak, and Carmen cut him off. "I don't want to talk about them anymore," she said firmly but without anger.

He gave a silent affirmation and then moved on to his next question. "May I ask you about your time at the facility?"

"Why?"

"For all our science, we're not terran," Rauon said with yet another groan. "Sorten science is generally more advanced, but when studying themselves, terrans will always have the advantage of perspective. It's possible they discovered something about Clairvoyants that we either overlooked or didn't even know to look for."

Carmen nodded slowly. "What do you want to know?"

"Anything you feel open to telling me. Remember, please be as complete and truthful as you can."

She nodded again, and her gaze dropped once more while she thought. It was difficult to know exactly where to start. No one had ever really asked her that either. The facility was so far behind her that it never really entered her daily thoughts. She didn't see how the question mattered.

"You don't have to tell me if you don't want to," Rauon said.

"No, no, it's fine," she uttered quickly.

While she figured out a proper response, she subconsciously touched her chest where Janus had shot her all those years ago. The wound was without any form of scar, such was the state of medical technology, but she could still find the exact spot without needing to reflect.

"The majority of the facility is underground. I don't know why," she began, her voice monotone.

"What is its name?" Rauon cut in.

"I don't know," Carmen replied after a little searching. "It has a name, but I don't know it. The facility just kind of...*is*. Everyone refers to it that way—staff, handlers, everyone. It's the facility. That's all it is. I've never wondered what its name was before."

"Go on."

She nodded and continued. "Time was always very weird there. We had no windows or clocks. There were no annual or monthly events, as far as I knew. I mean, no one celebrated birthdays or anything like that. You just knew what needed to be done for that day. Each day was basically the same." She shuddered. "I'd wake up in the middle of the night sometimes and not know if it was day or night, if I was dreaming or awake. Occasionally, my handler would come for me and I wouldn't know it wasn't a dream for hours."

"What was your average day like?" Rauon asked.

"My handler would collect me in the morning and I'd fight constructs. Then I'd go to class, and after that I'd have another fight. I was usually done after that," she said matter-of-factly.

"So basically just fighting?"

"Yes," Carmen said with a sharp nod. "My handler would talk to me, trying to teach me all sorts of stuff. It never really ended. I just fought constructs on and on and on, every day," she added. "But I do remember one day when I was very young when I had to levitate a room full of sand."

"A room full of sand?" Rauon asked.

"Yeah," she replied, unable to help a small smile. "I learned a lot from that—how to think, how my abilities work. Before that everything was so conscious. If I wanted one of my dolls to fly across the room, it did. If I wanted a cookie, it came to me like magic. But I was aware that I was doing it."

"What about after?" Rauon asked eagerly.

His enthusiasm made Carmen laugh. "I don't really think about it," she said.

"What do you mean?" he asked, obviously miffed.

"Exactly what I said. I don't really think about it. I still don't know how I can do what I do, but I just am, just like you just are. I don't really consciously think of any of it… most of the time." She could see the confusion on the sorten's face and decided to elaborate. "It's like breathing, walking, running, or your heart beating. You don't think about it, it just happens. A master painter doesn't think out each and every brush stroke. It—"

"Just happens," Rauon said, finishing for her.

Carmen nodded. "For the most part, that's it. At least, that's the best way I can explain it."

He gave his acknowledgement and then moved on to his next question. "Were there any other events at *the facility* that stand out for you?"

"Let me think," Carmen said as her hand went to the scarless spot on her chest.

She eventually realized what she was doing and quietly

moved her hand away, closing her eyes as she did so. In that moment, her twelve years at the facility endlessly churned in her mind. No one event or day came into focus. Her thoughts didn't sway to Mikayla, Janus, or Kali. She didn't relive every moment of her first fight or her first kill. She'd long analyzed, rationalized, and compartmentalized every memory she ever had of the place. There was her time with Janus, and there was her time with Kali. There was her time alone with Mikayla, and there was her time with her handler. Of course, there was also her time after Mikayla, when she was just alone. She could find no real meaning in any of it and doubted Rauon could either. There was nothing that *stood out*, not really.

Despite that, all the same feelings, never completely forgotten, were readily summoned despite no wish to do so. The same fear Carmen had felt on an almost daily basis coursed through her veins in a cancerous rot that, just like then, sapped the whole of her strength. The smiles that had come to her face mere moments ago were a barely remembered dream of another person she'd never be fortunate enough to meet again. Her body quaked. The feeling of all-pervading powerlessness drenched every moment, just as it had in those long past tear-filled nights.

"I'm sorry," she said after taking a deep breath and opening her eyes. "There really isn't anything. It all kind of blends together after a while," she continued, staring off into the distance as she spoke.

"You sure?" Rauon asked, visibly disappointed.

"Yes."

"All right. Anyway, you said earlier that you were taken to this facility for training and adjustment. What was the purpose of this adjustment?"

Carmen looked away for a second to think. "I don't really

know," she said.

She sat back in her chair and, with no real thought, played her fingers through her hair as she had when she was a kid, before she ever went to the facility. The tie for her ponytail, however, restricted the adventures her fingers could take to only a small range of what was possible. On and on her fingers went, constrained to the same tracks over and over again, even though they were unaware of it. She tired of the journey and rested her hair on her shoulder. It was long enough for her to get a good look without having to turn her head too much.

"I honestly don't really know what the adjustment is for. I just know that it happens."

"What do you mean?"

"Well, I was a handler for a period of time," she began. "So, I know both sides. When I was in the facility, I always assumed there was some grand plan the handlers followed. I assumed they were three or four steps ahead all the time. But when I was a handler for the facility, I never really got any direction. I could ask for advice, of course, but I was implicitly trusted with all aspects of my charge's life."

"What did you teach your charge?" Rauon asked.

"Not really much of anything," Carmen said with a shrug. "I wasn't a very good handler," she added.

"So, then why were you allowed to be one?"

"I don't know," she said yet again. It was now Rauon's turn to look at her hard, and it was easy to see she wasn't being very helpful. "I got the impression that handlers were assigned based on personality to their prospective charges."

"You and your charge were a lot alike?" the sorten interrupted.

"No, not at all," she said quickly. "Ph—he," she started, stopping herself from saying his name, just in case. "He was fiery," she continued, looking away as she thought of him. She smiled. "He was always looking for a fight."

"And that's obviously not like you...I hope," Rauon said.

Carmen took the joke for what it was and smiled again. The conversation, however, took her spirits away too much for her to actually laugh. "No, that's definitely not me," she agreed. She reflected on Phaethon some more. "But there was something else about him. Deeper. He hid that side from me. I suppose all assets keep something from their handler, yet it..." Her voice trailed off as she tried to find the right word.

"Yet it what?" Rauon asked.

She glanced at him. "It was hopeful."

"I see," he said solemnly.

"...No," Carmen replied, "you don't."

Rauon opened his mouth to make a comment but then thought better of it. The two of them sat in silence for a short while till he realized she had nothing else to say. He turned his attention to his PDD.

"I thank you for your input. I know it doesn't seem like much, but it is helpful," he said as he took notes. Carmen nodded. "I'll just be a few minutes." With that, he went back to his PDD, and she got comfortable.

She watched him as he studiously wrote down everything. She had never been one for notes or journaling, like Phaethon. Most of her time was spent trying to forget. There was no perfect account of her past. Even if there were, she would be hard-pressed to believe any of it. She didn't believe it when it was happening. Like almost everything in a Clairvoyant's life, it just was. There was no intrinsic meaning behind any of it.

She wasn't content to just sit in silence as the scientist continued his work. "What do you use the interview for?" she asked. "It can't really be that useful."

"I'm not sure what I can use it for. Not yet," Rauon responded. "With things like this, Clairvoyants and really everything, it's hard to know what is relevant or important in the moment. Years from now," he said, holding up his PDD for emphasis, "this interview could be the key to solving the mystery. Anything is possible."

"I doubt it," Carmen said.

"You never know. It's my job to always be open to the possibility. That's the entire point of my research: the possibilities."

Carmen shook her head while pursing her lips in disbelief. "How do you do it?"

"Do what?" Rauon asked.

"Do what you do. You're receptive to almost everything. It's...different," she said. "You're nothing like Caelus or Mugal."

"You've suggested that before, but we all want the same thing. The project leader and the security director have their ways. I know you don't agree with them, but they are just as reasonable as I am. Maybe more so."

Carmen shook her head again. "I think you're selling yourself short. Like, I'm sure you have a life outside of Solitary. I can't imagine Caelus doing anything other than driving himself crazy as he tries to figure out something or another about Clairvoyant beasts," she said, trying to imitate his tone.

"No," Rauon said. He seemed confused by the suggestion. "Most everyone here is solely focused on our end goal and nothing else."

She didn't respond right away. She thought about his quarters and the single-minded focus evident in every inch of the space, but then she thought about the picture in his room of the other sortens that said "Never Forget."

"You don't have a family?" she asked, confused.

Other than a brief pause in his note-taking, it seemed like Rauon didn't hear her words. He went back to his work like he had no other concern. Carmen waited, and for the first time since she'd been in Solitary, the head technician ignored her.

"Well?" she asked again.

He glanced at her. "I had a family."

"Had?"

"Yes, *had*," he answered coldly, taking her aback. "They died in this war, in the destruction of our home worlds by the terrans. I would have been with them, but I decided to forgo my vacation to finish some research I was doing here."

"I'm sorry," Carmen muttered, at a loss for anything else to say.

Rauon seemed completely unmoved by the apology. "I used to have long, philosophical discussions with the project leader before…then. I was always struck by how hurried he was. Every test result and analysis never came fast enough. It didn't make sense to me. Clairvoyants have been studied for decades and will continue to be studied for decades—centuries. What difference did it make if some bit of research was delayed by a day or two?" Carmen nodded slowly. "His reply was always the same. 'You don't know the Clairvoyant beasts as I do. Their Dark is always set against us, all of us. It has been too late for us from the moment we discovered the vermin. We will lose the whole of our kind unless we discover some defense against them. I fear the fires of their wanton destruction will touch every corner of the galaxy.'"

In that moment, Carmen thought of some of the things Kali had said about sortens. She'd spent most of her energy during those conversations trying to block out her old handler's bile. Despite Kali's intent behind what she said, there was still an element of truth to it.

"Everyone in Solitary is here for their own personal reasons. We accept only volunteers," he continued. "Over twenty-five billion have been lost in this war on all sides, and it hasn't even been a year."

"But the sortens surrendered," Carmen pointed out.

"Yes," Rauon agreed. "Yes," he said again softly, reflexively. "But our work is still important. There is no home for most of us to go back to. I was never for the war or our occupation of your kind. After witnessing the horror of it all, the mass destruction, I can offer no rationalization for any of it." He paused for a moment. "What is it that Clairvoyants like to say? Things just are?" he asked, his tone almost patronizing. "I understand the purpose of the attack. I understand what it meant for the war—why it happened. But, in an instant, all that I knew no longer existed…"

He took a deep breath, and it seemed like he was holding back from saying more. Then he looked around the room slowly. "We're safe here in Solitary, studying, researching… while the galaxy plays out its own drama, none the wiser. All there is is Solitary, its endless corridors, and our goal. No one here would say there's anything else. Not now."

Carmen nodded slowly, and the two of them stared at each other, neither saying nor even thinking about saying a word. They were mere feet apart, but in that moment, the gulf between them seemed insurmountable. The sorten had long since finished with his PDD. The Clairvoyant sat still, unsure if he was waiting for some type of response.

Rauon mercifully ended the silence first. "We have other tasks."

She nodded, and they left the medical bay for the endless corridors of Solitary.

18

TRUTHFUL DECEIT

Inertia stared at Carmen for a moment. His face was focused and serious. *"Tell me what happened one more time, please,"* he spoke.

She nodded and once again went over every moment of her time with Rauon earlier in the day. She spoke quickly but with as much detail as she could. Her haste was borne out of the simple fact that she didn't know if they would be interrupted before she could finish. The sortens were having a meeting of some sort, which allowed the two of them to be together in the meantime. There was no telling how long that time would last.

Inertia nodded solemnly when she finished. *"This complicates things."*

* * *

Mugal looked at Rauon for an uncomfortably long time. Caelus stood by them, simply watching the proceedings with no comment or reaction.

"She did what?" Mugal bellowed.

"As I said, she went into the communications room," Rauon answered again. "But, once again, I was conducting an experiment. She did not know where she was going. Nothing was compromised."

"And who gave you permission to conduct experiments at will, let alone one so foolishly naïve?" Mugal asked.

"I believe the project leader did," Rauon said, looking at Caelus. "If I may quote, 'I give you full license to uncover all the secrets of the Clairvoyant beasts. Question and be suspicious of everything, no matter how small. The tiniest clue could lead to the solution we're looking for.'"

Mugal was quiet for a long moment. The security director stared at him with thoughts Rauon could only guess at burning behind his mirthless eyes. Rauon wished he hadn't found out what had happened.

"And what did you hope to achieve with your experiment?" he asked.

Rauon hesitated for a second as he thought. "I wasn't sure what to expect, but there's very little about Clairvoyants that anyone objectively knows, particularly their intuition," he said. "They tend to *just know* information for no discernable or probable reason. Clairvoyants themselves don't even know how it's possible…"

Throughout his response, Mugal looked at him as if he were an imbecile. Rauon's voice trailed off before he could dare to make his next point. The security director seemed so annoyed by every word he uttered that Rauon wondered if he'd be vaporized for the insult. It was then that Caelus entered the conversation.

"Go on," the project leader said simply.

Mugal's eyes flashed Caelus a look of betrayal before he turned his attention back to Rauon.

* * *

"*It seems as I suspected,*" Inertia said.

"*Well, we always knew they had two bases,*" Carmen replied.

"*Yes,*" he said with a nod, "*but remember what you said. Whoever was on the other end of that comlink said they were transiting to a new position.*"

"*Yeah,*" she muttered, her gaze dropping as she thought through the event. Her eyes moved wildly back and forth behind closed eyelids as she shifted through the available information, meager as it was. "*A starship?*" she finally exclaimed.

Inertia stood and strolled around the small room they waited in. "*It makes the most sense. A planetoid in the middle of nowhere and a starship that is always moving. And, by that communique, it seems that this place and that ship will have a comms blackout till it arrives at its new position. Then who knows what happens.*" Carmen sat back in her chair and considered what he said. "*We will have to act quickly,*" he continued.

"*Why is that?*" she asked.

"*That starship can go anywhere. It's probably something unambiguous, like a freighter or passenger ship. Any unexplained loss of communications with this base and I bet they disappear. Just like that, gone,*" he said, snapping his fingers for emphasis.

"*Which means we have only a week to get what we need here* and *find that ship,*" Carmen said, the gravity of it all hitting her for the first time. Inertia nodded slowly. "*That does complicate things.*"

* * *

"Fine, the experiment *might* have been justified," Mugal said. "But I don't trust them."

He looked at the security monitor next to them, which showed the two Clairvoyants talking. He'd give all four of his legs to know what they were discussing, undoubtedly some subterfuge. Solitary didn't have any need to spy on its personnel, though, so an audio recording system had never been installed. The male paced around the room slowly while the female sat. He noted after some more study that, while they appeared to be talking, their lips weren't actually moving. A chill crawled up the sorten's spine.

"What do you think they're discussing?" Mugal asked no one in particular.

"Probably why we left them alone in a room," Rauon suggested. The security director shot him a glare, but he was undeterred. "Yes, we must be careful. However, nothing they've done warrants your suspicion. We sought to hire powerful Clairvoyants and powerful Clairvoyants made themselves available. They have fully cooperated with our every request."

Mugal heard everything Rauon said but seemed unmoved. "That is what concerns me. Charon made threats. Charon set limits. Yes, he willingly worked with us, but it was no secret that he hated us as much as we feared him. Hate I can trust. These two Clairvoyants, in that regard, give no such certitude," Mugal said.

Caelus laughed out loud, catching both sortens off guard. "Yes, if there is one and only one constant we can trust, it is that the Clairvoyant beasts seek our complete destruction. Other than those in service to that, they have no stratagems. The destruction of our home worlds should have made that abundantly clear," he concluded with a more serious tone.

"If you believe that, why did you allow them to come here?" Rauon asked straightaway.

"I have already given you that answer."

"You have?" he asked back.

"Yes. As you said, 'I give you full license to uncover all the secrets of the Clairvoyant beasts. Question and be suspicious of everything, no matter how small. The tiniest clue could be the solution we're looking for.' Remember?" Rauon gave his assent, and Caelus continued. "If need be, that includes inviting even our most lethal enemies to our doorstep. It is clear that the Clairvoyant scourge can be answered in no other way."

He suddenly got a faraway look in his eye. "All of my life I have studied the demons. The more I learn, the more certain I become that we will not continue if we remain as totally defenseless against them as we are. There are billions of terrans throughout the galaxy. Now they are weak, but if even ten percent of them gained the self-awareness of their inborn ferocity, the beasts would raze our civilization to the very ground! They have but one ultimate purpose: destruction. It has never changed in the whole of their existence."

"All of them?" Rauon asked. "That's what they all want?" Caelus made no reply other than to look at his subordinate curiously. Rauon turned his attention to the security monitor. "I don't think it's all of them."

Mugal let go a small sneer. "You're referring to the female. I've noticed he is quite taken by her," he said to Caelus.

Rauon turned to look at them both before he looked at the monitor again. He wondered what the Clairvoyants were talking about. Surely nothing as serious as this.

"Perhaps I am," he admitted simply. "There's something different about her."

"She is Clairvoyant through and through," Caelus cut in. "Her wiles even gave me pause. I see the hate in her eyes, though. It betrays her. Do not fall prey to her guile. I don't know when, but they will kill us all. Death is and will always be the Clairvoyant's purpose."

* * *

"*We have to kill them all,*" Inertia said simply.

Carmen froze so completely that her heart even skipped a beat. "*Must we?*" she asked. In the back of her mind, she knew Solitary needed to be destroyed. Still, the stark imminent reality of the possibility made her quake.

"*It's too much to risk otherwise. If that starship gets any warning—any warning at all—we will never find it, which would mean our mission would be null and void.*"

"*Our mission?*" Carmen asked, more to herself than to him.

Inertia looked at her silently. He didn't appear angry. No, he was a long way from anything approaching anger. She looked him in the eyes and saw only calm patience.

"*I know the only reason you are here is for Phaethon,*" he began. "*I know you have no care for myself, my mission, the war, or anything but your charge. But let me remind you that Charon works for the sortens. How many charges has he taken or will he take? Look at the work they're doing. Those Clairvoyants will be dissected and studied with no mercy or compassion. Just like...*" He hesitated. "*Just like Phaethon probably has been,*" he finally said.

"Don't say that," Carmen muttered out loud, her voice quiet.

Inertia didn't respond right away. "It's most likely the

truth and you know it," he said, his tone firm and dispassionate but not harsh.

Carmen slowly shook her head in disbelief. Then she looked at him with pleading eyes. "Don't say it," she repeated.

He was silent for another few seconds. The worry on his partner's face gave him a pained frown. "*I'm sorry you have to be here. I'm sorry for the situation. But I need you, and this is where we are. We have to attack, and soon. And we will probably have to kill every single one of them.*" Inertia took a deep breath. "*What do you say?*"

She nodded glumly and then swallowed hard. "*All right.*"

"*Do you think you can find that comm room again?*"

"*No,*" Carmen said without wavering.

"*Shit.*"

* * *

Rauon looked at Mugal, then at Caelus, and finally at the Clairvoyants on the monitor. The two sortens stared back at him. It stayed like that for what felt like an eternity. For the first time since he'd begun his work at Solitary, Rauon questioned the purpose of it. The two lethal Clairvoyants stayed where they were told, neither bothering nor harming anybody.

He looked at Caelus then. The scientist casually watched him. The intelligence twinkling in his eyes seemed to pierce all that their gaze set upon, unravelling the mysteries of the universe on but a trifle. It was his most dominating feature. But, on second thought, that was too near-sighted a conclusion. Rauon cautiously eyed the project leader's artificial arm and leg. Caelus rarely told the story of how he'd come to have the prosthetics.

Rauon had only heard it told once, which seemed odd now on reflection. It didn't seem to be a painful memory for him. The project leader practically used it as cautionary tale for the new recruits, laughing and even joking about his own foolishness.

In his story, Caelus spoke of how he once had a Clairvoyant lab assistant whose abilities were helpful in his work, and whose open demeanor had lulled him into a false sense of camaraderie. One day, this assistant stole his access codes to free the other Clairvoyant research subjects. Caelus said he confronted the Clairvoyant on the nature of his betrayal and their working relationship. The Clairvoyant supposedly made no reply—save one. Rauon remembered Caelus's uproarious laughter at this point in the story before he continued. The Clairvoyant burned off his arm and leg and then, after ensuring he wouldn't die, left him there. Caelus had laughed lightly while explaining that the sorten military wanted to use Clairvoyants as living weapons and had thus conditioned them to always fight to the death. The insult of being only maimed by a Clairvoyant was clear. Caelus rarely talked about what happened, but he was quite fond of saying, "That Clairvoyant could have killed me a thousand times with the effort of just a thought."

The project leader stood over both Rauon and Mugal, as always on his hind legs. His patches of burned flesh and his arm and leg made of metal had long since escaped notice, but now, in this moment, Rauon noticed. The planetoid, down to its most minute detail, was Caelus's construct through and through. He was the foremost author and practically father of Clairvoyant research. This sorten, this great sorten, was the progenitor of nearly it all. Rauon looked up at him, unsure of what he was about to say.

"Sir," he began, "I don't believe you have the best perspective."

Mugal looked like he'd been struck by lightning. Caelus, however, only leaned slightly back as he considered Rauon's words.

"Explain," the project leader said simply.

Rauon steeled himself with a deep breath. "With complete respect, Project Leader, I believe your prior experience with Clairvoyants negatively influences you more than you realize."

"Mind your place," Mugal barked.

"No, please listen to me," Rauon pleaded. "We have an opportunity here that's almost undreamed of," he said, gesturing to the monitor. "Two Clairvoyants—*two* of them— willing to work with us. It's only been a day and Psyche has already been very helpful, and you'd have the security director cast them out the nearest airlock." He paused and looked at the Clairvoyants on the monitor. "I don't know about Inertia, but with Psyche, when I look in her eyes, I don't see hate. I don't know what I see, but it's definitely not that. I…trust her."

Mugal scoffed loudly and groaned. "Before you get too enamored, don't forget yourself. How do you think the Clair- voyant countermeasure we develop will be used? Natural Clairvoyant or Construct, the interest of the military has remained the same," he said. "How could it not? We deserve blood for blood for the billions the terrans slayed. Don't you think your children deserve at least that much?"

Rauon could think of no reply. He eventually looked at Mugal and gave a small nod. Caelus said nothing either. He walked past his two subordinates like the master and commander he was and stopped in front of the monitor to watch the Clairvoyants for a time.

"Trust," he said as he turned around. Then he looked down at his artificial arm. "We must not forget ourselves to the vexing ways of those cursed creatures. Do not begrudge Rauon, my old friend," he said to Mugal, the twinkle in his eye returned anew. "It is the nature of our work that we get lost in it from time to time. I appreciate that he had the courage to light the way."

"Thank you, Project Leader," Rauon said.

Caelus waved the apology away and looked at the monitor again. "Our guests have been waiting long enough. I will see them now."

* * *

"*Why do we have to go back to the comm room?*" Carmen asked. "*Can't we just blow up the planetoid?*"

"*You misunderstand. Getting back to the comm room is not about killing the people there. Not exactly,*" Inertia responded. "*It has to do with how communications systems work. Signals can't be sent in random directions with any hope of a response. Not with the distances involved.*" Carmen nodded, and he continued. "*The starship said they would communicate again in a standard week. That means this facility would have to have some idea of where the starship is at that time in order to talk to it, probably down to the sector at least.*"

"*And how helpful is that?*"

He paused as he thought through his answer. "*Finding one single starship that could be anywhere in the galaxy is like trying to find a needle on a planet.*"

"*And since we don't know what the starship is, there are multiple needles that aren't the right one,*" Carmen said, thinking it through herself.

Inertia nodded slowly. "*Determining the sector is like*

trying to find a needle in a country instead of a whole planet —difficult but vaguely possible."

She looked away to think. *"Maybe we could just let Gungnir...and Widget know,"* she said, stopping herself from rolling her eyes as she thought of her. *"They can check it out while we just stay here. Both places would be covered."*

"Sure, great plan. Only a few problems with it," he began, his tone even and factual. *"The only long-range transmitters that we know of are in the comm room or* The Lady. *I quite doubt they'd let us use the comm room. Considering their response to you stumbling upon it, I think it's safe to say we weren't supposed to even know it existed. As for* The Lady, *we could either ask them to let us make a transmission, which I doubt they'd oblige, or we could sneak aboard and transmit, which they'd detect. Besides, Gungnir needs to be ready in case Charon makes another attack."*

"Do you think Charon will attack again? Do you think he already has?" she asked, slightly changing her attention.

"No, I don't think he has," he said. *"If he abducted any Clairvoyants, it probably would have gotten very busy here."* He took a deep breath and let it go pointedly before he continued. *"Unfortunately, we're completely in the dark about everything. Any intel Gungnir has can't get to us here, and everything we know can't find its way to him."* Now I know why the sortens call this place Solitary, Carmen reflected. *"It's part of the job. Nothing I haven't experienced before, but it is damn annoying,"* Inertia continued.

She nodded and then rested her head on her outstretched hand. She thought of all the death to come and wondered why it still gave her pause, considering the trajectory of her life thus far. Everything seemed almost laughably inevitable, despite her best attempts. Different circumstances and different choices, yet the same outcomes. What was the bother?

She put any further reflection on hold, though, and turned toward the door. Inertia looked at it as well. Someone was coming. Caelus walked into the room a moment later. Mugal and Rauon were right behind him. Caelus's expression of arrogant, smug superiority was as unabated as ever. Mugal had the look of someone grinding diamonds to dust between his teeth. But Rauon seemed oddly pleased. He gave her the sorten equivalent of a smile, and Carmen looked at him curiously. She could only guess he'd managed to dissuade any possible negative consequence from their little trip to the comm room. At least, that was what she hoped. If so, she was sure he'd tell her about it later.

Caelus walked directly toward her and stopped right in front of her. Carmen, still sitting, looked up at the sorten. He said nothing, just stood and stared, which made her feel like a child about to be scolded. For some reason, she thought of Janus and Kali, and even how Phaethon acted around her. She looked back at Caelus expectantly, but nothing came forth. She gave Rauon a curious look, who returned it with the same expression. Then she turned to look at Inertia.

"No mind of your own, beast?" Caelus asked. "Don't look to another. What I need from you is very simple. I trust you'll accommodate me."

Carmen looked at him again, but once again he said nothing. She'd just accepted that there were levels of odd depravity Caelus was capable of descending to, but this was a new one.

"So…what do you—" she tried to ask, but she was cut short when the sorten slapped her hard across the face with his artificial hand.

The shock of the action stung more than the actual pain.

Carmen's hand went to her face by reflex while she tried to process what had just happened.

"Our dear Rauon says I may have lost perspective," Caelus said. "It is hard to know with certainty. What say you, creature?"

"*What do I do?*" she asked Inertia hurriedly.

"*I have no idea.*"

Caelus looked down at her. Her hair was mussed, her lip was bleeding, and her cheek was red. She still cradled it. The animal looked up at him. Her manner supported the ruse that had beguiled so many. She looked actually hurt—not physically, not completely. No, the affront seemed to sap her so much that a passerby would think he could stamp her out like so many flowers. He wouldn't be fooled by it. He'd been in this situation before with so many of her kind.

"What, no comment? I expected more out of a Clairvoyant."

Carmen stared at the madman with no idea of what he was looking for. He suddenly slapped her again, this time on the other side of her face. Both Mugal and Rauon flinched in surprise when it happened. She even saw Inertia take a quick step forward to intervene before he stopped himself. She didn't know what Caelus wanted—seemingly no one in the room did—but she did know she wasn't going to be slapped again.

He moved to hit her once more, and she grabbed his hand before it could make contact. She glared at him and squeezed as hard as she could. Caelus made no reaction. Perhaps he couldn't feel pain through his artificial limb. Strangely enough, he seemed pleased.

"Yes, it's there. I always knew it was there," he said softly to himself. "You see, Rauon? You see the hate in her eyes?" Caelus asked, turning to his colleague before returning his attention to Carmen. Rauon said nothing. "Tell me. Surely you see it now?"

Carmen glanced at Rauon. Her expression didn't change, despite that she harbored no ill will toward him. She'd been disgusted since she'd been here. She'd been horrified, terrified, and many other things. But, for the first time in a long time, she was truly angry. The feeling surged within her, and it was shockingly difficult to contain. It wasn't from the pain of being slapped; she'd suffered far worse. It wasn't from the knowledge that this psycho had probably butchered her charge without a shred of remorse. No, it was simpler. He thought her an animal, a beast, a *monster*, and she had given in to his presumption after his crude provocation. She hated that he was able to do that. More important, she hated herself for the fact that it had happened so easily.

"Yes, I see it," Rauon muttered, but he sounded like he just wanted the experience to be over.

Carmen looked at Caelus then. The sorten stared her in the eye. She couldn't remember the last time a non-clairvoyant had done so without wavering.

"Why don't you kill me?" he asked, though it seemed like he was talking more to himself than to her. "You would like to. Yes, you would very much like to. Even now, you try to harm me despite your restraint."

It was then that she realized she was still squeezing his hand. She let go by practically throwing his hand away. Caelus laughed lightly and took a couple of steps back. Carmen pressed her lips together. She looked at Inertia, silently voicing her displeasure. His face was serious, but it was obvious he was thinking four moves ahead. She cared about none of that, though, not at the moment. She glared at Caelus again. He was right. She did hate him, and there was no point in hiding that. He laughed again before he turned to leave the room.

Then he stopped next to Rauon. "I hope *this* experiment was instructive," he said.

He left the room after that. Carmen glared at him the entire way.

19

MONSTER

Carmen rested an arm on the padded, heat resistant wall of the fight room and then leaned her head against it. She tried to forget about the dead Constructs littered about the room. Rauon was presently overseeing their removal, allowing some time for her mind to wander.

She closed her eyes. "*Why are we here?*" she asked Inertia telepathically after a sigh. He was overseeing everything in the observation booth with Caelus and Mugal.

"*To find out why the sortens are seeking Clairvoyant mercenaries,*" he answered.

When she opened her eyes, she noticed there was still blood on her hand. She rubbed it against the wall and then turned around, still feeling unclean.

"Sorry for the delay, Psyche. We'll be able to begin again shortly," Rauon said.

Carmen glanced at him. "Take your time," she said softly. As soon as the room was clean, there would just be another battle. It was constant battle.

"Thank you," he said before getting back to the cleanup.

Sorten thoroughness was certainly in full display. They

didn't simply remove the bodies so she could slaughter a fresh batch. No, they took pictures and recorded the exact cause of death before each dead Construct was removed. Presumably, just "death by kick to the face" or "death by heat beam" wouldn't do. She ignored their mechanizations and looked at the observation booth as she took a deep breath.

"*I know that,*" she spoke. "*But what's the point anymore? This place is a dead-end.*"

"*This place isn't a dead-end. It's death,*" Inertia replied.

Carmen agreed at first, but her eyes dropped as she considered the whole of her time here. Her thoughts eventually coalesced on one true description for the perpetual despair of Solitary. "*It's not death, it's lifeless. All of it, all the people who work here, lifeless.*"

"*Perhaps, but I don't really see a difference,*" Inertia responded. She even saw him visibly shrug in the observation booth.

"*There is,*" she spoke. "*This place is lifeless, sure as the planetoid itself. No one realizes it. It's normal to them. I don't know how that can be, but it is. That scares me.*"

There was a long pause before Inertia said anything else. She looked at him, and he stared right back. She was well aware that he was evaluating the status of his partner, and it was then that she realized she actually *was* his partner. She'd been too focused on Phaethon, Charon, and everything else to really consider Inertia. He was always so professional, so confident in everything he did, that the idea that he was just as trapped here and dependent on her as she was on him had never crossed her mind. She looked away and swallowed hard as the thought took on its full weight.

"*You aren't going to crack, are you?*" he asked.

Carmen looked at him again. "*No. No, I won't.*"

"*Good,*" he responded.

Nothing else was said for a moment. The relaxed but ready poise that carried through Inertia's entire person was heartening. Carmen, however, couldn't pull herself from her distraction. Her mind reflected over and over on long-buried memories as it had since she first arrived at this place. As always, there was no one image or thought when her subconscious went on this seemingly circuitous journey. She dimly remembered Mikayla's fur and what it felt like to run her hands through it. She had to remind herself of the confusion she had felt when she first met Kali. Janus's harsh words echoed in her skull every day but were barely heard. And then there was Michael. He seemed as forgotten as the ghostly image of her parents.

"*Are you all right?*" Inertia asked.

Carmen glanced at him. She guessed she looked uncomfortable. She looked away to think. "*It's just...*" she began. "*When I was girl, I used to go to a bluff and just sit. Mostly alone, just sitting, watching the clouds and the waves crashing. Just...still, I miss that peace. I've spent almost three quarters of my life fighting, constantly fighting. Can't really win and can't really be defeated either. Only loss,*" she concluded. She looked at the blood stains all around her from the dead constructs. Then her gaze dropped, putting a silent exclamation point on her thoughts.

Inertia watched her but said nothing.

"*I'm fine,*" she spoke, feeling prompted to reassure him in some way. "*But—*"

"*I know you're fine,*" he spoke. "*Unfortunately, Caelus seems to have taken some perverse interest in you. I don't know why.*" Carmen felt her cheek when he said that. "*He knows you don't like fighting. I think he's trying to provoke you.*"

"*Why?*"

"*As I said, I don't know.*"

She looked away and took a deep breath. "*So, what are we waiting for? Let's just attack.*"

"*Not yet. Soon, but not yet.*"

"*What are we waiting for?*" she asked again.

"*I still haven't figured out how their computer system works. I'm hoping we can use it to find the comm room. From there, we can track down their other base. Maybe there will be other details of their operation in the computers as well. It's quite obvious that neither Charon nor the captured Clairvoyants have been here for some time. There's nothing really to be gained on that lead.*"

Carmen gave a sharp nod. "*Right.*"

Rauon turned to face her. "Psyche, if you're ready, we may begin."

"Sure. Just a moment," she said. "*Anything else?*" she asked Inertia.

"*Nothing I can think of right now,*" he replied.

She nodded, though she was no longer looking at him. Two Constructs entered the room, and she got ready. The ones she fought today were stronger than any of the other Clairvoyant Constructs she had fought before. She guessed that all the data collecting and cataloging the sortens were doing was already paying off. These Constructs were armed with swords similar in construction to hers. She was bare-fisted, as had been the case with all of her fights up to this point. One day, every day.

"Psyche, we'd like it if you'd please use your weapon for this test," Rauon said.

She didn't need to be told twice. Her sword rested against the wall on the other side of the room. A mere thought caused it to fly to her waiting hand.

"You may begin," he said.

* * *

Inertia watched the battle with visible intent but only casual interest. Caelus and Mugal stood near him, as did a contingent of Clairvoyant Construct guards. The guards were new additions for today. He figured it wouldn't take too long before Mugal realized sorten-only security was a waste of time against a Clairvoyant.

The guards were not Inertia's chief concern, though. They were simply one complication among many. The status of his partner wasn't much of a worry either. Despite Edge's reluctance for fighting and killing, she was quite capable of it when she needed to be. No, his concern was the computers, always the blasted computers. Reading the sortens' minds to obtain passcodes and the like was the expected child's play. Large databases, which were probably secured by allowing only certain terminals access, could be sifted through for hours before anything relevant was found. He doubted he'd have that kind of time when they finally made their move.

Caelus looked at him. "Our copies seem to be making a better show of themselves," he said proudly.

Inertia turned his attention to Edge. She was quite the actress, and the battle was certainly spectacular. Each move and counter, from both sides, seemed to flow like a grand opera. The stress and strain on her face was painfully palpable. Death appeared entirely likely and even imminent for any of the participants at any time. But all that was only for the untrained eye. Somehow, the Clairvoyant always seemed to be in the perfect position to just barely avoid an attack. It was also curious that her opposition was never able to get any real momentum. Any attempt to crowd her or put her completely on the defensive only summoned a swift but not deadly reprisal that simply maintained the status quo.

He had always asked her to be herself, and she was doing just that. It was ironic that reluctance to kill meant prolonged battle, but if she was comfortable, he had no complaint. He didn't want the sortens to know how powerful she actually was anyway. He had never told her as much, but she seemed to intuitively understand that it was prudent to hold some of her raw potential in reserve.

"Yes, it seems that way," Inertia said.

"And you said never," Caelus replied dismissively.

Inertia pursed his lips nervously as Edge took a rather obvious step back in lieu of a killing stroke. Mugal watched the scene with his usual intensity, and when the moment came and went, he glanced in Inertia's direction before watching the battle once more. No comment was made, and the Clairvoyant hoped her little misstep went unnoticed.

"Yes, I did," he said, turning his attention back to Caelus. "You still have yet to change my mind."

"I haven't? Well, in short order, we'll have the results of her bioelectric field compared to archived data and our predictive model. We'll see how changed your mind is then."

Inertia looked directly at the sorten. "I'll save you the suspense. Not at all," he said.

"How do you know this?" Mugal asked pointedly.

"…I'm a Clairvoyant," Inertia said simply.

Caelus laughed at that. Mugal only narrowed his eyes.

"I admit I find your humor at the security director's expense entertaining. I hope you enjoyed it, as I doubt there will be many opportunities for it in the future. The universe is reason, utterly and completely. All that is needed to understand its machinations is to observe its ways long enough. Clairvoyants are no different," Caelus said. "They play at being mysterious and unknowable, but all that is needed is the proper insight."

"I wasn't joking," Inertia said, though he truly had been. The vexed annoyance currently on Caelus's face made the minor effort worth it. "After all I've taught you, you still don't understand the basics." The project leader's face transitioned from annoyance to disdain, and Inertia wished Edge was here to see it. "Clairvoyants are servants, slaves even, of the Dark. The Dark isn't some mystery that can be explored and charted. The Dark is mystery itself. There is nothing wholly rational about its whims. It is any and everything, formless and omnipresent, unstoppable but barely heard. It simply...is."

"Utter nonsense," Mugal muttered.

Caelus silenced him by raising his artificial arm. "We will see, Inertia. We will see." Inertia noted it was one of the few times Caelus had referred to him by name instead of *beast* or *monster*. "Do we have a cross-correlation ready?" he asked one of the technicians.

"Yes, Project Leader, momentarily," one of the technicians said. "Results coming in now." He paused for a few seconds. "Correlation for our copies is at ninety-three percent."

Inertia gave Caelus a questioning glance.

"Variation among our copies is not unexpected at this stage," the sorten said confidently. "There is as much art in crafting their gnomes as science. That, of course, will change over time." Inertia conceded the point with a nod.

"Correlation for Clairvoyant Subject 427111 is at...sixty-four percent," the technician continued.

"Ah, you see? Amazing progress in such a short amount of time," Caelus said. "I swear to you, even the deepest, most guarded aspect of your consciousness will be mapped and catalogued. It is always just a matter of time." Inertia made no response. Truth be told, he seemed totally disinterested in the proceedings. Caelus stomped his foot. "No words for me now, beast? Surely some mocking barb is ready and waiting."

Inertia didn't answer right away. Instead, he changed his focus to Carmen. "*Edge*," he spoke.

"*Yes*," she responded as she stepped out of the way of another attack.

"*It's time to give them another curveball. In about thirty seconds or so, go all out and then throttle back.*"

"*Okay.*"

"An impressive achievement," Inertia said, turning his attention back to Caelus. Mugal eyed him carefully as he spoke. "But I suspect ultimately for naught."

"Explain!" Mugal demanded impatiently. Caelus seemed just as anxious.

"The Dark is not only specific from individual to individual but moment to moment as well. Your model may match Edg—Psyche—at sixty-four percent now," he said, once again having to remember to use her ridiculous alias. "That, however, is just now and only for Psyche. A minute from now, your model may read ninety-seven percent and minute after that only five."

Caelus's eyes became narrower and narrower as Inertia spoke. And then, as if on cue, Edge went into action. A Clairvoyant going "all out" was hardly ever some breathtaking display of strength or speed but of decisiveness. Small sparks rippled along her arms, indicating a rapid change in her bioelectric field. Inertia couldn't help rolling his eyes despite that. She just couldn't go all out even when she was asked to. Some measure of reserve always remained.

In any case, the Clairvoyant's actions took on an added air of graceful efficiency, flowing between and through the Clairvoyant Constructs who appeared almost clumsy in comparison. The effort didn't last all too long. She stepped into one of her opponents' attack at an unexpected moment and then killed him with a stab to the chest in one smooth movement. Then Edge went defensive, pirouetting out of the way of an attack from the other Construct that could but ultimately didn't come. There was a quick pause in the action as she took a deep breath, and just like that it was done. She was back to her previous level.

The sortens made no comment. Mugal, however, looked back and forth between the two Clairvoyants, anger more and more apparent in his features. "The two of you are communicating through telepathy. I should have known. They are toying with us, Project Leader. Purposely skewing the results to hamper our research!" he bellowed. "Guards!"

The Clairvoyant Constructs rushed toward them, but Inertia didn't even glance at them. With the Constructs at his flank, he folded his arms, his attention fixed on Caelus. The sorten stared back.

"Is that true?" Caelus asked.

"Of course, it is," Inertia said. "It's not abnormal for Clairvoyants to communicate telepathically."

"Why would you want to skew the results of the research?" he asked, his tone making it quite obvious that the scientist's curiosity was fully engaged. Mugal bristled with such visible rage that it was a wonder he didn't combust into hellfire.

Inertia laughed, which caught both sortens off guard. "Skew the results?" he asked incredulously. "It's obvious that you've learned nothing from me. I told you from the beginning it was impossible. Yet, foolishly, you've continued the farce. You may as well be obsessed with banging your head against the wall."

"You've gone too far, terran!" Mugal yelled. "This ends—"

Inertia stopped his tirade by shaking his head. Then he glanced at the security director before rolling his eyes. The Clairvoyant Construct guards stood at the ready, tense for the command to attack. The sorten technicians cowered feebly behind their workstations, awaiting the inevitable battle. Yet, for Inertia, even a baby sleeping in his mother's arms had more apprehension.

By this time, Carmen had killed the other Construct, despite her middling effort. With nothing else to do, she and Rauon waited in the fight room, unaware of what was going on in the observation booth.

"Tell me," Inertia said. "If your model truly worked, how could I skew it?" The comment stopped Mugal so completely that he didn't even breathe or blink in response. "How could anything she does in that room matter to your model if it was accurately able to predict and reflect everything about her? As I said, your efforts are a joke."

Caelus suddenly appeared lost. He took a hesitant step away from the Clairvoyant and visibly shrunk. His eyes darted back and forth, searching. "Yes, yes," he muttered. "Foolish," he said to himself. Mugal looked at him, unsure of what to do. The few seconds of silence that followed seemed like hours. "Perhaps I was too hasty in saying the mystery was solved." He swallowed hard. "How…how do you suggest we proceed?" he asked, sounding at a complete loss.

Mugal's mouth fell open. Inertia, however, was waiting for those exact words. He walked past the Clairvoyant Constructs, telekinetically pushing them out of the way, and took a seat at the nearest computer console. The chair was never meant to support a terran frame, but he could manage. The computer, like the chair, was never meant to be used by terrans either. But, at last, he was finally able to examine the system.

"Wh...what are you doing?" Mugal asked, flabbergasted.

Inertia glanced at him and then looked at Caelus.

"The Clairvoyant is right," Caelus said to Mugal. "I think it has come to this. Maybe a less...*refined* mind can uncover the secret. All his insights have proved true thus far."

"But sir, I must protest," Mugal began. "The possible compromise to our operational secur—"

"That is enough, Mugal!" Caelus barked. "You forget yourself! We must finish our research by any means necessary. Employing the services of the Clairvoyant beasts is only a small measure of how far I'd go to ensure our success." He took a breath to calm himself. "No one here seems to genuinely understand the horrors that beset us. If you did, you'd urge me on instead of forestalling my every step."

"Project Leader?"

"Get out of my sight," Caelus spat.

Mugal opened his mouth to say something but then slowly it closed. He dropped his head and walked to the back of the room. Caelus turned his attention to Inertia.

"Shall we begin?" the sorten asked.

Inertia nodded, but he wasn't really listening. His focus was on the computer, and though the layout of Solitary was a bewildering, maddening mess, the computer system thankfully wasn't. Caelus barked orders to some of the technicians, but Inertia didn't pay attention to it. He instead smiled to himself as he slowly figured out how the machine worked. He'd used sorten systems before, but alien logic didn't always flow as expected. That didn't seem to be the case here.

But just then, something else captured his attention. He looked up and noticed the lights were flickering. One of his eyebrows rose curiously. It was unlikely that it was some sort of power failure, not in this place. He knew, even with just his cursory glance into the computers, that there were backups upon backups to prevent that from happening. He also suspected the lights were hardened against Clairvoyant bioelectric interference. There was no reason they wouldn't be. And there was something else. A power was approaching them.

It was different from the Clairvoyant Constructs. The energy of this Clairvoyant was a fiery, angry mass—malcontent personified. Inertia had never known its kind. The lights raged even wilder. The sight, combined with the raw power approaching, struck Inertia as oddly captivating, like a thundering waterfall. Every sorten was completely silent as they looked into the fight room with fretful awe.

"*Inertia!*" Edge said frantically. "*Inertia, what do I do? Talk to me!*"

He couldn't really see the fight room from his position, so he shot to his feet and rushed to the observation booth glass. His partner stood in place, seemingly unharmed by whatever peril was making her so hysterical. Yet her breath was quick and her cheeks were ashen. Her hands even looked like they were shaking. It would be hard to call Edge a paragon of confidence. He couldn't even imagine her carrying herself that way. Still, she had a Clairvoyant's self-assuredness, which he had yet to see waver...till now. Across from her stood the force of nature that would presumably be her opponent. It was a teenaged boy.

He was not a Construct, that much was obvious. Even standing still, the natural Clairvoyant wielded a dynamism those robots could never possess. The entire room was bent to him. There was no denying his presence. Sparks rippled along his body in the flickering dark, casting an almost demonic air to the scene. He was a standard, true blood Clairvoyant through and through. But there was something *off* about him.

His clothes made him look like a well-dressed lab animal. They were simple, durable, and new. But his hair was a tattered mess, with no attempt having been made to tend to it. His skin also looked worn and dirty, as if he couldn't or didn't care to clean himself. One of his most striking features, though, were the scars. Scars were a relic. Modern medicine meant that healing with scarless precision was the pride of every doctor, or at least those who cared about their patients. The scars covering the boy's face, neck, and arms were thus no testament to sorten incompetence. Then there were his eyes. The piercing, focused gaze of the Clairvoyant remained. Underneath the fiery visage, however, was dull, broken emptiness.

"Is that—"

"Phaethon," Carmen finished. *"Yes, that's him."* She paused. *"At least, what's left of him."*

As her old charge stared at her, she had no read on him. Hate, love, fear—there was nothing. There was only a Clairvoyant ready for battle in front of her. He was so primed that even a hair or two on her arm stood on end. The lights stopped flickering and the sparks disappeared, yet Carmen remained frozen in place. She had dream of this day. She had hoped and even prayed for its fruition. Now, standing here, she had no idea what to do.

Rauon stood behind her taking notes, completely unaware of the significance of the moment. She looked at the observation booth, and her partner stared back. His tense face mirrored her own. She looked back at her charge.

"Phaethon?" she asked telepathically. There was no reply. He gave no reaction at all. He just stared at her, if that was even an accurate description. She wondered if he even processed that she was right in front of him with the glass-

eyed way he existed in the world. "*Phaethon, it's me, Edge,*" she tried again.

Inertia could only watch. Telepathy was more direct than verbal communication, and he couldn't hear what was said between them. The body language, however, wasn't encouraging. Phaethon stood almost completely motionless while Edge's hands shook back and forth with pleas Inertia could only guess at.

Caelus turned to him. "Shall we begin?" he asked.

Inertia glanced at the sorten and then looked at his partner still pleading with her charge. He hesitated. The situation dictated action, but the timing wasn't right. He had only just accessed their computer system. Edge looked at him in that moment, at a complete loss. He had no direction for her.

He turned his attention back to Caelus. "Let's begin," he said. Then he walked back to the workstation.

Carmen saw Inertia walk away, and her eyes grew wide. She was on her own. She looked at her old charge. He stared right back at her.

"*Phaethon, what's wrong with you?*" she asked.

"Get out of my head!" he snapped. Carmen smiled. The response, though not what she expected or wanted, was at least a response. "You're not going to trick me. You're not Edge."

Her smile left just as quickly as it had come. "*Of course I'm Edge. Who else would I be?*" she asked telepathically while wishing Phaethon had the prudence to do the same. Rauon was already looking at the two of them strangely.

"I won't believe it. I *can't* believe it! Edge is gone. I'm never seeing her again. You keeping trying your best to break me, but I will never give in to you."

Rauon took a step toward them. "Psyche, do the two of you know each other? And who is Edge?"

Just what I need, she thought with gritted teeth. "No, we don't know each other," she replied under her breath.

Phaethon heard her anyway. "Ah, you see? Even you admit it!" he said. "I don't know who or what you are, but you're not a Clairvoyant. No Clairvoyant would work for this filth."

"*You don't understand!*" Carmen said, throwing her hands up in frustration. "*I am Edge. Remember all those games of chess I made you play?*"

He paused for a moment. "The sortens could easily know that. Maybe one of those machines they prodded me and cut me up with could read my mind or whatever," he said, which made Carmen wince. "It doesn't matter that you know that."

Carmen opened her mouth to respond, but Caelus spoke through the intercom system before she could say anything. "Beasts, this will be to the death. Begin," he said.

Phaethon assumed a guard and took a step toward her. She remained still.

"*I'm not going to fight you,*" she spoke.

He halted his advance. Indecision was a unique form of torture for the monsters of the Dark. It made the Clairvoyant's hands shake slightly till his eyes narrowed.

"Then just stand there and die!" he yelled.

Carmen was unprepared for the speed and violence of his attack. She could only watch, transfixed, her eyes ever widening, as he aimed a kick at her head. The blow was like none she had ever felt before. It sent her tumbling, end over end, into the nearest wall. Her head still spun after she hit, despite that she was no longer moving. It felt like hours passed before she realized she was lying on the floor and even longer to remember how she got there. She stood, and Phaethon was on her almost instantly.

She made no counterattack. The experience of every

battle, every fight, and every contest she'd ever had, in any form, was called upon. She could beat Phaethon; she was quite sure of it. His efforts were rage incarnate, seeking to overcome her by overpowering her fully. She remembered the chess games they played. He was falling into his old traps. There was only so long that she could hold him off while just defending herself, though. Her body shuddered as a punch slipped through her defenses. She groaned as a kick landed home, doubling her over. And with each landed blow, it became harder to thwart his attack. His jaw clenched tight when his punch made her stagger away and then fall to the ground.

"Psyche! Psyche, what's wrong? Fight back!" she heard Rauon say.

She glanced at him. He looked horrified. She looked at Phaethon again and did her best to ignore the sorten. She coughed blood before she came to her feet again.

"*I'm not going to fight you. You know I won't,*" she told him.

"You're not Edge! You can't be!" Phaethon screamed, though his voice sounded weak.

Carmen simply stared at him calmly, resolutely, despite her raspy breath and the blood trickling down her face. He cursed at her before he continued his savage attack.

* * *

Inertia could feel the violence even though he could not see it. Battling Clairvoyants were like no other force in the universe. He could also feel his partner weakening with each passing second...yet she also wasn't. It was a strange dance between her and Phaethon. He could feel that Edge, in totality, was being beaten to a pulp. He could even hear her groans and screams from time to time. Nevertheless, the bulwark that made Edge herself—the frustrated reserve that drove her half-crazy most of the time—could be easily sensed by anyone with the means to do so, now more than at any other time while he'd known her. It wrapped around her like a warm blanket. Oddly, though, that same reserve appeared to provoke ever more fury from her charge, like its very existence was an affront to everything he held dear.

Inertia, however, tried to ignore the battle. Their entire effort here was for nothing if he couldn't figure out the computer. Despite that, his thoughts and his duty were in opposite directions. The tension had his fingers tapping on the table while his eyes madly flickered back and forth, studying his screen at a frenetic pace. He looked up suddenly. This was pointless. He abandoned the computer and walked to where Caelus stood to look into the fight room.

"Your mate is a strange one," the sorten said. "For some reason, there appears to be no fight in her. Pity."

Inertia watched silently. Phaethon's attack looked near desperate. Her young charge forsook any attempt at fighting technique. Inertia slowly shook his head while Phaethon whaled away on her. She blocked almost every blow, but the force of them were making her legs visibly buckle. Phaethon didn't want to just beat her; it seemed like he wanted to pound her out of existence. The spectacle was as decidedly un-Clairvoyant as it was disturbing.

"*Edge, he's not going to stop. You have to fight back,*" Inertia told her. "*He's too far gone. They broke him. You have to fight back.*"

She gave no reply, which made him mull over his options. He was well aware that he could intervene. He could go down there himself and fight Phaethon. He'd probably have to kill him to get him to stop. Inertia thought about what that would do to Edge. Then he shook his head and looked at Caelus.

"Call it off," he said. The sorten looked at him with a start. "Call it off, Caelus. I'm sure you've got everything you need already."

"I thought Clairvoyants always fight to the death?" Mugal asked from the corner of the room where Caelus had banished him.

Inertia glanced at Mugal but ignored the question. Caelus ignored it as well. "Why would I do that?" he asked innocently. He motioned with his head toward the fight room. "You told me before that a Clairvoyant's Dark influences their every action, consciously or not. You even said nothing would happen in that room that she didn't intend. If she wishes to die, who am I to stop her? This is unexpected, but it's a data point nevertheless."

Inertia's jaw clenched and his hands balled into fists. He looked nervously into the fight room, his thoughts running a hundred miles a minute.

* * *

Carmen felt pain all over. One of her eyes was swelled closed, and she had no idea how many bones were broken. There was shooting pain through one of her legs if she put any weight on it, making it difficult to stand without the aid of telekinesis.

Phaethon's eyes blazed defiantly at her. She'd never seen him so enraged. "Fight back!" he screamed.

She shook her head. "No," she said softly, struggling to even speak.

The boy breathed hard. Behind the wrath steadily grew a gnawing disbelief. His eyes drilled into her, and it seemed like he was on the verge of crying. "If you were Edge, you'd have mercy enough to kill me."

Carmen frowned but said nothing. She dropped her hands and stood completely open with no attempt to defend herself. Phaethon recoiled from the sight, stepping away from her. His expression soon recovered from its first moments of shock and transitioned to raw, unbridled fear.

"You can't be her. She wouldn't have come," he muttered softly to himself. "No one would. Not for me. Not for me!"

He raised both of his hands and blasted her with two heat beams. The pure radiation blew her off her feet, impacting her against the far wall. She gave an earsplitting cry. Her bioelectric field and the body armor she wore resisted Phaethon's onslaught, but only just for a moment. Her vision burned with a white, searing light that seemed to come from everywhere while pain overcame her body. Phaethon screamed and cursed at her, but she could hardly make out anything he said. She was even distantly aware of Inertia yelling at her telepathically and Rauon's terrified scream in the fight room. None of it really mattered, though.

An unusual calm overcame her. For the first time in her life, Carmen felt whole. She felt no fear, no nothing.

Inertia, mouth agape, watched his partner die. The attack lasted only a few seconds, but that was enough. When Phaethon extinguished the beams, Edge lay bare in all her glory. Most of her upper torso and arms were blackened char, as was part of her face. Some of her hair still burned.

Everything was silent. No one moved, Clairvoyant or sorten. Inertia couldn't remember the last time his eyes blinked, and his heart had yet to resume beating. Smoke rose from Edge's corpse, slowly filling the room. Inertia's lips trembled.

Caelus gave the sorten equivalent of a shrug. "Well, had to end sometime," he said to himself.

Inertia looked at him with a piercing, soul halting glare that only a Clairvoyant could give. It was hard to come up with a reason not to kill him right then and there.

Caelus looked the Clairvoyant in the eye but appeared completely unconcerned. "Order a cleanup team to the room. I want a full autopsy."

* * *

Perception slowly pierced Phaethon's nightmarish stupor. The first sensation to peer through the fog of the past few seconds was his hard-panting breath. The last drops of adrenaline filtered through his body, making it shudder uncontrollably. The stink of burnt flesh was inescapable. Then, at last, he was finally able to see what was plainly in front of him. Edge, his now former handler, was dead. He'd killed her. It had been impossible to even dream that he'd see her, or anyone, ever again. Yet here she was…and she was gone.

This couldn't be happening. No one would come for him. Not here, not at the facility, not anywhere ever. It was almost laughable to believe otherwise. Clairvoyants couldn't even touch someone or be touched without hurting them. Clairvoyants were killers—wild, uncontrollable, feared horrors of the Dark. There was nothing else. It simply was and all that would be.

He felt an odd trickle down his cheek. His hand went to it and was wet when he pulled it away. He fell to his knees. It was too difficult to stand.

"What have I…" he said softly, his voice trailing off. He paused as what he was about to say was forced from the forefront of his mind. He dug his nails into his palm. "What did they make me do to you?" he asked, his tone getting harsher with each word. Then he stood with a start. "Sortens!"

He looked at Rauon with violence in his eyes. The technician seemed to sense the malevolence and backed away from Phaethon, well aware that the Clairvoyant could kill him with just a thought. There was no alternative, though.

All of a sudden, Rauon stopped in place, frozen by shock. His reaction made Phaethon stop as well. The sorten wasn't looking at him, nor did his expression carry the same mortal terror from before. It touched even deeper than that, like he had just witnessed stone turn to gold or someone walk on water. Phaethon turned to see what it was, and he was also immediately pinned in place.

There was a pained groan and even a curse, which was rare for her. Carmen stirred on the floor, coughing and hacking from the effort. Every contortion of her burnt skin made her wince and let out stuttering cries. Her first attempt to get up made her scream. The effort soon proved too much, and she fell to the ground again. Her breath came in rapid pants. All watched, transfixed, when after a few second of rest, she made her second attempt. This time, she worked to get her knees under her. From that platform, she was able to rest her torso on one of her forearms. The other was too badly burned to put any weight on.

Inertia couldn't believe what he was seeing. *"Are you okay?"* he asked telepathically.

Carmen breathed hard. Even just sitting on her knees took more exertion than any other endeavor in her life. Her entire body was racked with so much pain that she was on the verge of passing out.

"No," she responded.

The cleanup team entered the room.

"Stay away from her!" Phaethon yelled.

The sortens didn't even have time to have a reaction; Phaethon telekinetically crushed the first pair, and their screams echoed throughout the fight room. The second pair received a more humane death, simply falling to the ground with broken necks. Rauon ran out of the room.

Phaethon turned around to face the observation booth.

"Everyone down!" Mugal screamed.

Seconds later, the boy's heat beam ripped into the booth. A technician was cut in half by it. Another lost her arm. Caelus narrowly missed having his head vaporized by diving out of the way.

"Code 1! Repeat, Code 1! All suppression teams report to combat lab 223! Lethal force is authorized!" Mugal ordered.

Inertia could feel the sortens rushing to their position. It felt like a flood. Phaethon could sense their approach as well. He looked at Carmen, holding back his revulsion at her appearance.

"I won't let them hurt you anymore," he said. The pain of speaking made her reply unintelligible.

The first sortens entered the room with foam cannons and projectile weapons strapped on their backs. The soldiers moved like cats, with agility and speed. This first wave fired wildly. Some of their bullets even impacted the observation booth. Phaethon dispatched them with ease. The second and third waves entered a mere moment later. This group was protected by shielded, powered exoskeletons. The Clairvoyant's heat beams ablated off the armor in spectacular sparks but to no effect. Punches and even kicks impacted with dull, harmless thuds.

Phaethon regrouped at the other end of the room and then launched a powerful telekinetic attack. The metal of the exoskeletons strained but eventually gave way under the force of the Clairvoyant. The sortens' arms and legs were telekinetically ripped off before they were crushed into balls. Heads were ripped off also. And, in the end, the Clairvoyant stood triumphant, though clearly suffering from fatigue. The fourth, fifth, and sixth waves rushed into position.

"Call your teams off," Inertia said.

There was no way Phaethon would ultimately win. He was powerful, but he fought sloppily, seeking to simply overpower his opponent. Now was not the time to make the move against Solitary.

"What?" Mugal asked disbelievingly.

"He only wants to protect Edge," Inertia said, realizing all too late that he'd let her real name slip. "If you stop attacking him, he might calm down."

"Calm down? That's madness!" the security director replied.

Caelus made no response, other than to give Inertia a curious but knowing tip of his head. The Clairvoyant saw him mouth "Edge" to himself and then get a faraway look in his eye.

The battle continued in the fight room. The sortens absorbed tremendous losses, but their well-trained discipline was having an effect. With each sorten felled, his comrade came closer to hitting the mark. Wild shots became near misses. A sorten armed with a foam cannon managed to trap Phaethon's arm against the wall. A second shot nearly encased the young Clairvoyant. But then, all at once, they stopped.

The soldiers stood pinned in place, as if cast in stone. It wasn't by Mugal's order or by some sudden compassion on their part. Eyes, both in the fight room and the observation booth, grew wide as they made witness to the utterly impossible. Standing between the sorten contingent and Phaethon with arms outstretched to hold off the horde was Carmen. Her broken, battered body trembled, and her chest rose and fell with each haggard breath. But she didn't *simply* stand there.

Her bioelectric field seemed to erupt from the pit of her stomach, course up her spine, and play out from her fingers in wild array. More than half of the sortens in Solitary fainted from the disturbance of the Clairvoyant's power. The remainder vomited uncontrollably where they stood. Computer consoles outright exploded in the observation booth. Lights blew out in spectacular sparks. There she was for the first time, Edge, raw, unreserved, and complete. But the monster of the Dark wasn't preparing for battle. The seemingly half-dead Clairvoyant had moved like a shot. And now the entire effort, the sheer force of will, was solely to keep her standing. Her unbridled power and determination were like Atlas holding up the sky.

"Incredible," Mugal muttered softly.

Stunned silence hung in the air a while longer, till the mood was broken by laughter.

"Yes, most unexpected," Caelus said. "Most unexpected indeed." Carmen looked at him. "You've impressed me, Edge. No easy task." He paused before he spoke again. "Security teams, you may withdraw. Medical team, report to combat lab 223 at once." The sorten laughed again. "Quite impressive," he said to himself as he exited the observation booth.

Inertia watched him go. Then he looked at Mugal and finally at Carmen. She sank to the ground to rest against the wall and looked at Inertia. Despite her badly burned face, and despite that she looked like she was struggling to even stay conscious, her triumphant relief was quite apparent.

20

THE MASK OF TWISTED REFLECTIONS

The approach to Solitary was always the same. 1227231 normally didn't even waste its time powering up until the docking was complete. Today, however, that was not the case. The sudden and immediate summoning by Solitary's master, Caelus, was odd enough, but even that paled in comparison to the peculiar nature of 1227231's co-passenger. It was an extraordinary circumstance for an Eternal starship to even have a passenger. Their starships were unique in that they needed no crews. Only transport ships were designed for the capability of carrying passengers of any sort. Damage control was ably handled by each ship's host of repair drones, and they were just as part of the ship as cells were to a living creature's body. Yes, the Clairvoyant sitting quietly across from 1227231 was a curious event.

The Clairvoyant made no acknowledgement that 1227231 even existed. A cursory check of the logged encounters between Eternals and Clairvoyants revealed that was not atypical. Clairvoyants liked to claim that each was an individual, unique and ever-changing, but reality showed they were more monolithic than they liked to assume.

In any case, this Clairvoyant was dressed in the usual Clairvoyant manner of passive intimidation and dramatic effect. It was difficult to tell how successful the Clairvoyant was in that. 1227231 could be crudely called a machine and wasn't given to such emotionally generated flights of fancy. The Clairvoyant's clothes weren't very well constructed. They wrapped around his thin frame in haphazard fashion, flowing and billowing every time he moved. On the Clairvoyant's face was a rather strange mask. Its kind had never been recorded before. The mask's mirror-like metal finish reflected everything in imperfect detail. Not one image was presented as it actually was. The mask distorted everything, almost maddeningly continuing each and every reflection in a circuitous, never-ending maze.

Curious, 1227231 cross-referenced the Clairvoyant's garb and mask with terran psychological research to gauge its effectiveness. As always, that was rather difficult despite the large amount of data to draw from. Clairvoyants were keen on pointing out that Eternals were not alive, at least not by the traditional sense. Eternals were sentient, could reproduce in a sense, and were aware of and could change their environments. The cold machines, however, were just that: machines. 1227231 measured and studied the Clairvoyant's bioelectric field. It could not *feel* it, though, leaving that dimension completely unexplored, and no probe, sensor, or catalogued research could bridge that gap.

The Clairvoyant stood and to 1227231 he was frustratingly little different from a rock rolling downhill or a gust of wind. He was just a physical construct that could be observed and perceived but not truly known. Further study was warranted, but for now, 1227231 filed its observations and prepared to disembark. It was almost time.

The ramp opened slowly to reveal Solitary's lone hangar

bay, which contained another surprise. Parked next to their transport was a small, fast attack Corvette of terran construction. The type was quite common, Archer Class, well known for being a favorite on the black market of mercenaries and other similar sorts. The arrowhead-like planform was unmistakable. Though it was quite common throughout the galaxy, its ilk had never been seen here. Even the Clairvoyant paused for a moment to gaze at it.

That moment came and then went, and the Clairvoyant continued on his way. 1227231 followed and could only marvel at the Clairvoyant. He moved swiftly, gracefully, and efficiently, like all Clairvoyants, but most fantastically, he seemed to know exactly where he was going. By what means that was possible couldn't begin to be determined. 1227231 had been here before, as had other units. Mapping programs, tracers, inertial navigation, database sharing, and even reasoned guessing failed to make sense of Solitary's never-ending corridors. Yet, somehow, this Clairvoyant was able to casually discern what the plodding machinations of logic could not.

Boom, boom. The Eternal's heavy steps sounded behind the Clairvoyant. By contrast, the Clairvoyant's movement could barely be heard. He seemed to exist and not exist at the same time, ghostly yet as present as a tidal wave. *Boom, boom.* The Clairvoyant turned his head slightly and telekinetically opened one of the panels hidden in the corridor wall. Then he seemed to effortlessly flow into the new corridor. *Boom, boom, boom.*

* * *

"You're crazy. You know that? You're fucking crazy. And if you ever do anything like that ever again, I'll kill you myself."

Carmen wasn't completely sure Inertia was joking. Nevertheless, his comment made her smile, even though it hurt to do so. Her body was more patched together than healed, even after the services of Solitary's doctors. She lay in the medical bay still. Inertia was with her, as was Rauon. Her partner made no mention of her appearance, but Rauon had said that, while all of the life-threatening injuries she'd sustained had been repaired, her scars would have to be taken care of at a later date, if they even could be removed. Carmen didn't much care about that at present.

She smiled again. "Did I ever tell you I don't like cursing?"

"No. Why is that?"

"Long story. Wish I could tell you," she said after a pause. "Anyway, where's Phaethon?" she asked.

Inertia glanced at Rauon, who sat on the other side of Carmen, and then looked at her again. "I don't know," he said. "I know he's still alive," he added quickly before she could frown. "But I don't know where he's being held. He was never brought here. He wasn't seriously injured in the attack." Then he looked at her hard. "*Prudence, Edge, especially now,*" he told her telepathically.

She turned her head to look at Rauon, wincing from the pain as she did so. Pain killers had a muted effect at best on Clairvoyants. Her opinion on what she was changed like the phases of the moon, but now, with the pain receptors of her broken body assaulting her, she quite wished she wasn't a Clairvoyant.

"*Sorry,*" she replied telepathically, looking at Inertia again. "*So, what now?*" she asked.

He rolled his eyes and then slowly shook his head. Upon realizing what she said, Carmen pressed her lips together in a guilty smirk.

"*We'll be ready soon,*" Inertia replied. "*In fact, I am meeting with Caelus after this to analyze the data from the fight. Every moment I spend with the computers, the closer we get.*"

She nodded. "*Don't forget Phaethon. We need to find out where they're keeping him.*"

"*Of course,*" Inertia spoke. He was silent for a second or two as the Clairvoyants simply looked at each other until he placed his hand on her shoulder and patted her gently. The action made them both wince. It was difficult for Clairvoyants to touch anyone, let alone each other. "*I'm glad you found him,*" he said softly.

Carmen looked at Inertia's hand, looked at him, and smiled. She couldn't think of any sort of reply, but none was required.

"Rest. I'll be back later," he said. Then he turned and walked out of the room.

Carmen watched him go. This time, however, she wasn't left with quiet feelings of dread for being left alone in this awful place. No, not this time. She smiled again as she thought of Phaethon. Not this time at all. The expression, however, left her quickly when she turned her head and was reminded that Rauon was still with her.

"Psyche?" he asked, his voice exploratory and unsure.

Carmen returned him a puzzled look. There was something different in his eyes. He had the countenance of someone questioning their faith. He also looked like he was containing physical disgust as he looked at her. The effort to avoid looking at her without seeming like he was avoiding looking at her was obvious. She had no idea how she appeared, but the blistered, leathery mess that was her arm was a good clue. Her gaze traveling from her arm to Rauon and back caused him to redouble his efforts.

"Psyche, why didn't you fight back?" he asked.

She didn't expect the question. A response came to mind —a lie. It was a misnomer that Clairvoyants never lied. Their entire time at Solitary was a lie. Still, it was a distasteful practice, and as she looked at him, she couldn't bring herself to give another. She lay back on the bed, plain faced, and said not a word.

"Well?" Rauon asked. Carmen turned her head away from him, which made him pause. "Who is Edge?" he asked, his voice low.

Her only response was a deep breath. She heard Rauon get up and walk slowly in front of her. She looked at him.

"I fear there is more about you than I first assumed," he said.

No one said anything else. Carmen's unwavering eyes stared at him. Rauon stared back. She could have read him at any time and known exactly what he was thinking, but it was unnecessary. He, like so many before him, backed away from her slowly, as if she were a dangerous animal. Carmen watched him go, much like she had with Inertia. In this instance, though, she felt no elation.

* * *

Mugal was waiting for Inertia in the corridor. He had four Clairvoyant Constructs with him, as well as several sorten security members. Inertia looked at the unusually heavy escort and paused.

The security director noticed his hesitation. "You are to

come with us, Clairvoyant. The project leader wishes to see you."

"That I know, but all this?" he asked, gesturing to the force arrayed against him.

"Extra precautions in light of previous events. Project Leader's order," Mugal said. "As is this," he added, producing a set of binders. Inertia's eyes narrowed when he saw them. "You don't object do you?"

It was only a second, but in that brief instance, Inertia made a calculation. "No, I don't object," he concluded as he held out his arms.

Mugal stepped forward and placed the binders on him. It was only a few seconds before the Clairvoyant's hands went to his head and he fell to one knee. The corridor felt like it was spinning.

"They were calibrated for your mate. Should be more than strong enough for you," Mugal commented. Inertia glared at him but said nothing. "Come."

He got to his feet after a wobble and joined the sorten contingent. They moved swiftly with the security director and security members in front and the four Clairvoyant Constructs behind. Inertia did his best to keep up in the center. It was then that he realized there was something different about Mugal. The purpose and tenseness in his movements weren't birthed from his usual militant readiness. It was difficult to know what had caused the change.

Inertia considered the possibilities. Yesterday's events had reset the landscape. That much was inescapable. But what changed, and to what degree, was still only an educated guess.

He had never thought they'd see Phaethon, other than finding out in some computer record that he'd been killed. Now the sortens knew Edge's real name—well, her Clairvoyant name anyway. What could be done with that was hard to say. Phaethon had probably been interrogated on who Edge was and his relation to her. Inertia let his mind explore that realm for a moment. It was doubtful they'd found anything incriminating. They would probably kill or at least attempt to kill them if so. Inertia looked at Mugal. The sorten was certainly filled with purpose. To an outside observer, it looked like the Clairvoyant was being taken to his execution. Inertia looked at the binders and wondered if cooperating wasn't the best idea. It didn't help that Edge wasn't much of a threat to anyone in her current state.

In short order, the group eventually arrived in an average sized room. It wasn't a fight room or observation booth. There were computer terminals, but no one was at any of the workstations. In fact, no one was in the room at all. The sorten security and Clairvoyant Constructs took vigilant positions throughout the room, save two of the Constructs who stayed close to Inertia. Mugal walked a little away, but not before he shot the terran an accusatory glare.

What's going on? Inertia wondered, but there were no clues to go off of. Caelus wasn't even in the room. It didn't seem like they would be removing the binders. No direction was given. Inertia decided to not let the opportunity go to waste; there was no other option anyway. He took a seat at one of the computers, eyeing Mugal as he did. Mugal watched him in turn.

Inertia's search of the computer system proceeded in frantic spurts that were punctuated by his quick surveys of the room to make sure it was still safe to proceed. Mugal made no active attempts to stop him. It seemed more like the security director was waiting for something. Mugal glanced repeatedly at the door. Unfortunately, the binders did their job quite well. A purple clown with a bouquet of roses could have been behind that door, for all Inertia knew. But just then, there was a strange noise.

It sounded *heavy* and came at regular intervals. And it was getting closer. *Boom, boom, boom.* The sorten security team was no longer watching Inertia. Their attention was firmly fixed on the door. Inertia no longer studied the computer and looked at the door as well. *Boom, boom, boom.* It was right outside the room now.

A quiet second passed—several, in fact—and each was agonizing. Just then, the silence was broken by the sound of gears whirring and the hiss of hydraulics energizing. The door opened to reveal an Eternal attempting to fit through it. The ungainly machine clopped and staggered as it determined the optimum way through an entrance that was a size too small. Inertia couldn't help turning his nose up. Limbs were retracted, angles were adjusted, and the Eternal was finally able to make it into the room, where it rose to its full height.

Inertia looked up at it. The machine was charcoal black in color. Quite oddly, its construction was completely, if sometimes subtly, asymmetrical. The unnatural aesthetic of the unnatural contraption was intentional. This unit had yet to talk, but Inertia was already quite certain its synthetic voice would randomly change stress, tone, and tempo as it spoke. The ultimate purpose was to make whoever they encountered uncomfortable. It had to provide some type of advantage in some situations; Clairvoyants often used similar tactics. In any case, Inertia had dealt with Eternals before. It had been brief, but it was more than enough time for him to learn that he hated each and every one of them.

Boom, boom, boom, boom. The Eternal walked toward him, and it was a surprise craters weren't left everywhere it went.

"Where is the other Clairvoyant?" it asked, its voice

changing stress as he'd guessed. "I would like to study both of them."

Inertia pressed his lips together and took a deep breath. He had no doubt he was currently being scanned by every type of sensor in the known galaxy. It was just the Eternal way. No one knew exactly where they came from or who built them. They claimed they were the products and legacy of a long extinct race now lost to the histories. That explanation was as good as any other, and just as irrelevant. All that really mattered was that they weren't alive, despite their protests otherwise. Inertia would read nothing behind this unit's metal exoskeleton if he weren't wearing the binders. Each and every Eternal went about its purpose with the mindless abandon that only a machine could muster. That purpose, in almost all cases, was scientific research. An Eternal could spend months cataloguing each and every blade of grass in a field.

Caelus walked into the room with a small security escort of sortens. "In time. She is recovering in our med bay. The incident I told you about," Caelus said to the machine.

"Is there any threat that the female could expire? If so, I'd prefer to analyze her before," the Eternal said.

Caelus gave a soft chuckle. "No," he said. "I believe, for now, she will survive." He looked at Inertia as he spoke.

Inertia stared right back, and just then another player entered the room. Every soul subconsciously stiffened. The Clairvoyant's clothes swayed and billowed with every movement he made. The reflection of everyone's image in his mask, really all of creation, was bent, corrupted, and inverted on itself, on and on for eternity. Even Caelus took a few steps away.

"Beast," the sorten said, referring to Inertia, "this is 1227231." He gestured toward the Eternal. "And this is—"

"Charon," Inertia interrupted.

Caelus's face flashed with a look of surprise. Charon's countenance couldn't be discerned.

"Do you two know each other?" Caelus asked.

A Clairvoyant's bioelectric field was as distinctive as a fingerprint. Unfortunately, Inertia couldn't read much of anything with the binders on. Nevertheless, he knew of no Clairvoyant who used similar theatrics.

"No," Inertia said. "But I know of him," he added after another quick mental calculation.

"Explain," Caelus demanded.

"I wouldn't be here if it wasn't for him. My wife and I didn't even know sortens would accept Clairvoyant assistance until we heard of Charon's attack on New Earth," Inertia said. Half-truths were always the most effective.

"How did you know sortens were behind the attack?" Mugal asked.

"It made sense," Inertia replied. "Who else but the sortens would have the means to create Clairvoyant Constructs? And who else other than the sortens would *have* to use Clairvoyant Constructs because natural Clairvoyants won't work with them, especially not in numbers?"

That answer seemed to satisfy Mugal, who didn't say anything else.

"How industrious of you," Charon said. His voice, though not exactly deep, reverberated throughout the room. "Unfortunately, not all Clairvoyants seem as enterprising. I've been hounded by a particularly tenacious pair ever since that attack… Though one of them is not a Clairvoyant, despite how capable she is."

The comment caught Inertia's interest. "And what happened to them?" he asked, knowing in the back of his mind that the pair was more than likely Gungnir and Widget.

"They can't track me here. I will set out again after a time. That is all you need know," Charon responded.

Inertia gave a respectful nod and thought it wise to hold any further questions for the time being.

"It is fortunate that Charon could join us, never mind the circumstances," Caelus said, sounding almost respectful. "Now I must ask him, do you think our efforts here are wasted? Inertia has said since the beginning that I will never succeed."

1227231 spoke before Charon could. "All that is needed is time. Nothing escapes the relentless pounding of logic, given a long enough timeframe and enough variables to compare. A complete understanding and duplication of Clairvoyants is inevitable."

"I quite agree," Caelus said.

Charon and Inertia ignored the automaton.

"This entire facility and its purpose are a laughable construct," Charon said simply.

The sorten looked taken aback. "How can you say that? Why did you not say anything before?" he asked hurriedly.

Charon looked at Caelus. His mask split the sorten into wild disarray. "My opinion is immaterial. I get paid regardless of your success," he said.

Mugal glowered at him. Inertia couldn't help thinking that Clairvoyants were Clairvoyants, no matter their allegiance. It was refreshing.

"I tire of this. See me when you are finished here," Charon said to Caelus. Then he left the room without pause.

Caelus stood still for a moment, time Inertia used to study the computer. He was close. The sorten looked at him and noted how busy he seemed to be.

"Why continue working if you think it is futile?" he asked.

Inertia didn't look up from the computer. "Clairvoyants are wrong as often as anyone else. They are just seldom in doubt," he said simply.

The scientist considered his words and nodded. "What do you need to proceed?"

"As you said, time," Inertia responded, but he smiled a few seconds later. He had found everything he needed. He looked at Caelus. "I could use one thing," he said, holding up his bound hands.

Mugal shot the project leader a look but said nothing. Caelus didn't speak either, instead pausing for silent consideration.

"No, those will stay for now," he said. Then he took a deep breath. "I will return in a moment. I must speak with Charon."

Inertia looked at 1227231 and Mugal, wondering when the best time to strike would be now that he knew exactly how to get to the comm room and how to use the computers. He'd have to reconnect with Edge and figure out some way to find Phaethon.

Caelus left the room as Inertia made his final calculations.

* * *

Charon patiently waited for Caelus in the corridor. The beast's services were invaluable, and his loyalty was without question. Despite that, being around him made Caelus's skin crawl.

"You said there were two of them?" the Clairvoyant asked.

"Yes, the male, Inertia, who you just met. He's provided technical assistance. His mate, who is more powerful, was used as a baseline. I'm not sure what to call her, though. She claims her name is Psyche. However, yesterday, one of the previous subjects you brought us referred to her as Edge, and the two of them even defended each other," Caelus said.

"Which subject is this?"

"His Clairvoyant name is Phaethon," the sorten replied. "Of course, we interrogated him, but he revealed nothing. Unfortunately, a mind scan takes some time and is yet to be completed." Charon made no response. "Does the name mean anything to you?"

"What did she say?" he asked back.

"She's yet to be questioned."

Charon was silent for a moment. "I can't be certain. I need to see her."

"That can be arranged," Caelus said.

He started walking and Charon followed. They disappeared into a room only a short distance down the corridor. The sortens in the security station stiffened when the Clairvoyant entered, relaxing only when Caelus gave a reassuring nod.

"Show me the med bay," he ordered.

The security officers responded dutifully. "On the main screen now, Project Leader," one of them said.

Caelus stepped out of the way to allow Charon a clear look. On the main screen was Edge. She lay on her bed quite peacefully in the medical bay. The burns on her face and arm were clearly visible.

"I know this one," Charon said. "There were reports of an extremely strong Clairvoyant fitting her description years ago at the facility on New Earth."

"The same facility where you collect Phaethon?" Caelus more remarked than asked.

"Yes."

"Do you know anything else about her?"

"I do not. She got the attention of many when she was younger, due to her extreme power. But she was basically forgotten after she graduated."

Caelus stared at the monitor hard. "So, she and Phaethon are from the same facility, know each other's names, and defended each other. You also said two mercenaries have been following you since your attack on New Earth. Too many coincidences," he said.

"Indeed," Charon muttered, folding his arms. "Kill her and her partner. Do it immediately."

21

INTO ACTION

Charon didn't return to the room. Caelus entered alone sooner than Inertia had expected. Other than glancing in Inertia's direction from time to time, the sorten largely ignored the Clairvoyant. Inertia bit his lip. It was impossible while wearing the binders to tell if Charon was waiting outside. He'd never had an objective be so close yet feel so far away. If only he could capture or kill Charon... But the opportunity seemed ever more fleeting.

Caelus spoke quietly to Mugal while Inertia considered his next move. He couldn't hear what was said, and it wasn't easy to intuit. It was then that he realized how much he passively read minds to discern alien body language. With the binders on, the sortens were opaque to him. Mugal listened more than he spoke. By Inertia's best guess, Caelus was probably giving a series of commands. That was nothing out of the ordinary. As impossible as it seemed, however, the always solemn security director's features turned more severe the longer Caelus talked, drawing all of Inertia's attention.

Boom, boom, boom. "What are you studying, Clairvoyant?" 1227231 asked as it lumbered toward him. Its tone seemed curious instead of accusatory.

Inertia cursed under his breath. He preferred to not be distracted from whatever was going on with Caelus and Mugal.

"I'm reading the baseline comparison results between different batches of Clairvoyant Constructs," he said while trying to figure out how to get the Eternal to go away.

1227231 shifted its position to get a better look at the workstation. Inertia already had the screen on the relevant data just in case. "What are your findings?" the machine asked.

Inertia couldn't care less about the sorten data, despite how extensive it was. He didn't waste his time answering right away either. Instead, he watched Caelus exit the room. Two of the Clairvoyant Construct guards left with him, which prompted a look of interested surprise from Inertia. Then his eyes fell on Mugal. The sorten stared back with icy readiness. Inertia turned his attention back to 1227231.

"I don't have any conclusions yet," he said, no word of which was a lie.

Mugal continued staring at him, even while he moved slowly from sorten guard to sorten guard. A few hushed words were exchanged from leader to each subordinate, but Inertia had no idea what they were. There was a silent edginess about the sortens. It couldn't be described as calm, but it was a far cry from the nervous dread Clairvoyants usually produced in all those around them. For the first time since he'd been in Solitary, Inertia felt anxious. He couldn't help a glance at his binders.

"How long have you been studying the data?" 1227231 asked.

Inertia looked at the Eternal and then back at Mugal and

tried his best to divide his attention between them. "Not long. It took quite a while for the sortens to trust us," he said loudly enough for the security director to hear.

Mugal made no reply. It didn't even seem like he heard him. Instead, he moved to the center of the room and faced Inertia and 1227231. The sorten guards slowly moved to either side of the room until all of them had a clear line of fire. The Clairvoyant Constructs were now at Inertia's flanks. He glanced at the binders and then looked at Mugal again, who stared at him like a waiting viper. *They're going to attack*, he realized.

"That is understandable," 1227231 remarked. "Surely you can understand that Clairvoyant-sorten cooperation will always be circumspect."

"Yes, that seems obvious now," Inertia said.

"That is a very reasonable view from you," the oblivious Eternal said. Mugal flashed 1227231 an annoyed look. "I hope this is the first of many such cooperations," 1227231 continued.

"It is difficult to be optimistic," Inertia said to the machine, though he looked at Mugal. He placed a silent bet with himself that the sortens wouldn't attack while the Eternal was still in the room. "What about yourself? Why are you here?" he asked.

"This is a joint Eternal-sorten project," 1227231 said matter-of-factly. "Development of an effective counter against your kind is existentially prudent."

"But the sortens aren't at war with us. At least not now," Inertia pointed out.

"That is true. However, even after surrendering, the threat persists. Terrans are the most violent and destructive species in the galaxy. Sortens have the most advanced research on Clairvoyants. It is perfectly logical for us to partner with them. Moreover, our kind and yours *are* at war," 1227231 responded.

Inertia nodded and noted to himself that, despite how violent and destructive terrans were perceived, they weren't exactly winning the war. The Eternal continued.

"Thus why I was curious as to why Clairvoyants would assist such an effort," it said. "I would like to see your mate to get her perspective."

"As would I," Inertia concurred. He looked at Mugal. "I'm done here for now. I wish to see Psyche. I'd like to take 1227231 with me."

If the sortens were stupid enough to put the Clairvoyants together, the odds of them getting out of here alive increased by several orders of magnitude. The only real question was how badly the sortens wished to avoid a fight with 1227231 as a bystander. The damage or destruction of an Eternal by sorten guards would certainly be an undesirable outcome, given their alliance.

Mugal's eyes narrowed. "That is not possible," he said.

"Why is that?" 1227231 asked.

"As the Clairvoyant no doubt guessed by now, she has her own company to attend to," Mugal said. The Eternal began to protest, but the sorten cut him off. "Enough of this prattle. 1227231, go to the project leader in the comm room. He will explain all that's going on. Go quickly," he snapped.

1227231 stood still. The machine, emotionless and driven by algorithms and numbers, seemed gripped by indecision. It made no response until, *boom, boom, boom*, it slowly walked to the door. The Clairvoyant and the security director stared at each other the whole time; they didn't even move. Numerous calculations and wheels within wheels played through their minds. Meanwhile, 1227231's gears whirred and hydraulics hissed, and eventually it fit back through the door.

Nothing happened after the Eternal's departure. The only change was the fainter and fainter sound of its booming weight as it continued down the hall. All were still. Nevertheless, Mugal's muscles were taut. Several of the sorten guards focused on the sights of the weapons mounted on their backs. The Clairvoyant Constructs reasonably aped the subjects they were copies of, betraying nothing other than the ready calm of a Clairvoyant.

Boom, boom, boom. 1227231 almost couldn't be heard now. Inertia took a deep breath and closed his eyes. Then he opened his eyes and let his breath go slowly. The Eternal could no longer be heard.

The sortens' first shot destroyed the workstation Inertia was sitting behind. By that point, however, he had already tipped out of his chair and onto the ground. Instinct drove him more than any conscious thought. Even diminished as he was by the binders, a Clairvoyant was still a monster of the Dark. The connection could never be completely severed.

He rolled under the table to the center of the room and stood. The sortens' bullets still tore through where he had been in a shower of sparks and noise. No one noticed the lights in the room flickering wildly. Just then, the Clairvoyant's eyes glowed, and all stood transfixed as they bore witness to the impossible. Inertia's binders shattered like glass. The sorten guards were impaled by the telekinetically-propelled fragments an instant later.

The two Clairvoyant Constructs leapt into the fray. Their offensive of wild punches and kicks forced Inertia to retreat, but his face betrayed no stress or worry. His movements were crisp, direct, and seemingly gaining in energy. One of the Constructs managed to catch his counterpunch and threw him across the room for the mistake. Inertia landed painfully but regained himself in fractions of a second.

Something changed in that moment. He seemed annoyed. The Constructs came at him again and, seconds later, one was tumbling across the room, dead. The second Construct fared little better. It was only a matter of time before an attack from Inertia, definite and clean, made the Construct fall to the ground, never to get up again. He turned to face Mugal.

"It's impossible," the sorten said, his lips trembling. "One of our copies bested you with one blow… And those binders were calibrated for your mate. She's more powerful than you are!"

"Is she?" Inertia let the question hang.

Mugal's eyes grew wide until the Clairvoyant telekinetically snapped his neck. Inertia took a second to look at the body at his feet. He brushed it aside after a second or so and made for the door. But before he could even leave the room, red lights began to flash and an alarm sounded. He cursed under his breath. An alert status was probably tied to Mugal's bio-med readings. He could already feel sorten security members approaching. That, however, wasn't Inertia's biggest concern. He couldn't sense his partner.

"*Edge! Do you hear me, Edge?*" he shouted blindly, but with nothing to focus on, he may as well have been trying to scream underwater. He hoped with all that was in him that she was just too far away to get any sort of read. It was just as likely, though, that she was dead.

He was out of time either way. The sortens were mere moments away. He bolted out of the room with the knowledge that he had only one real option. He had to assume Edge was dead, which meant he needed to somehow get to the comm room. There was too much to risk otherwise.

"Fire!" the leader of the approaching sorten contingent yelled.

Gunfire ripped through the corridor, ricocheting off the

bare metal to destroy all in its path. Inertia, however, had already escaped through one of the hidden hatches. There wasn't much to gain by risking an engagement. Just then, he ran into another security team.

A foam cannon trapped one of his legs to the corridor wall. A Clairvoyant Construct kept him occupied with a furious attack. Blow after blow came raining down. Despite his best efforts to block or move his body out of the way, trapped as he was, there were times he saw stars. The sorten security members moved precisely. Their well-drilled coordination made it seemed like they too could communicate through telepathy. A second shot from them encased the Clairvoyant in foam, except for a hand, which he shook about in a futile effort to free himself. The security team from the previous corridor joined them.

One of them keyed his communicator. "Project Leader, the male Clairvoyant has been neutralized."

"Excellent," Caelus said. "Is his body intact enough for study?"

The sorten security member looked at the foam tomb existing on the corridor wall like a cancer. Inertia's hand still fought but appeared weak and desperate in its feeble grasps for freedom.

"Yes, Project Leader," he said.

"Good. A medical team is en route to your position."

The sorten security member looked at the other team. "Team 6, you stand relieved. Thank you for the assistance."

Yet the members of team 6 didn't move off. "He should have suffocated by now," one of them said.

"Just a little more fire in this one. He'll be dead soon enough," a member of the other team remarked.

That truth seemed more and more likely with each passing second. Eventually, Inertia's hand fell limp, and both security teams breathed sighs of relief as the medical team approached.

"He's all yours," one of the security members said.

"No, he's not!" one of them screamed.

The foam mass quivered and bulged. Lights flickered wildly, several of which outright blew out. The medical team took flight down the corridor while the security teams took several cautious steps back. All of a sudden, half of the foam mass encasing the Clairvoyant blew away. The unbelievably bright light that was the cause was directed to the rest of the foam, and the assembled sortens watched in horror as it melted away. Inertia eventually emerged, down on his hands and knees, gasping for air.

"He's loose!"

The sortens with the foam cannons opened fire first. The foam was specifically designed to combat Clairvoyants. Heat resistant and capable of suppressing a bioelectric field, it was almost perfectly suited for the task. Inertia didn't attempt to resist the spray rushing toward him outright but instead subtly redirected the mass with telekinesis. It was enough to make the foam miss and impact on either side of him. Just then, a gunshot hit him square in the chest. His body armor, however, reduced the potentially lethal impact to nothing more than a dull ache. Inertia's response was immediate.

One of his heat beams cut a sorten armed with a foam cannon in half. Telekinetically redirecting the aim of another sorten encased half the security team in foam. One unlucky enough to only be hit in the face by the foam gave a muffled scream as he fell to the ground. His doom-filled cry, however, was unheeded by his comrades. A punch from Inertia ended a sorten that was only partially trapped. Another, also only partially trapped, was felled by a heat beam that left the remaining half of his body on fire. Inertia dodged out of the way of more gunfire before telekinetically snapping the offending sorten's neck. Then, at last, all that remained was the Clairvoyant Constructs. All five of them.

Clairvoyants, even crude copies of Clairvoyants, didn't fight in the expedient manner of overwhelming force like disciplined soldiers. There was a long pause in which nothing happened. Inertia breathed heavily for a moment, having yet fully regained his breath from his trial with the foam. The Constructs simply looked at him. What was to come wouldn't be a duel. There were, however, rules—unspoken codes of conduct that even these dim creatures had to be aware of in some vestigial way.

Inertia turned his head slightly to look at the Constructs at his back before focusing again at those to his front. No one assumed a guard, yet all were tensely ready. Time seemed to slow, seconds becoming minutes and even hours. Yet, the lights that weren't blown out in the corridor pulsated madly. In the background, the sounds of the suffocating sorten reverberated up everyone's spine until, at last, he stopped moving.

The two Constructs at Inertia's front flew toward him like a shot. He responded deftly, leaping toward them and short-circuiting their attack with a punch that cratered a Construct's jaw. The blow was enough to render him not much of a threat anymore, but a second punch doubled the Construct over, and a third crumpled him to the floor, dead. It was good to be sure.

Inertia had enough time to duck out of the way of a kick from behind him, but he suffered the full force of a heat beam. It ablated his heat-resistant body suit and left his arm and shoulder smoking but no worse for wear. His own heat beam ripped through the Construct and practically exploded against the corridor wall. Fiery, molten metal rained throughout the passageway. The pieces bounced off Inertia to no effect, as Clairvoyants couldn't be hurt by their own energy. Three opponents remained.

They came at him again. A few quick steps were all it took to place the Constructs on one side of him. The narrow corridor hindered their movement, and they got in the way of each other, stumbling and wavering, while Inertia only grew stronger. After each breath and each beat of his heart, he became more efficient, more direct, and more deadly. Every action he made seemed to have a destined finality about it. A series of punches bounced harmlessly off his shoulders, and each led to the almost effortless counterpunch that spun the Construct like a top as his lifeless body fell uncoordinatedly to the ground.

The natural Clairvoyant pirouetted away from an attack in that brief moment of vulnerability. An elbow at the end of his maneuver sent the attacking Construct staggering toward the corridor wall. Inertia extended his arm, and fire and smoke from the point-blank hit of his heat beam encased him. The smoke billowed and rolled around him, redirected by his bioelectric field, and he looked at his remaining opponent, who backed away slightly.

Inertia assumed a guard. The Construct remained ready and waiting. The next few seconds passed in a flash. The servants of the Dark wielded their power like the frightening forces of nature they were. This time, it ended with the Clairvoyant Construct dead at Inertia's feet.

Taking a deep breath, he surveyed the carnage all around him. His breathing was calm and his skin was cool. He had only one concern. *I need to get to the comm room.* He had a general idea of where it was, as impossible as that was to believe in the maze that was Solitary.

He moved quickly, nearly at a full run down the corridor. But he slid to a stop before he went through a hatch into the next. He could sense a sorten patrol passing by. They came and went, and Inertia made his way down the new corridor. If there was only one problem in getting to the comm room, it was that it was a floor below him. Undoubtedly, the elevator would be heavily guarded. Mugal had drilled his security teams too thoroughly to miss such an obvious oversight. Inertia went through another hatch. The elevator would be at the end of the hall, if he navigated correctly.

He flew, loaded for bear, but even so he was unprepared for what waited for him. A mere two sortens guarded the elevator. The Clairvoyant, for one of the few times in his life, felt surprise. The feeling passed quickly. He snapped their necks before they could even take aim, and then he entered the elevator. After selecting the proper deck, the elevator began on its way. Then it stopped moving. It didn't *just* stop, though. The lights shut off and dim emergency lights activated.

They cut the power, Inertia thought. He frowned. It hadn't taken long for the sortens to cover their lapse in guarding the elevator. He cursed loudly when he wasn't able to open the doors again, rendering him effectively trapped. Several solutions went through his mind, and the least sensible appeared to be the most prudent. He pointed his hands at the floor and melted a hole through it. Another heat blast blew a hole through the elevator doors on the deck below.

The comm room wasn't far. He dispatched another group of sortens with little care and less fanfare. His destination was in sight now, even in the dim corridor. It was unguarded. He entered the room. Power cut or not, the sounds and lights of the computers and communication systems were quite apparent.

Inertia went deeper. Sorten technicians were busy throughout the room as they carried out their tasks. Caelus was in the center of it, giving orders. 1227231 stood silently by. Just then, a Clairvoyant Construct leapt in front of Inertia from an unseen corner. Everyone turned to watch the battle.

Furious and violent though the assault was, the Construct never stood a chance. A quick punch slipped through Inertia's defense and he spat a curse, but that pain was brief. The tide turned in short order when he buckled the Construct's knee with a kick. The contest ended a moment later with a clubbing punch that dropped the Construct and produced a pool of blood where he lay. Inertia looked at Caelus and took a step forward.

"Halt, Clairvoyant!" 1227231 called.

Inertia looked at the Eternal, who placed itself between him and the project leader. Gears whirred, hydraulic hissed, and 1227231 produced an impressive host of various firearms mounted on various places all over its body.

"I have been designed and hardened for the explicit purpose of combating Clairvoyants! Surrender, or you will be destroyed," 1227231 said.

Inertia couldn't help rolling his eyes. The Eternal's end began first as a shudder that started at its feet. The shudder moved up the machine, growing in intensity until 1227231 shook with such force that the entire room vibrated. Gears whirred as they were ejected from its body. Hydraulic fluid puddled at its feet. In less than a minute, 1227231 collapsed in a pile of parts.

The Clairvoyant looked at Caelus again. "You know why I'm here," he said.

The sorten stared back. "Yes, yes... I've long known I was destined to meet destruction by your kind."

He rose to his full height, crossing his arms. Caelus stared the Clairvoyant in the eye for one long, solitary moment, his fiery intelligence blazing bright for all to see. What realization he came to in his quiet resignation could only be guessed at.

Caelus calmly stroked his artificial arm. "Do it," he said.

After casually raising a hand, Inertia burned the scientist down where he stood. Several of the sorten technicians screamed. Killing Caelus, however, was never his mission, nor even a secondary objective. He gave a quick snort and then sat at one of the computers.

"Beat it," he said to no sorten in particular, but they all got the message. They ran out of the room like rabbits, sparing not even a glance back.

Inertia got to work. The download of all the sorten data to *The Lady* was the first step. Despite that, his face was grim. He had hoped Charon would be with Caelus, maybe as one last line of defense for the scientist. Inertia wasn't sure how he'd match against him. At this point, it didn't really matter. Capturing or killing Charon *was* a mission objective, but he had no idea where he'd slunk off to. Compared to securing the data from Solitary's computers, it wasn't worth finding out. But just then, he thought of another Clairvoyant who perhaps wasn't as lost to him as he feared. He could only think of one thing he could do for her.

Gaining access to Solitary's intercom system was simple, as was his message. He just hoped Edge was still alive to heed it.

22

NIGHTMARES

Something happened. Carmen still lay comfortably in the med bay, but there was now a pinprick on her consciousness that itched like a mosquito bite. The sensation was a Clairvoyant's closest companion. She sat up and glanced around the room like an inquisitive cat. Nothing was readily different. The doctors and scientists still studied the Clairvoyant Constructs that lay dead all around her, and the beeps and hums of various life support and medical equipment saved the room from the silence it otherwise would have been filled with. She frowned. Closest companion or not, those pinpricks were never very forthright.

She leaned back and sighed. No one had said anything about how long she'd have to stay here, and the mounting boredom made her mind drift. The whirlwind of the last day was hard to put into focus. Her body still ached. She looked at the burnt mess that was her arm and then hesitantly touched the burnt side of her face. Both acts produced no emotion. But just then, she thought back to Rauon and felt decidedly cold.

She'd had few friends in her life. Probably most Clairvoyants would say the same. She wasn't completely sure what the word even meant when truly put into action. She thought of Kali. She'd been her handler, and despite how close they were and despite that Kali held no real responsibility toward her former charge now, their relationship remained as a shadow of what it had once been. It was the same with her and Phaethon, except in reverse. She guessed Artemis was a friend in some sort of way. She had no idea if Artemis was even alive, though.

And Inertia? She couldn't really say. Friends? Not really. She didn't even know his real name. Acquaintances? They were certainly more than that. He said they were partners, but that description didn't feel right either. She thought about him further and then rolled her eyes. She had no idea what they were.

Nor, so it seemed, did she have any answer as to whether she was actually friends with Rauon. They were completely different with unrelated backgrounds, but he came closer than anyone to what she would call a friend. She trusted him, as crazy as that was in this place. There were even times that the feeling seemed mutual. Yes, she terrified the sorten, but that fear was a mere byproduct of what she was.

Clairvoyants were terrifying, almost on an instinctual level. They could crush you in an instant. They seemed to know everything about you, even your deepest, darkest secrets. And their whims changed just as quickly as the currents of a typhoon. She wasn't like that, of course—she'd never been like that. She thought back, however, to how Rauon had looked at her earlier today. "I fear there is more about you than I first assumed," he had said. She considered his reaction and her mission and then swallowed hard.

The conclusion of her current course was inevitable; it had been from the start. Despite a small part of her that protested, she ultimately knew why she was here. She looked slowly around the room with the gnawing realization that every sorten here would die, probably from her hand. If Rauon were present, it wouldn't change matters. It was foolish for her to think they were or could ever be friends.

Just then, there was another stirring of her Clairvoyant intuition. She sat up quickly and panned her head around the room once again. She saw nothing of note, which made her narrow her eyes. She turned to one of the scientists.

"Excuse me," she asked. "Is something going on?"

The sorten gave her an annoyed look and continued his work without reply. Carmen pointedly rolled her eyes and took a deep breath but made no further comment. She did, however, notice the lights flickering. She looked at them curiously. She'd had more battles in Solitary than she cared to recall, and it was quite rare if the lights flickered during any of them. Before she could ponder what that meant, though, she became aware that someone was coming.

In fact, they were rapidly approaching, and it seemed like there were two of them. It had to be Clairvoyant Constructs. The sheer purpose, directness, and efficiency that currently soaked every aspect of their being was a match for any of her kin. If they were set before them, the Constructs would crash through boulders without even realizing it. Yet, that was all that they were: a machined tool that was just as unwavering as a hammer hovering over a nail. Carmen was sick of even being near them at this point. She was quick to note, however, that it was just Clairvoyant Constructs coming. They had no sorten escort. *Odd*, she thought. The sortens, until this point, seem so distrustful of Clairvoyants that they wouldn't even let their tools wander around without some sort of leash.

She could hear them now. As she stared at the door, their steps were like a countdown to their arrival. Constructs could have feelings—these did—but they were difficult to fully read, like music created on a synthesizer by a baby. There was only one thing she could really discern from these Clairvoyant Constructs: intention. She didn't know what it was, but it made her nervous.

She looked around the room hurriedly. The sorten doctors and scientists, however, carried on with their work, either unaware or unconcerned. Carmen tried her best to remain undaunted too. Her conscious mind produced several reassuring trifles that clouded the truth. While she consoled herself, her breath shortened, her heartbeat quickened, and her pupils dilated.

The door burst open so quickly that it was like an explosion. Several of the sortens screamed in surprise. The Constructs rushed in and locked eyes with Carmen. It only lasted a second or so—that instant in which no one was able to make a move—but it was the single greatest moment of clarity she had ever experienced. They were here to kill her. And she wasn't in the best condition to respond to the threat.

A thought sent the bed she had been lying on rushing at her attackers like a battering ram. Both Constructs dodged out of the way, and Carmen, after hovering in place for a moment, stood on unsteady feet. The pain shooting up her spine made the room spin even faster. She was acutely aware that she wasn't feeling one hundred percent. All the same, she was unprepared for just how far gone she was. In her current state, Carmen was little match against a glass of warm milk. She only just managed to raise her guard before they were upon her.

She groaned loudly as her burnt arm shielded her from a blow. It was enough of a distraction that she didn't see the follow-up punch coming. If the room spun before, now it gyrated and quaked as another hit sent her crashing into one of the many occupied beds. The half-dissected Construct landed next to her, coating her face and body with his blood. More screams filled the room. Medical equipment and diagnostic machines tumbled to the ground as the sortens rushed madly to get out.

Carmen paid attention to none of it. She was too busy scurrying away over dead bodies, equipment, and even people when they tripped over her. The Constructs pursued, telekinetically vaulting the mess out of the way. The frenzied chaos was such that she only dimly registered that she was against the wall. Over and over again her legs kicked out in front of her, only to propel her nowhere. Her predicament finally became clear after about the fifth time she felt the solid mass behind her.

She gave a defiant scream, raised both of her hands, and fired a heat beam from each with everything she had. The searing white light was like a great hammer crumbling the ceiling on the opposite side of the room. Clothing spontaneously combusted. An unlucky scientist lost the top of his head. The Clairvoyant Constructs, however, were able to avoid the attack. Carmen's spirits drop a touch upon seeing them unharmed. One reached out and grabbed her by the hair above her forehead. The interplay of their energy was a grand display of sparks and noise, and she screamed again from the pain of their bioelectric fields clashing. For the Construct, though, the effort was worth it as he rained blows down upon his now immobile victim.

As she struggled against his grip, the first punch hit like a tidal wave. The second sent a river of blood and spittle across the room. The third made her body tremble and her grip slacken, but the wherewithal to act remained. Her moment came in a flash. Almost by instinct, Carmen was able to just move her head out of the way at the last second. The

Construct's fist impacted the wall with the dull thud and crack of meat and bones breaking. It was enough of a distraction for the Construct that she was able to free herself and roll away.

She came to her feet then, breathing hard. The two Clairvoyant Constructs turned to face her. By this point, the room was empty of all living souls, save for the combatants. She well knew that, if she were fully recovered, this contest would have been over almost as soon as it began. She wasn't sure she could beat them in her present state, though, which got her mind working. Unfortunately, they started their attack again with a feint, stealing her small window of opportunity to ponder.

The feint did exactly what it was supposed to do and moved her out of position so she'd be vulnerable for the real attack. She managed to duck out of the way, even though she didn't really see it coming. A counterpunch held them in place long enough for her to dash to the relative safety of the other side of the room. And there they stood, ready to start all over again, yet again.

She took a deep breath. As before, one of them attacked before the other. This time, though, she spoiled the assault by telekinetically flinging one of the corpses strewn about the room directly at her aggressor. The second Clairvoyant Construct launched his assault by leaping at her while his comrade staggered. Carmen saw him coming this time. She fell to the ground underneath him, her hand rising to shoot a heat beam straight through his body. A telekinetic thrust bounced her back to her feet as soon as she hit the ground. The remaining Clairvoyant Construct, however, kicked her legs out from under her, and she crashed to the ground again. When she rolled back to her feet, they exchanged blows, which she didn't get the better of.

A particularly hard hit sent her reeling into the nearest wall. She only had enough time to look at him before she was attacked again. She couldn't think and felt strangely disconnected from her body. It responded aptly, if a touch too slow. She just couldn't come up with any response against such overwhelming force. At last, she simply screamed and head-butted the Construct in the face.

He fell back, cradling his injury. Carmen was able to hold her surprise long enough to take the opportunity given to her, and a clean punch knocked him to the ground. She raised her hand and produced in front of her a smoldering hole, out of which stuck the Construct's arms and legs.

Carmen dropped to the ground after that, utterly spent. It was only then that she finally noticed she was covered in blood. Most of it wasn't hers—the vast majority belonged to the dead Constructs the sortens had been studying. She telekinetically removed the mess. The same couldn't be done for her own blood, though. She breathed hard and was too tired to move, so a thought telekinetically retrieved some nearby gauze. It was convenient that she was already in the medical bay.

When she was done wrapping her wounds, she closed her eyes and took several deep breaths. She was practically panting. Sweat beaded all over her body. She barely had the energy to move. Yet all these things were mere diversions as Carmen tried to figure out what her next step should be.

Her eyes shot open. "Phaethon," she said to herself.

She stood as fast as she could, groaning as she did so, and steadied her wobbly legs by resting a hand on the nearby wall. For now, she had to trust that Inertia could take care of himself. But Phaethon...she had to find him. If only she knew where to look. In that moment, the room darkened, red lights flashed, and a loud alarm sounded. She didn't know what exactly that meant, but it couldn't be a good thing.

With no idea of where to go, she stepped out of the room. She could hear several sorten security squads approaching. She didn't *simply* hear them, though; the noise thundered down the corridor, seemingly shaking the whole of Solitary. It sounded more stampede than security contingent. She hesitated. Clairvoyants were terrible and destructive creatures. Any school kid knew that. Even so, in her present state, reputation and reality were not one and the same. For one long second, she considered challenging the sorten horde. Then she thought better of it and set off in the opposite direction, not knowing whether it was putting her closer or farther from her destination.

The problem of destination sent her thoughts running just as fast as her legs were carrying her. Phaethon wasn't as injured as she was. Inertia had said he hadn't been brought to the med bay. *Where would he be? Where would the sortens hold him?* she thought over and over. Her mind was focused, ready, and tense. When she disappeared through one of the hidden hatches, however, she promptly collapsed. Outright panting, her throat was raw. Her will remained undaunted, but her body was failing her. She didn't know why, but it seemed like she was running out of time.

Where would they hold him? Carmen thought frantically while she regained herself. Solitary was as much a maze as it was a dungeon. In fact, the purposes of both seemed to intersect and blend together. *Where is he?* she thought again as she existed deep in the dark hell of Solitary.

The sortens drew closer, and she began running again. She wondered if she'd be able to sense Phaethon. She was quick to remind herself, however, that she hadn't even known he was at Solitary until yesterday. The entire facility seemed hardened against Clairvoyants. Her best and only guess was that, since her former charge wasn't in the med bay, he might be wherever his living quarters were. Her only point of reference were her own living quarters, which were unfortunately not on this floor, and she didn't know exactly where the elevator was.

Her legs burned from their futile effort to speed her to safety. She was well aware that, by this point, she was only reacting to what was happening. That would get her killed. There had to be some way, somehow, to get off this floor. She scanned the corridor, hoping for a hidden hatch or elevator that could avail her or at least let her escape, if only momentarily. Then, all at once, she stopped in place as an idea took hold. The sortens chasing her had to be coming from somewhere. She doubted they'd garrisoned their security near the med bay. That seemed a bit pointless, since all the Clairvoyants were already dead by the time security got there.

The sorten pursuit was bearing down on her. It sounded like an army. Carmen took a deep breath and committed herself to the one and only option she could think of. The stupidly obvious simplicity of the plan was its chief virtue. She'd make herself invisible. She'd never done it before. She'd never felt the need. But she remembered assets turning invisible at parties back at the facility all the time. The idea wasn't so farfetched. The various energies of the universe already bent to her will. Why wouldn't light? The only issue was she had no idea how it was done. But her mind went back to her time at the facility, to a room full of sand. The knowledge of how to complete her task had escaped her then, just as it did now.

She closed her eyes as she had countless times before in her life and let the Dark take her. As always, it remained a part of her, despite how much she pretended otherwise. She was consumed by a sudden calm. Action, reaction, will, and force all existed on the same plane. Carmen opened her eyes and was taken aback. The world was presented before her in a wild array of color. At first, the image made her dizzy. Everything appeared in a splattered mosaic, like she was viewing the remains of a box of crayons dropped in a blender. The sight made her think, for a moment, that the sortens had used some sort of neurological weapon against her. However, hard as it was to see, she could just make out the security running toward her, and they seemed unconcerned that they were nearing a monster of the Dark. The lead sortens even ran right past her without missing a beat. But then the group slid to a stop—with her in the center of the mass.

She stood still. A sorten in the middle moved slowly in small circles. He had some kind of scanner in his hands.

"I don't understand it. She should be right here," he said.

"Perhaps your scanner is broken? Clairvoyants don't just disappear," another said.

"Actually, they can," a different sorten remarked.

They looked hesitantly amongst each other for a moment.

"Spread out. Find her. If you see anything suspicious, clear your line of fire and shoot it," the security leader ordered.

Carmen couldn't help but swallow hard and exhale sharply upon hearing that. It was precisely the wrong thing to do. The closest security member to her looked at her with a snap. He didn't see her, as his guns weren't yet blazing, but he did take a step closer. The sortens were mostly on all fours and came to just above her waist. This one moved closer while his comrades checked just as carefully in the other directions. He was now close enough that simply sticking out his tongue would have bridged the gap.

She took a small, nearly imperceptible step back. The

sorten stiffened, stealing her breath away. He must have seen some disturbance in the air from her movement. He aimed his weapon right at her chest, though whether he knew that was unclear. She had to do something, but she didn't know what. Then an idea came from one of the most unlikely of places.

"Ahh!" a sorten cried with surprise from down the corridor.

The security member in front of her ran to his aid, as did half the squad.

"What is it?" one of them asked.

"Something touched me!" the stricken sorten said. "I think it pulled out of some of my fur."

Carmen allowed a small smile as she thought of Widget.

"Your fur?" one of them asked.

"Yes, that's what it felt like."

They stood still for a long moment. Nothing was said as they looked at each other.

"She's not here," one eventually said.

"She has to be! Look what the gauge is reading," the sorten with the scanner protested, holding it up for all to see.

"That thing's broken," the security leader said. Then he looked at his squad. "Move out!"

The sortens assembled in a well-ordered line and bounded down the hall. Carmen watched them leave, breathing several sighs of relief. She eventually dropped her cloak of invisibility, and when confronted again by the sight of the world as it normally was, she was very nearly taken aback again. It seemed it was possible to get used to anything.

She ran back the way she came, still shaking her bleary head. She couldn't hear or sense any sorten security teams coming, so it looked like she was in the clear. After going back through the hidden hatch, she nearly flew by the medical bay. Sorten personal were inside, tending to the dead. They didn't even notice her go.

The elevator wasn't too hard to find, as it wasn't far from the med bay. More important, though, it was undefended. She could only guess the sortens had never expected she'd get this far. It was also helpful that she'd been with Rauon enough times to remember what floor she lived on. She pressed the appropriate button, thankful that her luck seemed to be changing. Everything seemed to be changing and for the better, for once. She just needed to find Phaethon and get out of here.

But when the elevator arrived, her lips morphed into a bemused frown. The doors weren't opening. She pressed the button to open them, and a second later, the power in the elevator failed. She let out a small sigh. Luck was with her for the moment, but it was by no means her best friend. She telekinetically ripped the doors open and leapt into the corridor, pausing a moment when a tremor rumbled through Solitary. She had no idea what it was, so she paid it no further mind.

She looked down the empty corridor to a destination she did not know. The usual anxiety of the aimless inevitability that was her life was nowhere to be found, though. She took a few hesitant steps forward before she was sure of what she was sensing. Phaethon was here, somewhere. A Clairvoyant's bioelectric field and its energy signature was as unique as a fingerprint, and as sure as she was breathing, she could sense his.

Pure elation clouded any other feeling. She bolted down the corridor, quick as Mercury and unstoppable in her purpose. The pain of the body faded away, its protests muted. Mind and body were a team. They were like moth to flame, drawn like a beacon to a feeling, a mere intuition of where they were needed. She twisted and turned through several of the hidden hatches along the corridor walls. She was a Clairvoyant, yes, but her senses merely gave her a direction, not a path. She stopped for a quick moment to consider exactly how to get to where she needed to go.

"There," she said to herself, darting through yet another of the hidden hatches.

After a short trek down a corridor, she went through another hatch. She was so nerve-rackingly close that it felt like she could reach out and touch Phaethon. The mere thought of it surrounded her in warm comfort, like a blanket. The feeling had seemed lost to her the day she arrived at the facility.

She went through another hatch and stopped in place. Phaethon stood before her. He was not alone.

"Rauon?" she asked curiously.

The sorten technician stood on his hind legs next to her charge. They were joined by a small security contingent who aimed their weapons at both her and Phaethon.

"Edge," Rauon replied.

Carmen slowly shook her head, not understanding. "What are you doing here?"

"I should have asked you that in the beginning," he spat, anger bleeding into his voice. "I knew you would come looking for him. Why is that?"

She didn't answer right away. The alarm blared, and the corridor alternated between flashes of red light and absolute dark, lending urgency to the proceedings. But to her, the scene seemed frozen like a timeless diorama.

She looked at Phaethon. He appeared unharmed. However, the security seemed ready and willing to modify that status.

Carmen swallowed hard. "He's my charge," she said,

looking at Rauon again. "I don't care about anything else—Caelus, your work here, none of it." Phaethon stared at his handler till he could only shake his head as his gaze fell.

Rauon's countenance didn't change. "That's it? All this, just for him?"

"Yes," she answered quickly.

"I…don't believe you. Not anymore," the sorten said.

"I'm not lying."

"What about your partner?" Rauon asked pointedly. "I somehow doubt his motives are as noble as what you claim." He took a deep breath and, when he looked at Carmen again, his eyes narrowed. "Caelus was right. He was always right. I now know why he calls you beasts. Clairvoyants only have one purpose. It is integral to everything they are. Destruction."

"That's not true," Carmen insisted.

"Everything about you is a lie," Rauon went on. "You even lied to me about your name. And your *real* name, Edge, isn't even your real name. Why should I believe anything you say?"

"What about you?" she asked in turn. "What were you going to do to my charge if I didn't come? This didn't start with us. We didn't start the war with you. We didn't enslave you. I've seen how you casually butcher Clairvoyants just for study. None of you seem to even notice the brutality!"

"Brutality?" Rauon said with a start. "A Clairvoyant speaks to me about brutality! My entire family is dead! Billions of innocent sortens are dead! And do you weep for them? I heard of the cheers throughout the Terran Empire when it was announced that the core of their most hated enemy was utterly destroyed. By your own words, terrans house their own children in vast facilities to do nothing but learn how to kill! You fear and hate us, but one of your newborns could rip our arms and legs off with a thought. And you wonder why we fret…"

"This is insane!" Carmen said with clenched fists. "If I wanted to kill you, I would have done so by now!"

"Yes, I agree. Insanity. But what do I have to thank for your prudence?" Rauon asked. "You disapprove of our methods. Well, I don't blame you. I used to cry myself to sleep every night when I first started here." The comment caught Carmen's attention. He continued. "I regret a lot of what I had to do for this project. I always hoped the collision course of our two species could be averted. I wished we could come to some sort of understanding. Then I lost everything I ever knew with the destruction of the home worlds. That was when I realized madness, true madness, is merely a factor of guilt. That is what justifies my actions. The knowledge that my work here, whatever its price, will go on to protect untold numbers of sortens far into the future from you and your kind."

The sorten said nothing else for a long moment. Carmen made no reply as her thoughts turned inward. Then Rauon nodded to one of the security personnel, who pressed his weapon against Phaethon's temple.

"What of you, Edge?" the head technician said. "I've seen how you look at Caelus. How much more would it take for your prudence to waver? What will it take for you to hate us, if you don't already?"

Carmen looked away and reflected on one simple fact. Her life, either directly or indirectly, had been almost completely dictated by sortens. From her time at the facility, which was modeled on sorten treatment of Clairvoyants, to why she was here now, it was all influenced by them in some way. She truly was the wolf in the forest. She thought back to how Kali spoke of sortens, how Eli spoke of sortens, how every Clairvoyant she had ever met spoke of sortens. They weren't unjustified. The horrors she'd seen in just the past few days were a testament to that. Except...the mirror image seemed just as true.

She looked at Rauon, her mind racing to place a million thoughts into a few words. "I don't want to hate anyone. I don't want to hurt anyone. I want...I want to stay good."

Rauon looked at her in utter silence. He rose to his full height, towering over everyone, before he diminished, as if releasing a great exhale.

"So do I," he said.

The Clairvoyant and the sorten looked each other in the eye for a long moment. She didn't read him. She didn't have to.

"All I want is my charge," she said softly, holding her hands high to be as nonthreatening as possible.

Rauon glanced at Phaethon and then at Carmen, who gave an encouraging nod. One of the security members stiffened.

"You can't seriously be contemplating that?" the guard asked.

Rauon didn't even glance in the security member's direction. "I'm not contemplating it. I'm doing it," he said as he turned to Phaethon. Then he motioned to Carmen with his head. "Go."

The boy began walking toward her. The sortens watched him leave. Carmen dropped her hands, unable to help an unabashed smile. But the feeling went away when she looked at Phaethon. His eyes were particularly drawn to her burnt face, reflecting a sort of pained disgust. It was then that a spark was lit. She had seen the look more times than she cared to count, usually at the end of their chess games. She shook her head slowly while her eyes gave a silent plea.

"No!" she screamed, leaping toward her charge.

But it was already too late. He turned his head and extended his arm. She grabbed him just as he shot his heat beam. She screamed from the pain of their interacting energies and was only able to spoil his aim enough to keep him from hitting Rauon full on. The beam instead hit him just below the waist, severing his legs. The sorten gave a pained cry of surprise before he fell into the burning pile of his own legs. The corridor filled with his desperate screams as he burned. The sorten security responded promptly, training their weapons on the threat. But by that time, Phaethon had been able to shake Carmen off him, and he burned the sortens down where they stood.

Carmen lay on the ground, her mouth agape. Rauon writhed and struggled in a vain attempt to escape the flames consuming him. She telekinetically snuffed the fire out before she looked up at her charge, who stood silhouetted in the dark by flames and the flashing lights of the alarm.

He looked down upon her. "You may not hate them," he said, "but *I* do!" Then he ran off down the corridor.

"Phaethon!" she called, but he didn't even look back.

She took a few quick steps after him before stopping in place. She was torn. Fists clenched, she ran to Rauon's aid while, over her shoulder, she watched her charge disappear down the corridor. The sorten was burned over most of his body. His legs were well and truly gone. He struggled to breathe, and Carmen didn't know what she could do. By instinct, she reached out to touch him, but long forgotten fears made her stop short.

"I'm sorry. I'm so sorry," she said over and over again, her voice breaking.

Rauon looked up at her. "Go, Edge. Go to your charge," he said, weak and pained.

Carmen only leaned back slightly. "I can't leave you here alone."

"This is Solitary," he said after a groan. "Go."

She took a few hesitant steps away.

"Go," he said again. "Go!"

She took off down the corridor after Phaethon. Rauon's voice echoed after her.

"Madness! This place is madness!" he yelled.

Carmen had never run so hard in her life. Her legs were almost a blur. Her body screamed at her, but she was too fatigued to fly. She could still sense Phaethon. That, however, wasn't her only guide. She guessed the sortens had sent reinforcements, because their dismembered bodies made a bloody trail of bread crumbs. Her lip curled in disgust. This was more than murder. Most of the sortens weren't even dead, at least not yet. Body parts were littered everywhere she could see. She even slipped and slid in the blood after making a tight turn. Screams of pain lashed out at her with such force that she screamed as well, simply to try to drown them out, while the smell of burned, melted flesh filled her every pore.

Eventually, her body protested too loudly and she had to stop. Her throat felt like it was on fire and her legs throbbed with each rapid-fire pulse of her heart. She looked down the corridor at the insane, bloody chaos. Just then, a construct grabbed her by her ankle, begging for his life. She wrestled her foot free after a small yelp of surprise. Next, a sorten reached out for her.

"Help," he muttered, blood spilling from his mouth. "Help me."

Carmen's eyes grew wide as the violence reached out for her. She seemed neck-deep in it. She ran off, not really after Phaethon but just to get away. Yet, over and over again, they came at her. She closed her eyes, but the image beset her still.

It was all that there was. It was all there ever was. Every direction she turned and every avenue she took made no difference. Here, trapped in the dark, there were no illusions, no comforting rationalizations, and no escape.

She spoke to the victims, though she talked to no one in particular. In truth, she was more talking to herself. Her words were of no consequence—just trifles she had used to comfort herself back at the facility. They came forth with no real thought or effort. It was just a small ritual, of her many, to forget the horrors of the day. But they no longer seemed to be working.

She went through one of the hidden hatches and stopped. A sorten stood in front of her. He had a bad wound to the chest.

"He killed me," he said as he staggered toward her. "He… he killed me. I'm…dying."

The sorten practically fell on her. The pain of touching a Clairvoyant was plainly visible on his face, and it continued until she was able to weaken her bioelectric field. She struggled to support his weight.

"There's nothing I can do," she said softly. She wasn't even sure the sorten heard her.

"Don't go," he pleaded, his voice weak. "Stay with me. Stay with…"

His eyes were still open. Carmen tried to avoid looking at their haunting emptiness as she eased him down. Just then, she heard a comforting voice. It seemed to pierce the insanity like rays of sun through dark clouds.

"Edge, make your way to *The Lady*. I will meet you there," Inertia said through Solitary's intercom system.

Leaving hadn't really crossed her mind at this point. She was aware consciously that she needed to, she *had* to, but that impossible goal had never even entered her wildest imagination. It felt like she'd been stuck in Solitary's insane maze her whole life, doomed to circle its endless corridors for eternity, so lost that she didn't know there was an exit.

She had to find Phaethon. He was nowhere to be seen, but she could still sense him. She was still surrounded by hands reaching out to her or severed limbs attempting to do the same, seeking salvation from a Clairvoyant after another had struck them down. It was hard to tell whether they were begging for mercy or trying to drag her down. She shook her head as the overwhelming mass gnawed at her. There were so many. She'd killed before—seen dead bodies before. One or two at a time, and maybe even a few or a small pile, but not the lot of them all at once. It was too much to take. In a fit of exasperation, Carmen took to the air. The death was with her still. It would always be with her. But at least she was no longer deep in the muck of the fallen as she flew along the ceiling.

The Clairvoyant streaked toward her charge, sensing the life slip away from each and every sorten as he killed them. At least his malevolence slowed him down. It was always hard to read Phaethon, but she was close enough now to get an impression. He wasn't the fiery ball of anger she expected. No, he seemed scared, terrified even, and the feeling grew in intensity the closer she got.

Indeed, she caught a small glimpse of Phaethon far down a corridor, and that only made her charge press on harder.

"Phaethon!" she called. "Phaethon, stop!"

There was no response. He killed two more sortens, making it a point to maim them just enough so they'd barely be alive when he finished. The task slowed him considerably, though it made Carmen wince throughout. She could almost touch him now.

Phaethon seemed desperate to get away. He took to the air

as well and jetted away from his handler. She found some hidden reserve, and it was just enough to keep him in sight. Her opportunity came when he slowed to go through a hatch.

She tackled him. He gave a loud grunt from the pain, but she didn't care. Their momentum sent them tumbling down the corridor, but she didn't loosen her grip as they went end over end. When they finally came to a stop, Carmen got on top of him and pinned her charge to the ground. He shocked her. He screamed at her. He cursed and spit at her. But she held firm.

"No more!" she yelled over his protests. "Not like this. We're not monsters!"

"How can you say that? Of course we are!" Phaethon sounded like he was on the verge of crying. "That's what we were turned into."

Carmen looked him in the eye and saw herself reflected back. She felt drained in mind, body, and spirit, but one small ember kept her from failing completely. "Except we don't have to stay that way," she said.

Phaethon turned his head and looked at the dead sortens down the passageway. His expression wasn't one of sadistic triumph, but there wasn't an indifferent lack of recognition either. When he turned to his handler, his entire being seemed to deflate.

"This is all that there is," is replied. "This is all there ever is."

Carmen looked away and couldn't stop her eyes from falling, if only slightly. "We have to try. What else can we do?"

"I don't deserve anything else," he said.

She paused. "Well, this is a bit different from overturning the chessboard when you're losing," she said after a deep breath. Phaethon looked at her but made no reply. "If you don't deserve it, then neither do I. Perhaps no one deserves redemption. I know one thing, though. I'm tired of being trapped in places like this."

"Is that you talking or Kali?" Phaethon asked.

Carmen took another deep breath. "It's me," she said. Then she extended her hand to help him up. "Trust me."

He looked at her and hesitated.

"Trust me," Carmen said again. Phaethon looked at her hand and took it. She pulled him to his feet. "We have to get to the ship."

"Do you know where it is?"

"No," she responded.

Just then, a long line of yellow lights appeared before them.

"What's that?" he asked.

Carmen smiled. It truly was nice to have a good partner. She could only assume Inertia was monitoring her progress from some sort of control room. She turned to Phaethon.

"Come on," she said.

The pair moved off at a slow run. She really didn't have the energy for much more than that. They opened a hatch to find a squad of sorten security waiting for them.

"Fire!" the squad leader said as soon as the Clairvoyants were in view.

Carmen extended an arm to prevent Phaethon from stumbling into the corridor, and the two of them were able to retreat back inside. She looked at her charge and could already see the first beginnings of a new blaze.

"No," she said sharply. He gave her a confused look while the bullets ricocheted all around them. "Clean," she said, holding up a finger to emphasize her point. "We're not monsters."

She closed her eyes, and Phaethon watched her. A few seconds later, the shooting stopped. He stole a quick peek into the corridor. The sorten squad lay dead on the ground, their necks broken. He turned back to his handler. She opened her eyes, looking woozy and weak.

"Come on," Carmen said.

At this point, even managing a fast walk was a struggle. She could feel Phaethon's concern, but he didn't say anything. She could also feel more sorten security closing in on them. They were relentless. Their shouts of horror at their fallen comrades echoed through Solitary, even though they couldn't yet be seen.

The yellow road of lights led to an elevator. She pressed the button to call for it and sighed when it became obvious the elevators were still shut off. Phaethon telekinetically ripped the doors open so she didn't have to. She groaned loudly when she looked up and down the empty elevator shaft. They would have to fly, though it was only a minor inconvenience, all things considered.

"Up or down?" he asked.

"Up!" Carmen yelled just as the sortens came into view.

The lead security member took aim at them and fired just as they entered the elevator shaft. The bullets ripped into the wall, causing a deafening torrent of noise but otherwise leaving the Clairvoyants no worse for wear.

They flew up to the next floor, opened the door, and saw no yellow lights. Two more floors, and no more luck. On the next floor, their path was laid out before them. Carmen was so exhausted. The room spun and it was hard to even know where she was. Her arms and legs shook from the sheer exertion. And more sortens were coming.

"Come on. We have to be almost there," she said, though it was Phaethon and not her who was ready to go.

He moved at a slow jog. Carmen followed a few steps behind. They went through a hatch and down a corridor for a long way, and then another corridor. Their passageway filtered into another, and she turned around and stopped for a moment. The corridor they just left had been one of three. She remembered the split. They were close. She ran with renewed vigor, and it was now Phaethon who was pressed to keep up. Then, at last, there was a door at the end of the passageway.

No grace and no modesty—she wanted out of this hell with all due haste. Carmen telekinetically ripped the door off its hinges and made straight for *The Lady*. As before, the ship sat alone quietly. Inertia was waiting for them. She ran toward him and collapsed in his arms. Phaethon watched the scene, his mouth agape.

"What happened? Is she all right?" Inertia barked at the teenaged boy.

"I, uh…uh…"

"I-I'm fine," Carmen struggled to say. "Get us out of here," she added, her voice weak and strained.

Inertia nodded sharply and picked her up. "Phaethon, find a place to strap in," he said before carrying her into the ship and closing the hatch.

Phaethon nodded, and Inertia, still carrying her, made his way to the bridge. He took a moment to strap Carmen in her chair, and she noticed how gentle he was despite his haste. He then took his seat, and his hands flew over his console. *The Lady* hummed and whined to life. Carmen maintained the wherewithal to turn on the external cameras. They showed the hangar, and a part of her worried that some trick of fate would strand them here. But then, eventually, *The Lady* began her escape. Up and up she went. A brief thought flashed through Carmen's mind that they would crash into the hangar door, but *The Lady* emerged from the confines of Solitary with no drama, only to accelerate farther and farther away.

Carmen watched the planetoid in her monitor as it receded. She noticed she was breathing in quick pants, and she swallowed hard. After a few seconds, she was able to calm herself. Inertia looked at her and nodded. She nodded back. They each let go a small sigh.

He tried to say something then, but she passed out as soon as he opened his mouth.

23

ATONEMENT

Carmen stood outside Phaethon's makeshift quarters on *The Lady*, unsure of what she was going to do. In the past few days since they'd escaped Solitary, she hadn't been purposely trying to avoid her charge. It didn't seem like Phaethon was avoiding her either, as far as she could tell. *The Lady* wasn't a large ship by any means, and it was impossible to keep from encountering each other. Nevertheless, both Clairvoyants did their best to pretend that the necessary and inevitable could be put off till eternity.

She stared at the hatch, her mind blank, steeling herself to bridge the last few inches to her goal. Long had she dared to dream of this moment, but now that it was here, she was at a loss. By this time, Phaethon had to have sensed that she was outside his room. He didn't open the hatch, though, so it seemed he couldn't span the gap either. It was then that she noticed her reflection in the dull, brushed metal finish of the hatch. Her hand went to the ghostly image, and there was only coldness under her touch.

A thought came to her as her eyes fell. "Edge, it's time,"

she said softly to herself. Except for the first time in her life, she was finally ready to face what may come. She moved to open the hatch but stopped short. "Phaethon," she called. "Phaethon, can I come in?"

There was no reply. She wasn't completely surprised. She opened the hatch with no further hesitation and immediately saw Phaethon. He sat expectantly, though not exactly comfortably, on the bed in front of her. She took a seat opposite him. No words were said. Phaethon wasn't even able to look her in the eye. His expression reminded her of a dog worried it was going to be scolded. She was able to determine quite quickly the reason for it when he cautiously glanced at the burns on her face and then looked away nervously when she noticed his attention.

With her good hand, she touched the burnt side of her face. "It doesn't really hurt that much," she remarked reflectively. Phaethon looked at her, and Carmen nodded slowly. "On balance, a fair trade I think."

"A fair trade?" he asked in disbelief.

"Definitely."

"But it was all my fault," he said.

"Yes," she agreed without pause, which made Phaethon shift uneasily. "But it was my fault for leaving you alone at the facility to get taken. The burns really don't bother me too much. I'm just happy I was able to find you."

They sat for a long while in silence. It wasn't awkward, though; just a quiet moment of reflection.

"I'm sorry," he said softly. She waved the apology away and shrugged. "You aren't going to make me play chess now, are you?" he asked sheepishly.

Carmen looked at him, nonplussed, for a moment. Then she laughed loudly when she realized he wasn't being serious. Her reaction made him smile—the first she could ever remember seeing.

"Unfortunately, I left the board back at Solitary."

Phaethon's face fell at her mention of that hell. The change was as sudden as flipping a light switch. Her laugh trailed off as the air grew heavy. He said nothing, and it seemed like nothing would be forthcoming.

"What's wrong?" she asked.

"Nothing...nothing. I don't want to talk about it," he muttered.

His face was neutral and his body rigid. Carmen noted both while she second-guessed her next question. She was loath to ask it. However, she was well aware that, if not now, it would be never.

"What did they do to you there?" she asked, not really wanting to know the answer. She didn't ask for her sake, though.

Phaethon looked at her, and it seemed like he was trying to decide for himself whether he'd answer. "I wasn't the only Clairvoyant they had," he began. "There were about a half dozen of us in all. I was the oldest."

Carmen nodded seriously. She remembered Rauon mentioning that they occasionally received children for study. "How did you know there was only a half dozen? I didn't even know you were there until I fought you," she asked.

Phaethon swallowed hard. "I don't know where they kept you, but we were all in the same room."

"Go on."

"They'd take us out one at a time. I don't know what they did to the others. No one talked about it. But they'd attach me to a machine that would make you see or hear things."

"What kind of things?" Carmen asked.

"Horrible things. Indescribable things. And every time, it was like I existed apart from myself. Like I was watching myself going through whatever motions they wanted me to. I don't know if anything that happened then actually happened. Sometimes I'd come back to the room covered in blood and I wouldn't remember why."

She was silent for a long moment as she considered everything he said. "Phaethon, what happened to the other kids? They're not still back at Solitary, are they?" she asked. "We'll go back right now if they are."

He glanced at her for a second and then slowly shook his head. Dread filled his eyes as memories flashed before them.

"Phaethon?"

"They're not at Solitary. Not anymore," he said, his voice cracking slightly.

"What happened to them? Where are they?" she asked.

"I fought them." He was quiet for a few seconds. "The sortens made me. One at a time, for their tests." His eyes fell to the deck when he finished speaking.

"You were the oldest and most experienced," Carmen remarked.

Her charge nodded solemnly. "I don't know why we had to be roomed together," he said, frustration and anger drenching every word. "I was the oldest. They all looked up to me and…wanted me to keep them safe. I used to hold them when they cried themselves to sleep. But they would take me and one of them, and only I would come back. None of them even knew what was going on. I had to make up stories."

Carmen felt weak just hearing him talk. The boy was a quivering mass. She reached out to him. "Oh, Phaethon," she said, not knowing what she could do but wanting to offer comfort all the same.

"Don't touch me," he said, batting her hand away. She held her place, but he couldn't even look at her. She retreated slowly as he started speaking again. "There was a girl there. She was the youngest, maybe six or seven years old. Her name was Anna. She kind of looked like you," he said, looking at her.

"What about Anna?" Carmen asked.

"I absolutely hated her. She just wouldn't shut up about when we were going to be rescued. She was convinced her parents would open the door at any moment and take her home. She'd get the rest of them going too. Most of them had given up hope, but she just had to make them believe. I just wanted her to shut up. Just one night without her squealing about how we were going to be saved," he said through clenched teeth. He took a deep breath.

"She was the last one. Maybe a day before I fought you, I fought her. She was the only one of them who didn't cry. She just stood there and accepted what was going to happen." He sounded like he didn't believe the words that were coming out of his own mouth. "She was only six years old," he remarked. "After it was done, I looked down at her body, and I was alone. And…and—"

"And what?" Carmen asked.

When Phaethon glanced at her, it seemed like he'd forgotten she was still there. "And I was happy she was dead!" He shook his head slowly as tears slid down his face. Carmen could only watch. She had braced herself for many things, but she never would have guessed this. "I just couldn't help it. There were no more kids. I wouldn't have to hear her again." Then he looked at her with an odd smile that contained no joy. "The worst part of it is, if you would have been one day sooner, she would have been right."

Carmen leaned back as she considered the possibility. She quaked at her conclusions. And to this point, she had thought she'd succeeded.

He looked at her, still trying to regain control of himself. He rocked back and forth as he spoke. "I wish you never found me. I don't deserve it."

"I had to," she said.

Phaethon looked around the room, shock and confusion on his features. "Why?"

"I've never been through what you experienced. I can't imagine it. I don't even want to try. But I've done many things I regret," she said, forcing a lighter tone for his benefit. "Things that I've realized over time still haunt me," she added. "They'll always haunt me. Just like this will always haunt you. It just *is*. I'm only just beginning to understanding that. We can't run from it or forget it. We just have to accept what has happened."

"What have you ever done?" he asked.

Carmen said nothing at first. "You don't know why I worked at the facility, do you?" Phaethon shook his head. "I needed money. My boyfriend was very sick. I told myself I'd do anything to make him well. But the reality is that I never really cared about him. Not really. Maybe not even from the very beginning. I just wanted to forget everything. I wanted a normal life without all this," she said, gesturing around herself. He nodded. "I was selfish. The only thing I did was keep him alive past any sense of dignity. I cheated him… I cheated you. I think we can both agree that I wasn't a very good handler."

"You weren't that bad," Phaethon said.

She slowly shook her head. "Thank you, but we both know the truth. Anyway, there are other things," she continued, thinking of Mikayla, Eli, Theodore and the others from her apartment building, and even Anna, who she had been too late to save. "But it is all about one thing. I don't think I ever really forgave myself."

"For what you did to your boyfriend?"

"No," she said quickly, shaking her head. "I…" She hesitated for a second. She'd never said it out loud before. "I don't think I ever forgave myself for being what I am."

Her charge looked away and closed his eyes for a long moment. "I think I understand," he finally said mournfully. "What we are is terrible."

"I don't know," Carmen answered after a short while of searching. "In the end, we're just people." She looked away as flashes of thoughts crossed her mind. "I've hurt people, killed people. People have been hurt and killed because of me. I guess it will have to be paid back in some way. In the end, though, I'm going to have to live with it and myself."

Phaethon went quiet again. It was obvious that he didn't like her answer, but she had nothing better to give. He looked at her. "Is that what you were trying to do? Pay it back in some way by coming after me?"

"A little bit yes, and a little bit no," she said without having to think about her answer.

"I don't understand," he muttered.

Carmen stood and walked toward him. She placed her burnt hand on his shoulder, wincing for a second or so from the interplay of their bioelectric fields.

"Phaethon," she said. He looked her in the eye, and she saw her own reflection. "I guess, in a way, I am like Anna. I came for you because no one ever came for me."

He looked away to consider that. The long silence between handler and charge was but one of many. Yet, after a time, Phaethon stood and hugged her. Carmen was so surprised that it took her a moment before she hugged him back.

"Thank you," he said.

She smiled, though he couldn't see it. This new silence had a different air, and they both took their fill before they let go.

"Will you be all right here? I have some things to take care of."

Phaethon nodded slowly. "I'll manage."

She patted him on the shoulder. "Let me know if you need anything."

"I know. You're my handler," he said.

Carmen smiled, Phaethon smiled in turn, and with that, she left the room. Her mood stayed with her as she changed her focus to Inertia, who was in the bridge. After a short walk, she saw him sitting at his console. He turned to her and nodded when she entered. She sat next to him.

He glanced at her for a quick moment before returning his attention to his console. "How is he?" Inertia asked.

"He'll be fine," Carmen said. "It's a lot to work through."

He looked at her again. She glanced back. Inertia, unlike Phaethon, never gave any reaction to her burn scars. It was comforting. In any case, she saw him hesitate, which was rare for him.

"How are you?" he asked after noting her interest in what was on his mind.

"I'm..." she began but trailed off to allow her thoughts to come into full focus. She gave a pained smile. "I'm in a good place now. It's been a very long time coming."

Inertia gave a knowing smile at that and nodded slowly, which brought a weary but satisfied smile to her features. No words were said to ruin the moment. After a time, he activated *The Lady's* communication systems. Gungnir's face appeared on the center console between them.

"We're both here," Inertia reported.

Gungnir nodded. "Good. I've received the report from the Space Force Special Forces team that took Solitary, and I've had Widget go through all the data you sent me."

"Were they able to find Charon?" Carmen asked.

"No," he said, regret palpable in his voice. "As Widget and I found when we were hunting him, he is very good at covering his tracks. It seems we will have to wait for him to make his next move. As for Solitary itself, it was mostly evacuated by the time the Space Force team arrived. Except, in their haste, the sortens weren't able to completely wipe their data cores. The information Inertia found has also proven most useful.

"And Edge, for what it's worth, the assault team was unable to find a sorten matching Rauon's description among the dead." Carmen nodded but didn't know whether to be happy or troubled by the news.

"Gungnir," Inertia said, "there's a spaceport not far from our present location. I will drop off Edge and Phaethon there. They can get transport back to New Earth, or wherever they want." Carmen looked at him sharply with a questioning face, but he didn't seem to notice.

"Very well," Gungnir replied. "Edge, this looks like the end of the road for you. Thank you, truly. I'm happy that, in all this, you were able to find your charge."

Carmen heard him but didn't listen to a word he said. Her mind was elsewhere. After a period of no one talking, she realized both Gungnir and Inertia were waiting for her to respond.

"You're welcome," she said with a weak nod. She was no

longer looking at the screen and didn't see Gungnir raise an eyebrow at her.

"Inertia, contact me once you're finished with them. I'm not sure the next task is even feasible," he said.

"We will see," Inertia replied. Then the men nodded, and the transmission cut out. He turned to Carmen, who still had a faraway look in her eye. "Are you all right?" he asked.

She sat still, glassy eyed, till all of a sudden, she broke into a smile. "Drop Phaethon off," she said.

"Okay?" he muttered quizzically.

Carmen laughed lightly and then slapped him playfully on the arm. "I'm your partner," she said matter-of-factly. "I'm not letting you do this alone." She relaxed in her seat. "There are more Phaethons out there," she added introspectively. "I have to do what I can. Charon has to be stopped."

He nodded slowly, a wry smirk coming to his lips. "Okay," he said again.

"What's this other task? Why is it unfeasible?"

Inertia stopped smiling. "Remember that second sorten base? The one they mentioned back at Solitary?" She nodded. "The data I pulled did have its current location. It's a freighter just like we thought. But..."

"But what?" Carmen asked.

"But it's deep within sorten space. We can't get that far behind their lines with a ship this small. Even if we could, I'm not sure how we could avoid getting blown out of the sky. Worse still—"

"The freighter will move when it gets no response from Solitary, so our info is only good for less than a week," she finished for him.

He nodded. "Exactly."

Carmen sat solemnly as she turned the problem over and over again in her mind. Inertia said nothing as well. Her eyebrows furrowed as no immediate solution became apparent. On and on she went till, at last, she looked at Inertia. He simply watched her as he rested his chin on a closed fist.

"All right, go ahead and say it. It's completely appropriate in this case," he muttered after an exaggerated sigh.

Carmen laughed and then pulled her lips into a guilty smirk. "So, what now?"

ABOUT THE AUTHOR

Yup, I'm the evil guy keeping you up all night to read, "Just one more page." A storyteller from birth, it was inevitable that I'd find my way to writing books. All of my works have a very strong focus on character and believable worlds.

Other than books, I'm a licensed pilot and certified jet nerd. I'm also interested in motorsports and a lover of the "sweet science."

Check my latest updates and join my newsletter at ktbeltbooks.com

CPSIA information can be obtained
at www.ICGtesting.com
Printed in the USA
LVHW031625281221
707357LV00002B/171

9 781954 913031